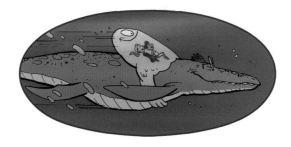

Copyright © 2019 by Gavin Aung Than
Original interior design by Gavin Aung Than and
Benjamin Fairclough © Penguin Random House Australia Pty Ltd.

All rights reserved. Published in the United States by Random House Children's Books,
a division of Penguin Random House LLC, New York. Originally published by Puffin Books,
an imprint of Penguin Random House Australia Pty Ltd., Sydney, in 2019.

Random House and the colophon are registered trademarks of Penguin Random House LLC.

RH Graphic with the book design is a trademark of Penguin Random House LLC.

Visit us on the Web! rhcbooks.com

Educators and librarians, for a variety of teaching tools,
visit us at RHTeachersLibrarians.com

Library of Congress Cataloging-in-Publication Data is available upon request.
ISBN 978-0-593-17512-5 (trade pbk.)
ISBN 978-0-593-17509-5 (hardcover)
ISBN 978-0-593-17510-1 (lib. bdg.)
ISBN 978-0-593-17511-8 (ebook)

The artist used Adobe Photoshop to create the illustrations for this book.
The text of this book is set in 11-point Sugary Pancake.
This edition's cover and interior design by Sylvia Bi and colorization by Sarah Stern

MANUFACTURED IN CHINA
10 9 8 7 6 5 4 3 2 1
First American Edition

SUPER SIDE KICKS

OCEAN'S REVENGE

BOOK TWO

Gavin Aung Than

Color by Sarah Stern

Random House 🏠 New York

PREVIOUSLY . . .

Four superhero sidekicks were sick of being bullied by their selfish grown-up partners, so they decided to form their own team. They are the . . .

SUPER SIDEKICKS!

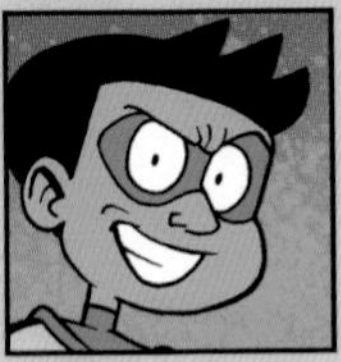

JUNIOR JUSTICE

Born leader. Expert martial artist. Brilliant detective. Assisted by Ada, the world's most advanced belt buckle.

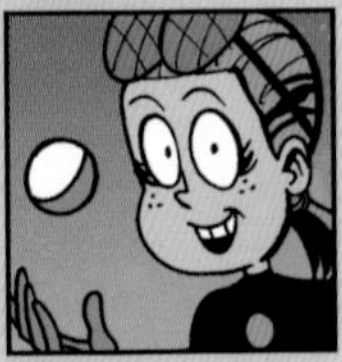

FLYGIRL

Acrobatic flyer. Bug whisperer. Cricket lover (the sport and the insect). Uses dangerous bug balls to subdue enemies.

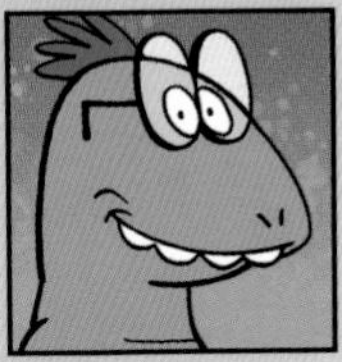

DINOMITE

Dinosaur shape-shifter. Physics professor. Poetry connoisseur. Would rather be reading a book.

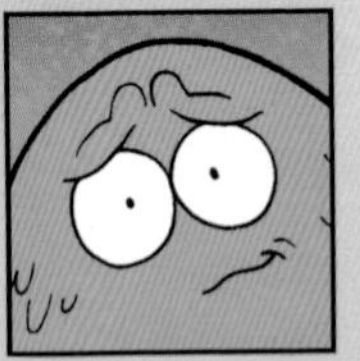

GOO

Limitless stretch factor. Untapped power potential. Still has nightmares about his past as a bad guy.

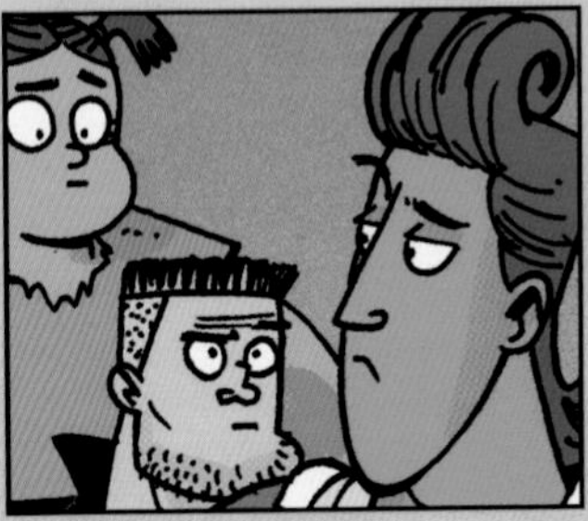

THE GROWN-UPS

Captain Perfect, the world's most beloved (and obnoxious) superhero; Rampagin' Rita, simple yet scary strong; and Blast Radius, who hasn't met a problem he couldn't solve by blowing it up.

Chapter

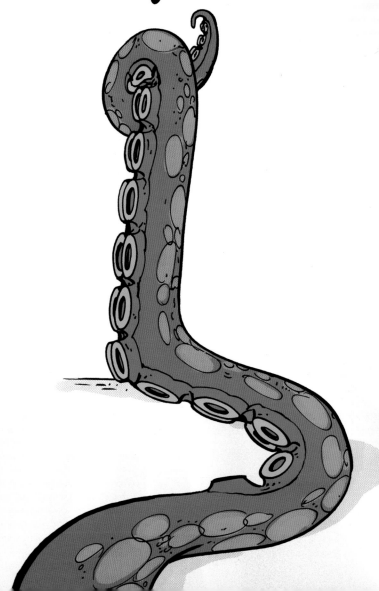

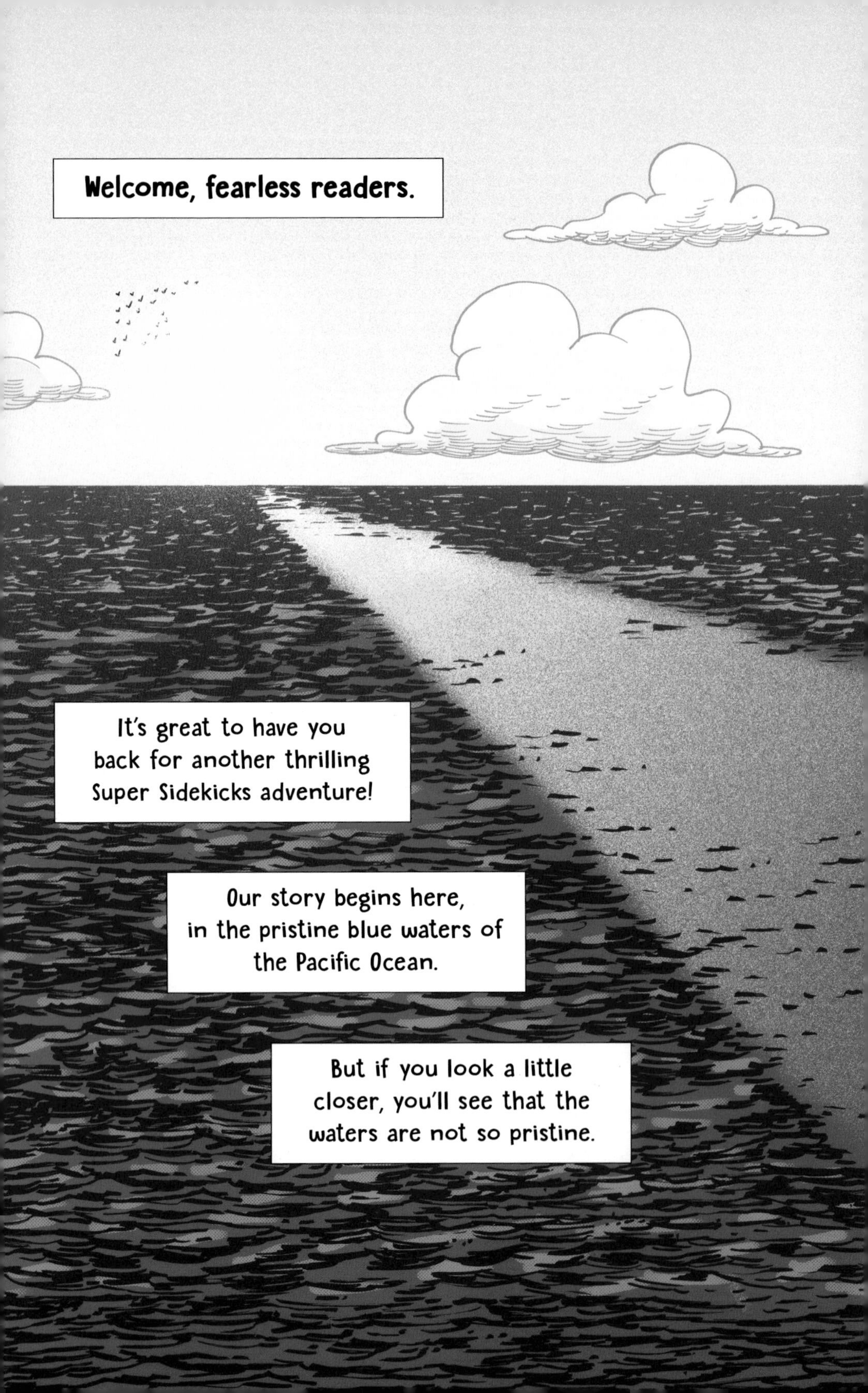
Welcome, fearless readers.
It's great to have you back for another thrilling Super Sidekicks adventure!
Our story begins here, in the pristine blue waters of the Pacific Ocean.
But if you look a little closer, you'll see that the waters are not so pristine.

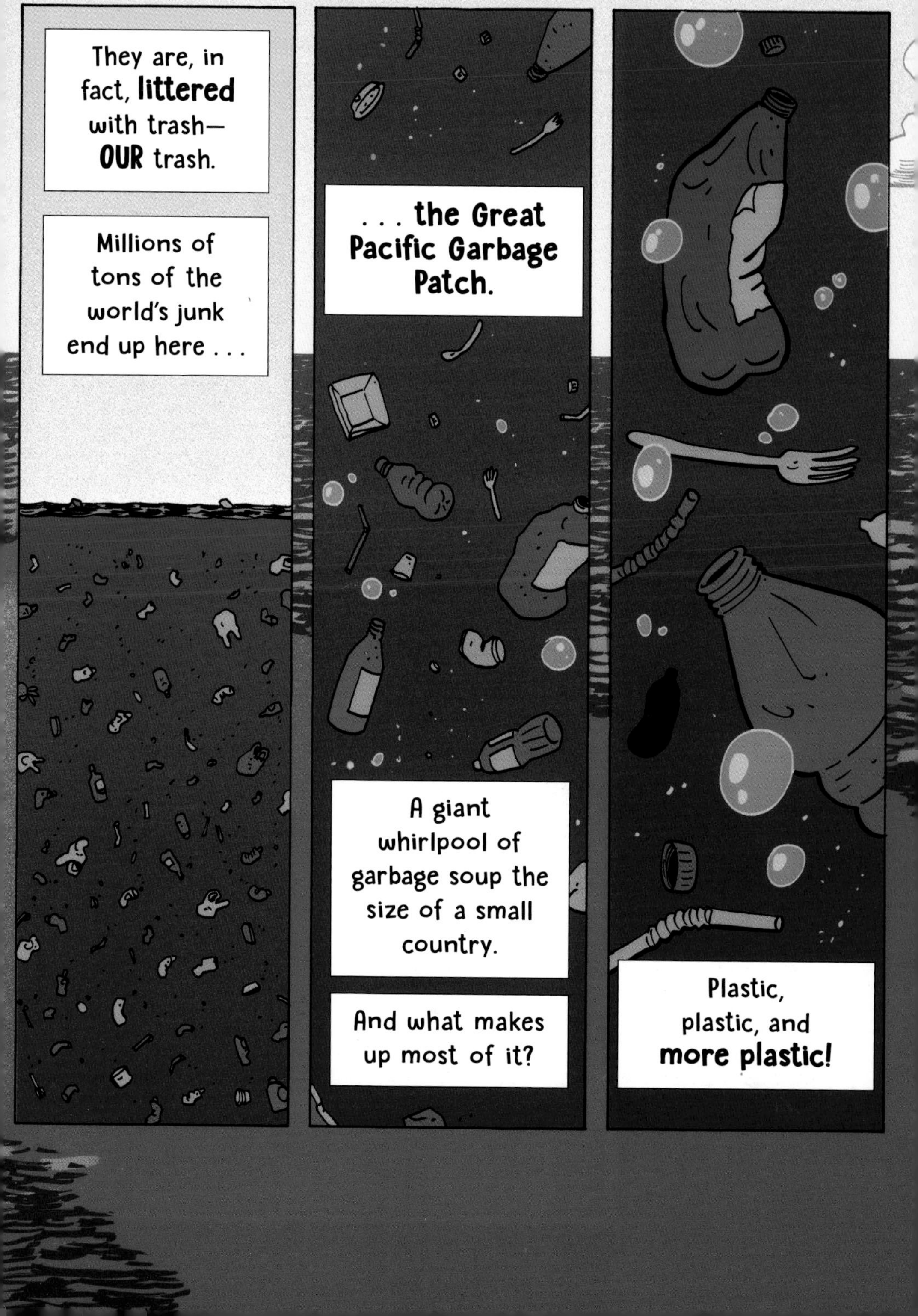
They are, in fact, littered with trash— OUR trash.
Millions of tons of the world's junk end up here . . .
. . . the Great Pacific Garbage Patch.
A giant whirlpool of garbage soup the size of a small country.
And what makes up most of it?
Plastic, plastic, and more plastic!

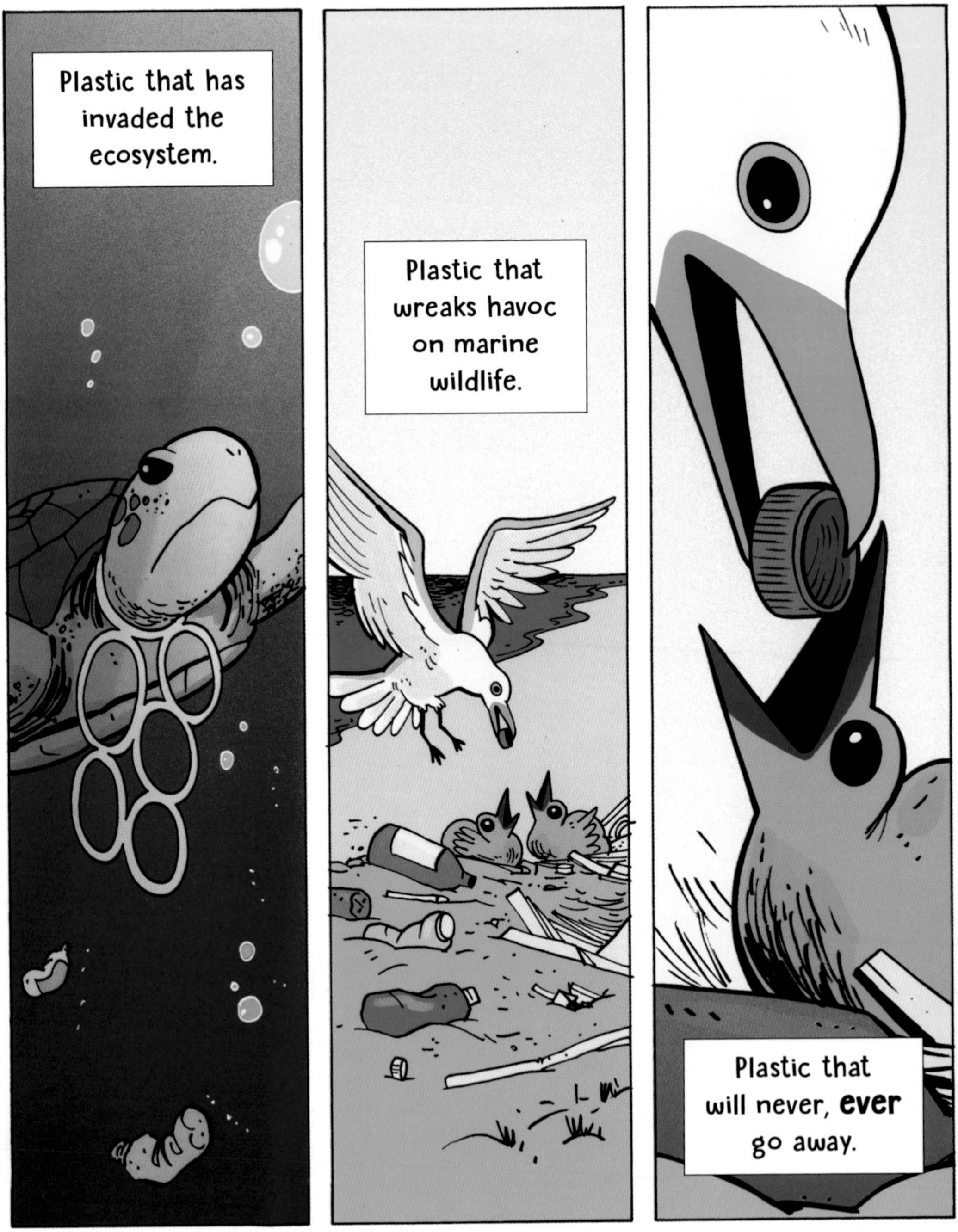
Plastic that has invaded the ecosystem.
Plastic that wreaks havoc on marine wildlife.
Plastic that will never, **ever** go away.

But what's this? Something strange is happening. The plastic trash seems to be joining together . . .

It's miraculously combining to form **bigger and bigger** pieces.

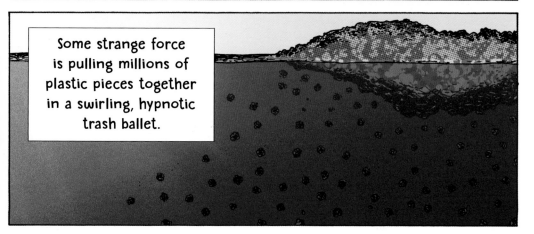

Some strange force is pulling millions of plastic pieces together in a swirling, hypnotic trash ballet.

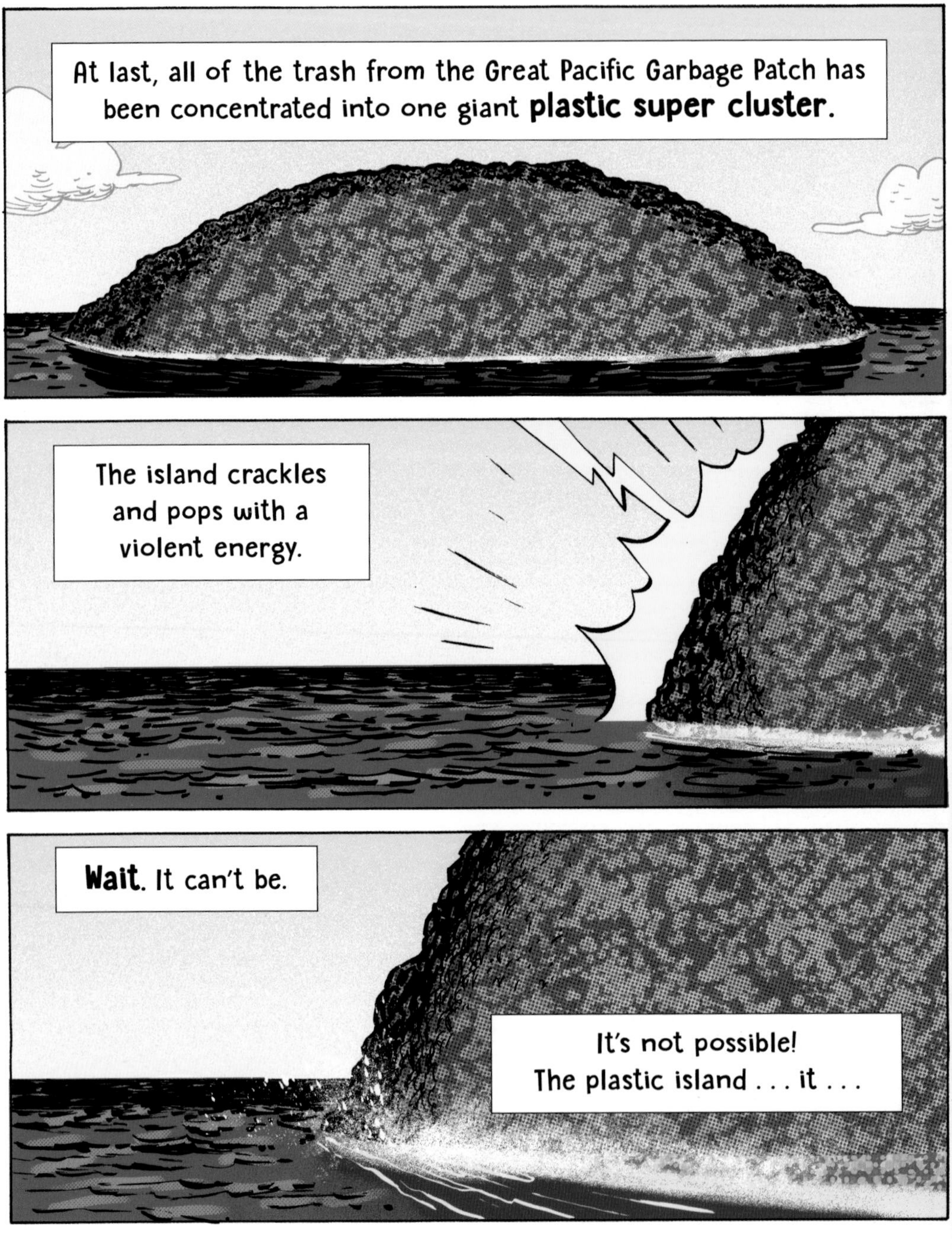
At last, all of the trash from the Great Pacific Garbage Patch has been concentrated into one giant **plastic super cluster**.
The island crackles and pops with a violent energy.
Wait. It can't be.
It's not possible! The plastic island . . . it . . .

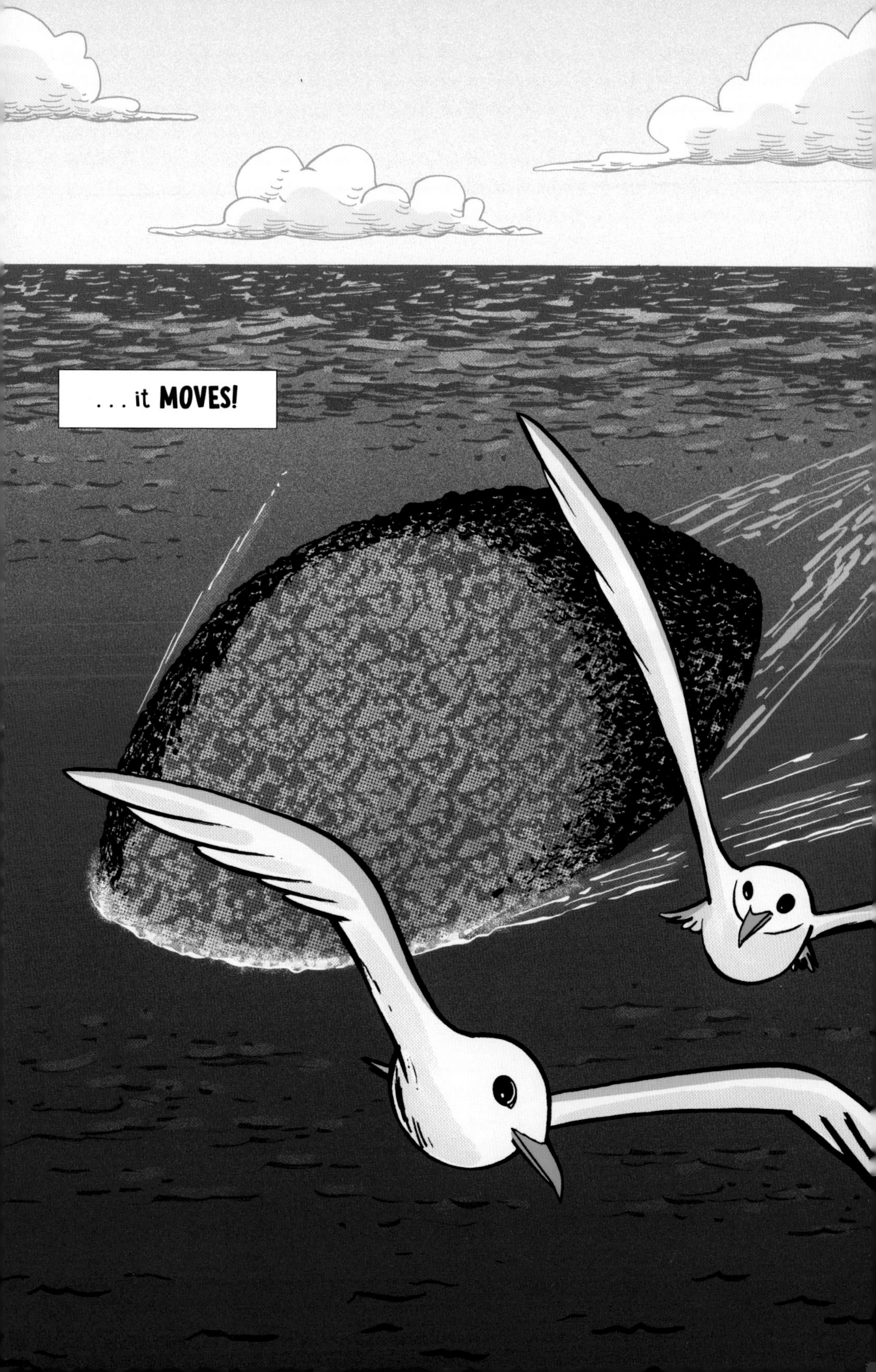
. . . it MOVES!

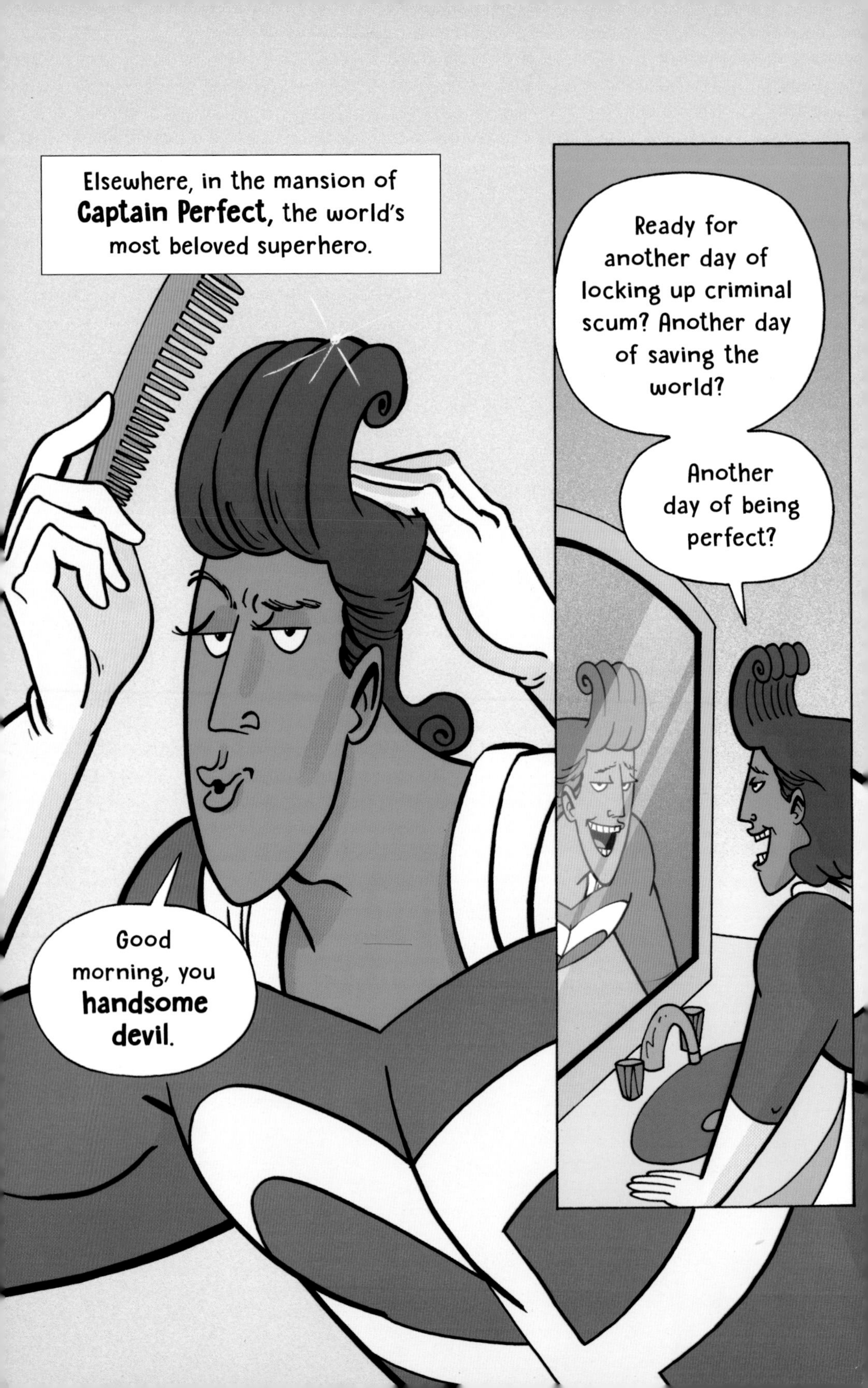

Elsewhere, in the mansion of **Captain Perfect**, the world's most beloved superhero.
Good morning, you **handsome devil**.
Ready for another day of locking up criminal scum? Another day of saving the world?
Another day of being perfect?

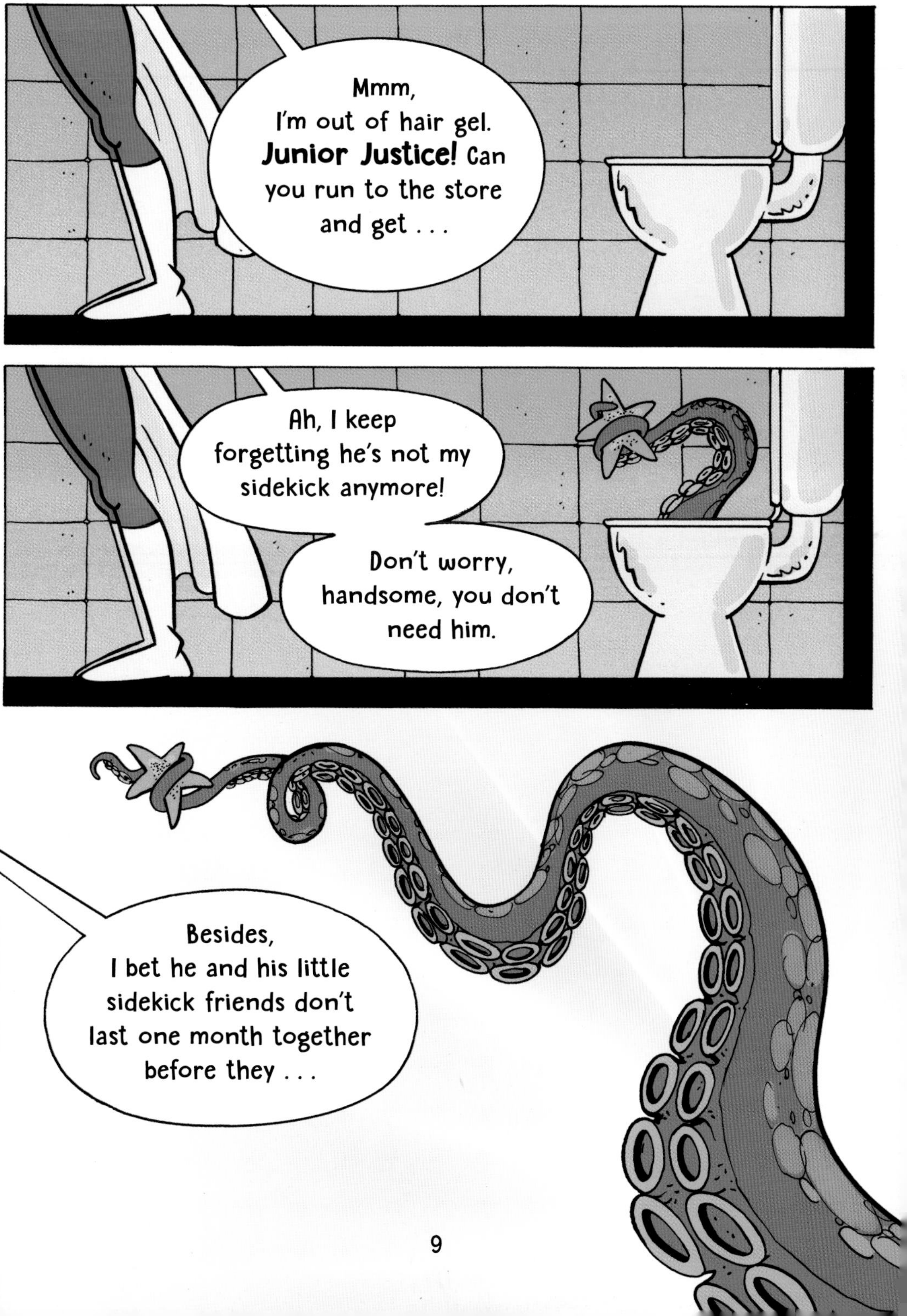
Mmm, I'm out of hair gel. **Junior Justice!** Can you run to the store and get . . .
Ah, I keep forgetting he's not my sidekick anymore!
Don't worry, handsome, you don't need him.
Besides, I bet he and his little sidekick friends don't last one month together before they . . .

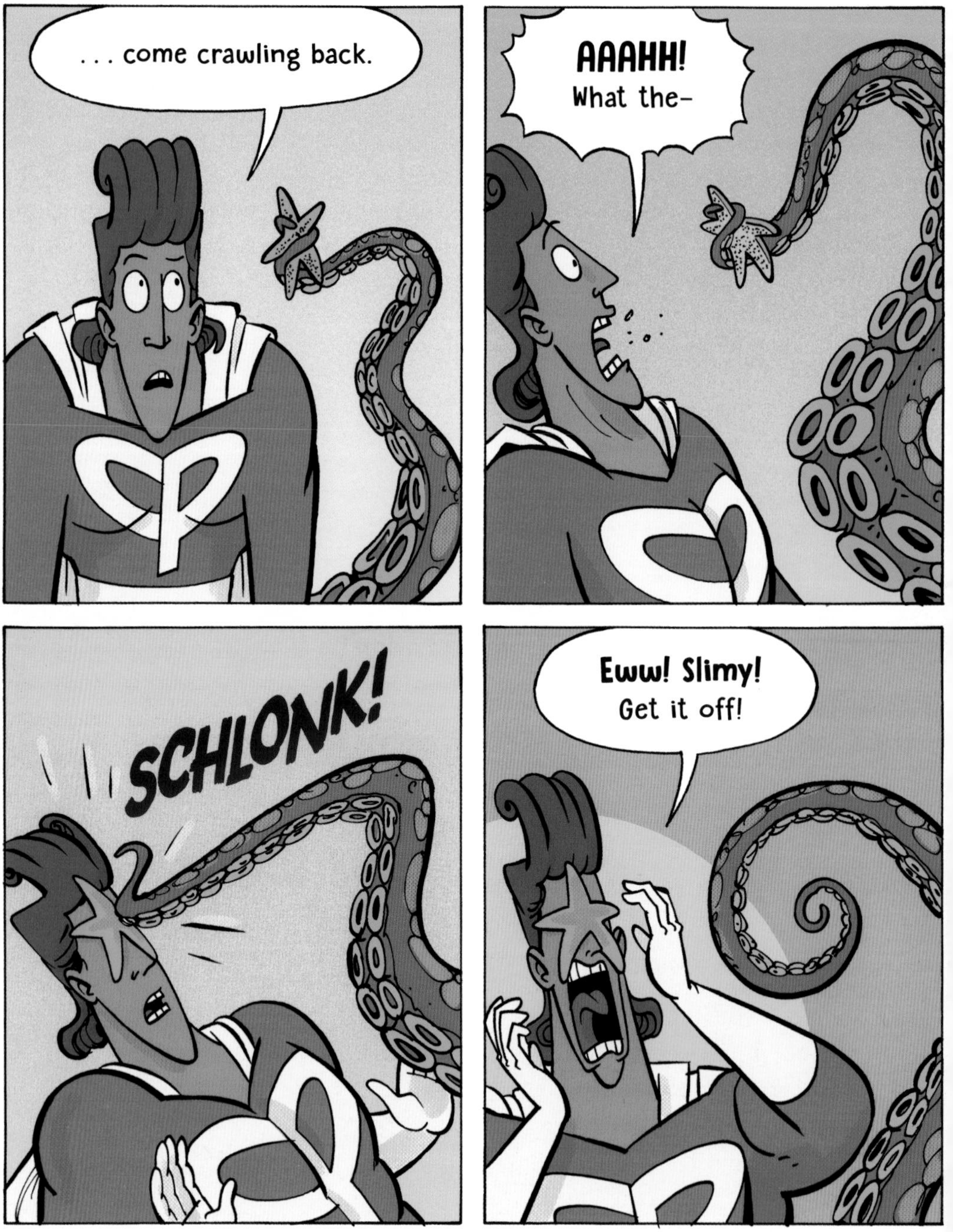
. . . come crawling back.
AAAHH! What the–
SCHLONK!
Eww! Slimy! Get it off!

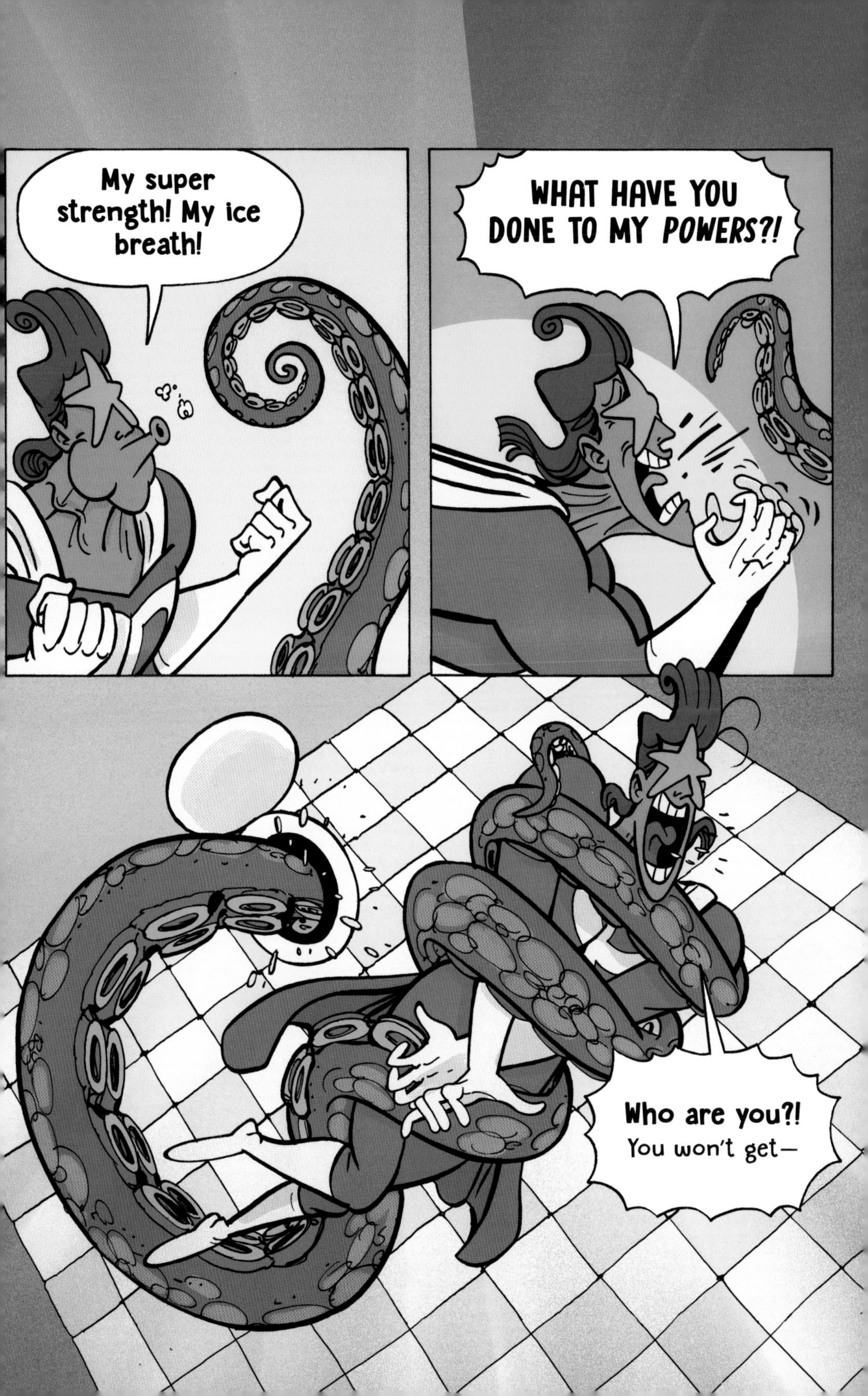
My super strength! My ice breath!
WHAT HAVE YOU DONE TO MY *POWERS*?!
Who are you?! You won't get—

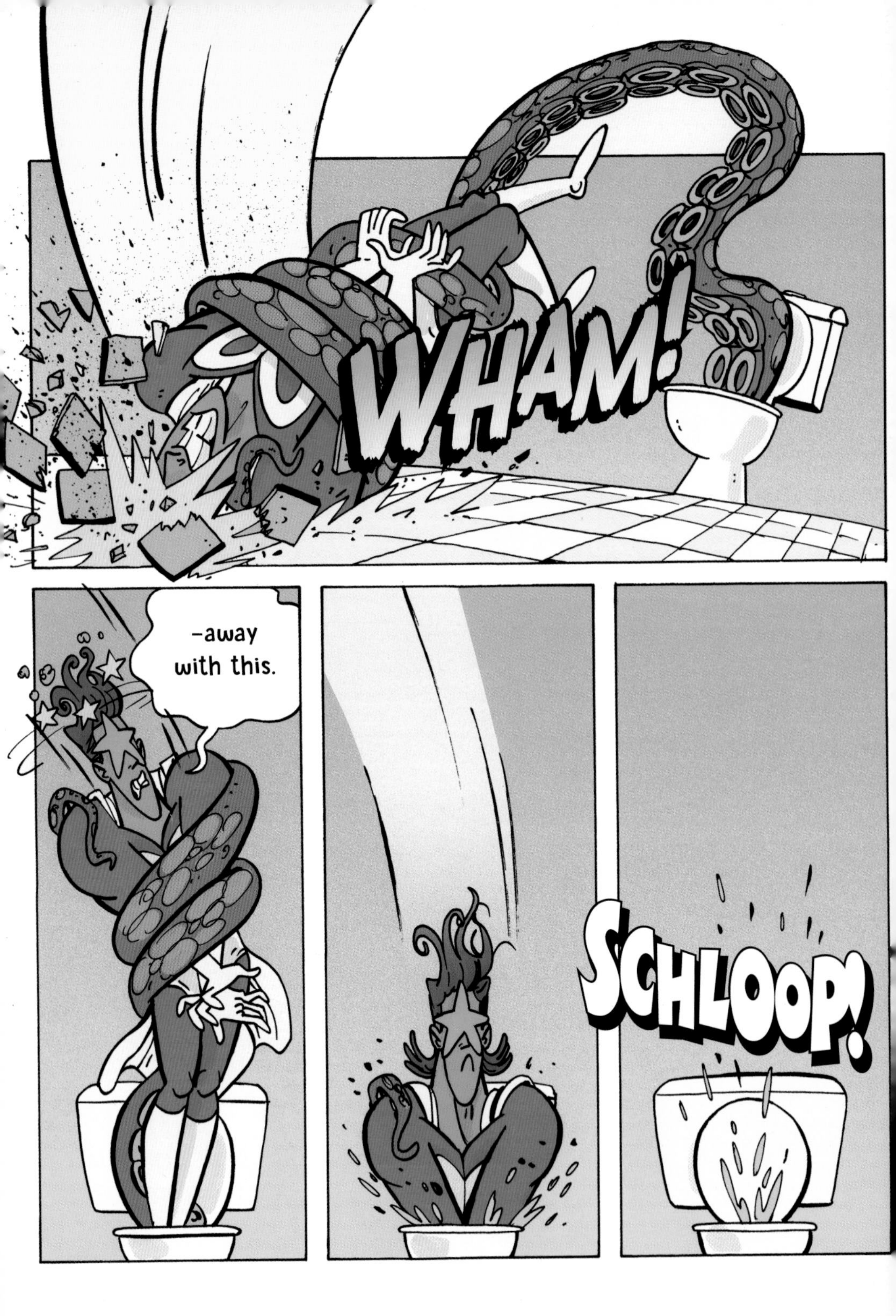
WHAM!
-away with this.
SCHLOOP!

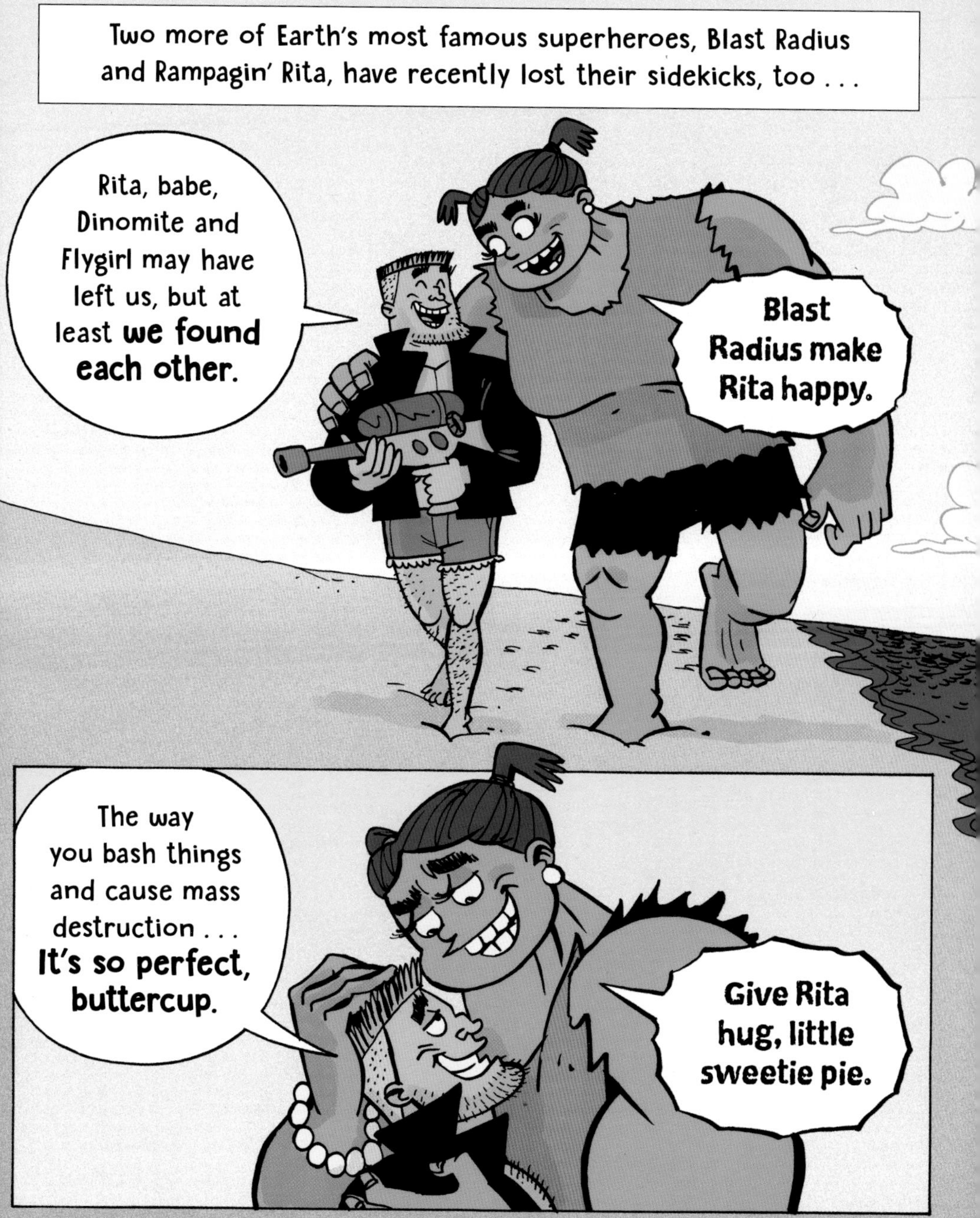
Two more of Earth's most famous superheroes, Blast Radius and Rampagin' Rita, have recently lost their sidekicks, too . . .
Rita, babe, Dinomite and Flygirl may have left us, but at least **we found each other.**
Blast Radius make Rita happy.
The way you bash things and cause mass destruction . . . **It's so perfect, buttercup.**
Give Rita hug, little sweetie pie.

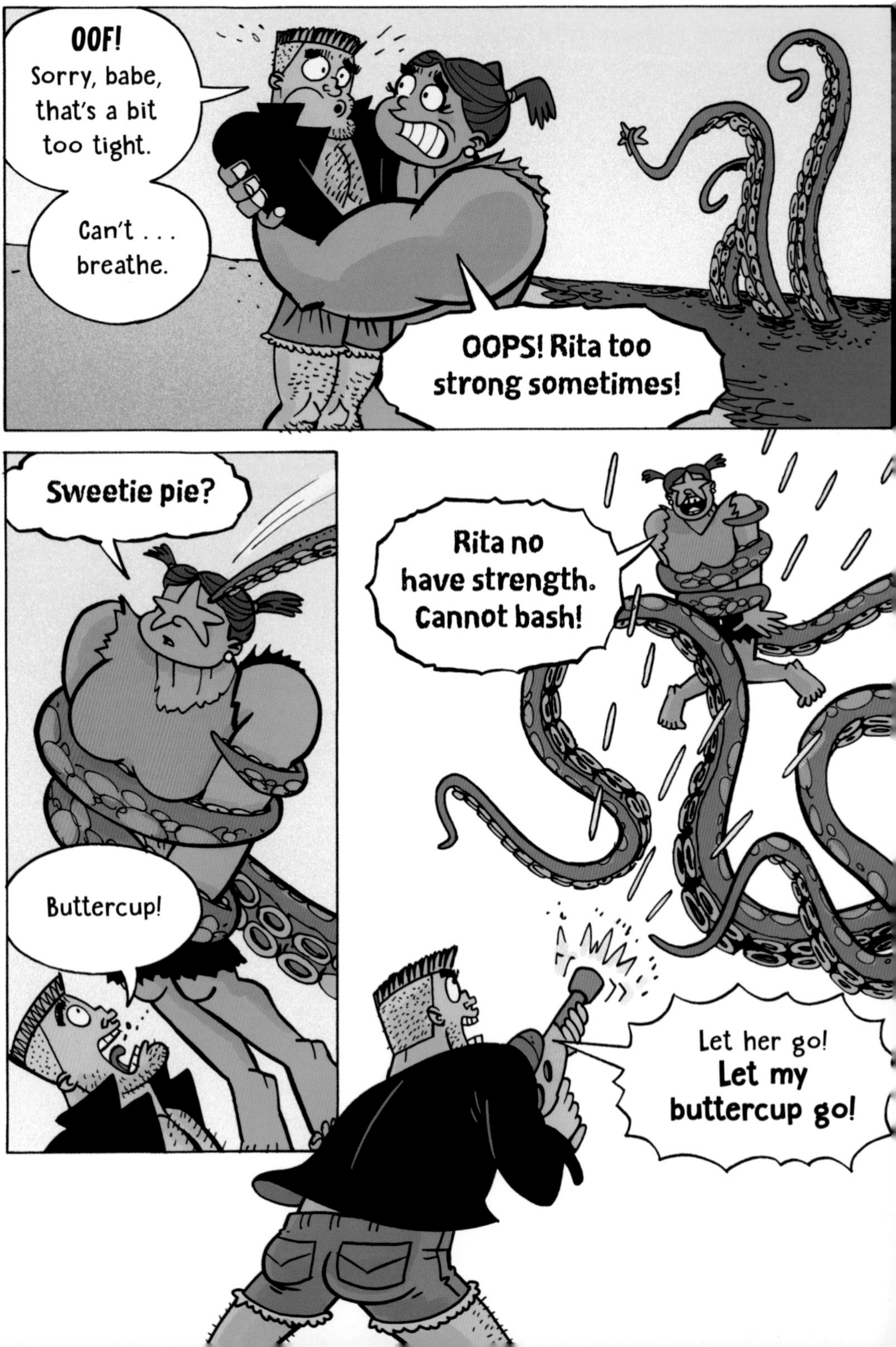
OOF!
Sorry, babe, that's a bit too tight.
Can't . . . breathe.
OOPS! Rita too strong sometimes!
Sweetie pie?
Buttercup!
Rita no have strength. Cannot bash!
Let her go!
Let my buttercup go!

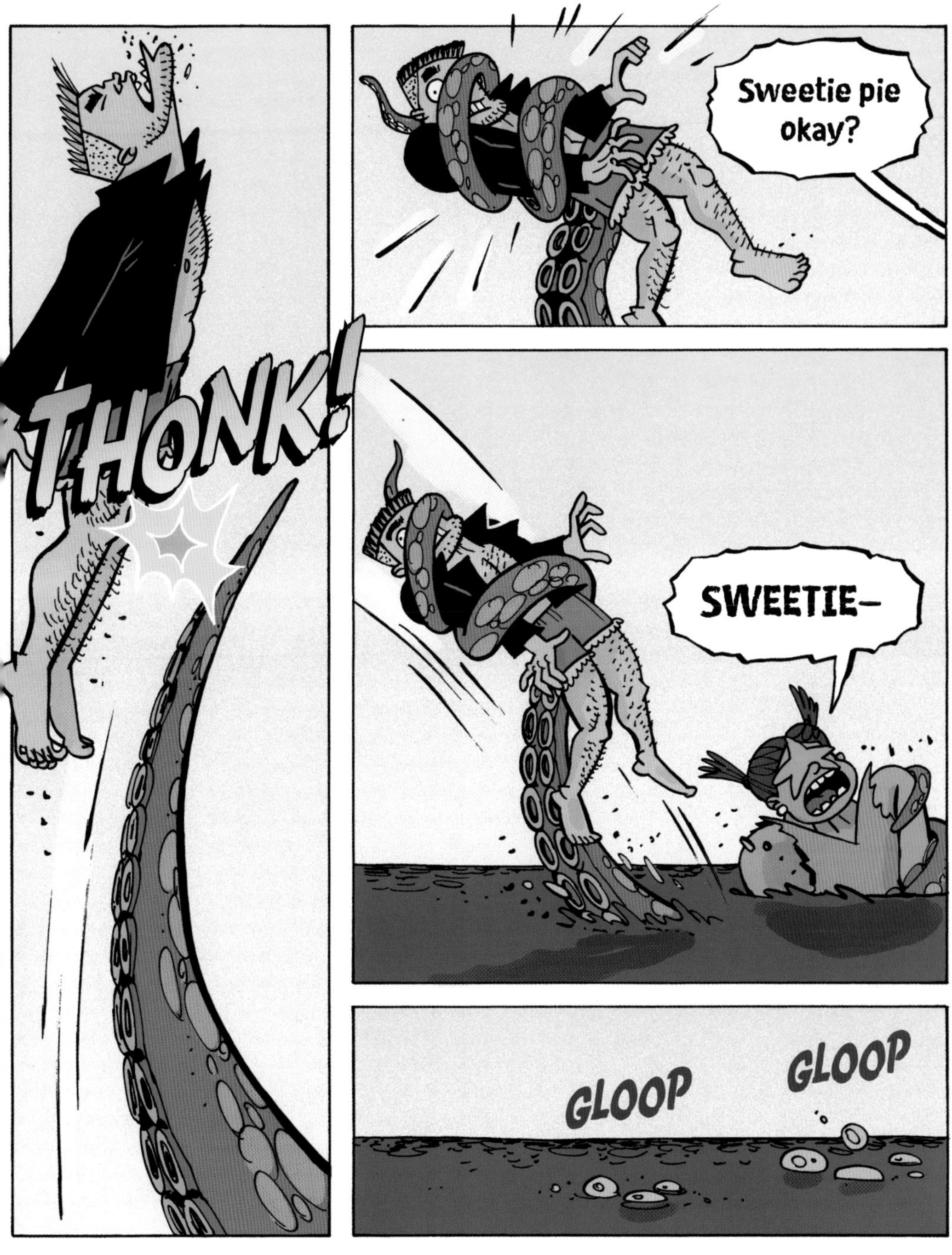
THONK!
Sweetie pie okay?
SWEETIE–
GLOOP
GLOOP

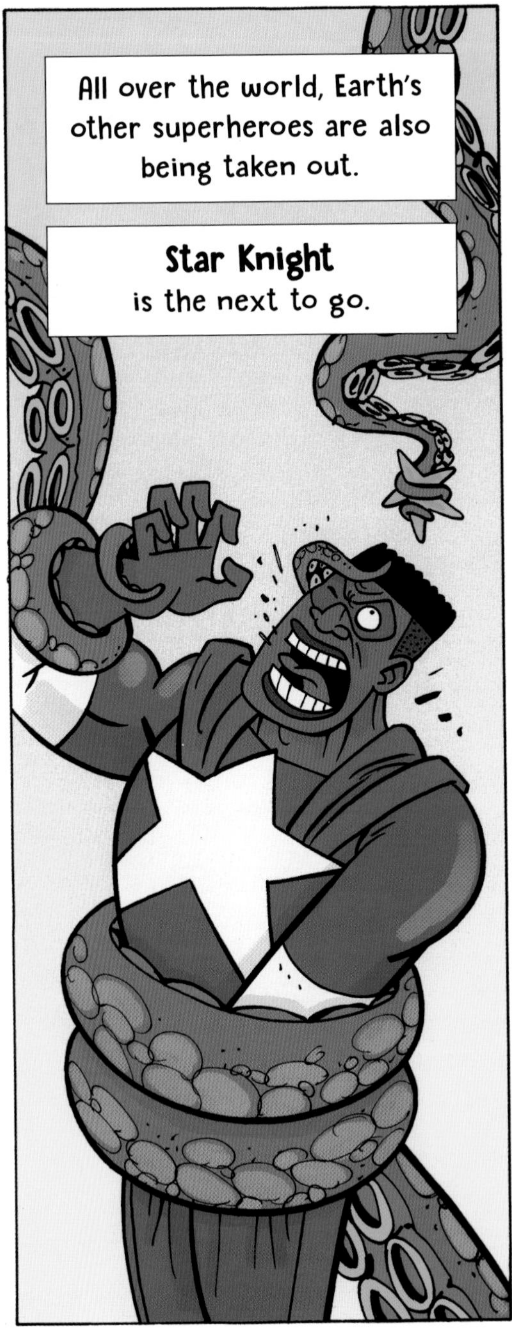
All over the world, Earth's other superheroes are also being taken out.
Star Knight is the next to go.

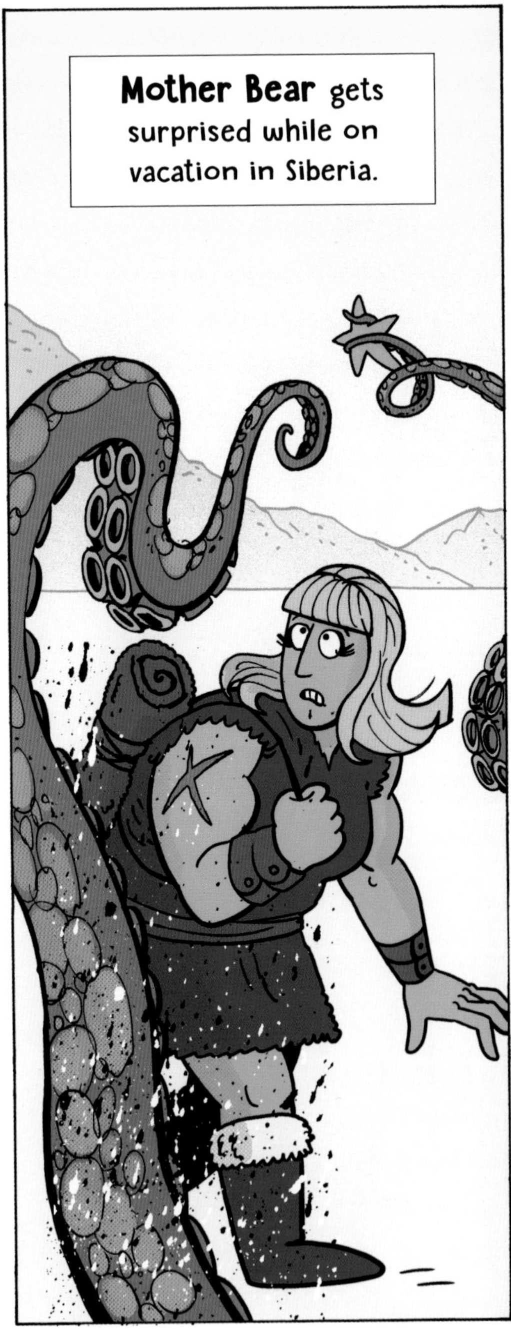
Mother Bear gets surprised while on vacation in Siberia.

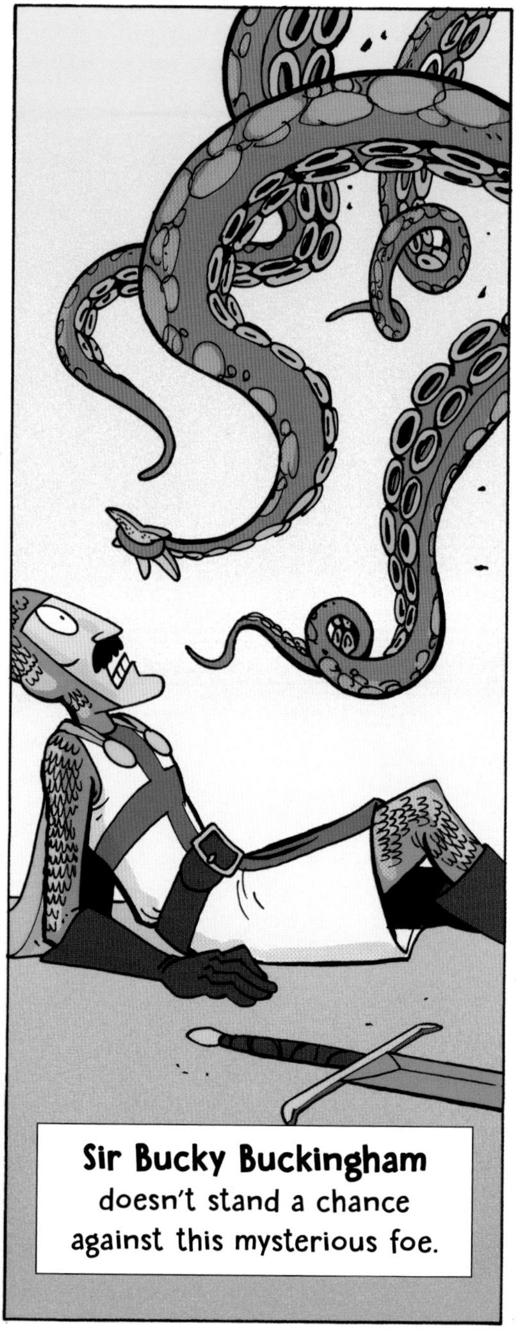
Sir Bucky Buckingham
doesn't stand a chance
against this mysterious foe.

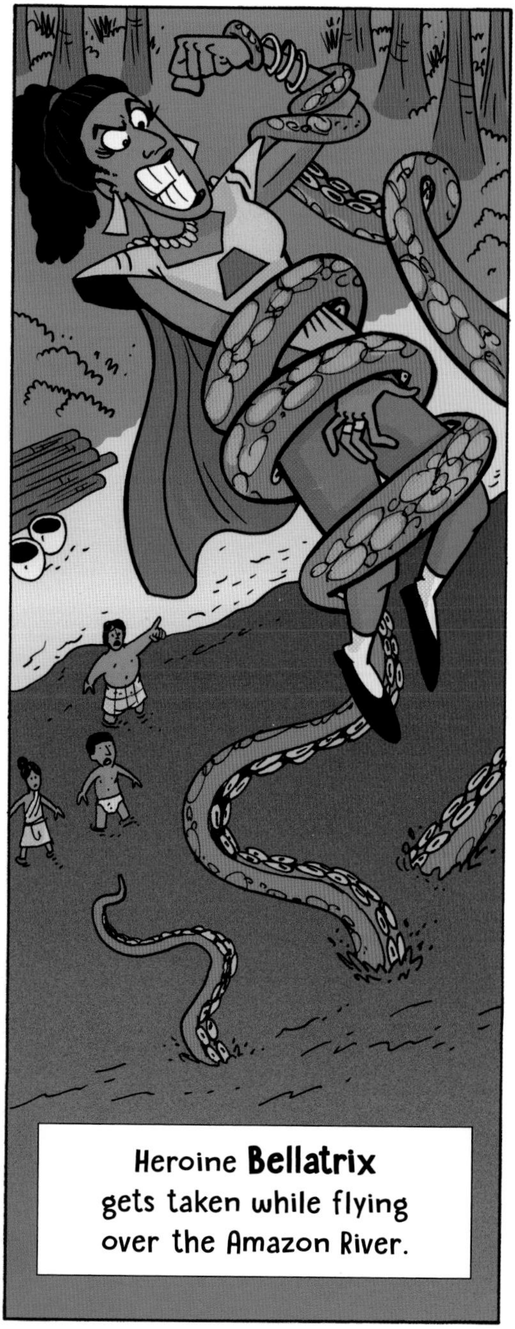
Heroine **Bellatrix**
gets taken while flying
over the Amazon River.

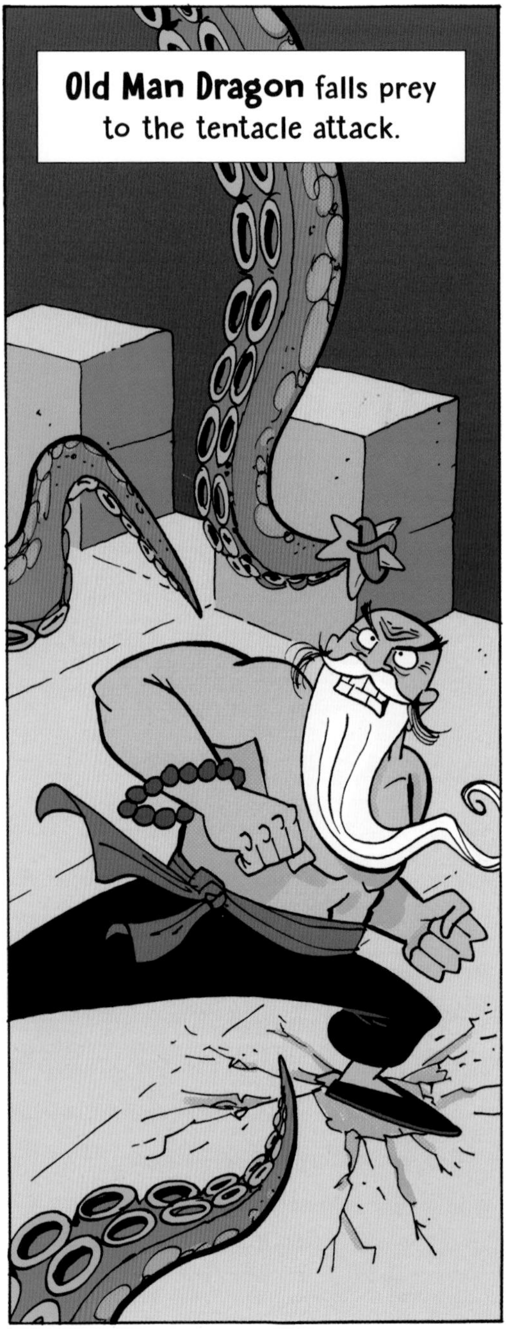
Old Man Dragon falls prey to the tentacle attack.

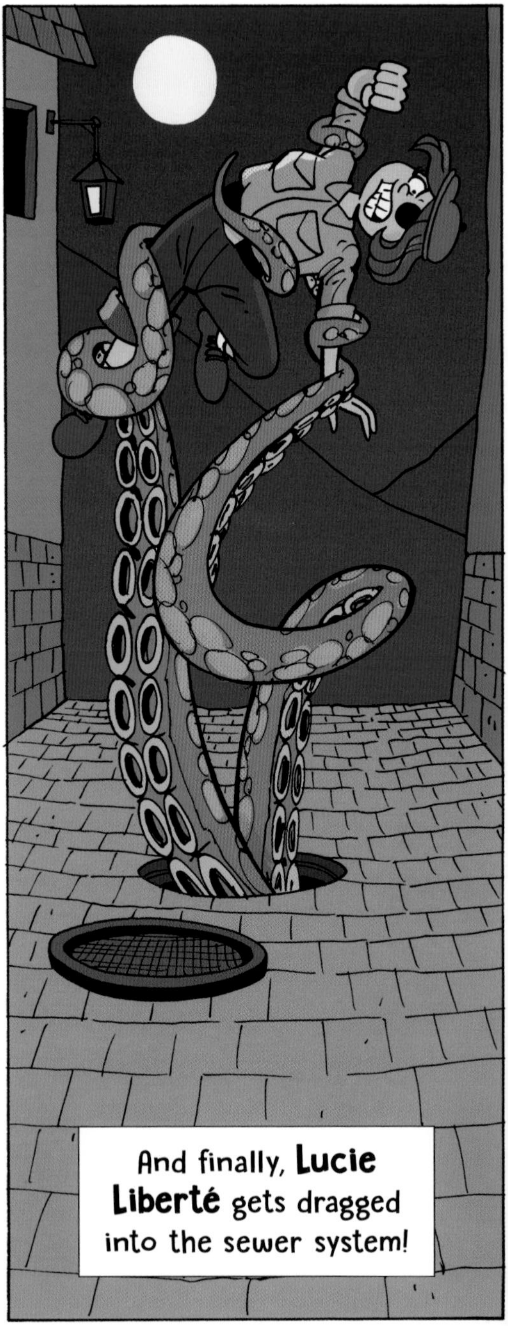
And finally, **Lucie Liberté** gets dragged into the sewer system!

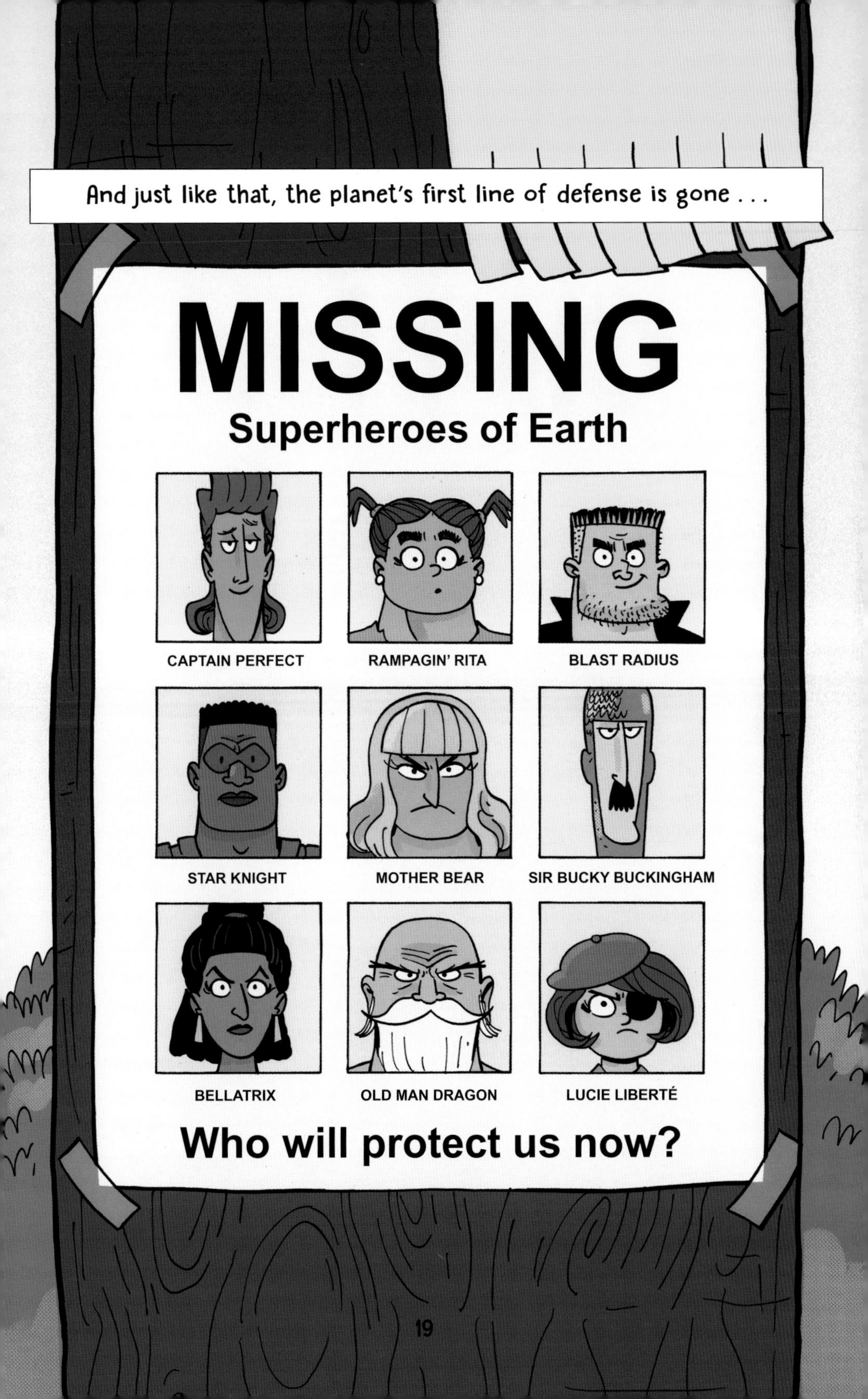

And just like that, the planet's first line of defense is gone . . .
MISSING
Superheroes of Earth
CAPTAIN PERFECT
RAMPAGIN' RITA
BLAST RADIUS
STAR KNIGHT
MOTHER BEAR
SIR BUCKY BUCKINGHAM
BELLATRIX
OLD MAN DRAGON
LUCIE LIBERTÉ
Who will protect us now?

Chapter

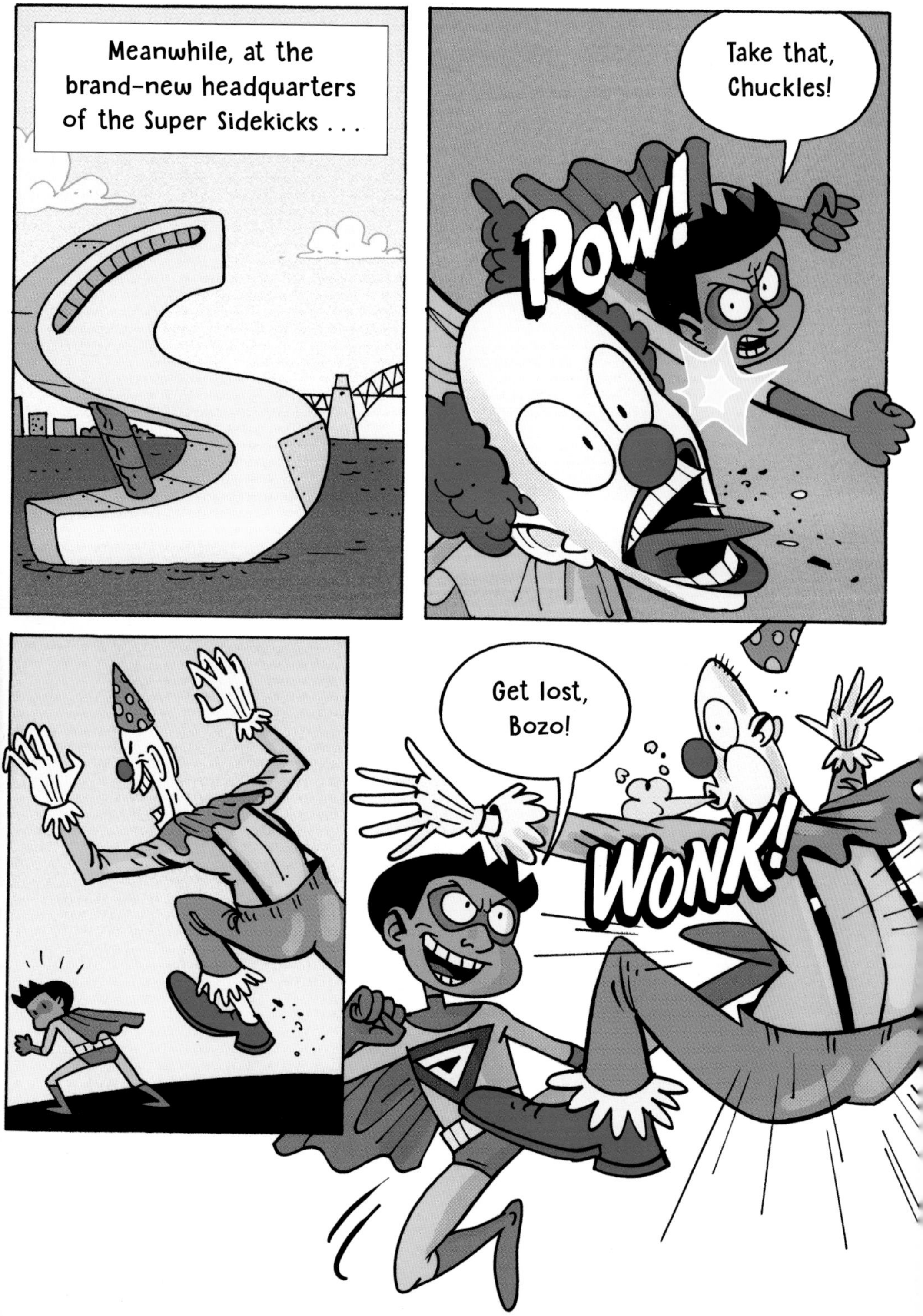
Meanwhile, at the brand-new headquarters of the Super Sidekicks . . .
Take that, Chuckles!
POW!
Get lost, Bozo!
WONK!

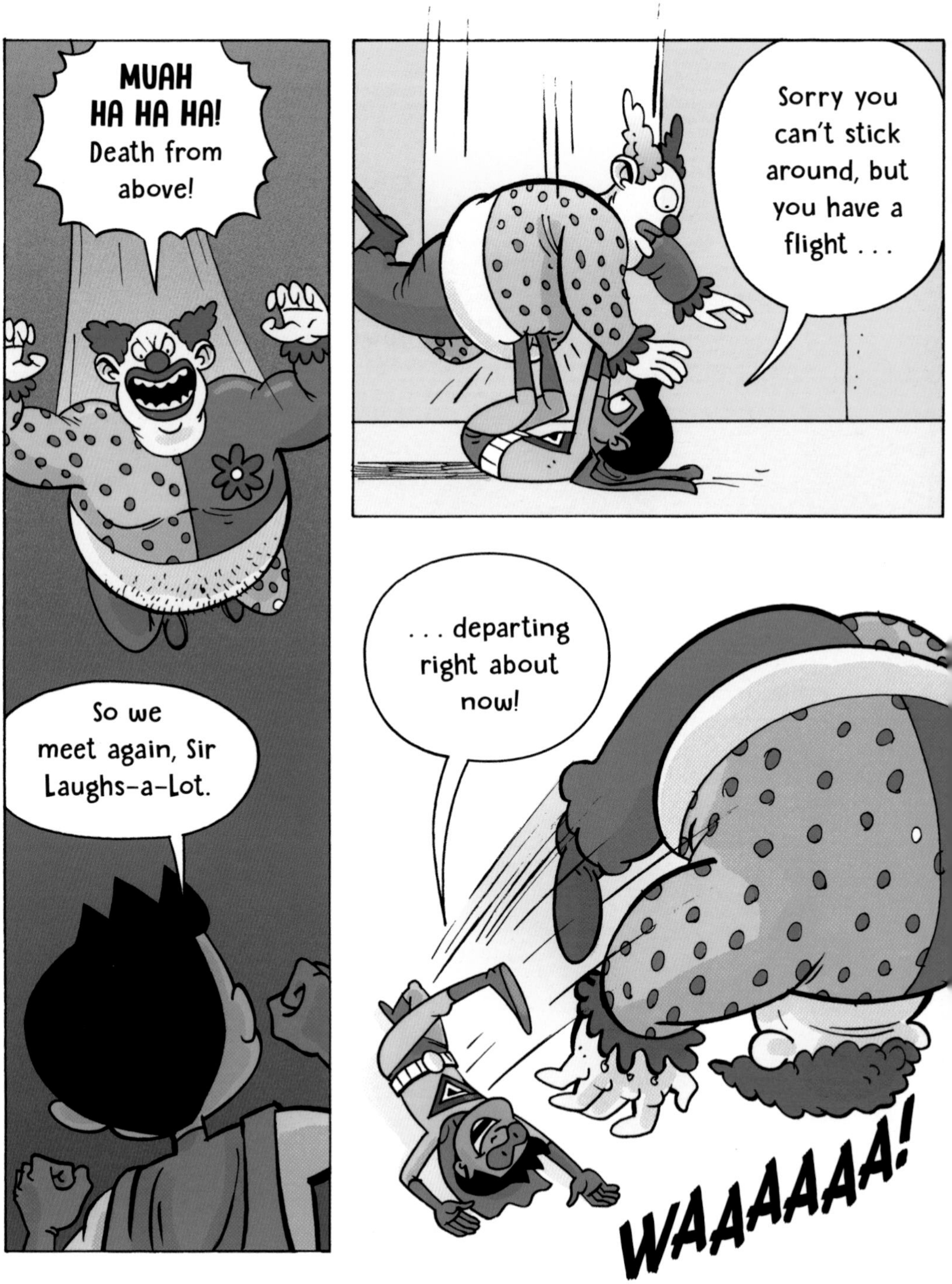
MUAH HA HA HA! Death from above!
So we meet again, Sir Laughs-a-Lot.
Sorry you can't stick around, but you have a flight . . .
. . . departing right about now!
WAAAAAA!

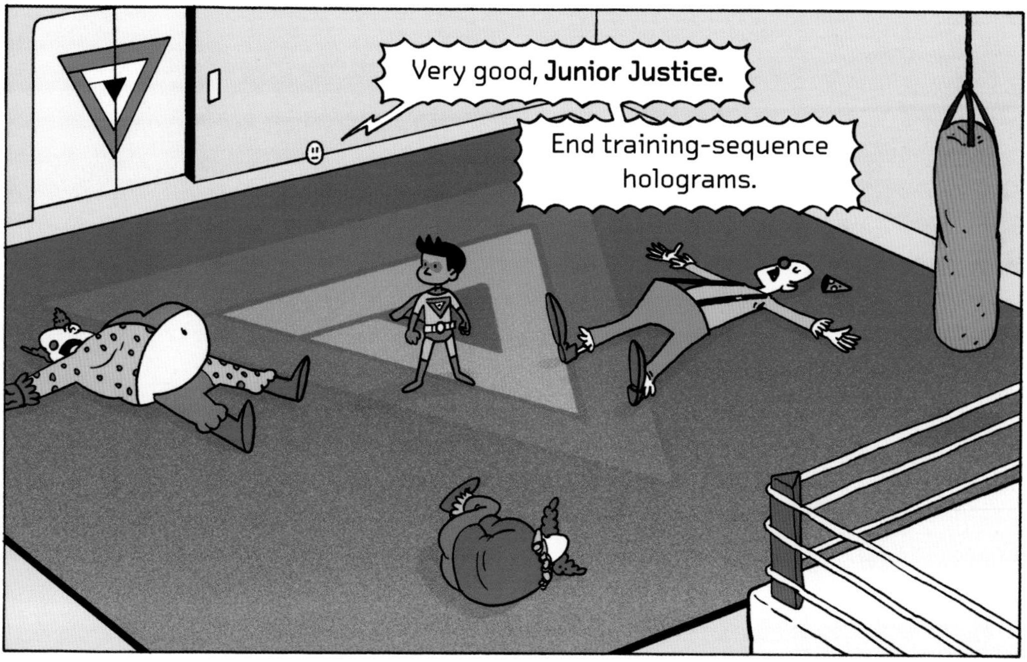
Very good, **Junior Justice.**
End training-sequence holograms.

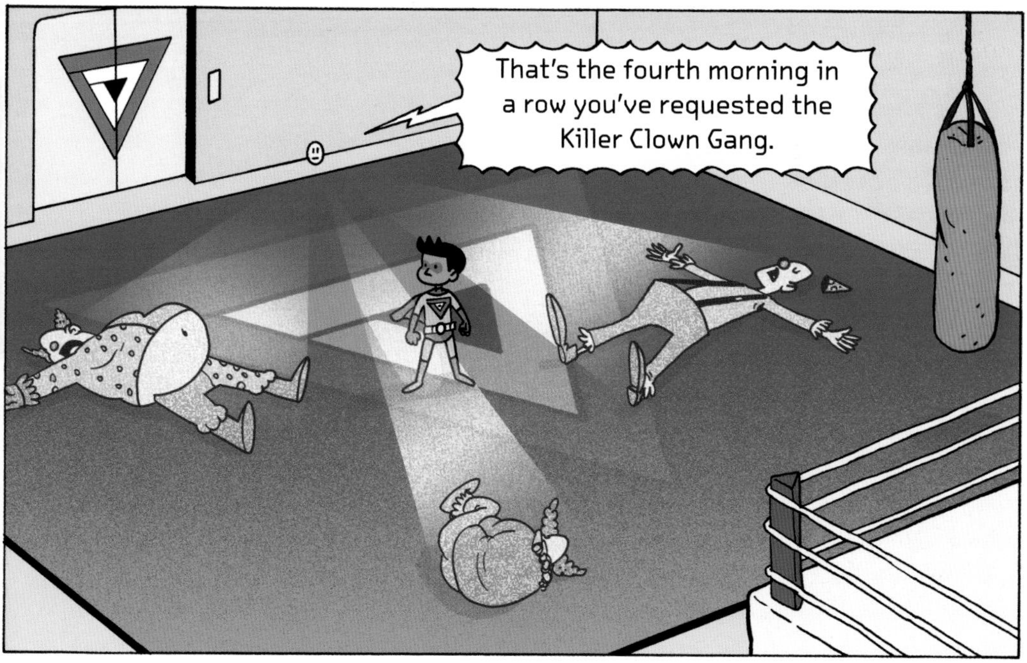
That's the fourth morning in a row you've requested the Killer Clown Gang.

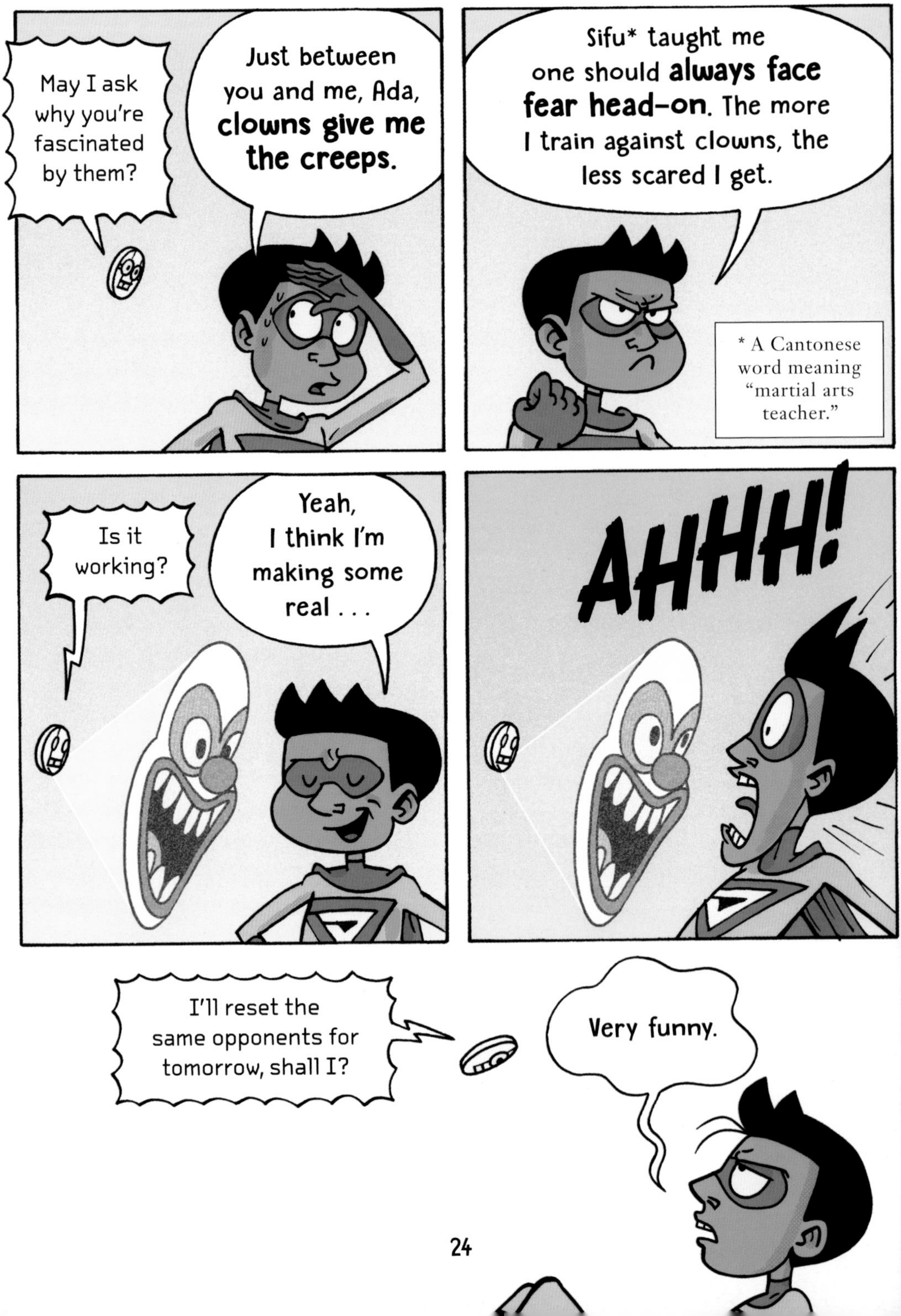

May I ask why you're fascinated by them?
Just between you and me, Ada, clowns give me the creeps.
Sifu* taught me one should always face fear head-on. The more I train against clowns, the less scared I get.
* A Cantonese word meaning "martial arts teacher."
Is it working?
Yeah, I think I'm making some real . . .
AHHH!
I'll reset the same opponents for tomorrow, shall I?
Very funny.

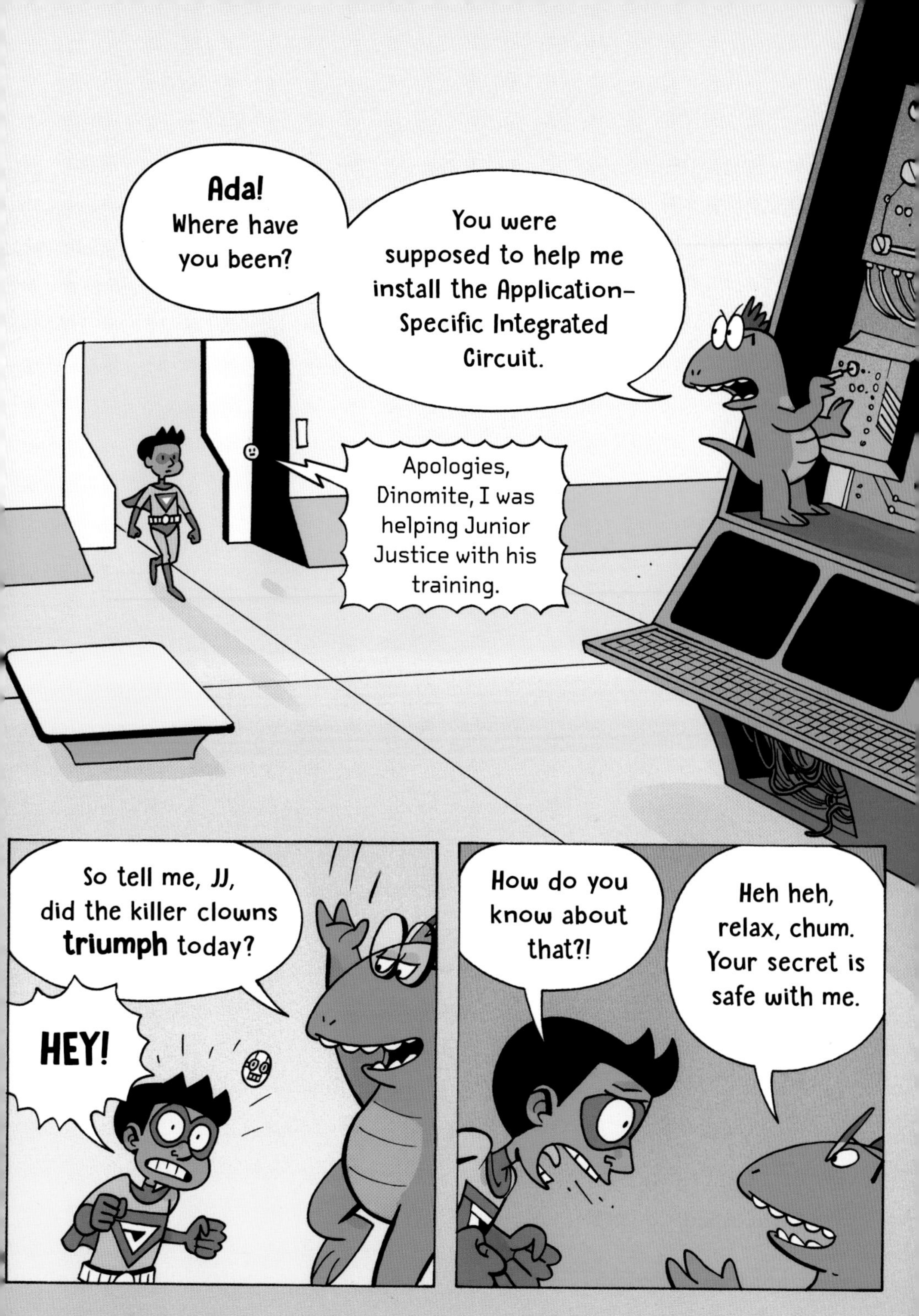
Ada!
Where have you been?
You were supposed to help me install the Application-Specific Integrated Circuit.
Apologies, Dinomite, I was helping Junior Justice with his training.
So tell me, JJ, did the killer clowns **triumph** today?
HEY!
How do you know about that?!
Heh heh, relax, chum. Your secret is safe with me.

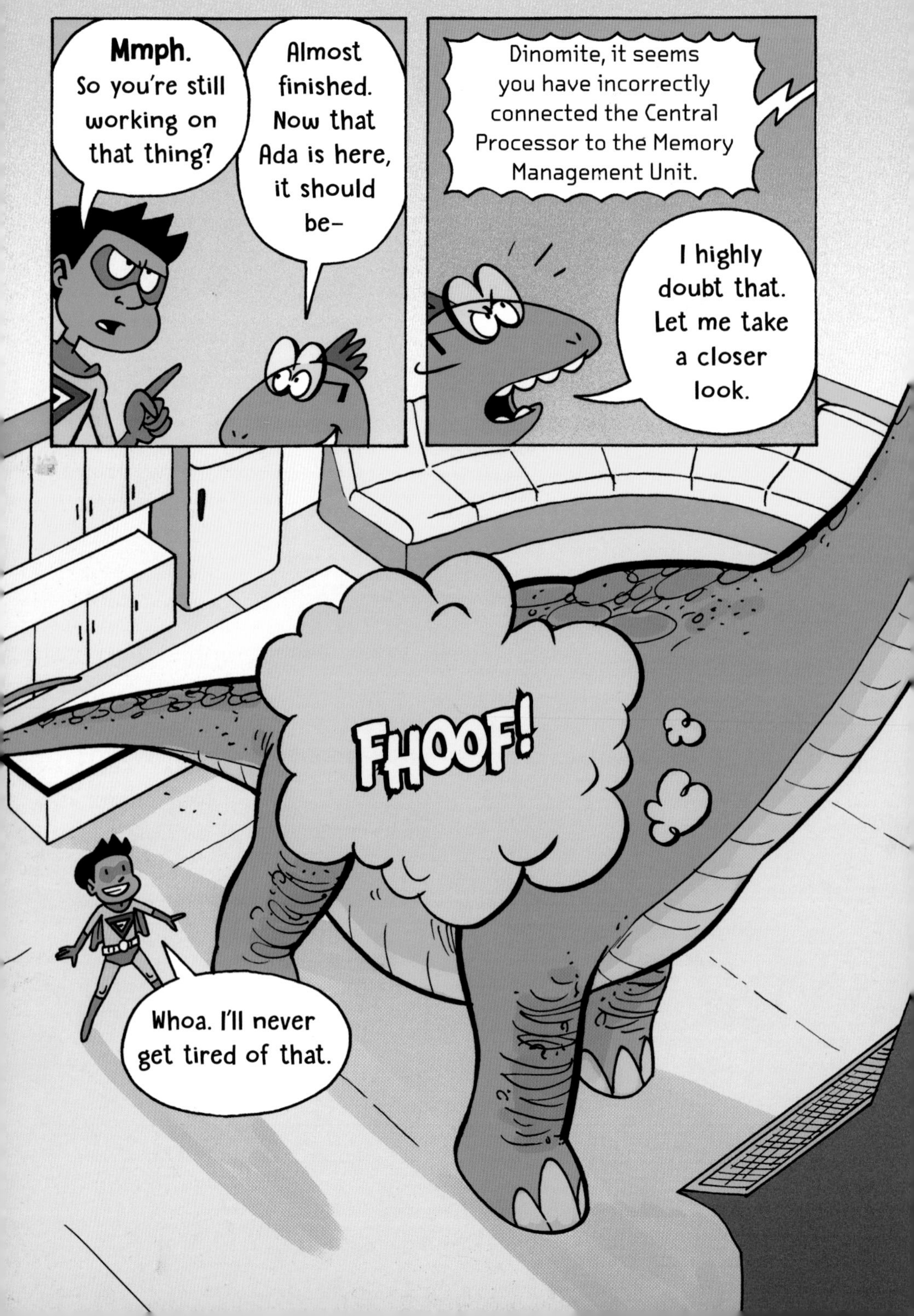
Mmph.
So you're still working on that thing?
Almost finished. Now that Ada is here, it should be–
Dinomite, it seems you have incorrectly connected the Central Processor to the Memory Management Unit.
I highly doubt that. Let me take a closer look.
FHOOF!
Whoa. I'll never get tired of that.

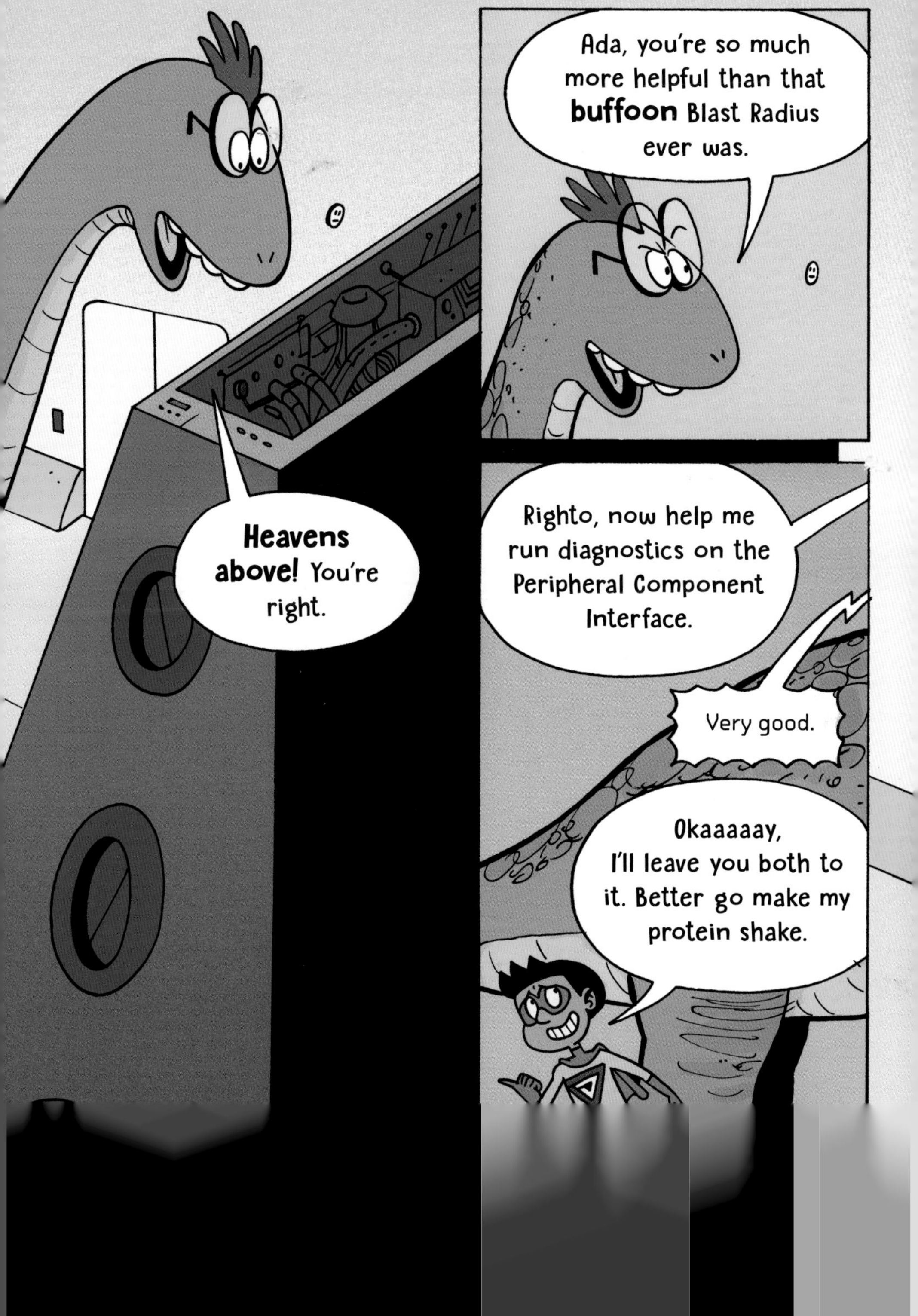
Heavens above! You're right.
Ada, you're so much more helpful than that buffoon Blast Radius ever was.
Righto, now help me run diagnostics on the Peripheral Component Interface.
Very good.
Okaaaaay, I'll leave you both to it. Better go make my protein shake.

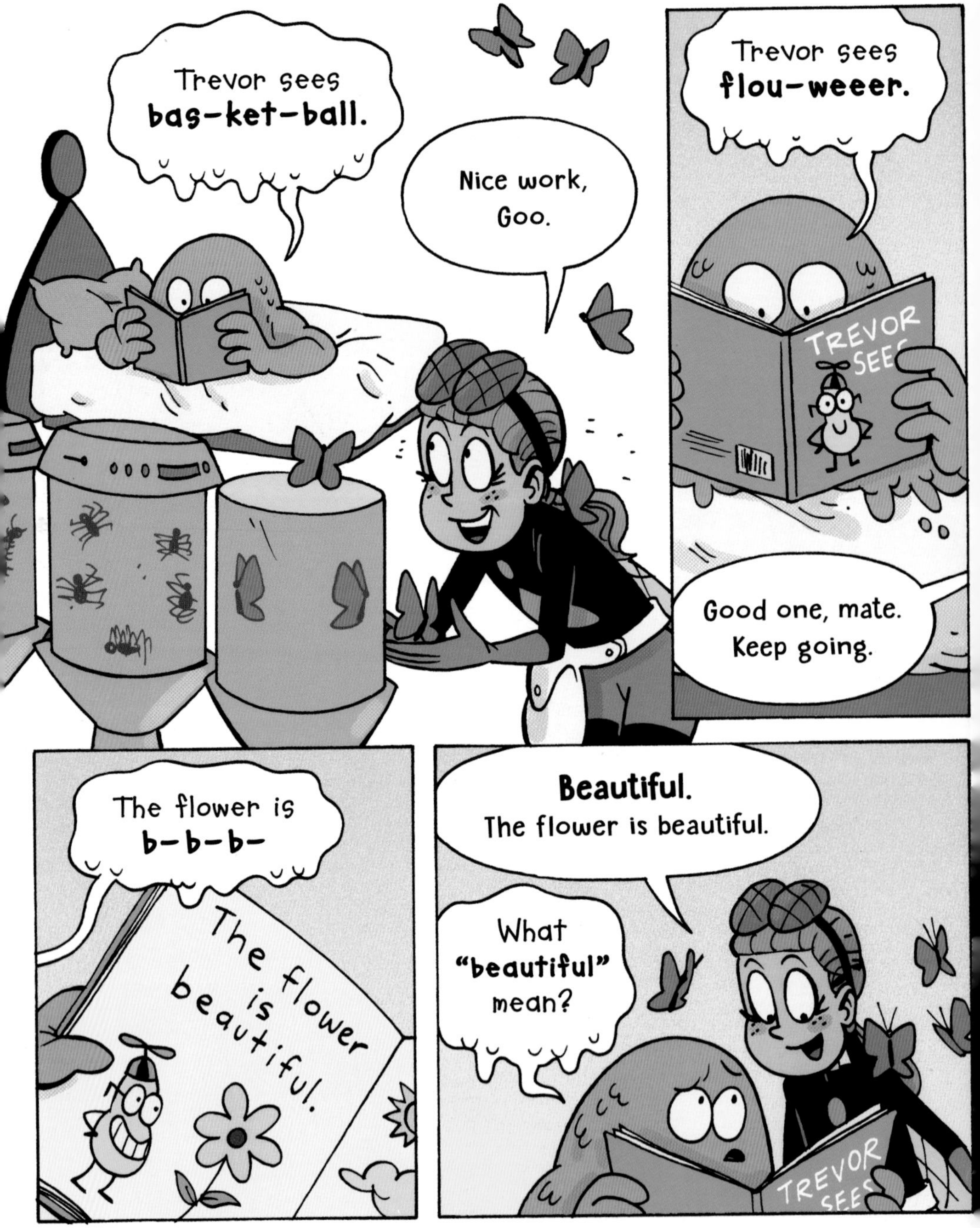
Trevor sees
bas-ket-ball.
Nice work, Goo.
Trevor sees
flou-weeer.
TREVOR SEES
Good one, mate. Keep going.
The flower is
b-b-b-
The flower is beautiful.
Beautiful.
The flower is beautiful.
What "beautiful" mean?
TREVOR SEES

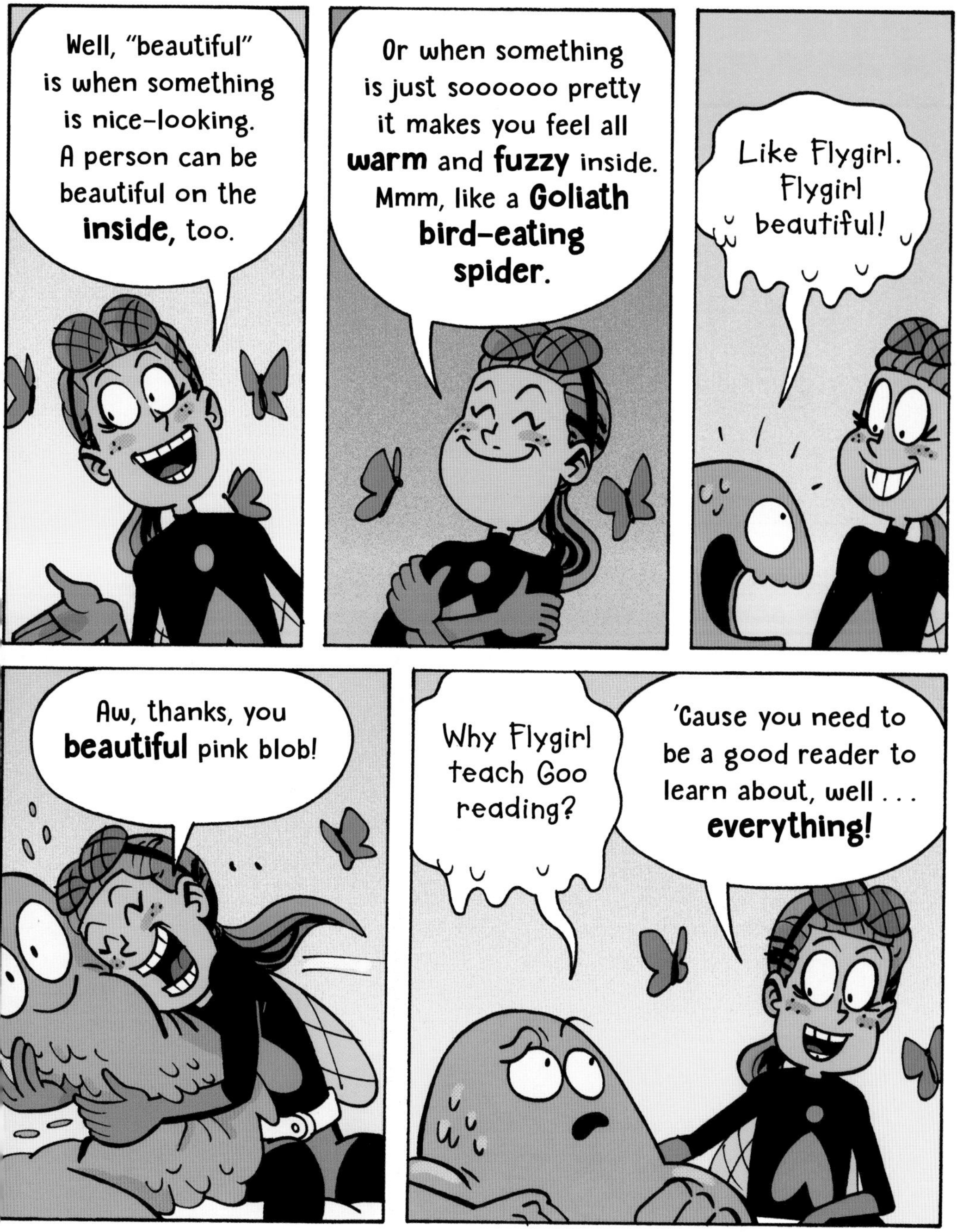
Well, "beautiful" is when something is nice-looking. A person can be beautiful on the **inside,** too.
Or when something is just soooooo pretty it makes you feel all **warm** and **fuzzy** inside. Mmm, like a **Goliath bird-eating spider.**
Like Flygirl. Flygirl beautiful!
Aw, thanks, you **beautiful** pink blob!
Why Flygirl teach Goo reading?
'Cause you need to be a good reader to learn about, well . . . **everything!**

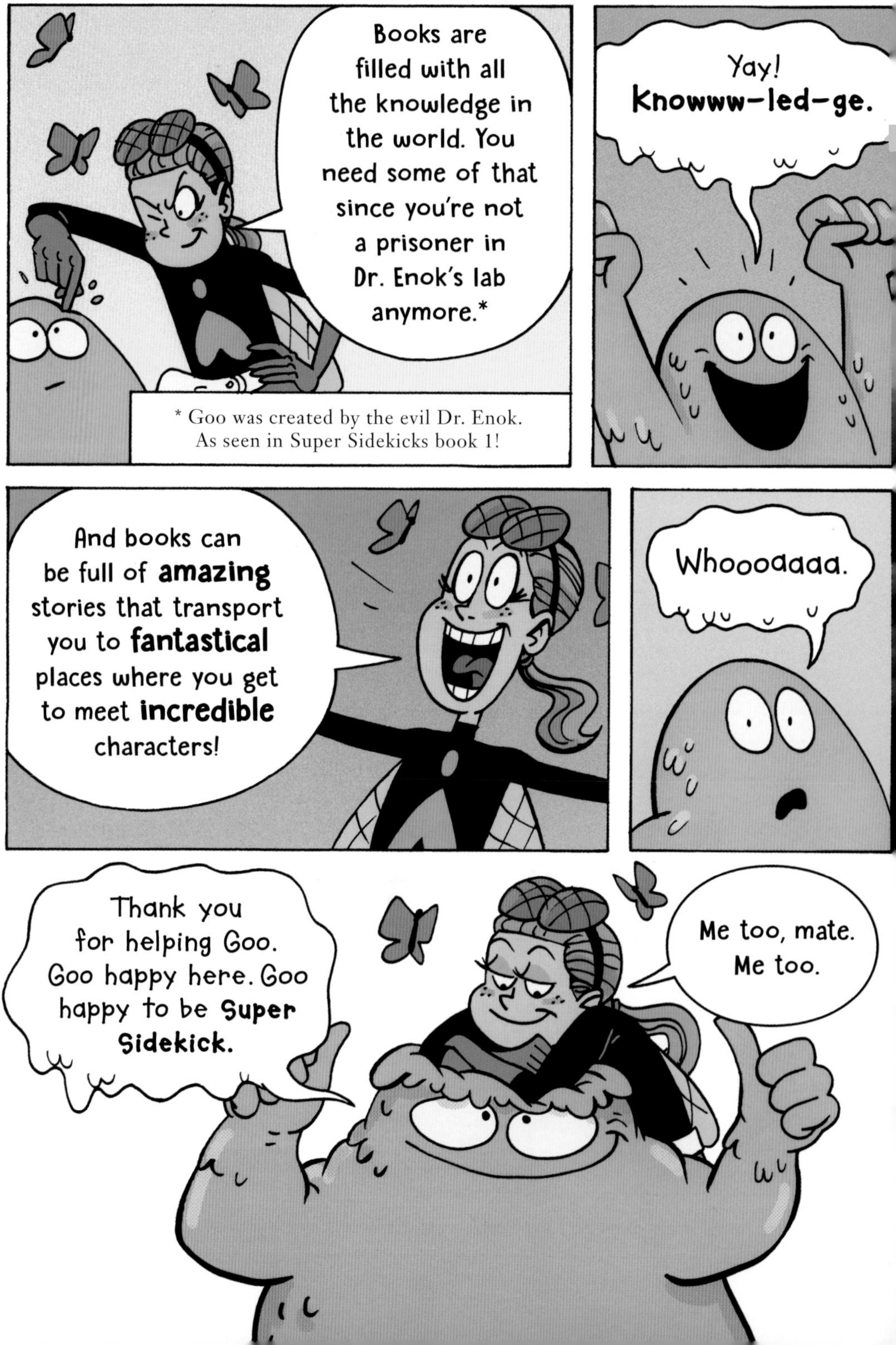
Books are filled with all the knowledge in the world. You need some of that since you're not a prisoner in Dr. Enok's lab anymore.*
* Goo was created by the evil Dr. Enok. As seen in Super Sidekicks book 1!
Yay! Knowww-led-ge.
And books can be full of amazing stories that transport you to fantastical places where you get to meet incredible characters!
Whoooaaaa.
Thank you for helping Goo. Goo happy here. Goo happy to be Super Sidekick.
Me too, mate. Me too.

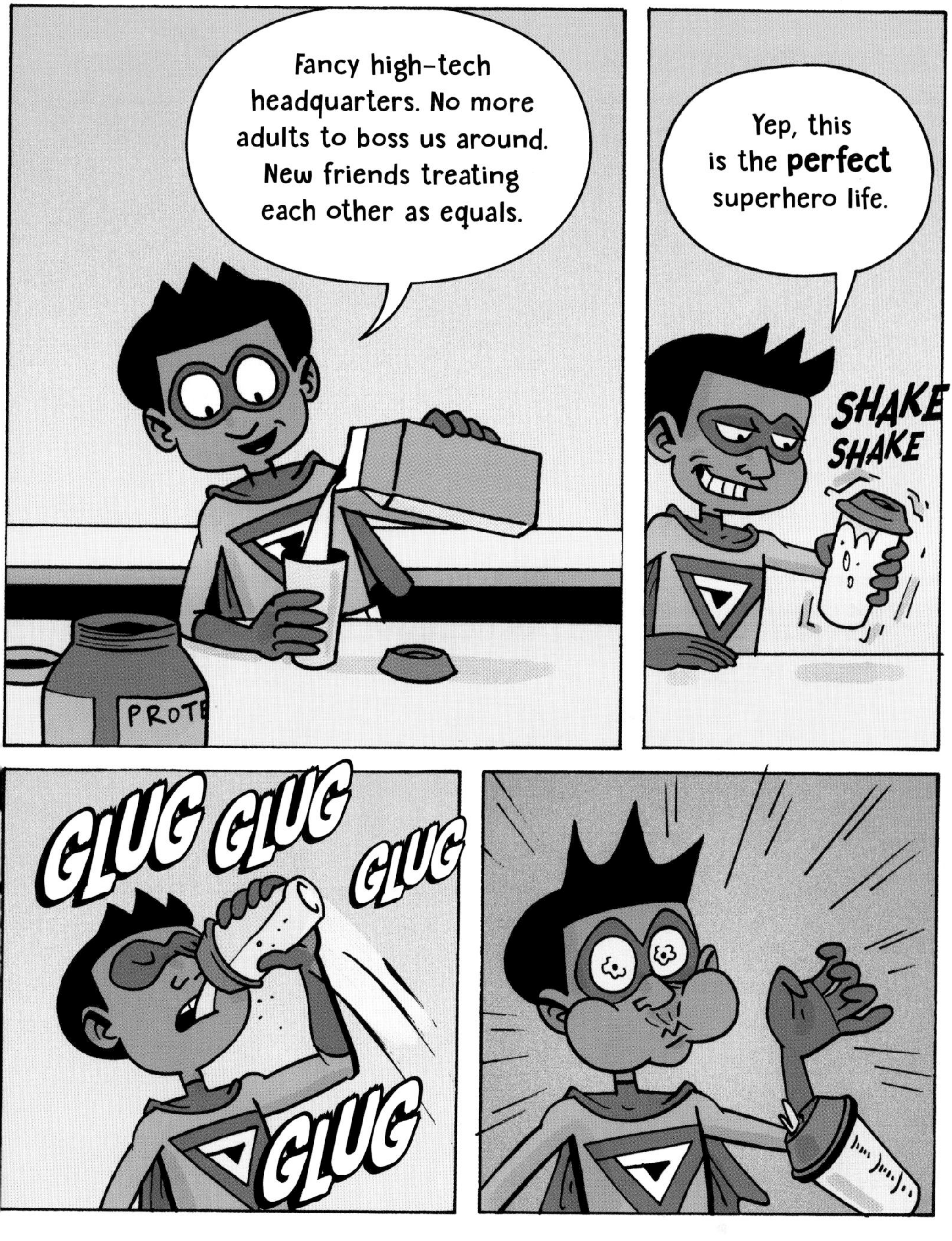
Fancy high-tech headquarters. No more adults to boss us around. New friends treating each other as equals.
PROTE
Yep, this is the **perfect** superhero life.
SHAKE
SHAKE
GLUG GLUG
GLUG
GLUG

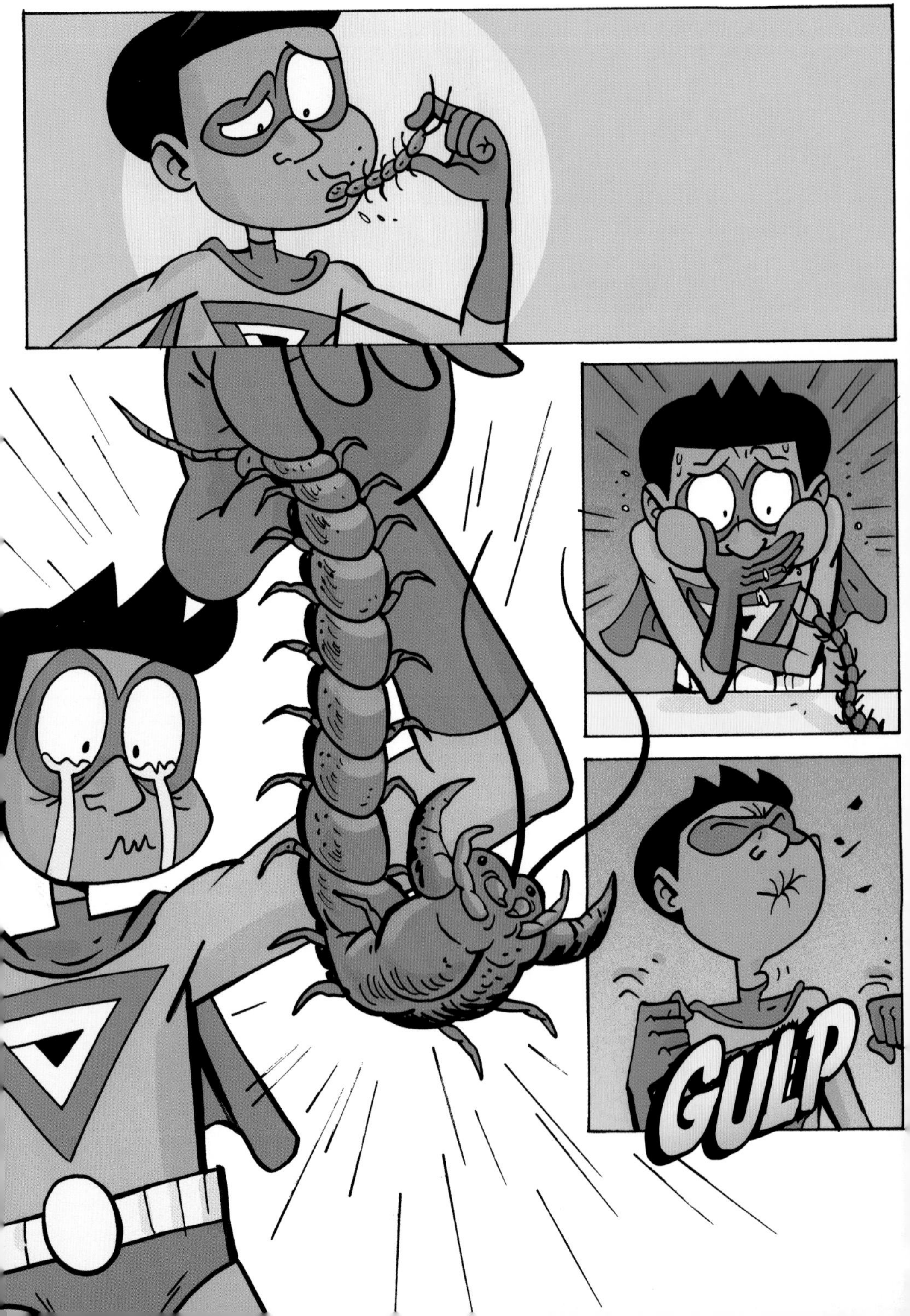
GULP

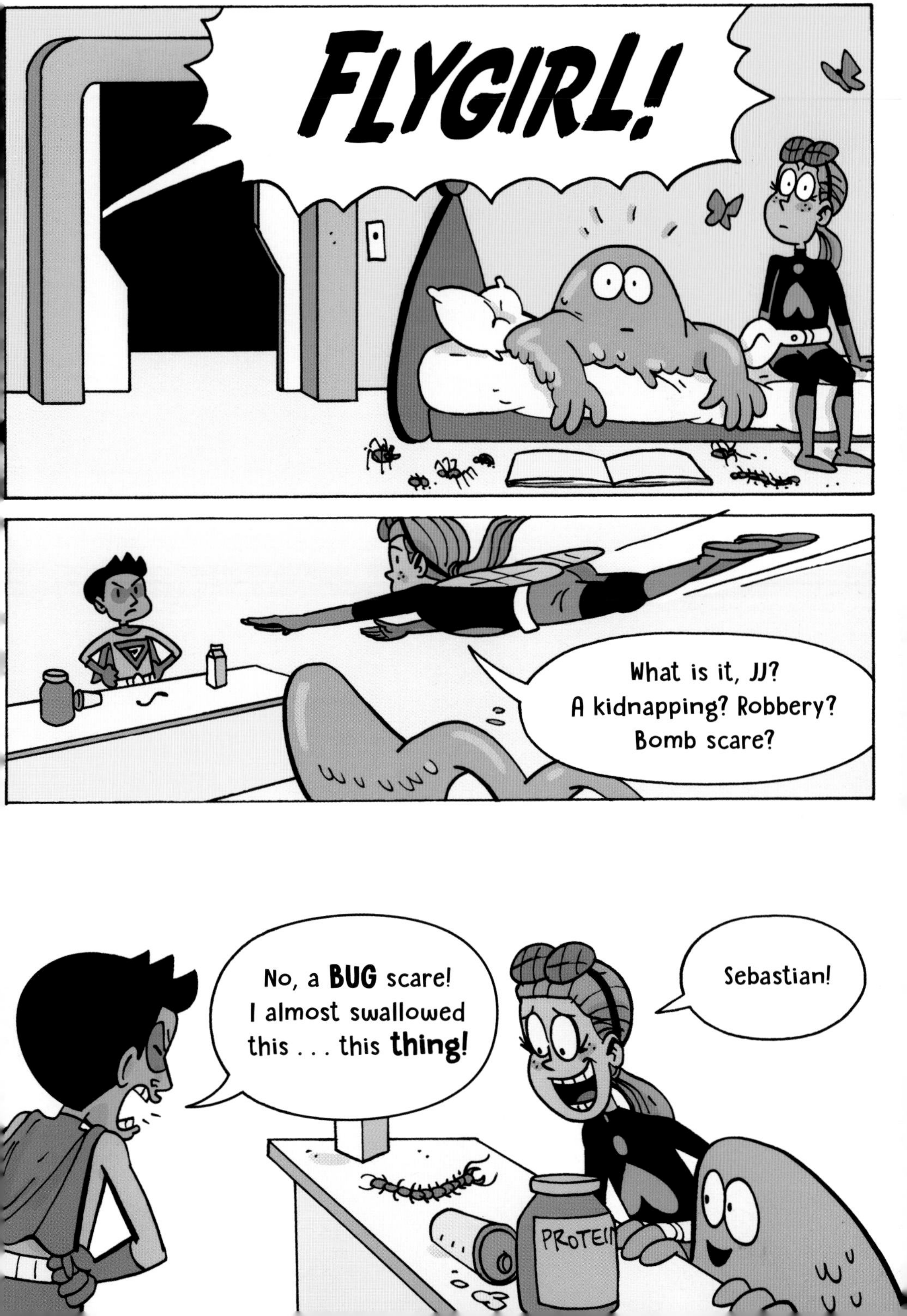
FLYGIRL!
What is it, JJ? A kidnapping? Robbery? Bomb scare?
No, a BUG scare! I almost swallowed this . . . this thing!
Sebastian!
PROTEI

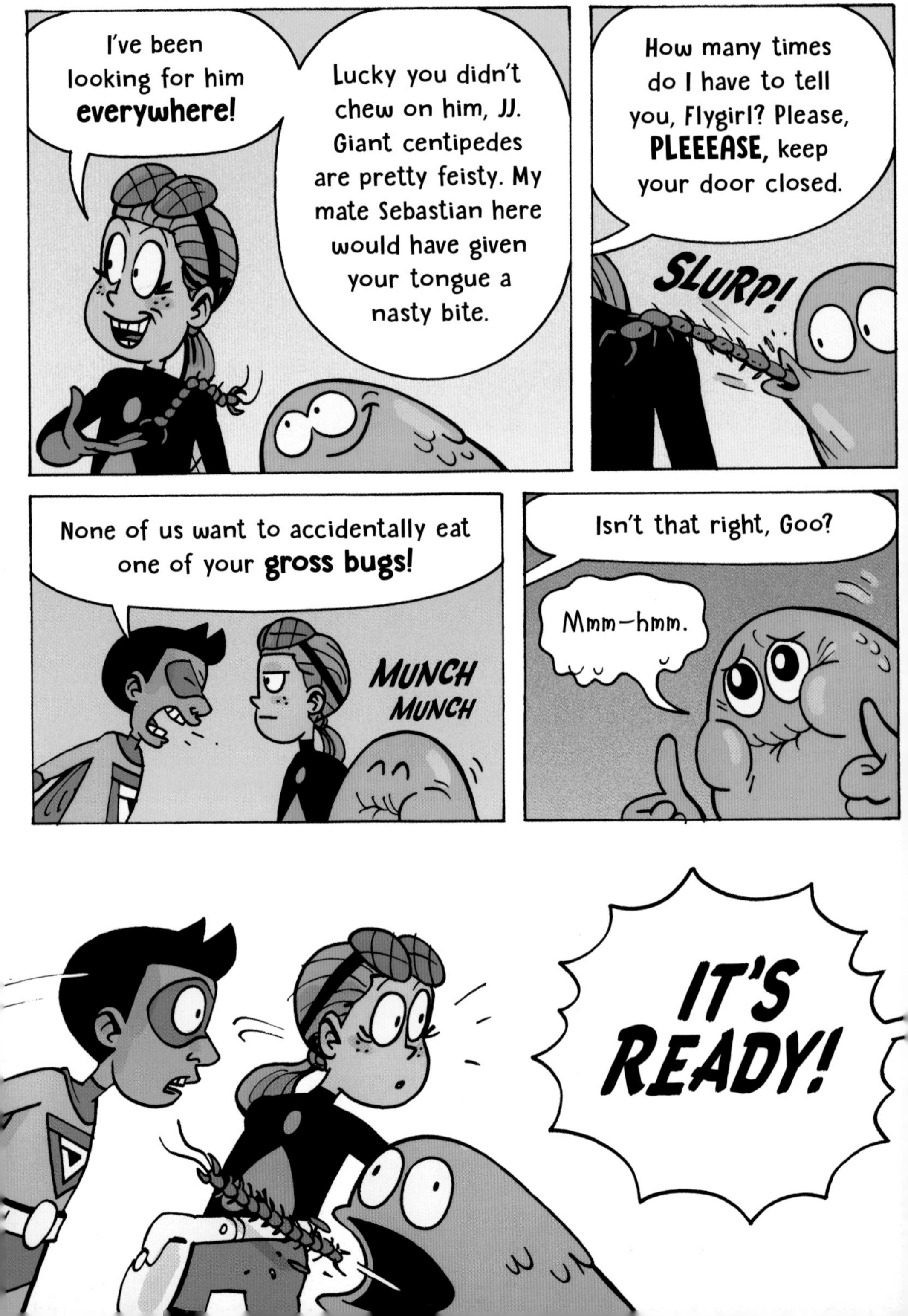
I've been looking for him **everywhere!**
Lucky you didn't chew on him, JJ. Giant centipedes are pretty feisty. My mate Sebastian here would have given your tongue a nasty bite.
How many times do I have to tell you, Flygirl? Please, **PLEEEASE,** keep your door closed.
SLURP!
None of us want to accidentally eat one of your **gross bugs!**
MUNCH MUNCH
Isn't that right, Goo?
Mmm-hmm.
IT'S READY!

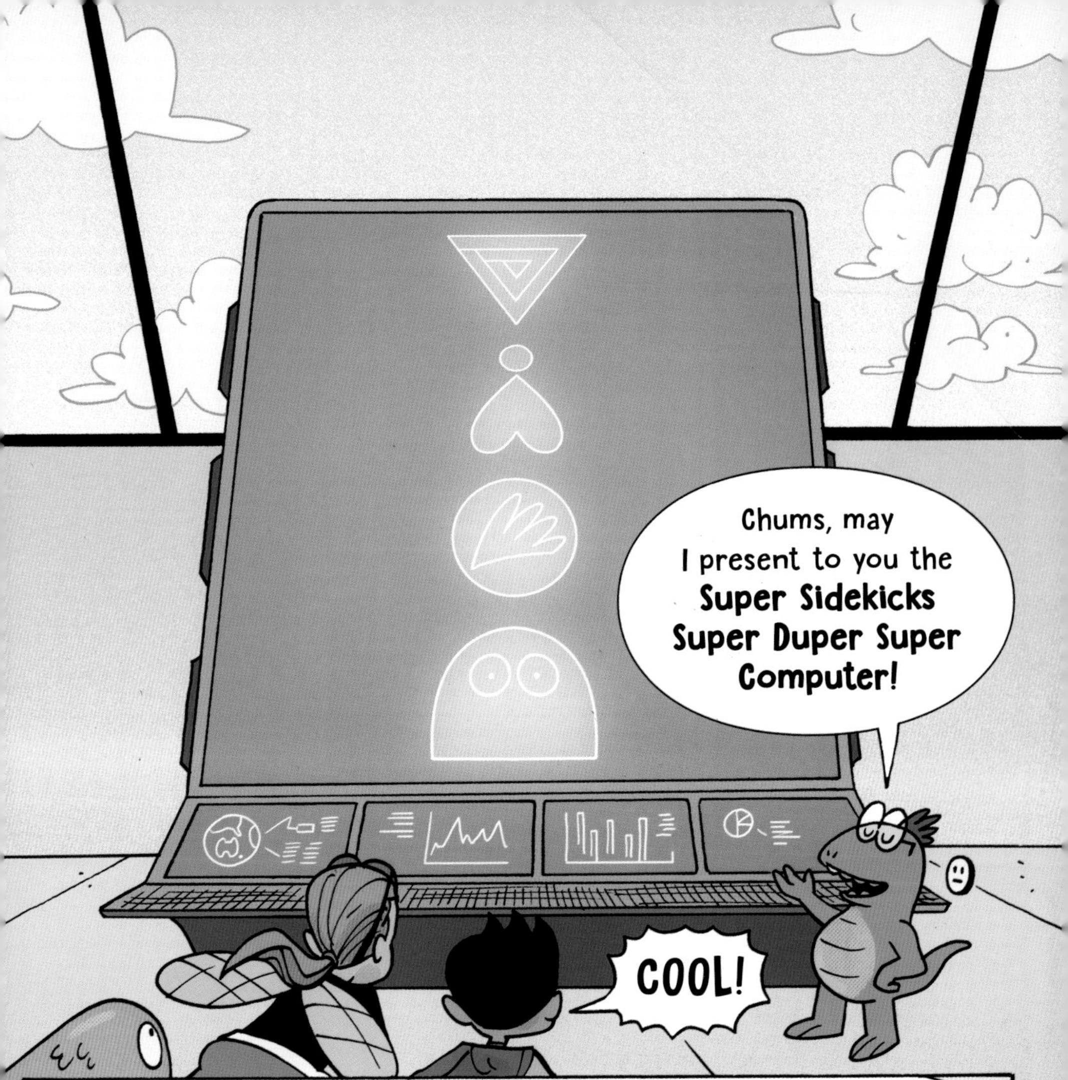
Chums, may I present to you the **Super Sidekicks Super Duper Super Computer!**
COOL!

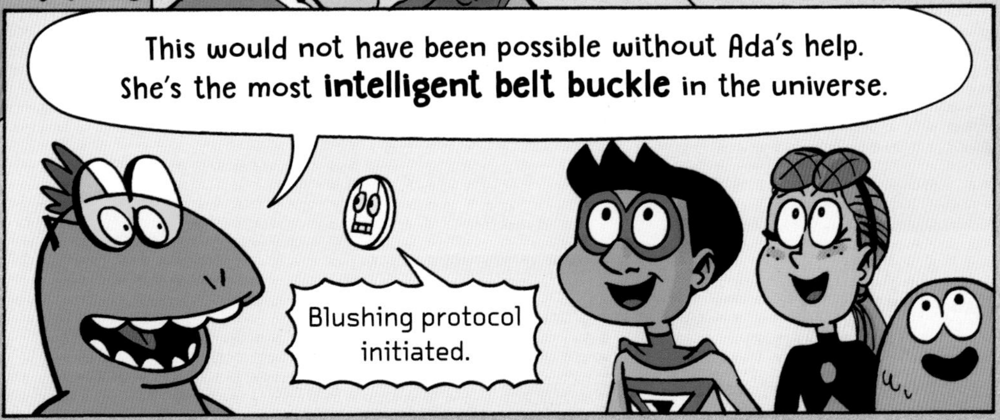
This would not have been possible without Ada's help. She's the most **intelligent belt buckle** in the universe.
Blushing protocol initiated.

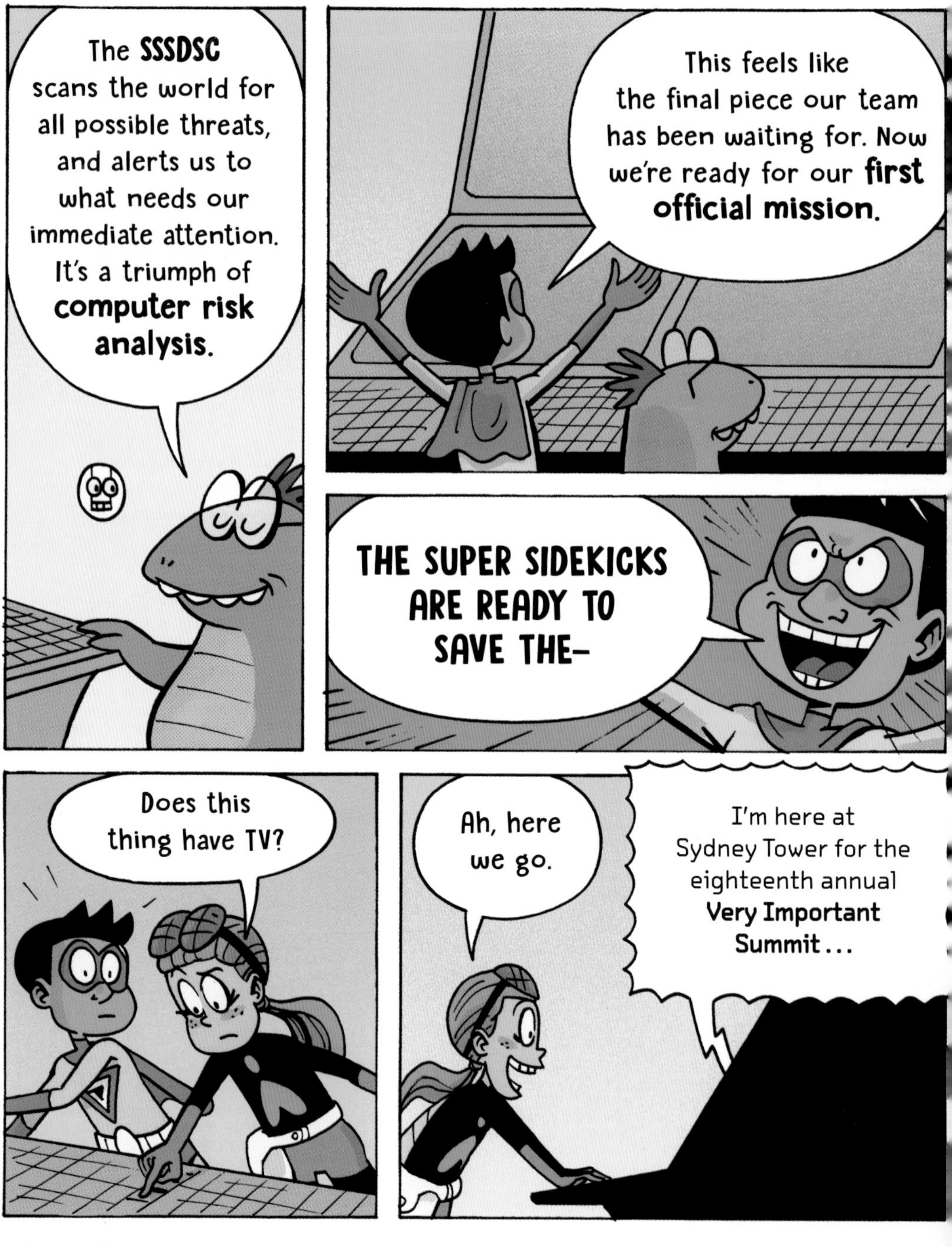
The **SSSDSC** scans the world for all possible threats, and alerts us to what needs our immediate attention. It's a triumph of **computer risk analysis.**
This feels like the final piece our team has been waiting for. Now we're ready for our **first official mission.**
THE SUPER SIDEKICKS ARE READY TO SAVE THE–
Does this thing have TV?
Ah, here we go.
I'm here at Sydney Tower for the eighteenth annual **Very Important Summit...**

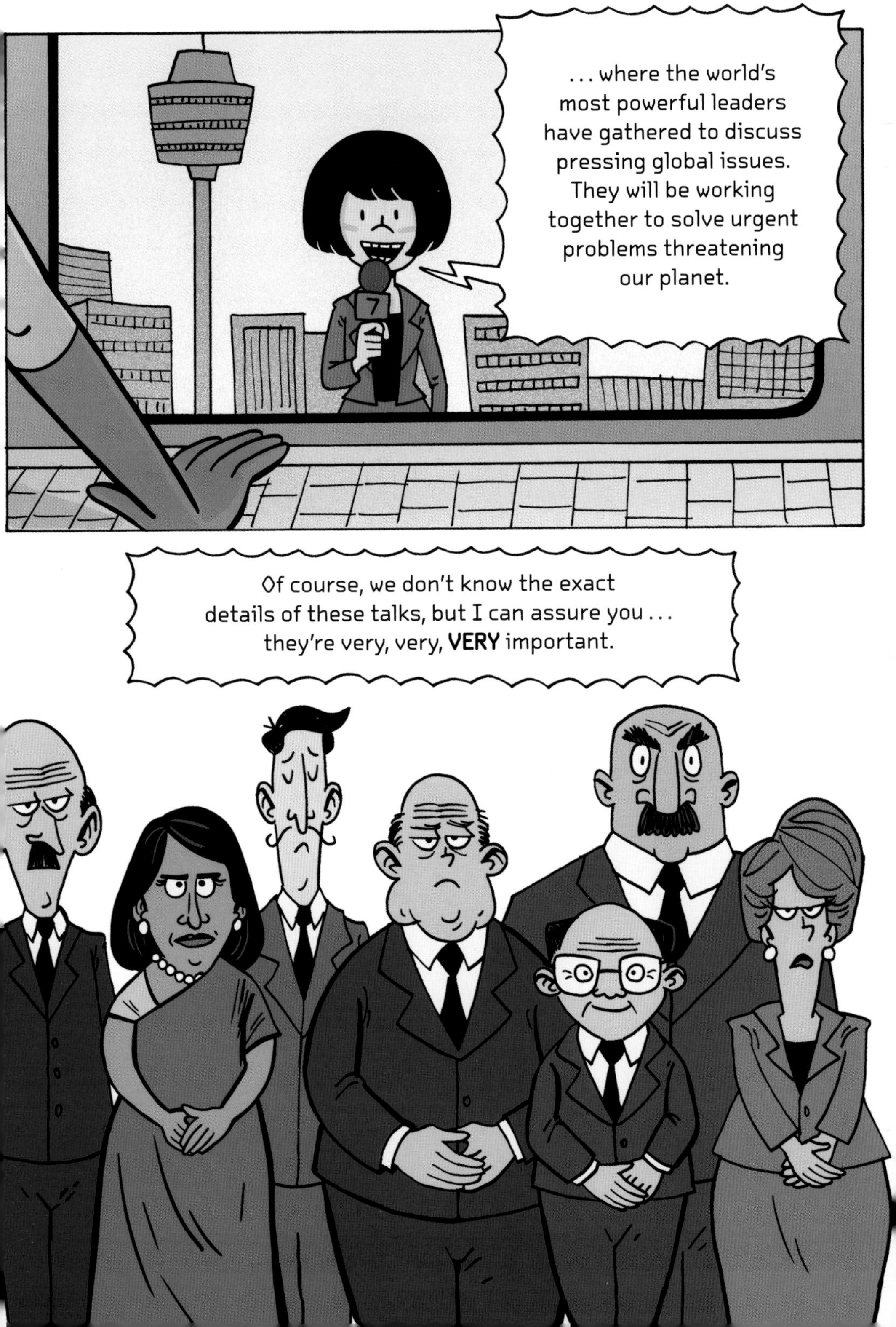
. . . where the world's most powerful leaders have gathered to discuss pressing global issues. They will be working together to solve urgent problems threatening our planet.
7
Of course, we don't know the exact details of these talks, but I can assure you . . . they're very, very, **VERY** important.

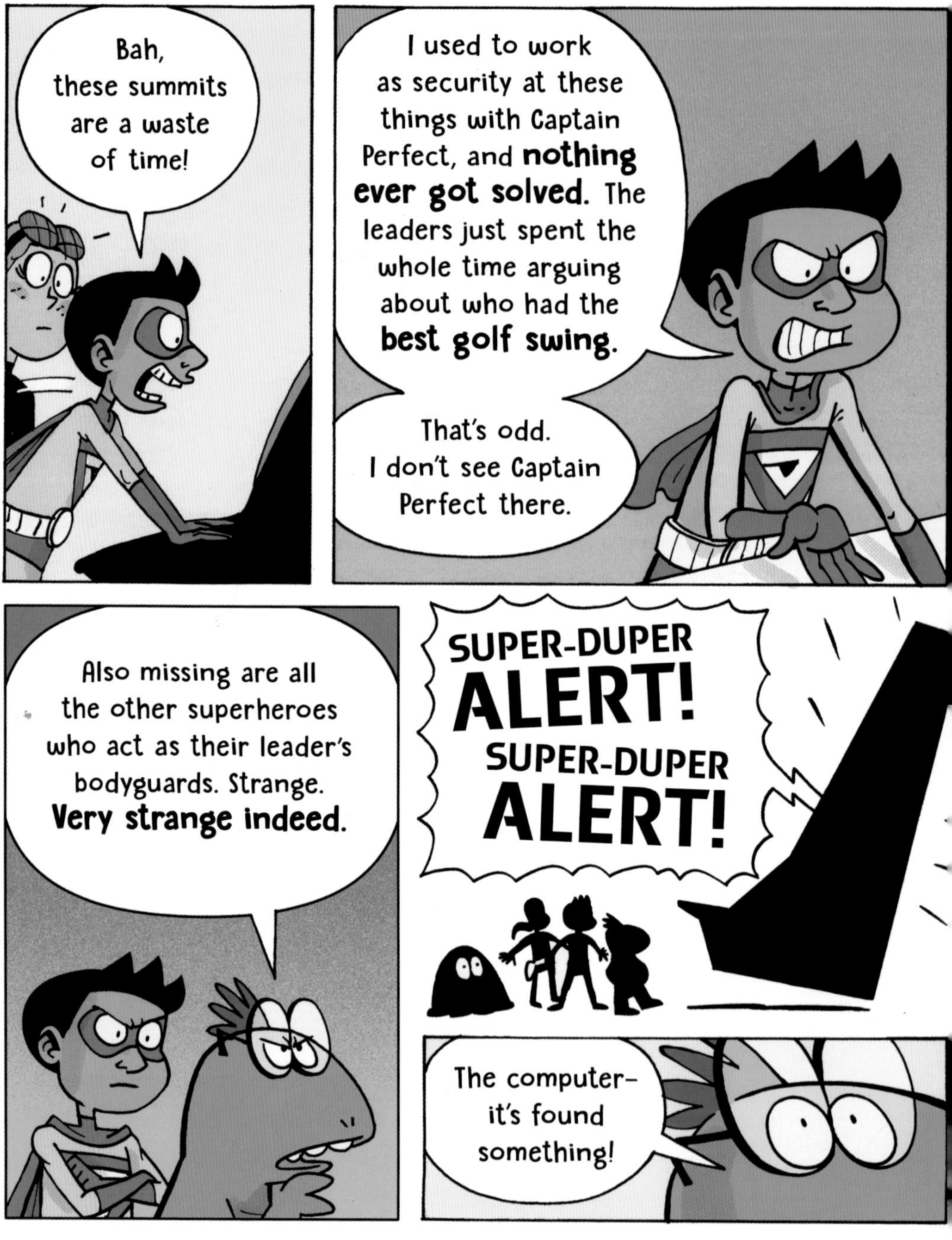
Bah, these summits are a waste of time!
I used to work as security at these things with Captain Perfect, and **nothing ever got solved**. The leaders just spent the whole time arguing about who had the **best golf swing**.
That's odd. I don't see Captain Perfect there.
Also missing are all the other superheroes who act as their leader's bodyguards. Strange. **Very strange indeed.**
SUPER-DUPER ALERT! SUPER-DUPER ALERT!
The computer–it's found something!

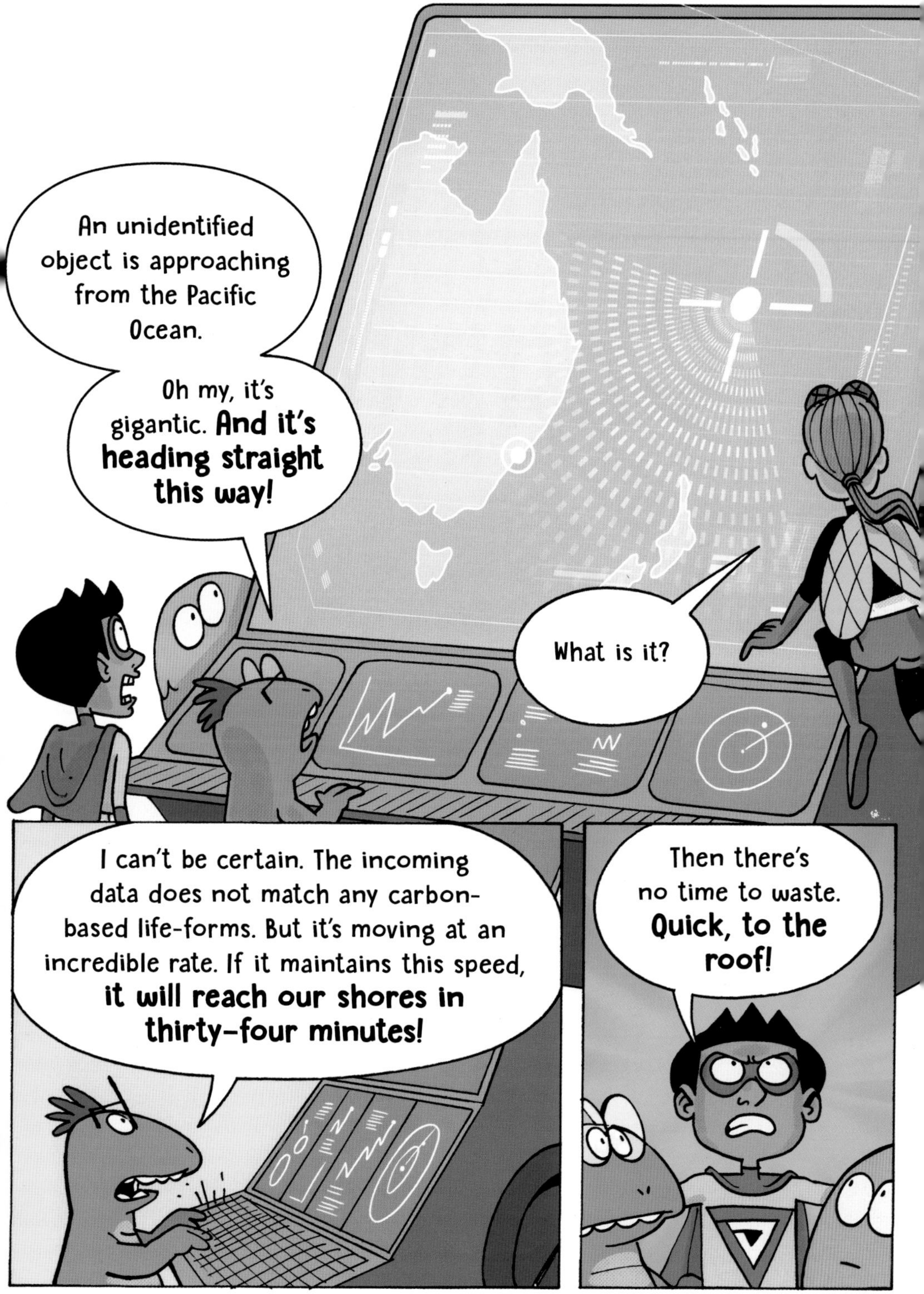
An unidentified object is approaching from the Pacific Ocean.
Oh my, it's gigantic. **And it's heading straight this way!**
What is it?
I can't be certain. The incoming data does not match any carbon-based life-forms. But it's moving at an incredible rate. If it maintains this speed, **it will reach our shores in thirty-four minutes!**
Then there's no time to waste. **Quick, to the roof!**

Chapter

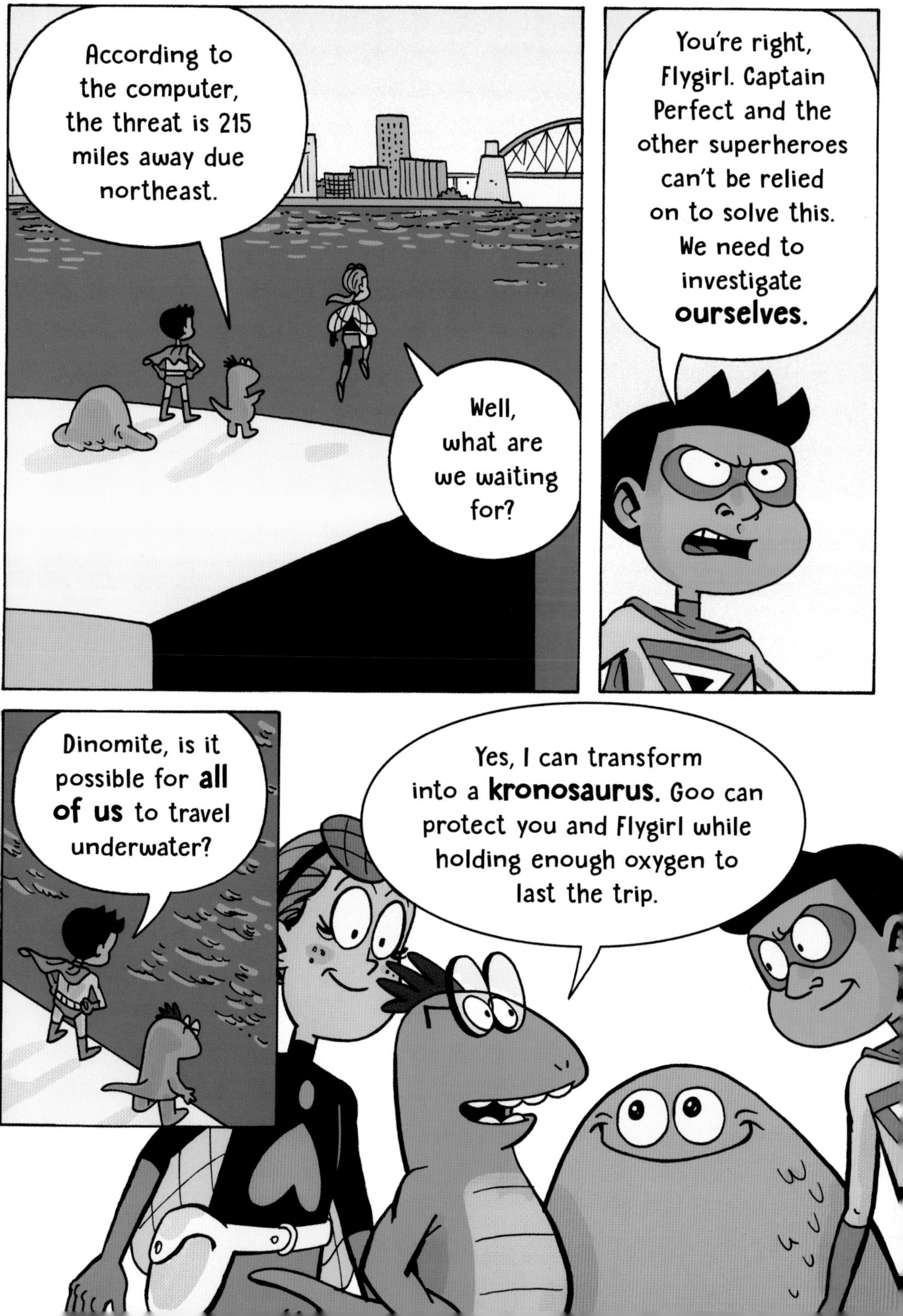
According to the computer, the threat is 215 miles away due northeast.
Well, what are we waiting for?
You're right, Flygirl. Captain Perfect and the other superheroes can't be relied on to solve this. We need to investigate **ourselves.**
Dinomite, is it possible for **all of us** to travel underwater?
Yes, I can transform into a **kronosaurus.** Goo can protect you and Flygirl while holding enough oxygen to last the trip.

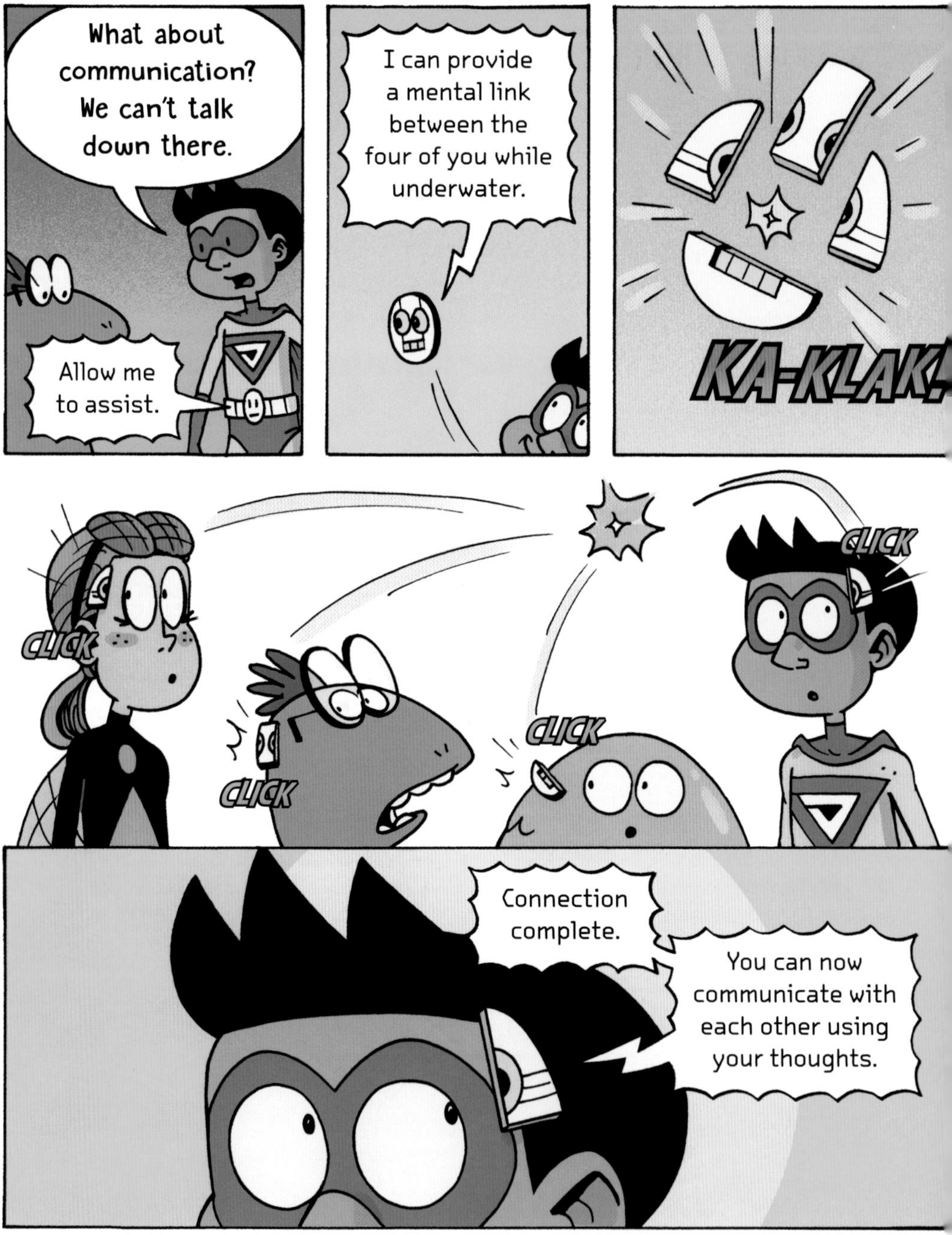
What about communication? We can't talk down there.
Allow me to assist.
I can provide a mental link between the four of you while underwater.
KA-KLAK!
CLICK
CLICK
CLICK
CLICK
Connection complete.
You can now communicate with each other using your thoughts.

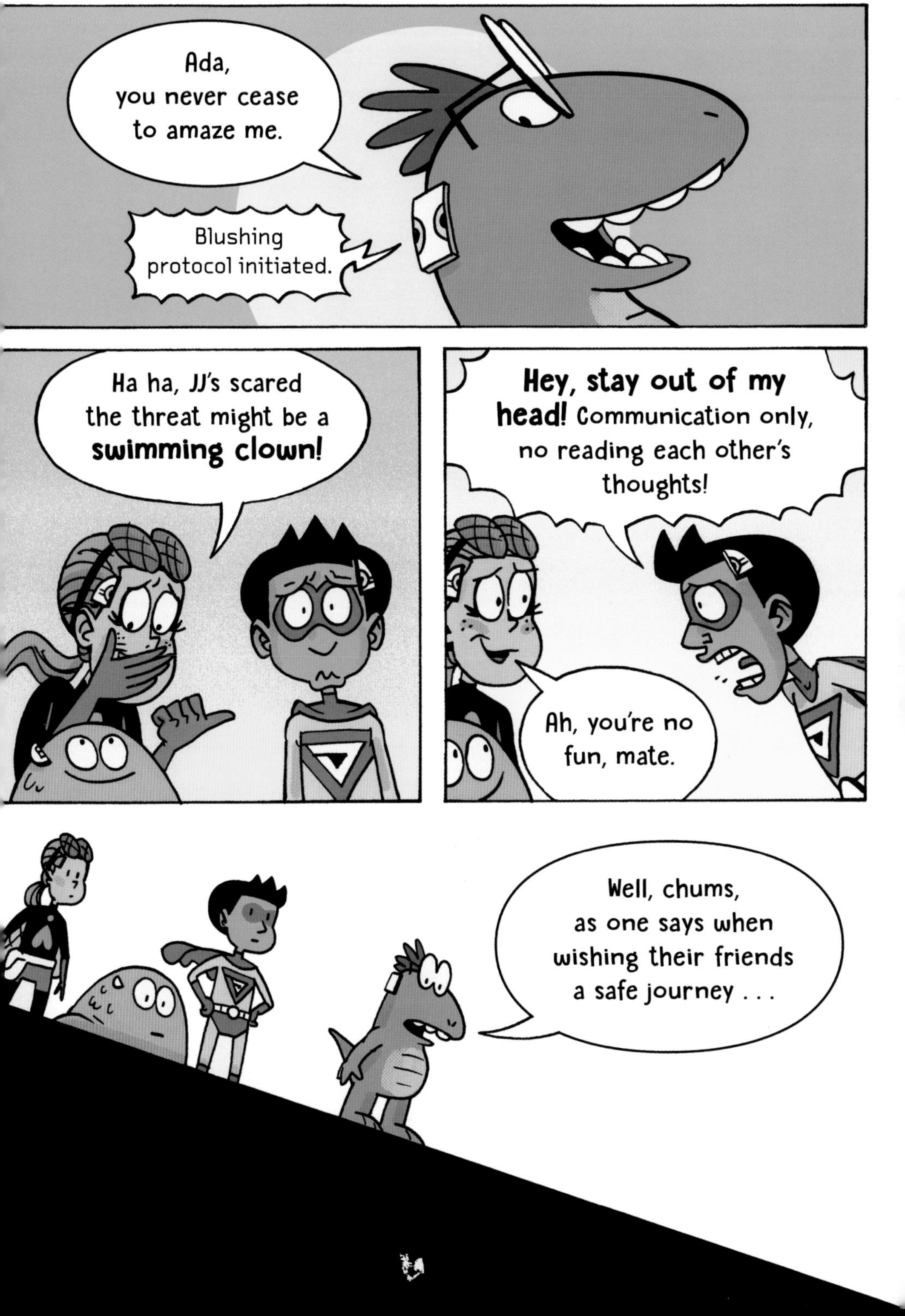
Ada, you never cease to amaze me.
Blushing protocol initiated.
Ha ha, JJ's scared the threat might be a **swimming clown!**
Hey, stay out of my head! Communication only, no reading each other's thoughts!
Ah, you're no fun, mate.
Well, chums, as one says when wishing their friends a safe journey . . .

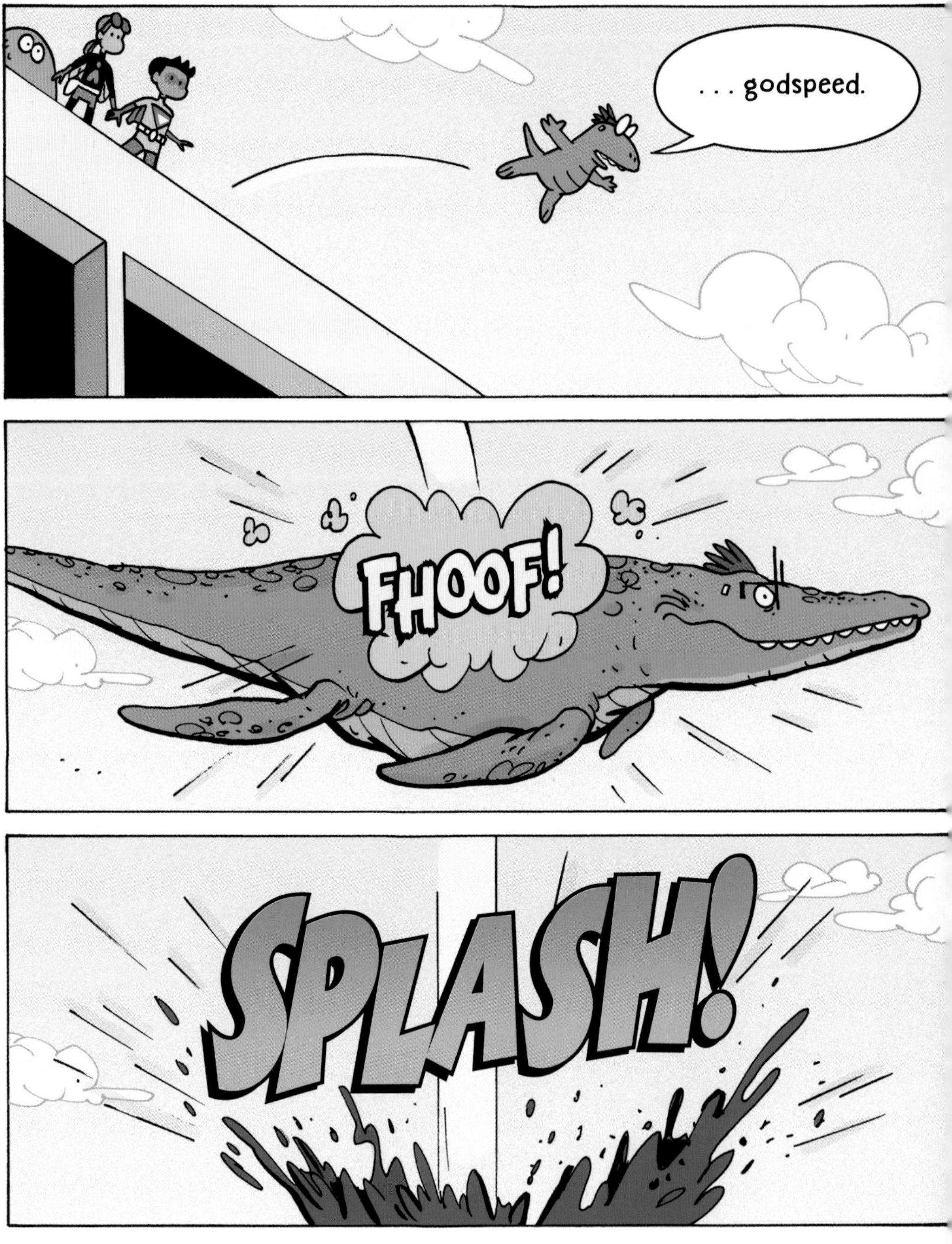
. . . godspeed.
FHOOF!
SPLASH!

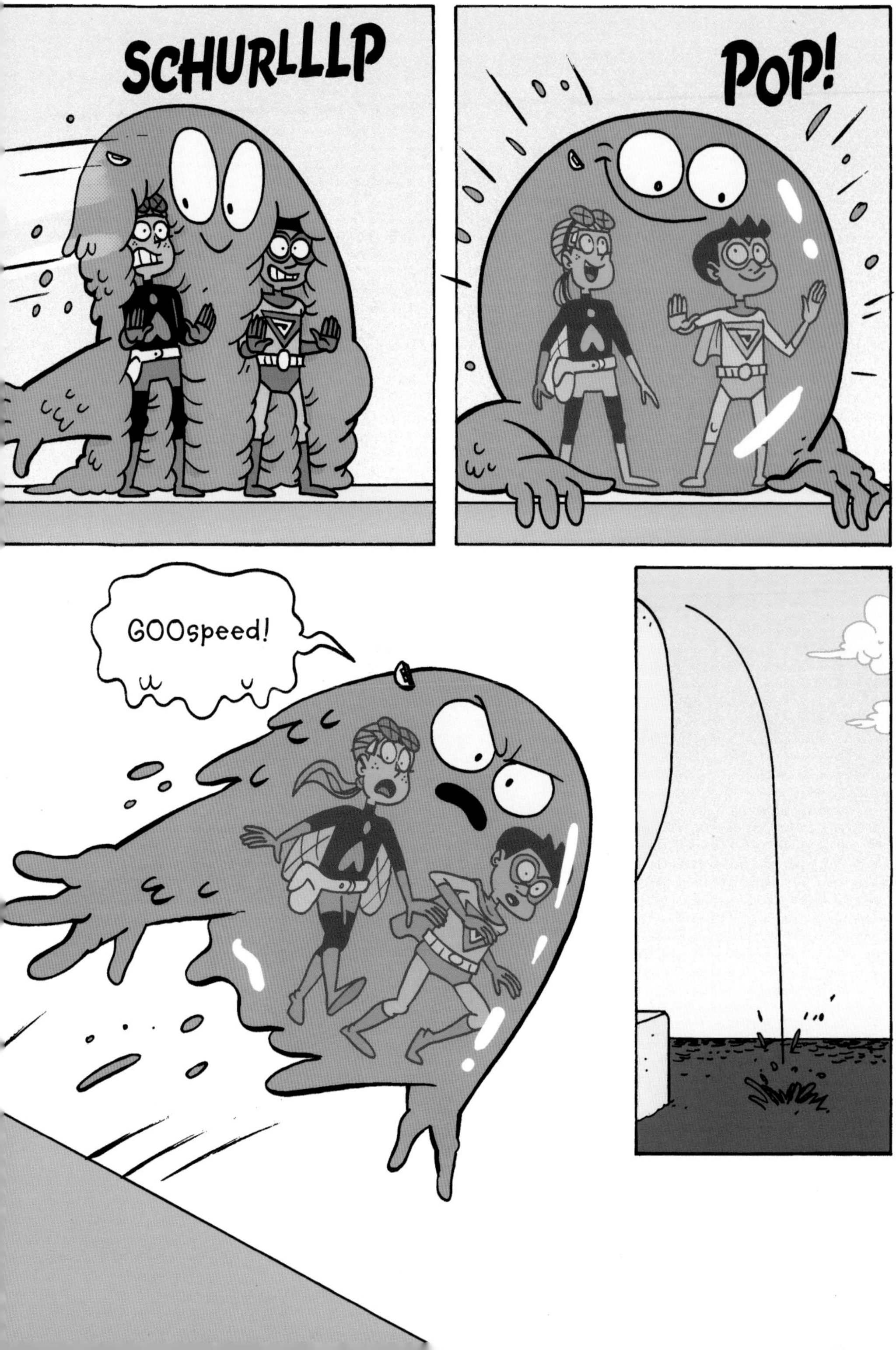
SCHURLLLP
POP!
GOOspeed!

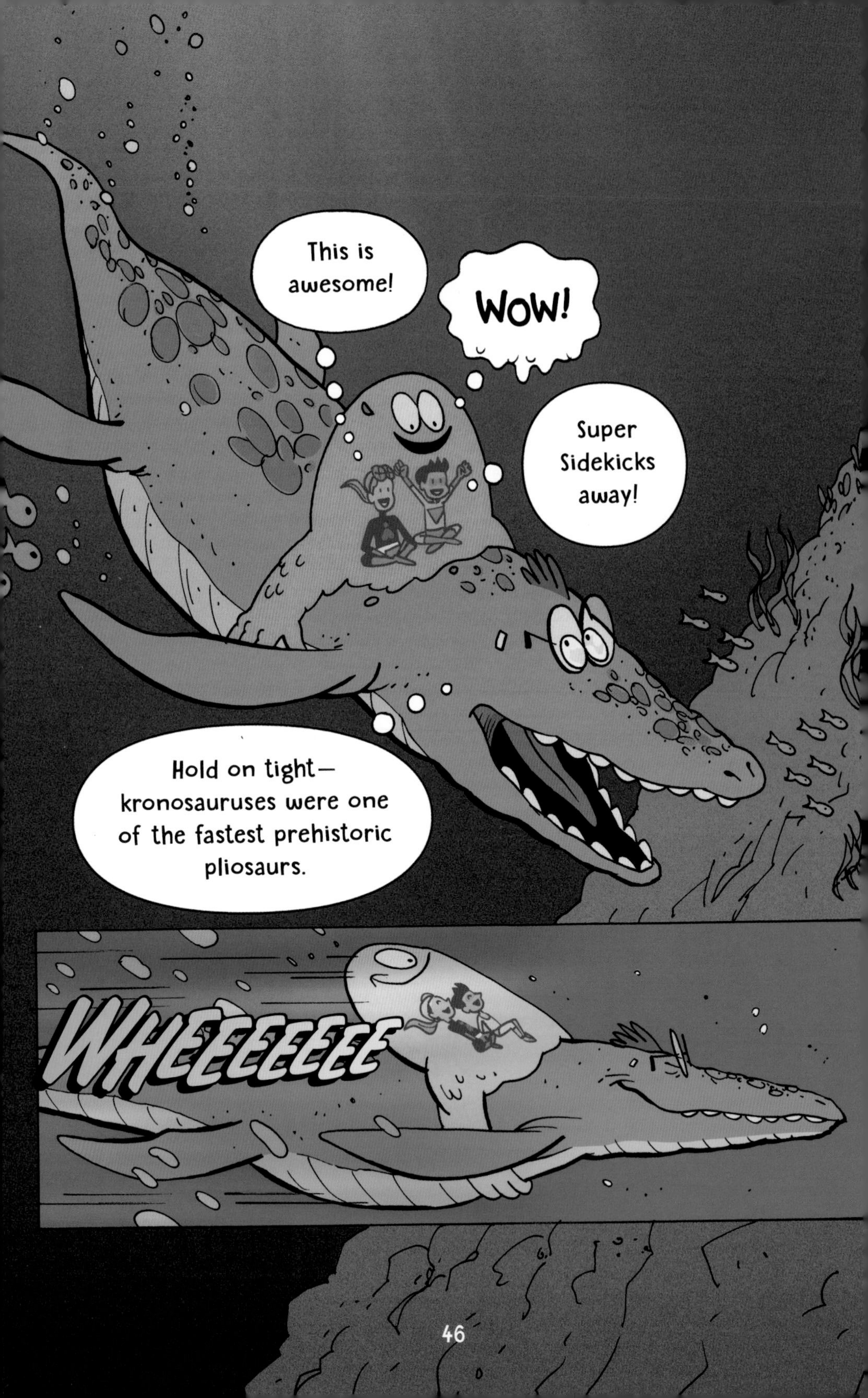
This is awesome!
WOW!
Super Sidekicks away!
Hold on tight—kronosauruses were one of the fastest prehistoric pliosaurs.
WHEEEEEEEE

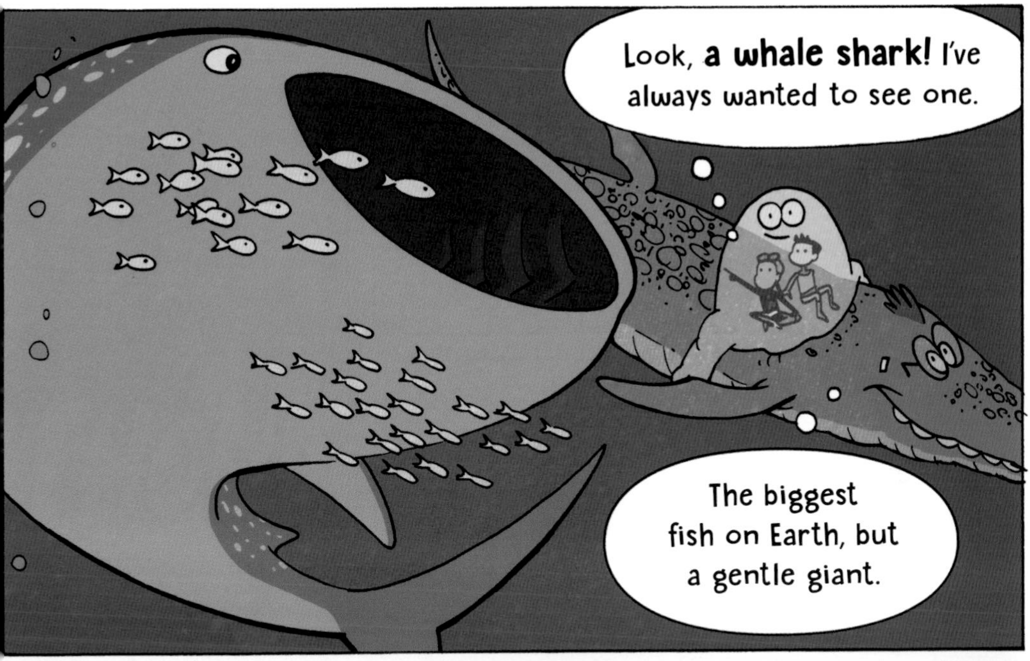
Look, a **whale shark!** I've always wanted to see one.
The biggest fish on Earth, but a gentle giant.

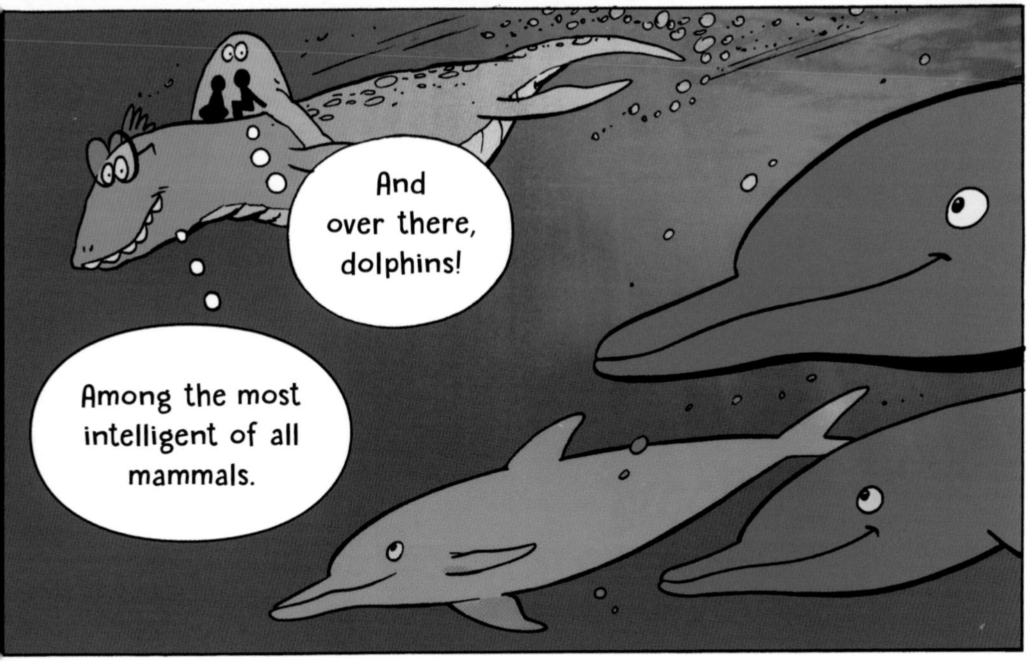
And over there, dolphins!
Among the most intelligent of all mammals.

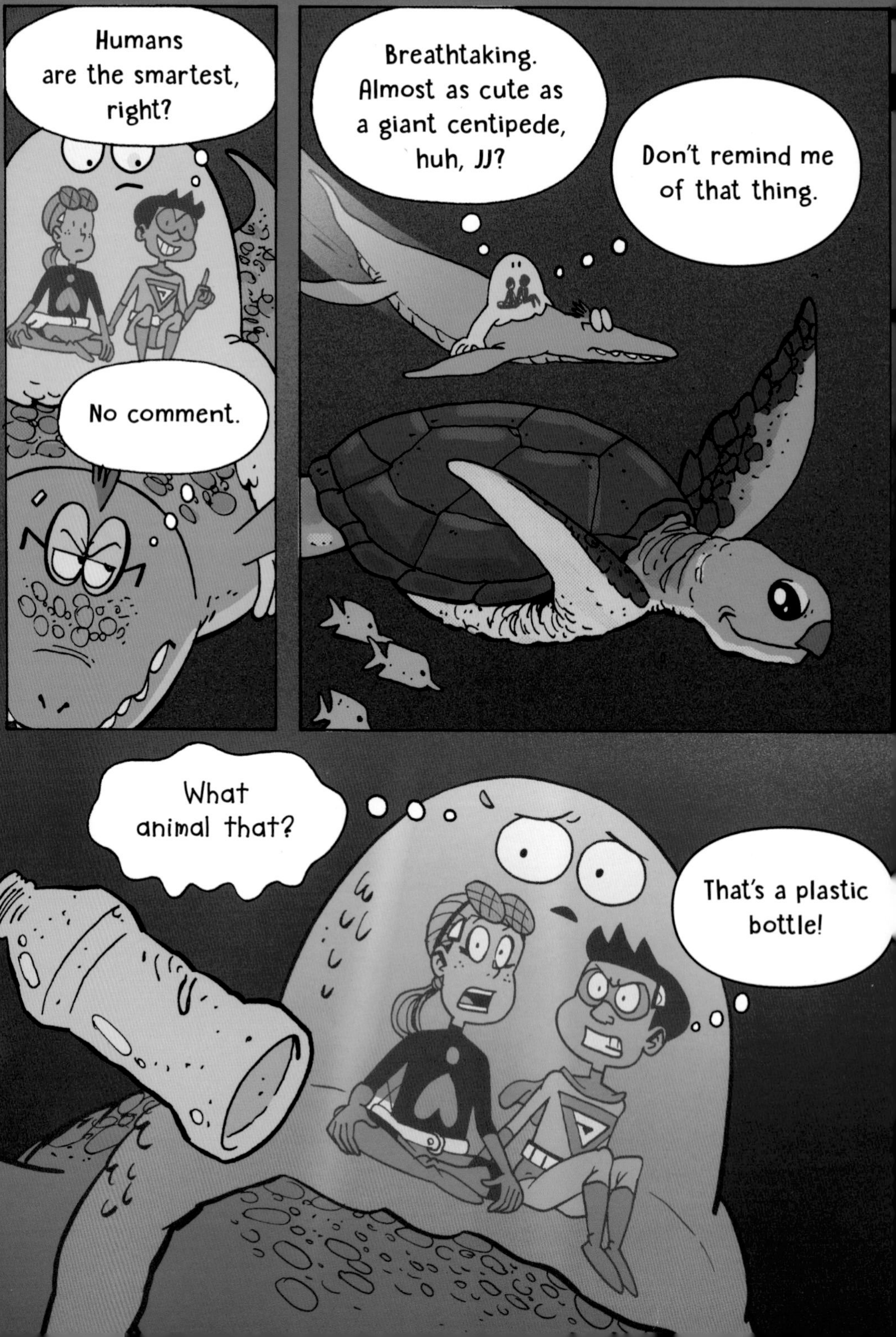
Humans are the smartest, right?
No comment.
Breathtaking. Almost as cute as a giant centipede, huh, JJ?
Don't remind me of that thing.
What animal that?
That's a plastic bottle!

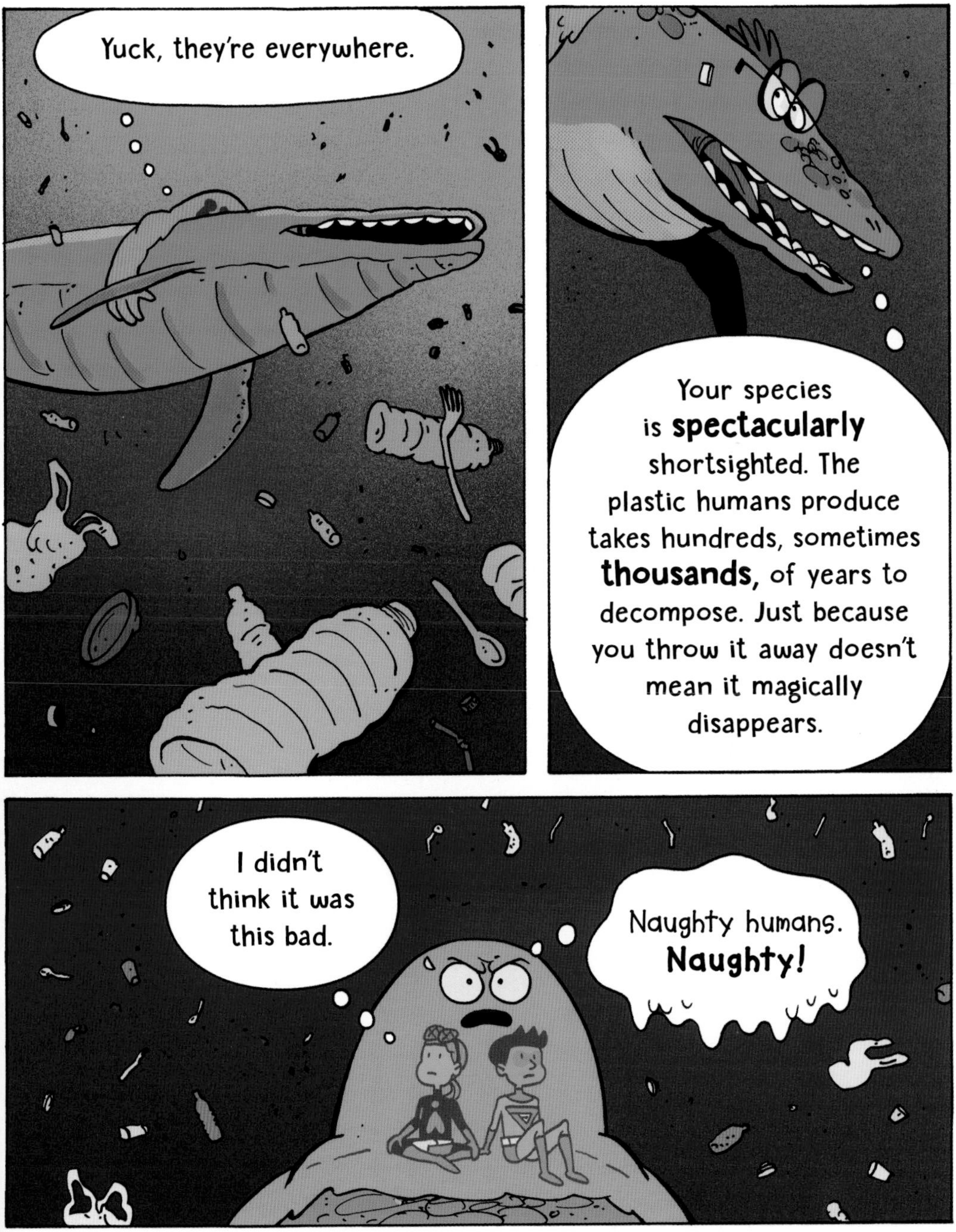
Yuck, they're everywhere.
Your species is **spectacularly** shortsighted. The plastic humans produce takes hundreds, sometimes **thousands,** of years to decompose. Just because you throw it away doesn't mean it magically disappears.
I didn't think it was this bad.
Naughty humans. **Naughty!**

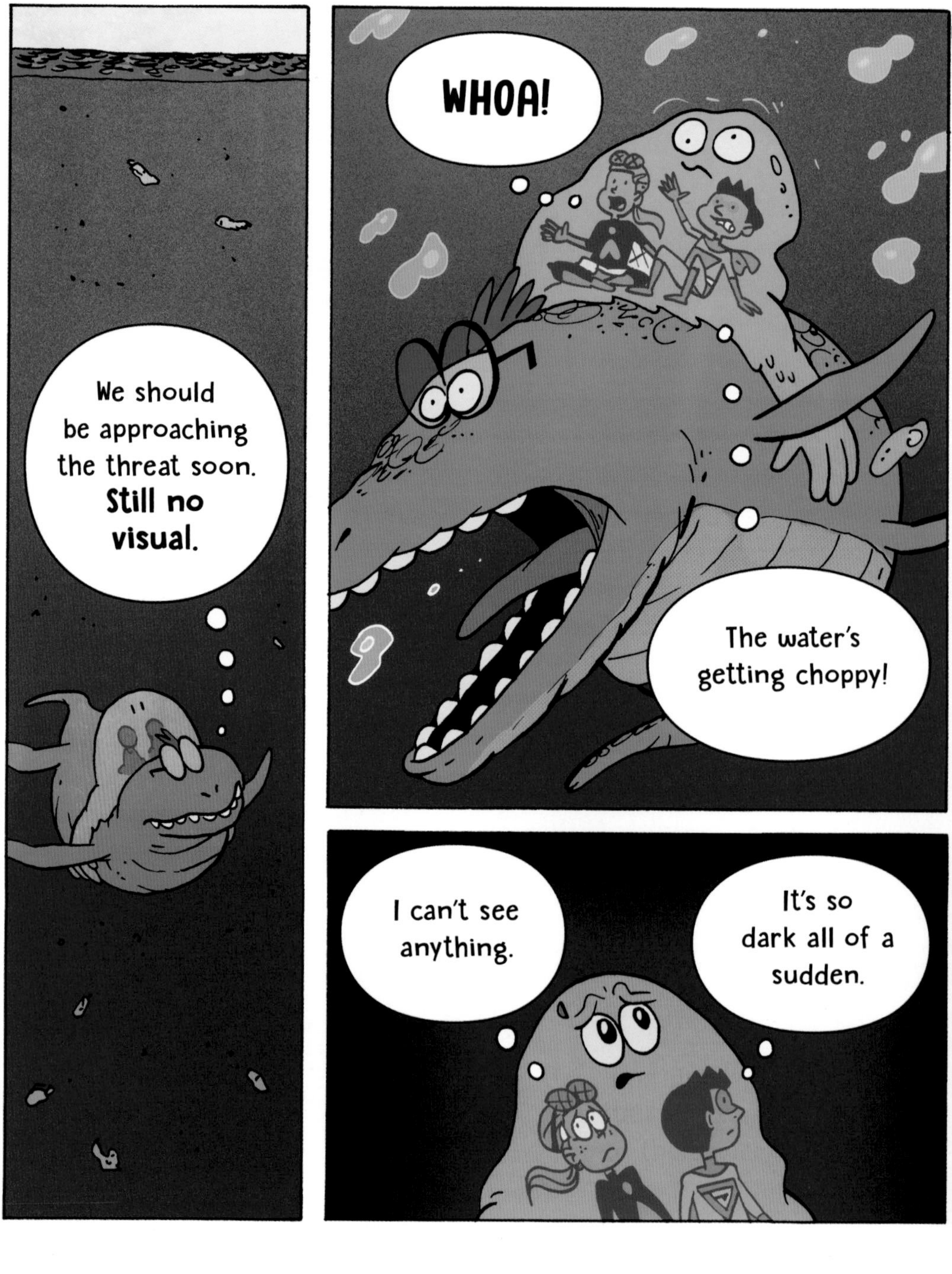

We should be approaching the threat soon. **Still no visual.**
WHOA!
The water's getting choppy!
I can't see anything.
It's so dark all of a sudden.

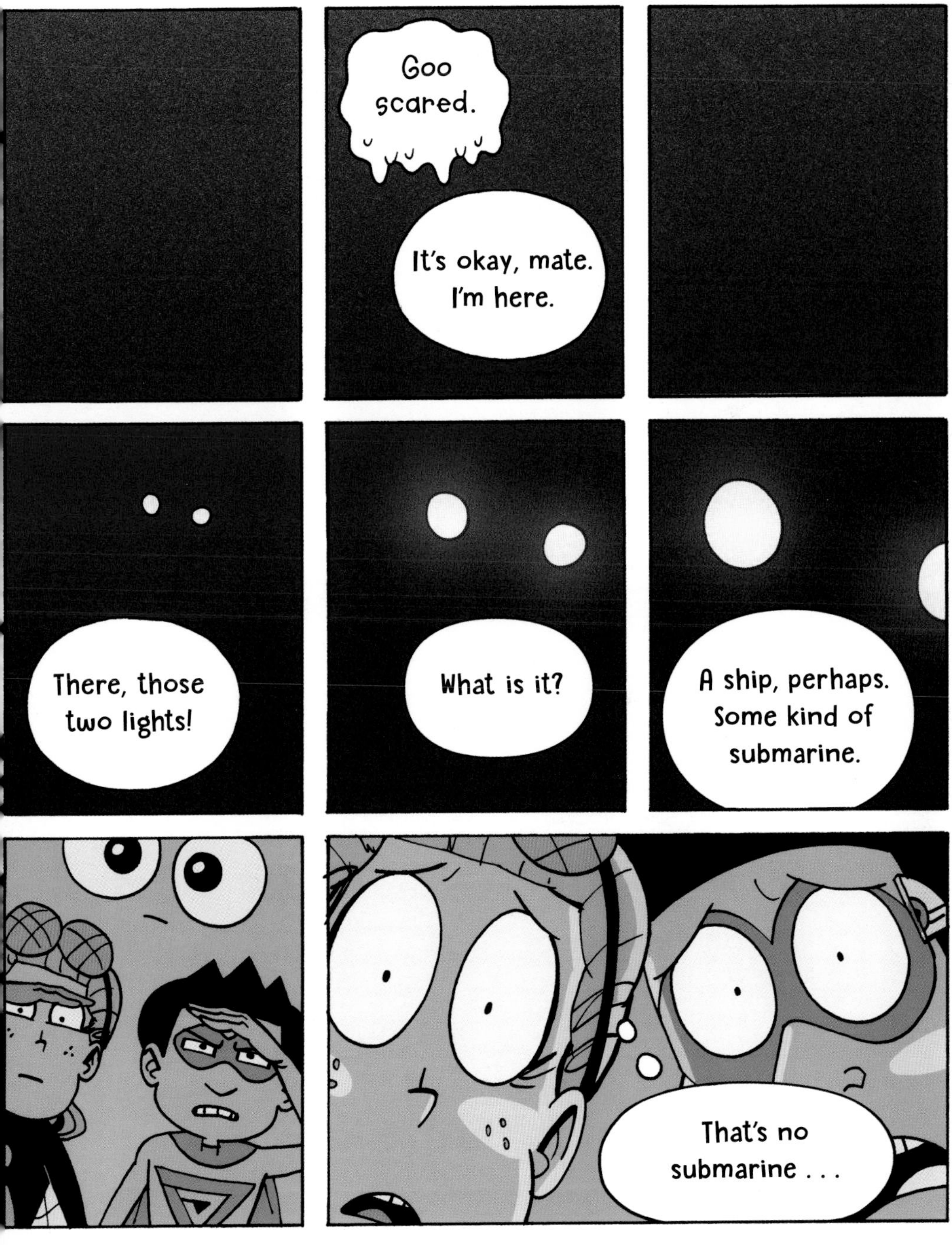
Goo scared.
It's okay, mate. I'm here.
There, those two lights!
What is it?
A ship, perhaps. Some kind of submarine.
That's no submarine . . .

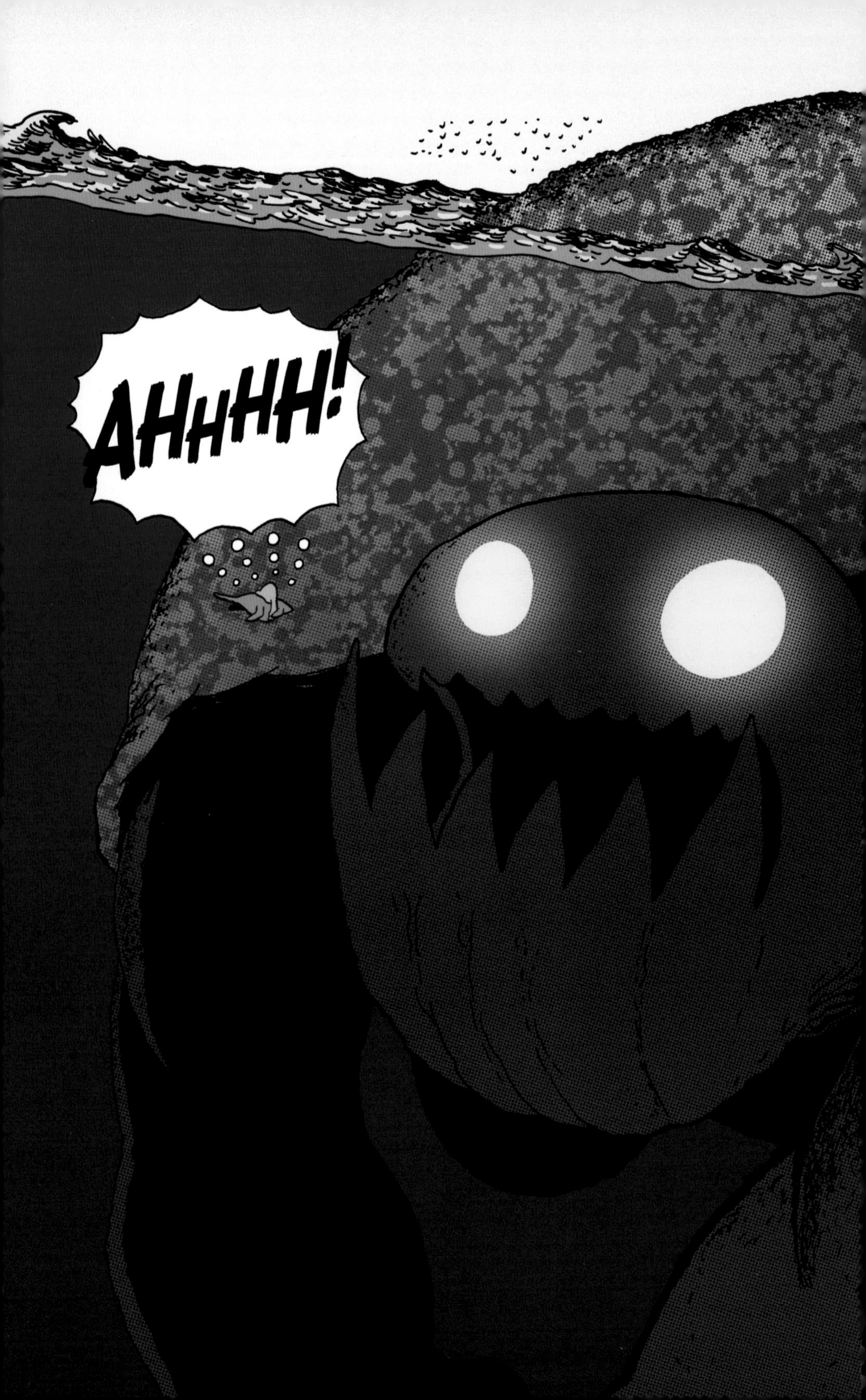
AHHHH!

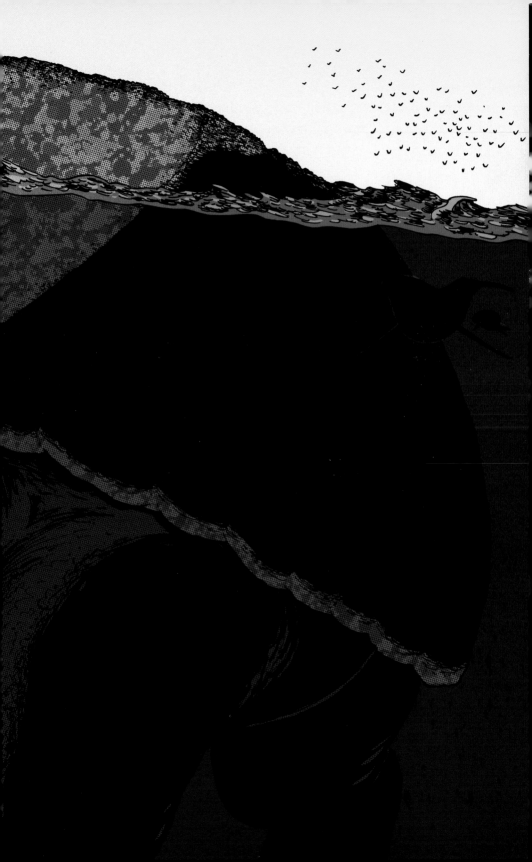

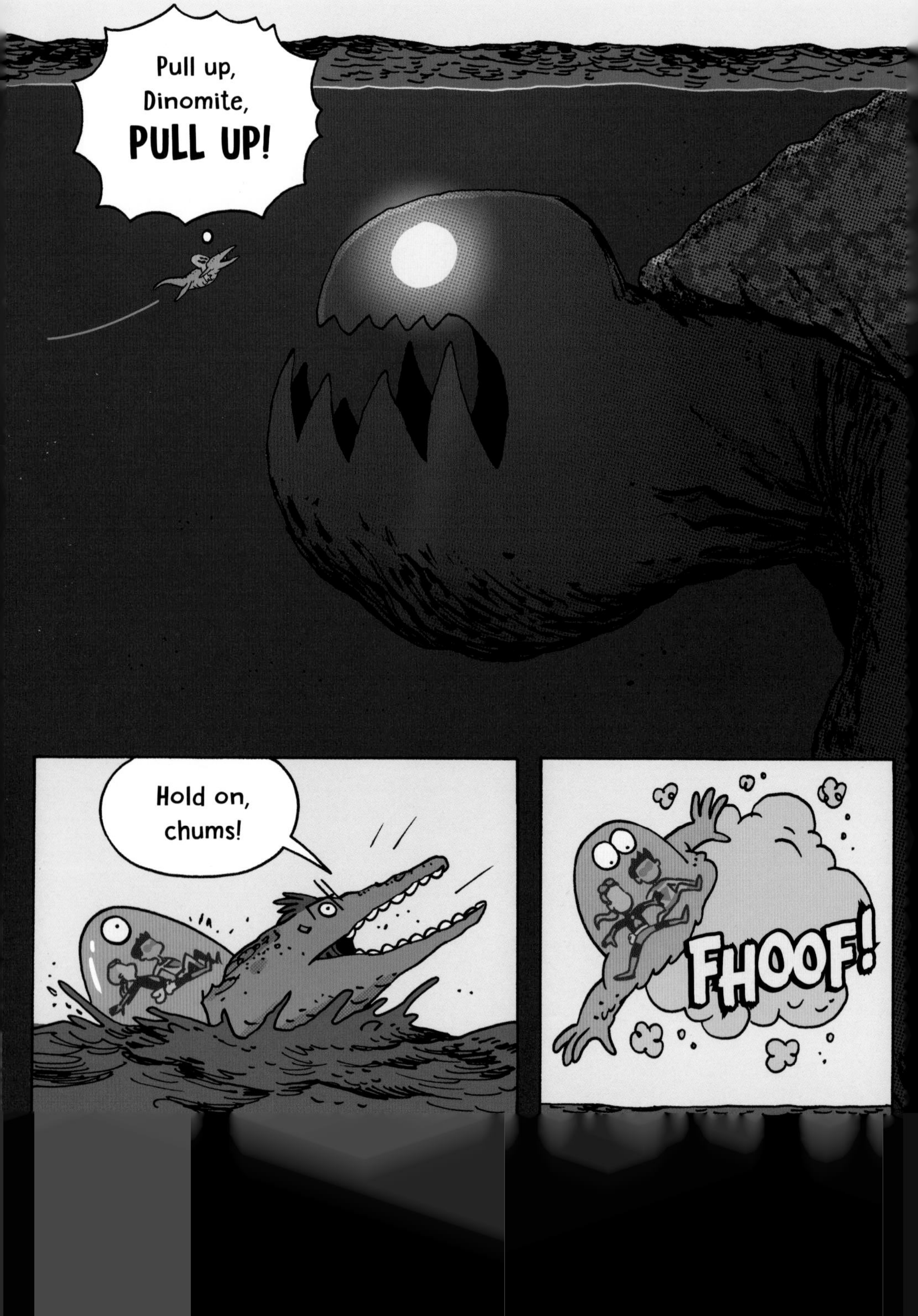
Pull up, Dinomite, PULL UP!
Hold on, chums!
FHOOF!

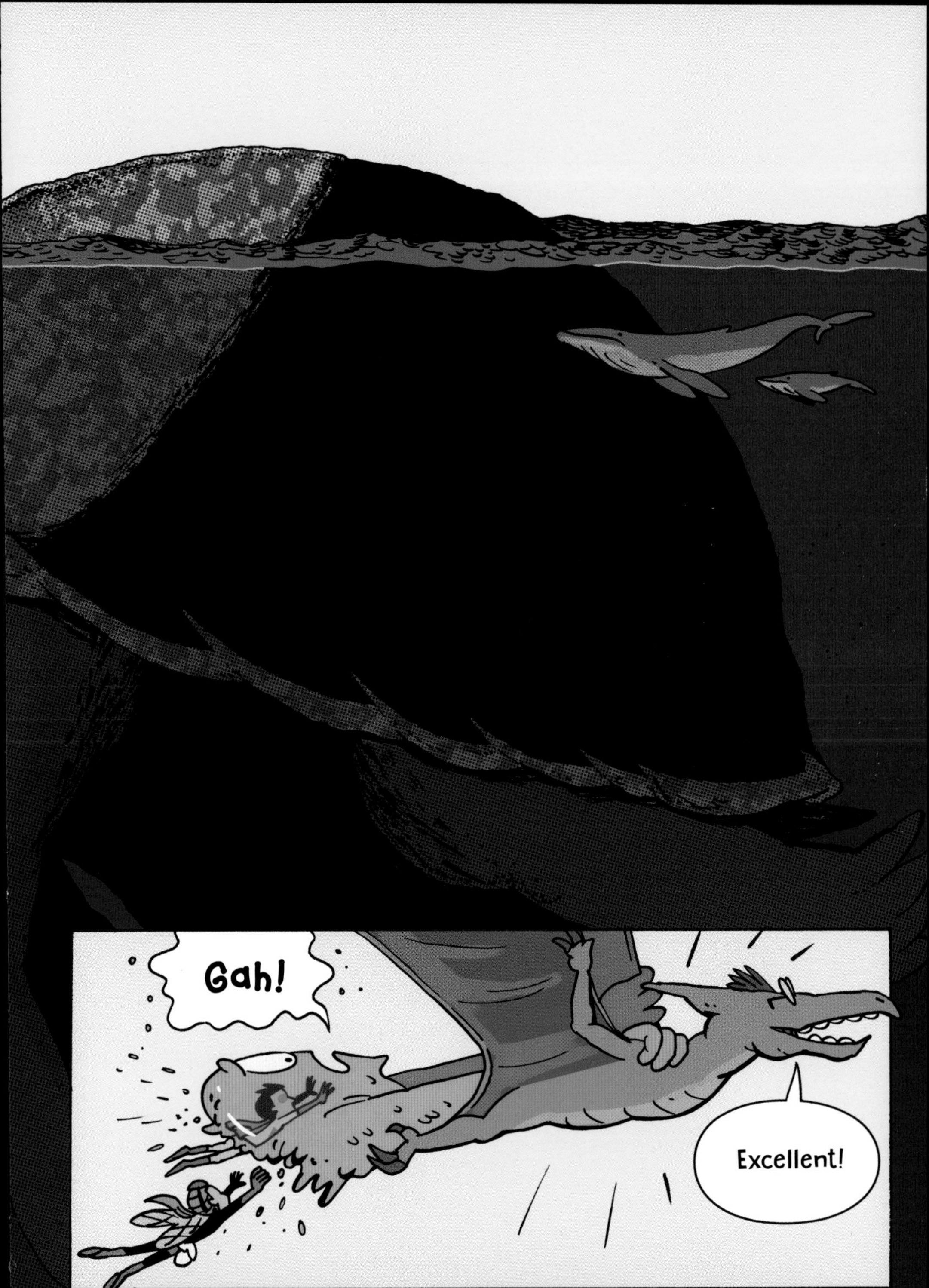
Gah!
Excellent!

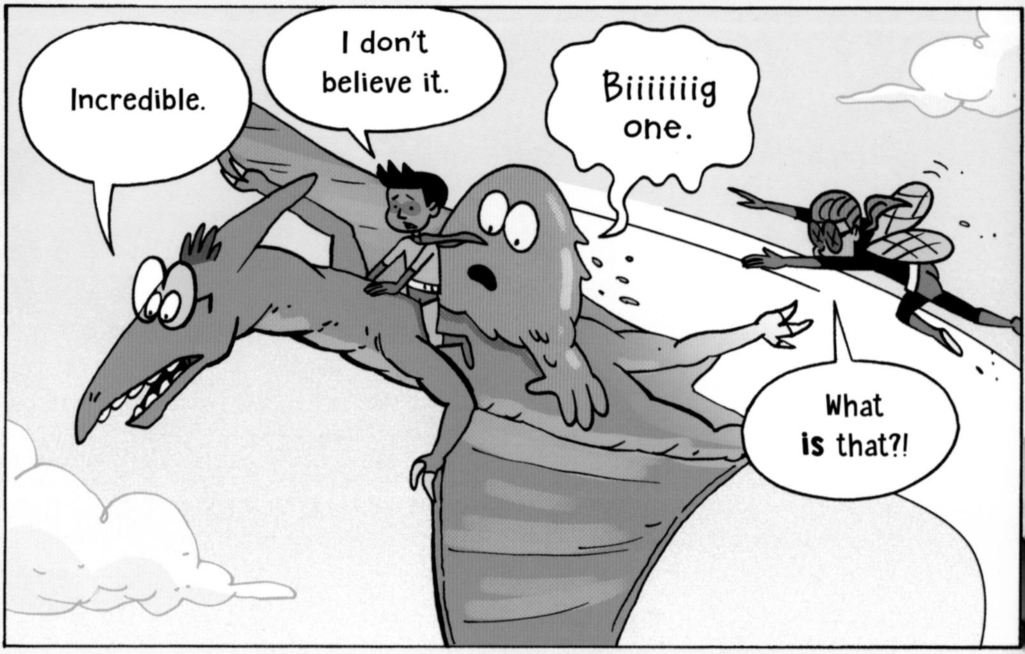
Incredible.
I don't believe it.
Biiiiiiig one.
What **is** that?!

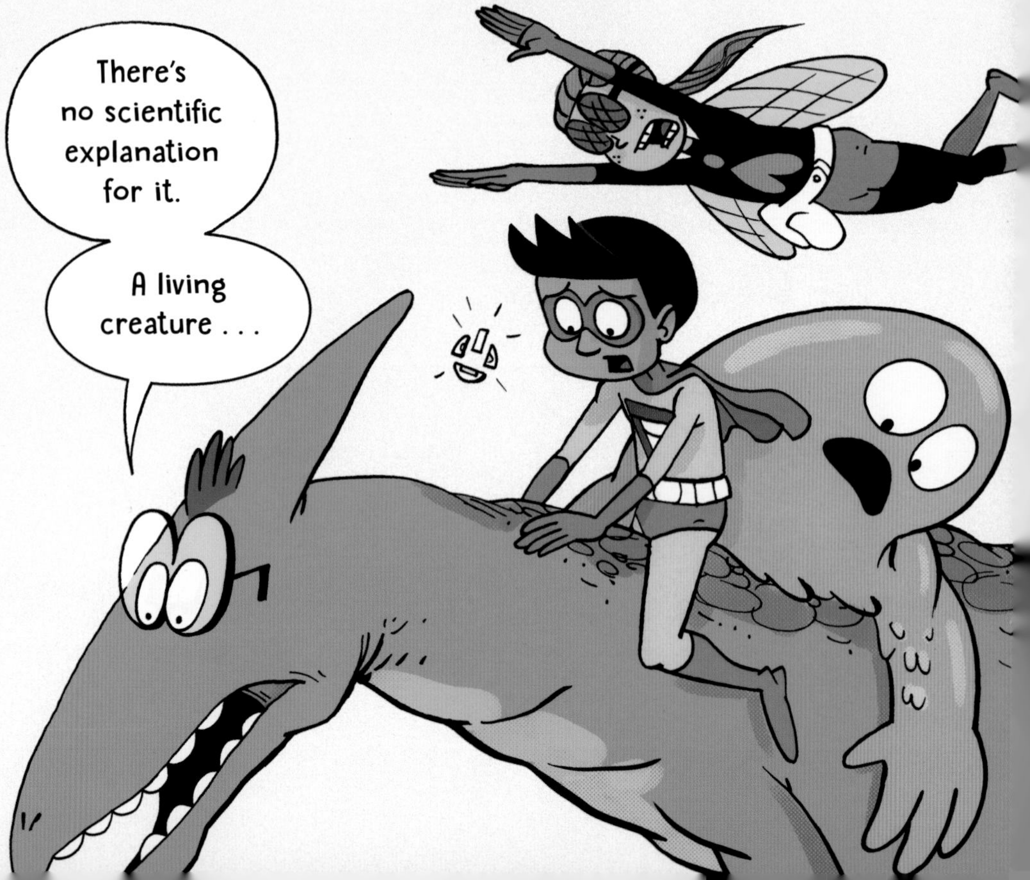
There's no scientific explanation for it.
A living creature . . .

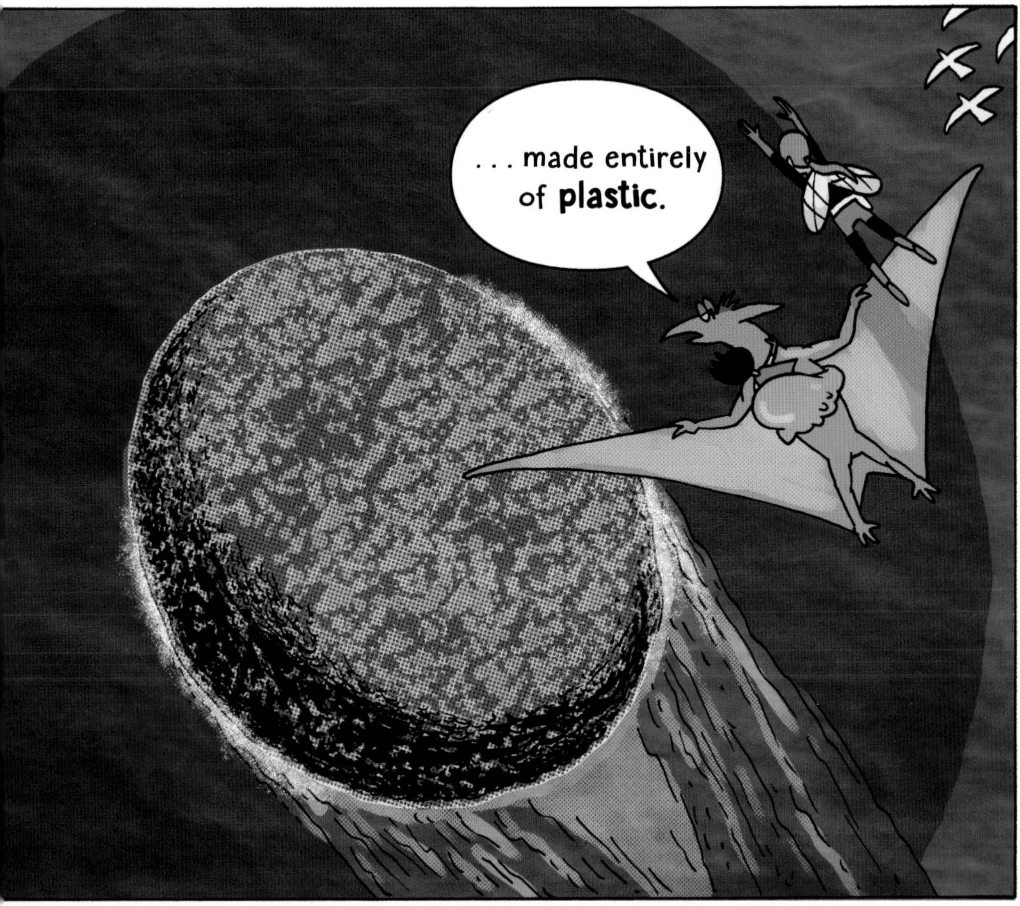
. . . made entirely of **plastic.**

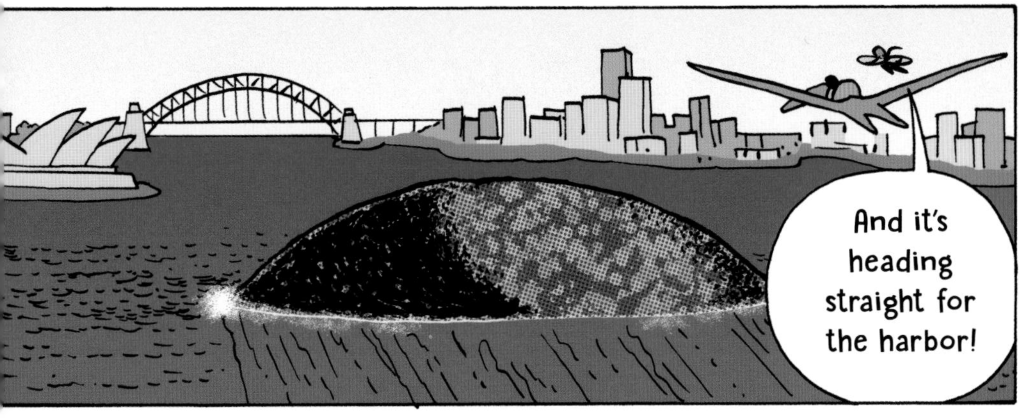
And it's heading straight for the harbor!

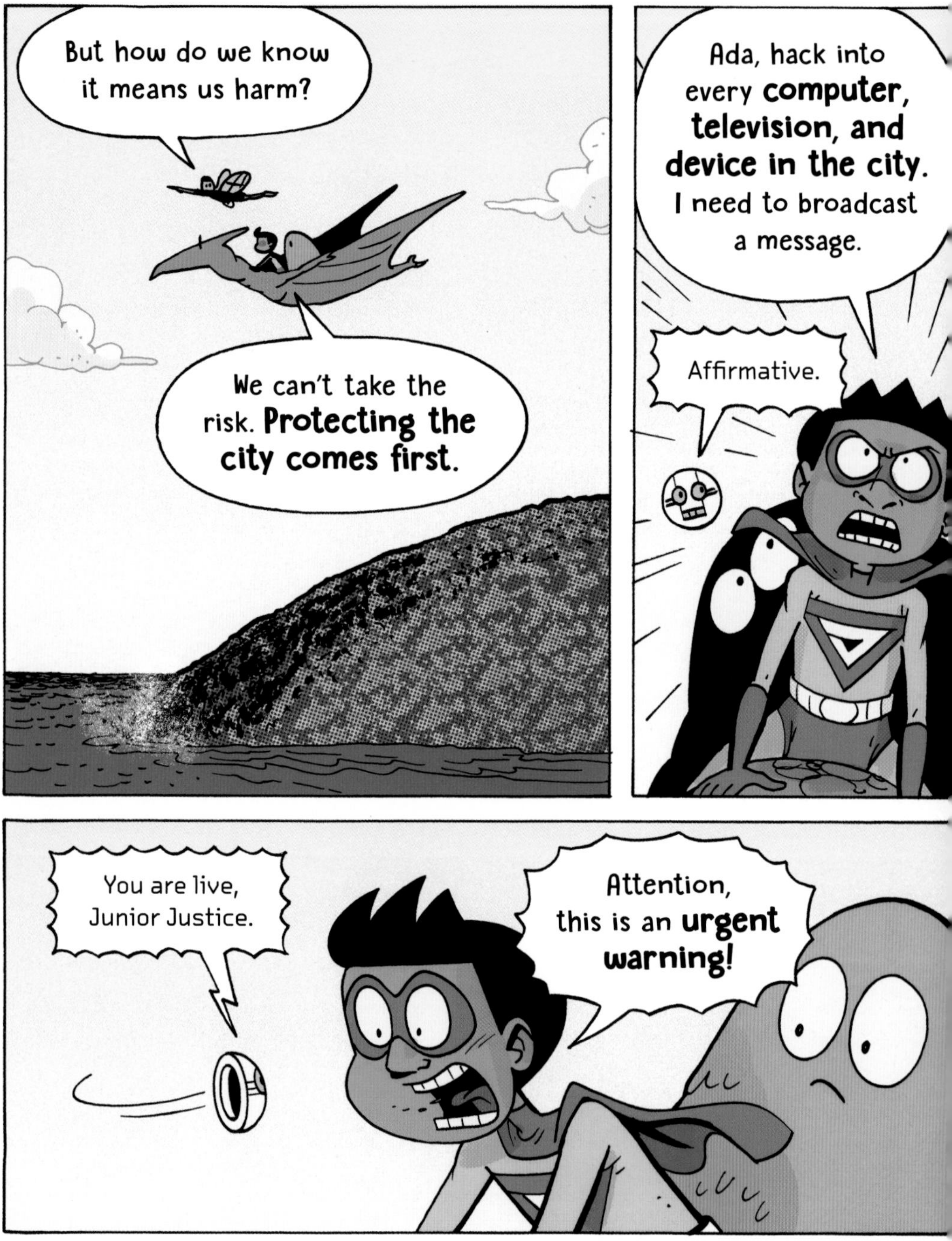
But how do we know it means us harm?
We can't take the risk. **Protecting the city comes first.**
Ada, hack into every **computer, television, and device in the city.** I need to broadcast a message.
Affirmative.
You are live, Junior Justice.
Attention, this is an **urgent warning!**

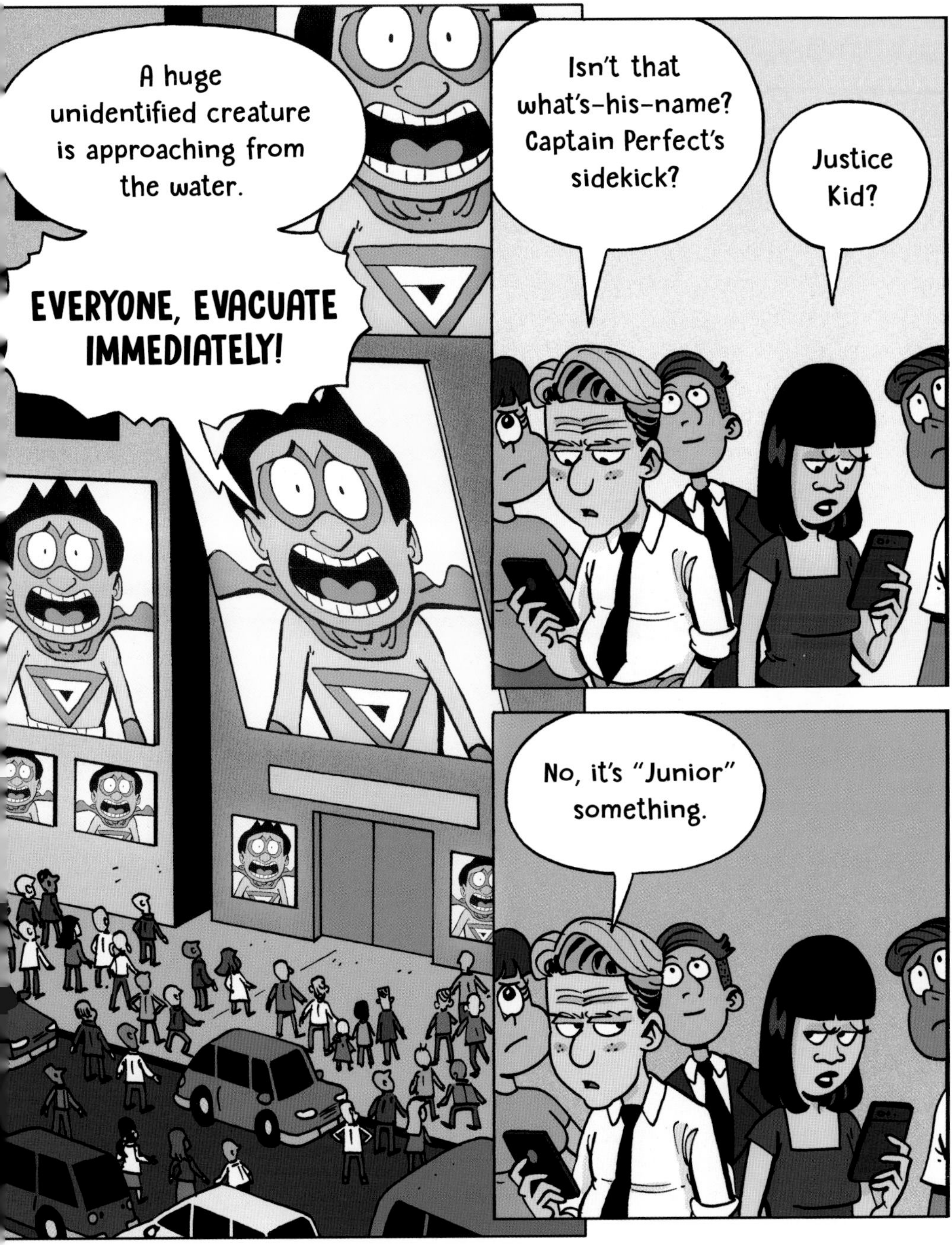
A huge unidentified creature is approaching from the water.
EVERYONE, EVACUATE IMMEDIATELY!
Isn't that what's-his-name? Captain Perfect's sidekick?
Justice Kid?
No, it's "Junior" something.

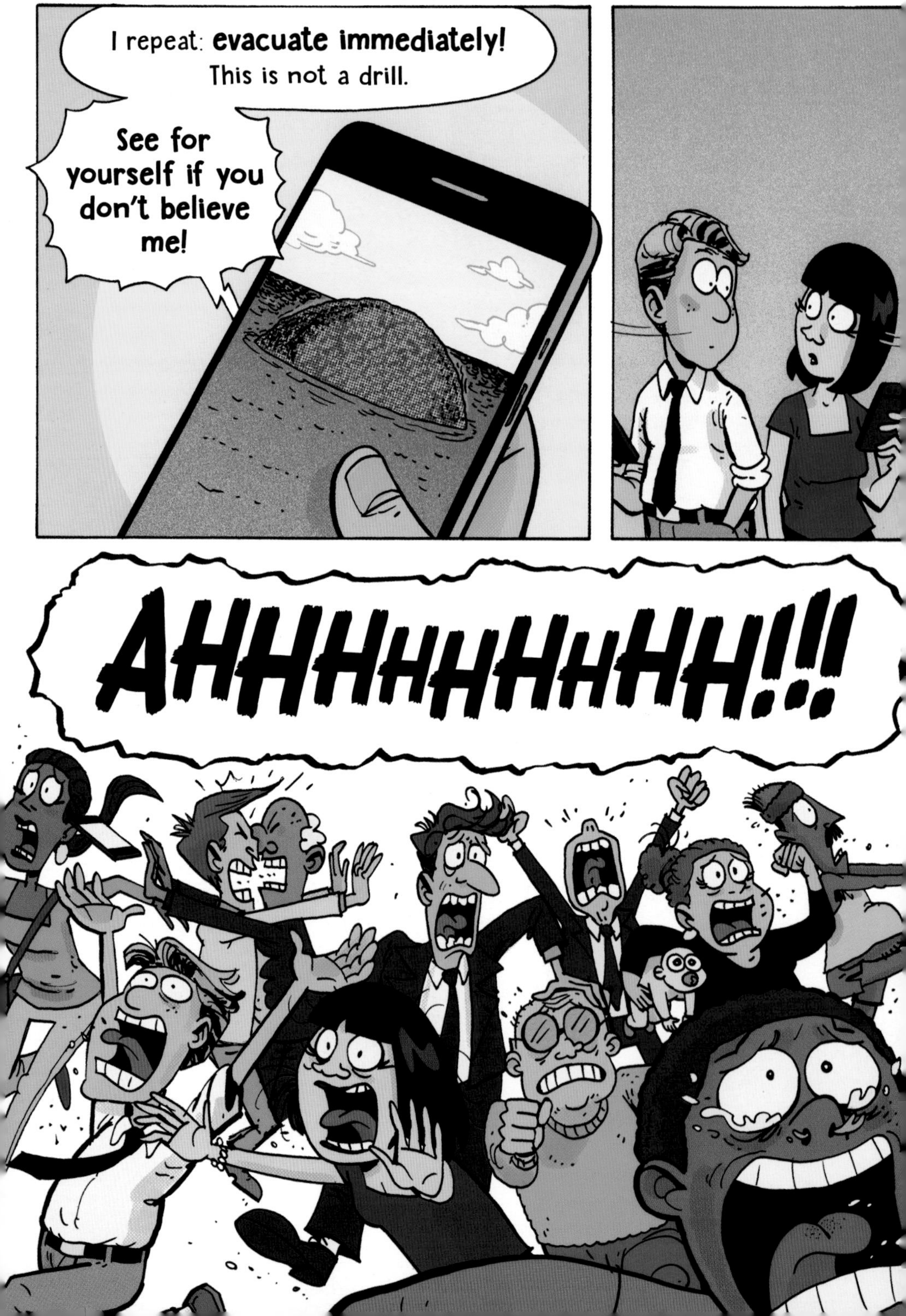
I repeat: **evacuate immediately!** This is not a drill.
See for yourself if you don't believe me!
AHHHHHHHHHHH!!!

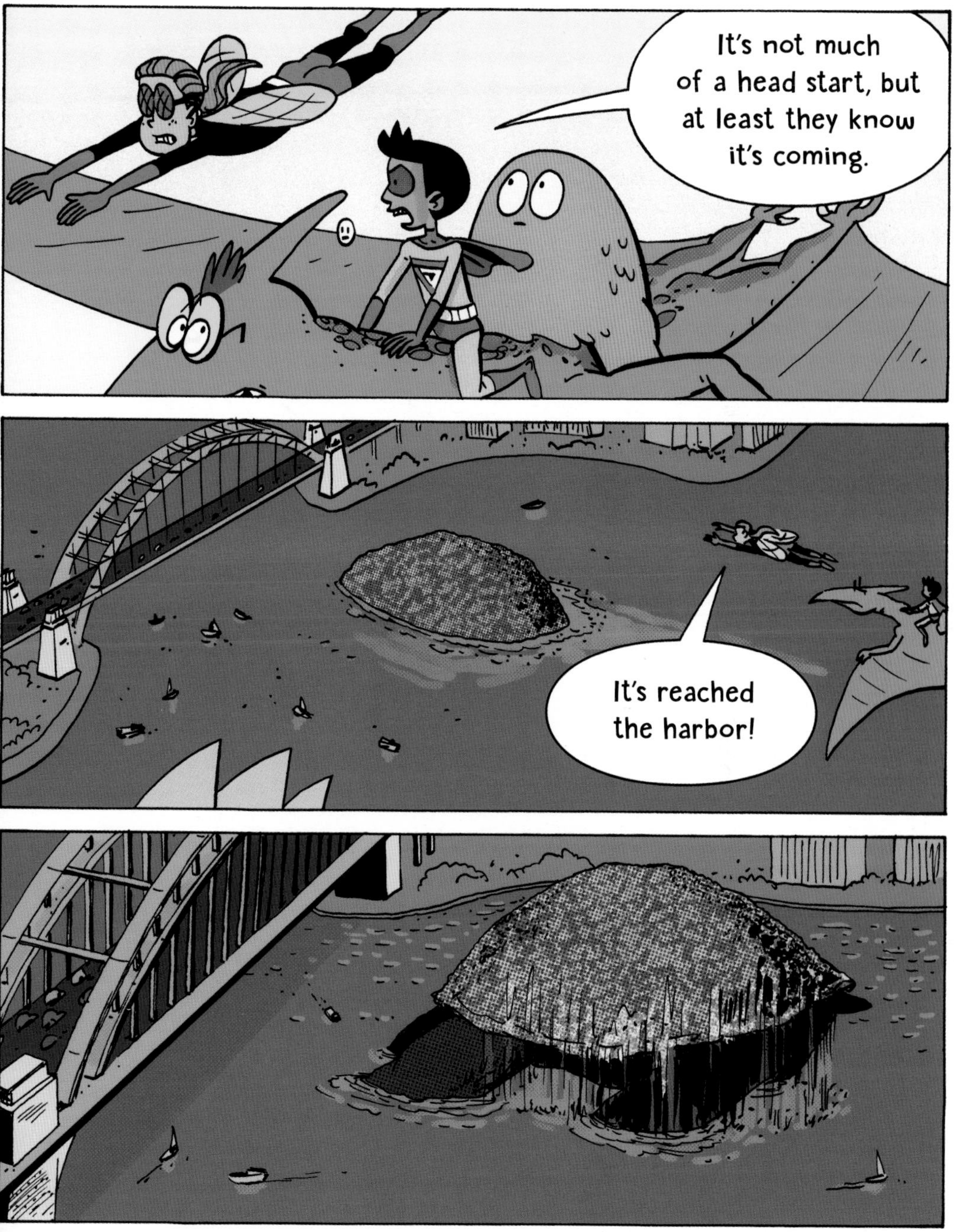
It's not much of a head start, but at least they know it's coming.
It's reached the harbor!

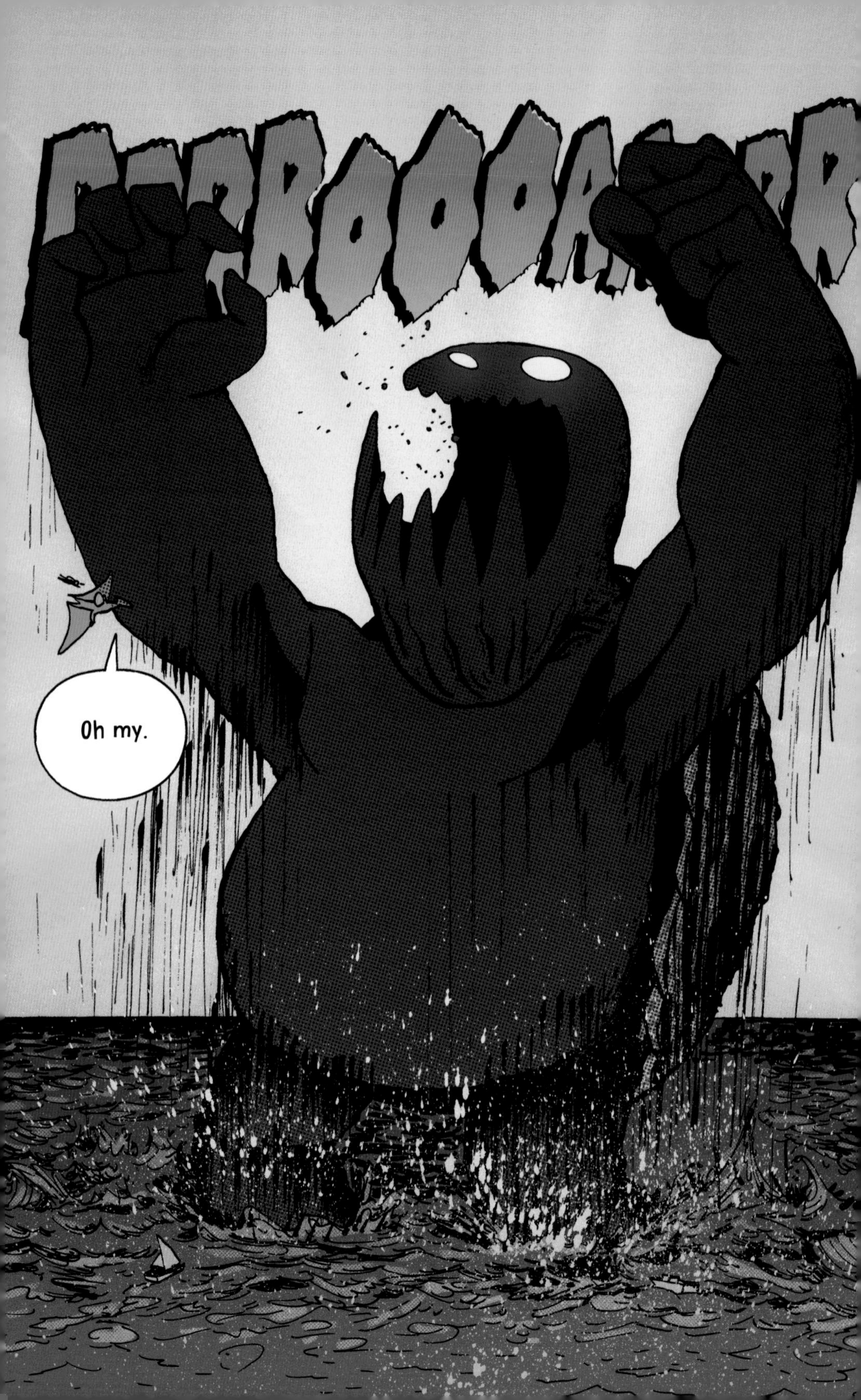
Oh my.

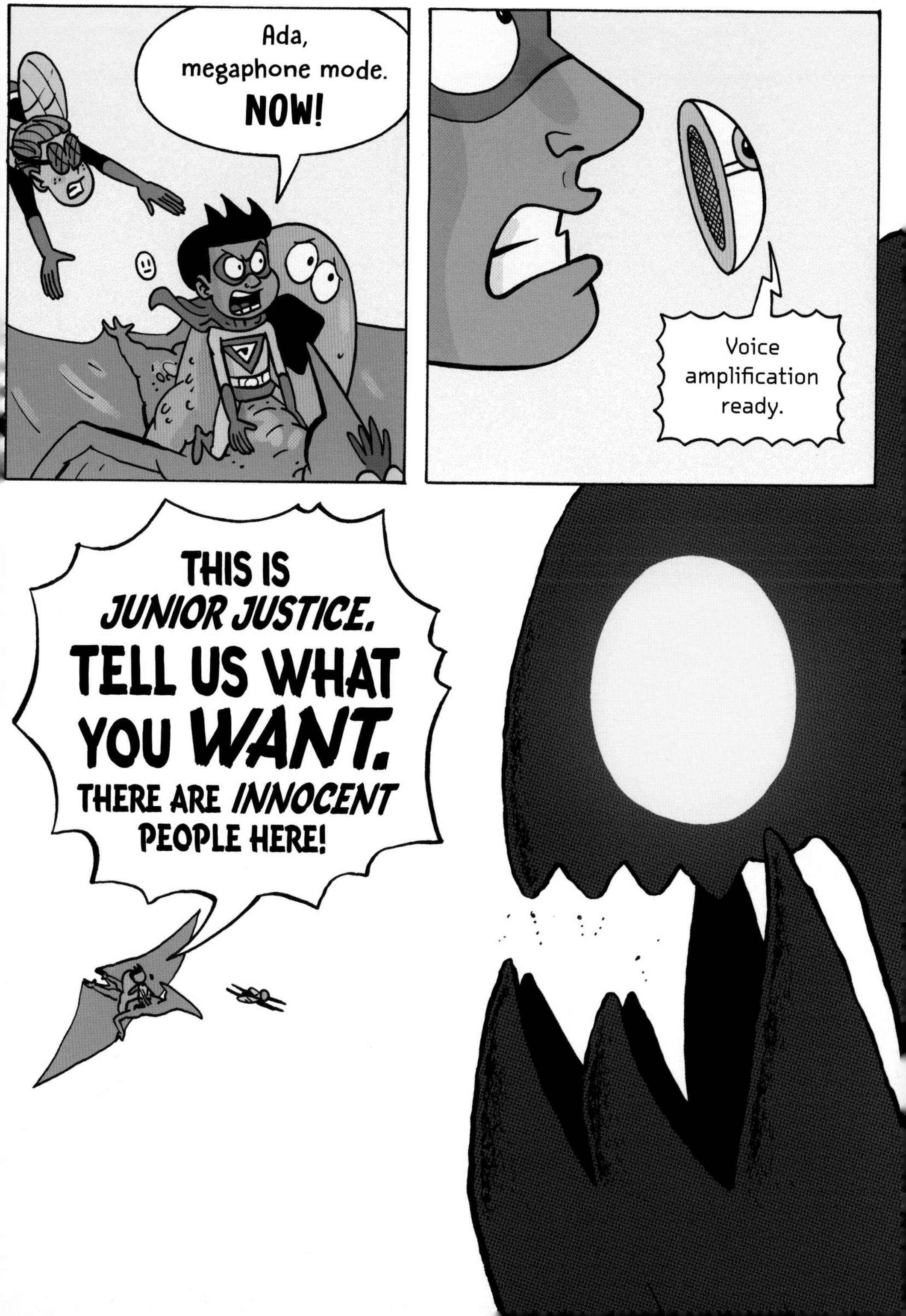
Ada, megaphone mode. NOW!
Voice amplification ready.
THIS IS JUNIOR JUSTICE. TELL US WHAT YOU WANT. THERE ARE INNOCENT PEOPLE HERE!

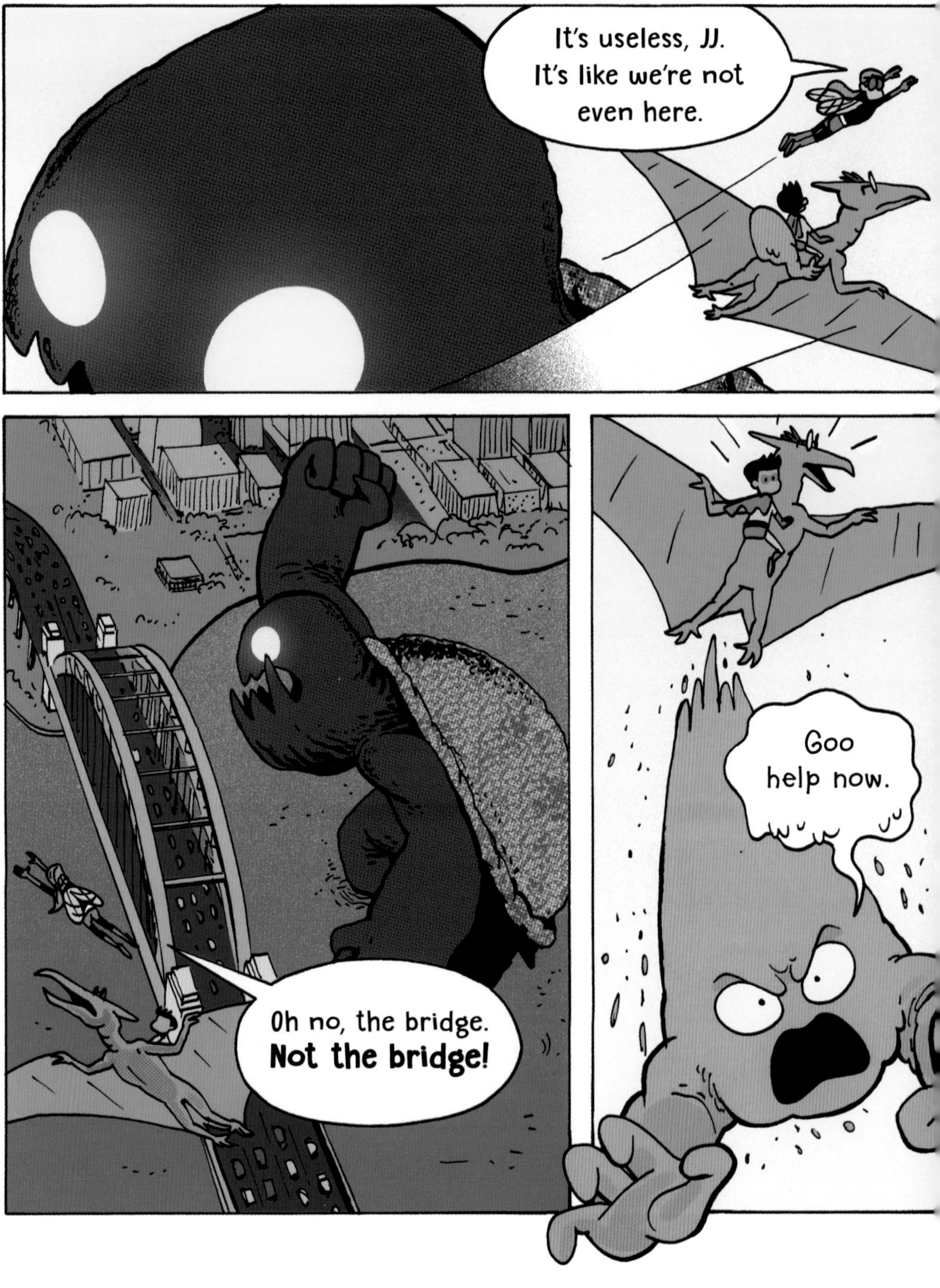
It's useless, JJ.
It's like we're not even here.
Oh no, the bridge.
Not the bridge!
Goo help now.

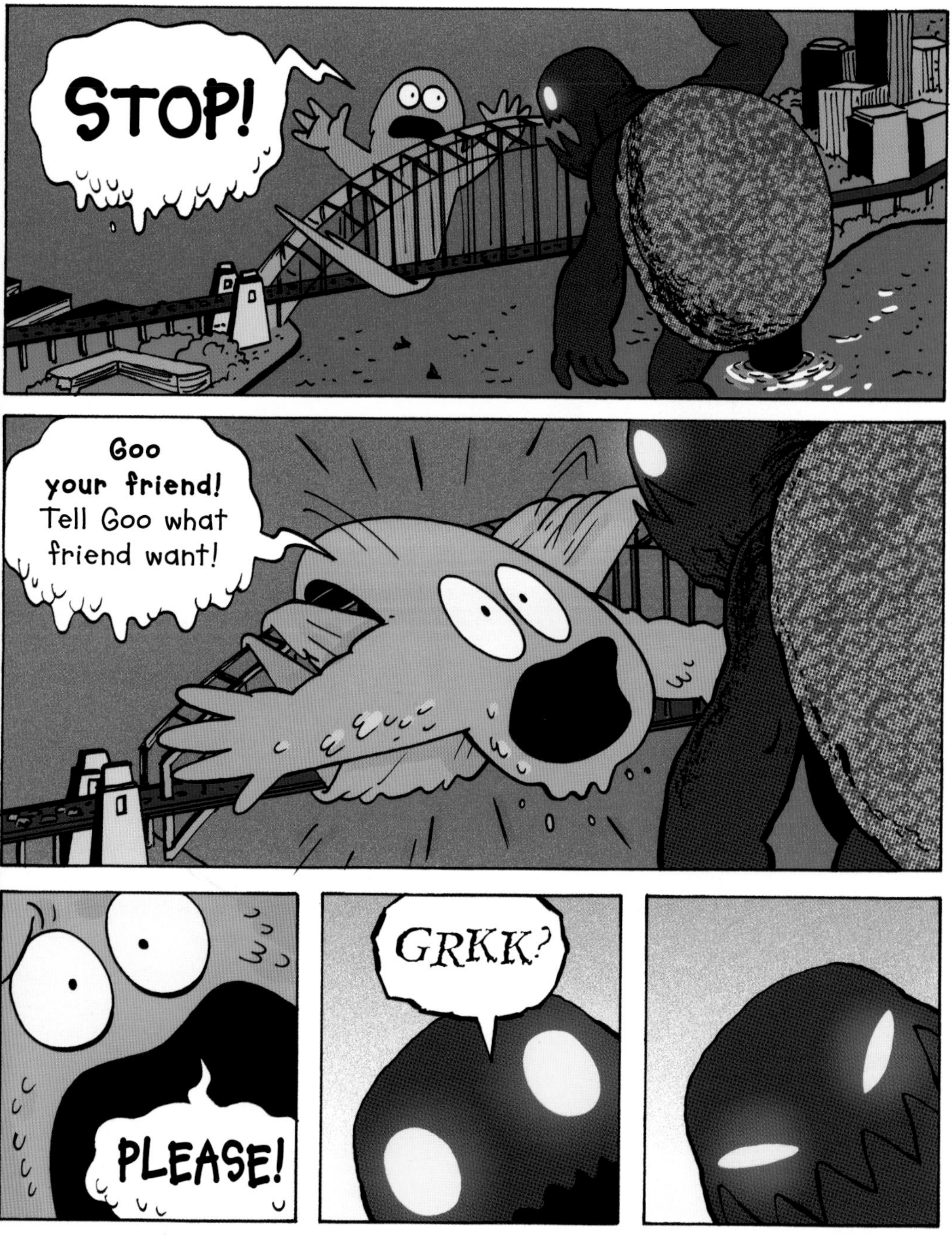
STOP!
Goo your friend! Tell Goo what friend want!
PLEASE!
GRKK?

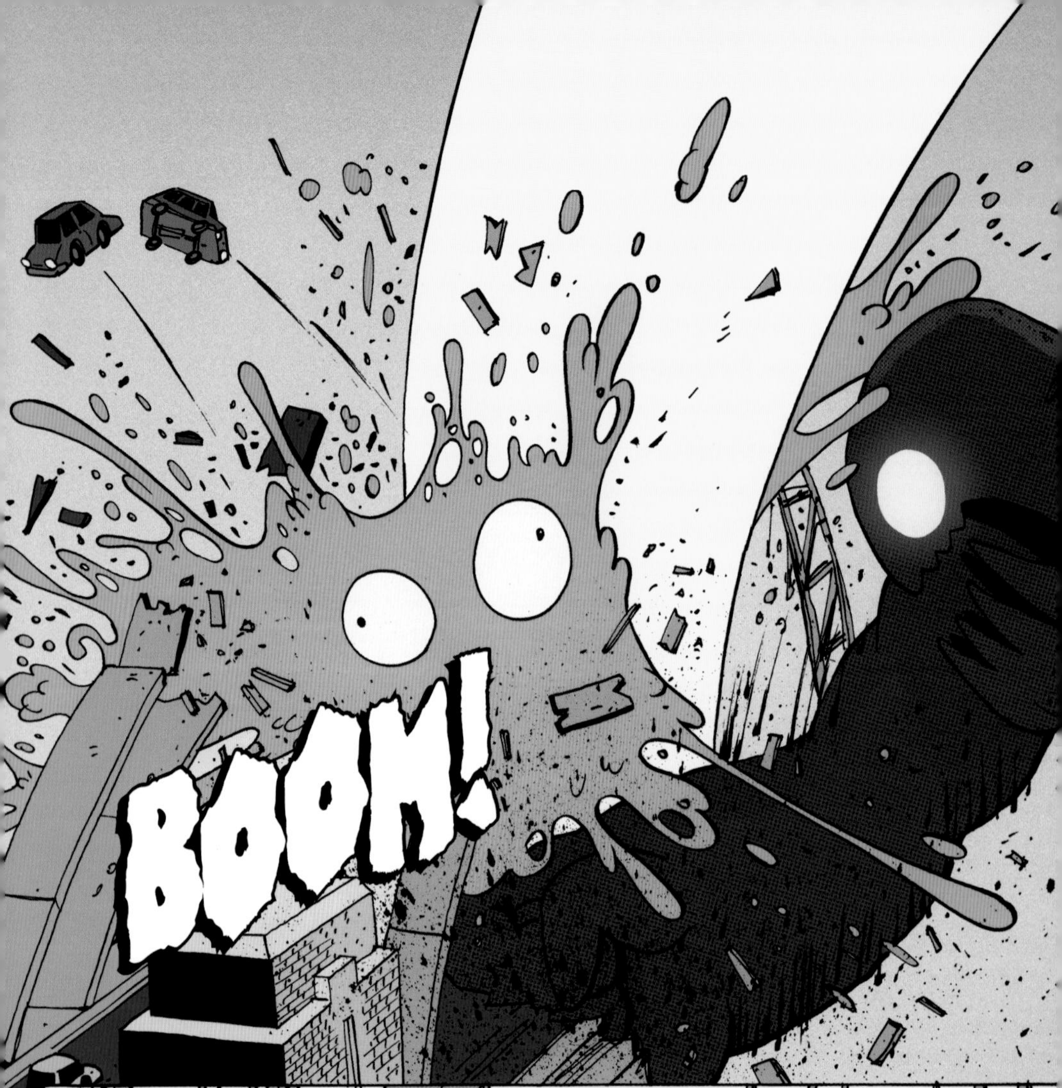
BOOM!

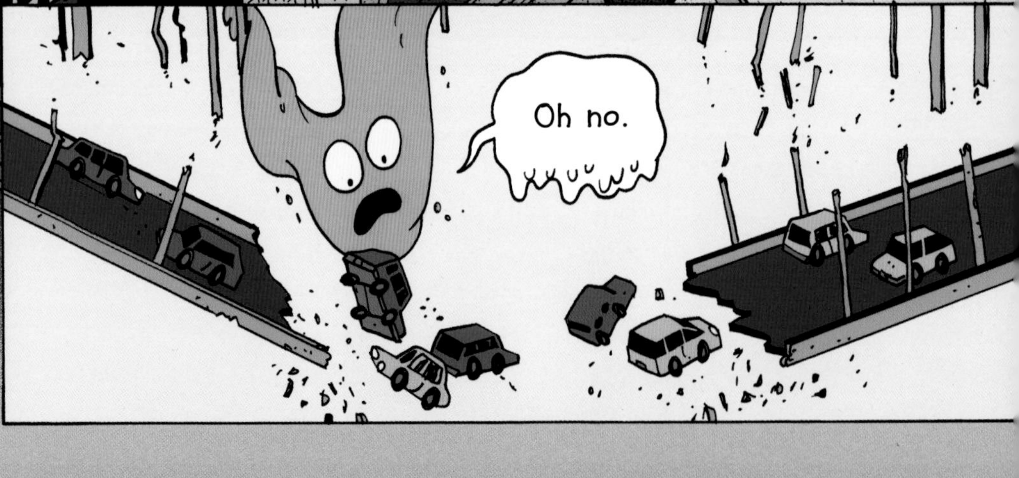
Oh no.

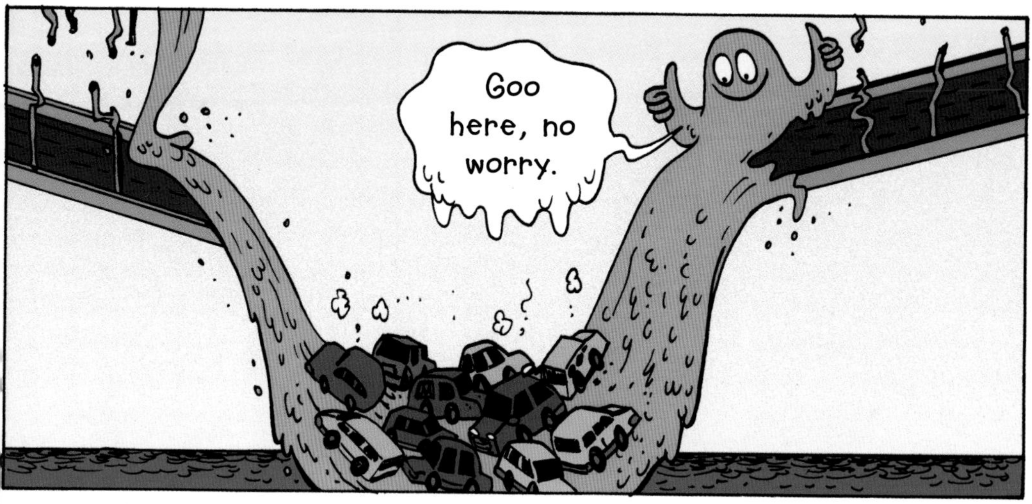
Goo here, no worry.

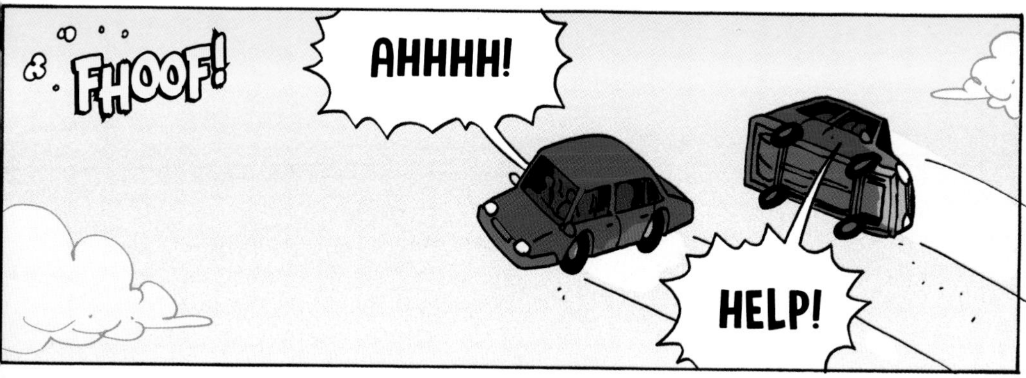
FHOOF!
AHHHH!
HELP!

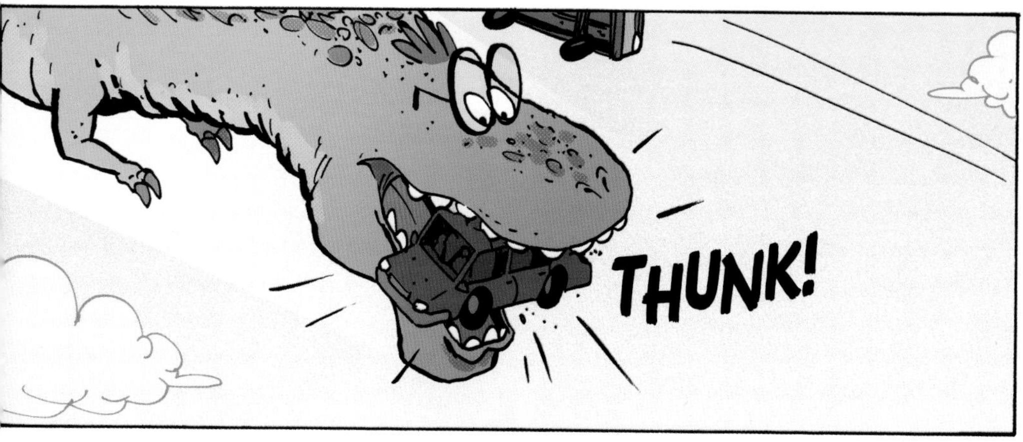
THUNK!

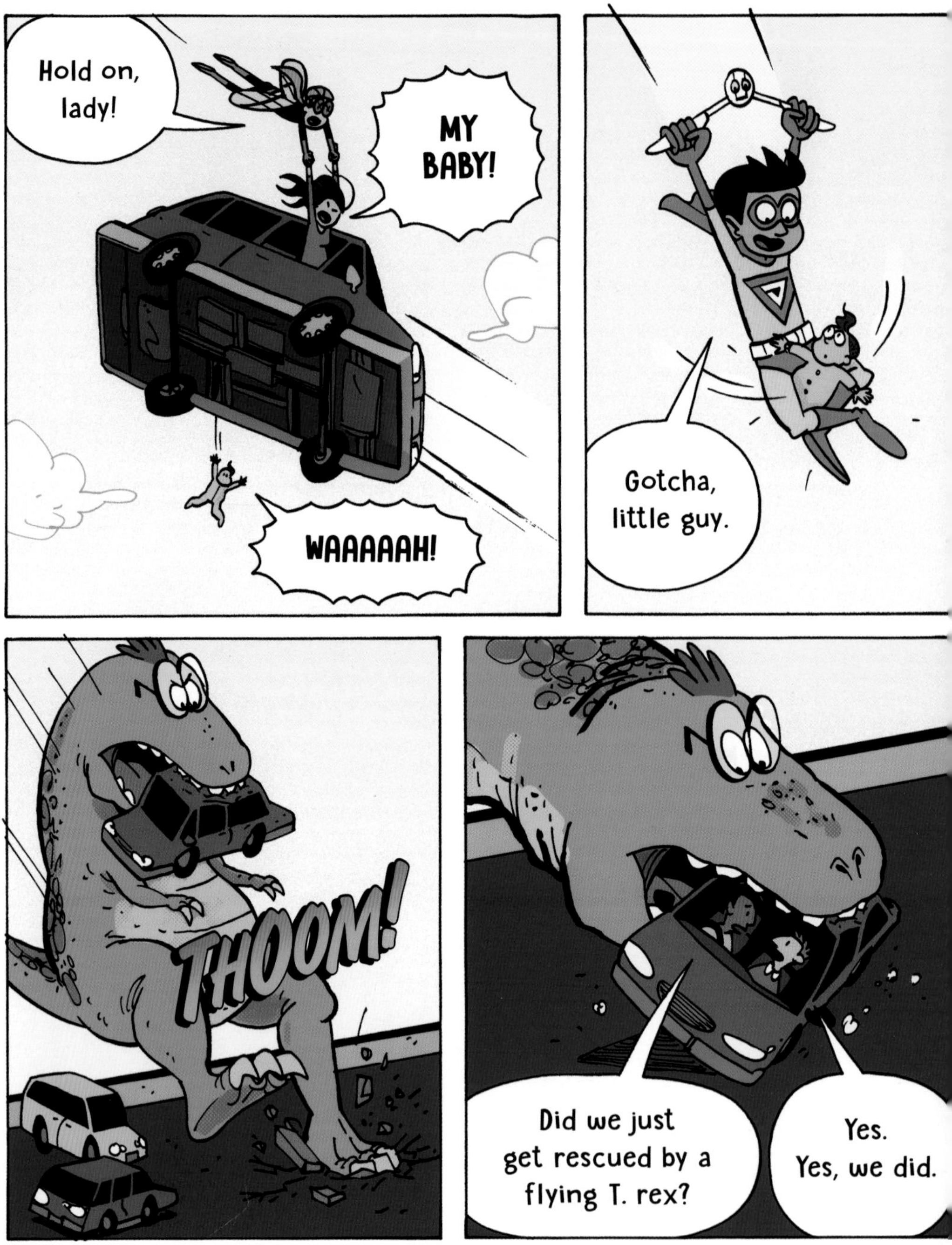
Hold on, lady!
MY BABY!
WAAAAAH!
Gotcha, little guy.
THOOM!
Did we just get rescued by a flying T. rex?
Yes. Yes, we did.

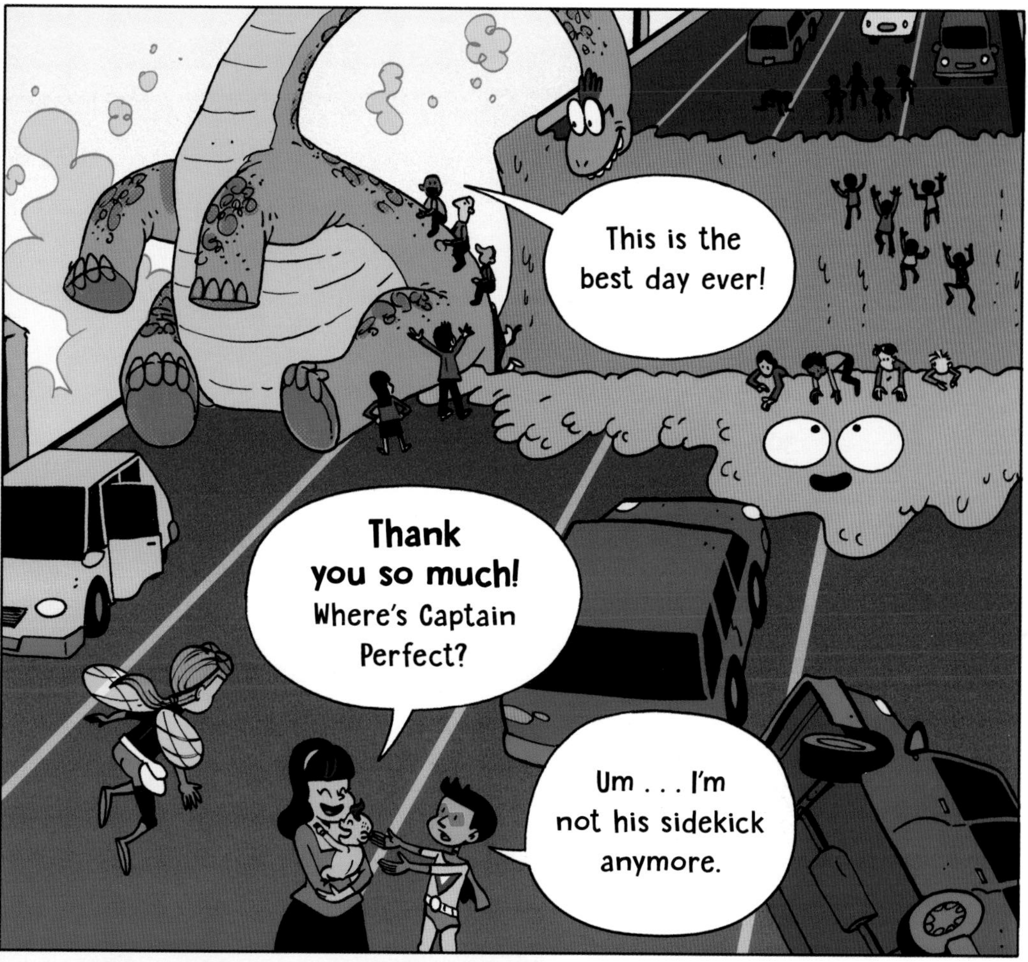
This is the best day ever!
Thank you so much! Where's Captain Perfect?
Um . . . I'm not his sidekick anymore.

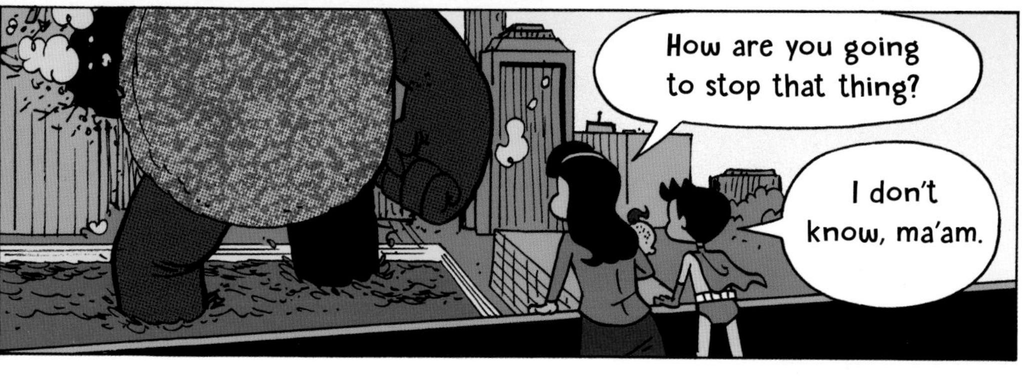
How are you going to stop that thing?
I don't know, ma'am.

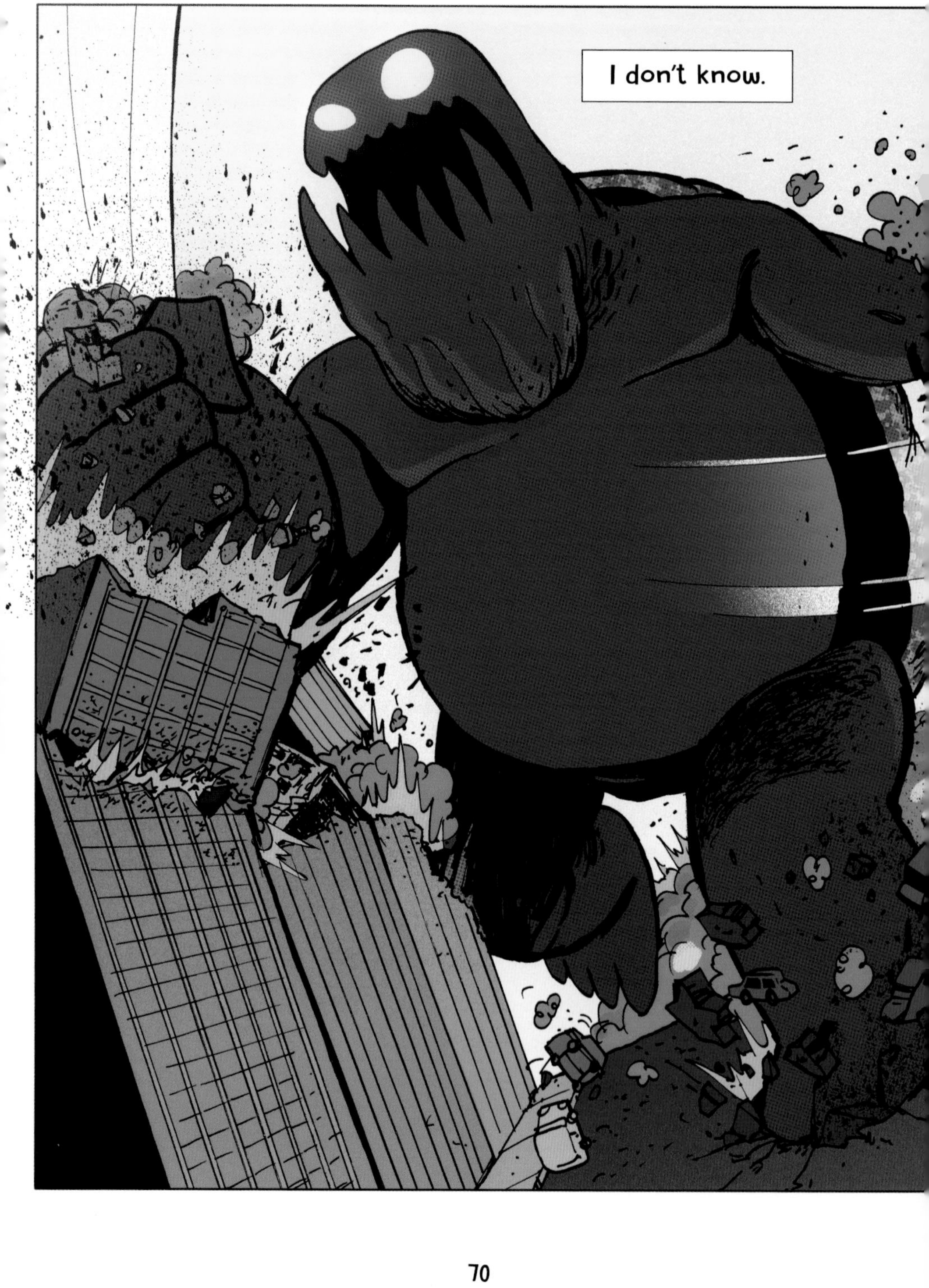
I don't know.

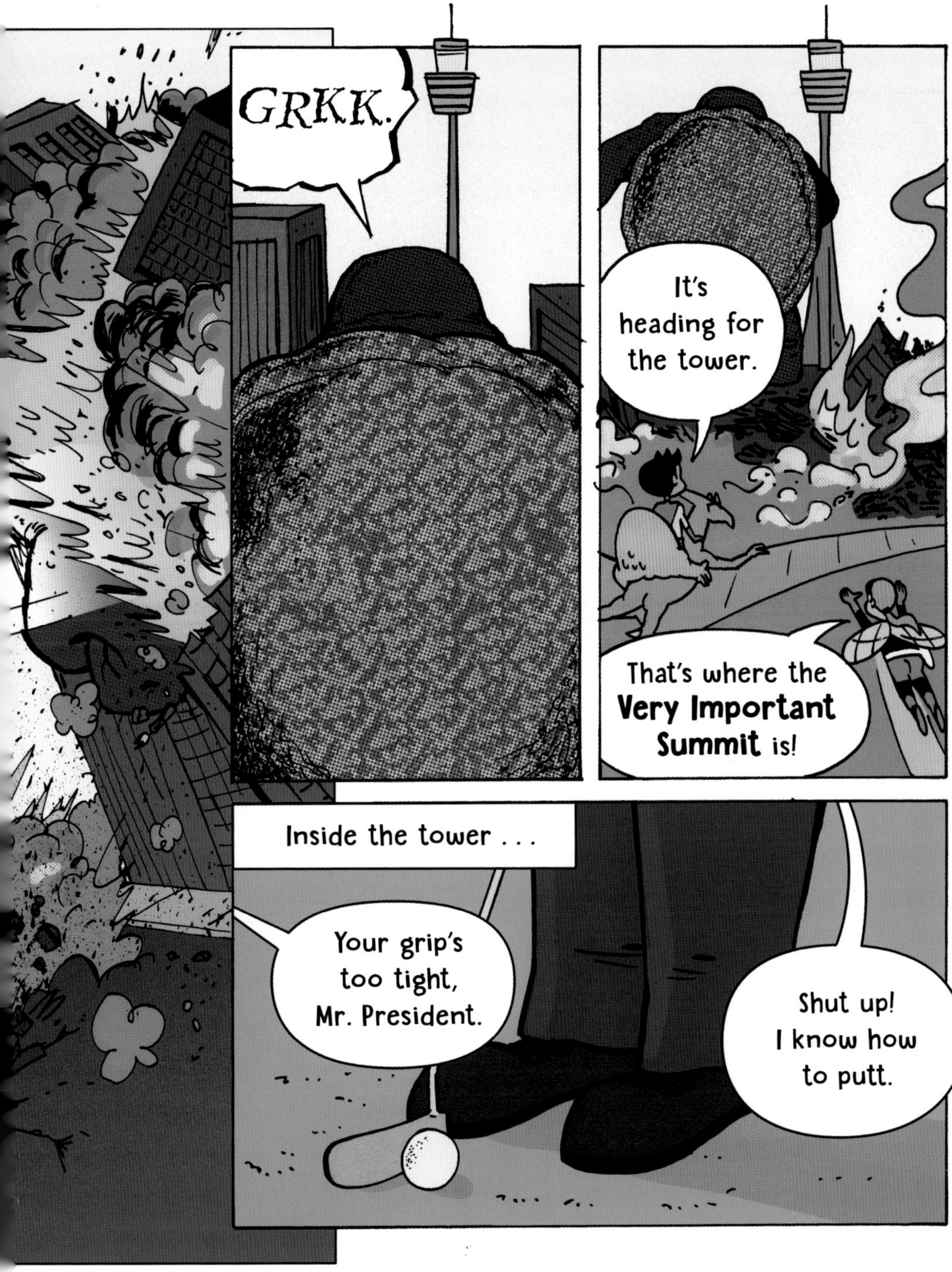
GRKK.
It's heading for the tower.
That's where the **Very Important Summit** is!
Inside the tower . . .
Your grip's too tight, Mr. President.
Shut up! I know how to putt.

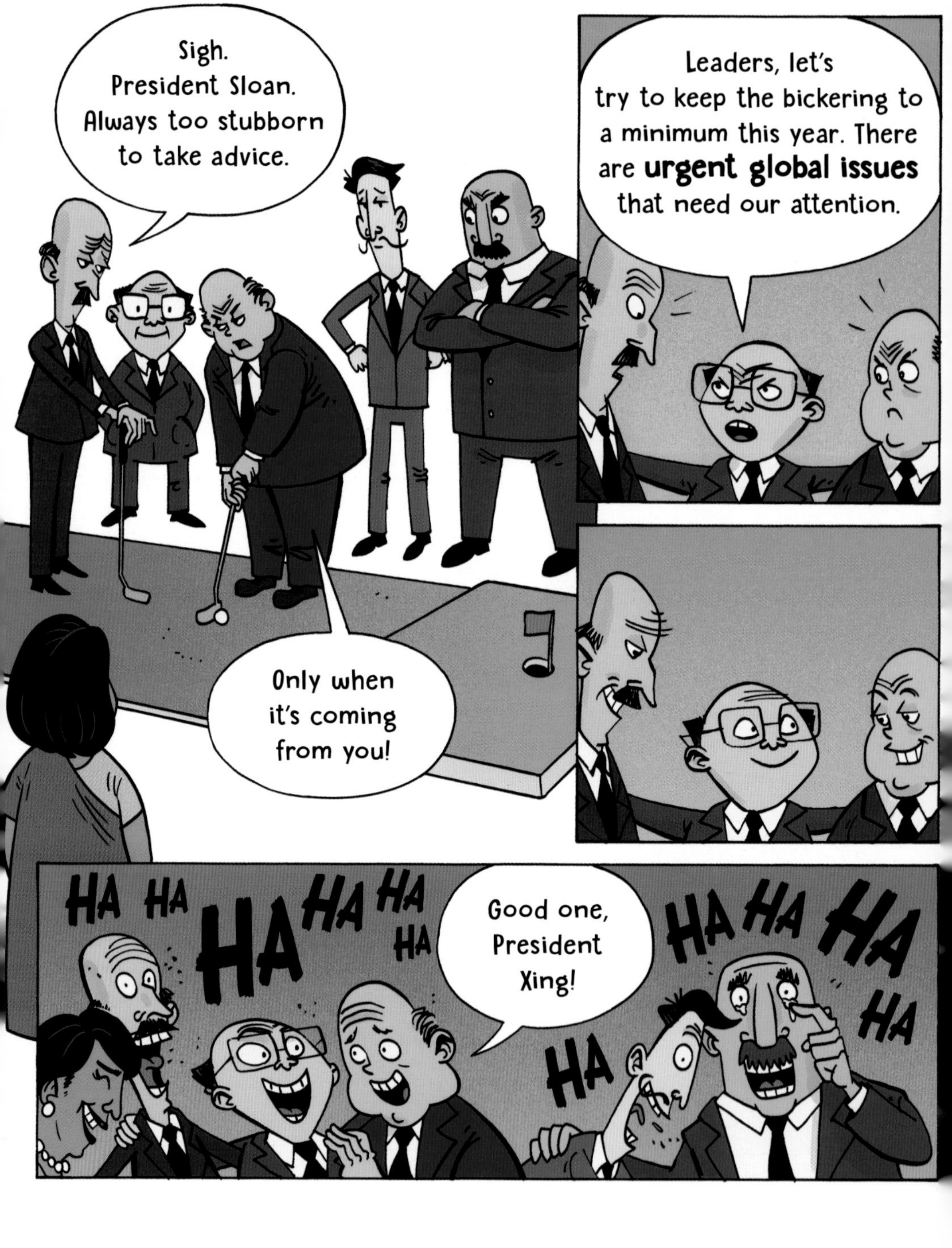
Sigh.
President Sloan.
Always too stubborn
to take advice.
Leaders, let's try to keep the bickering to a minimum this year. There are **urgent global issues** that need our attention.
Only when it's coming from you!
HA HA HA HA HA HA
Good one, President Xing!
HA HA HA HA HA HA

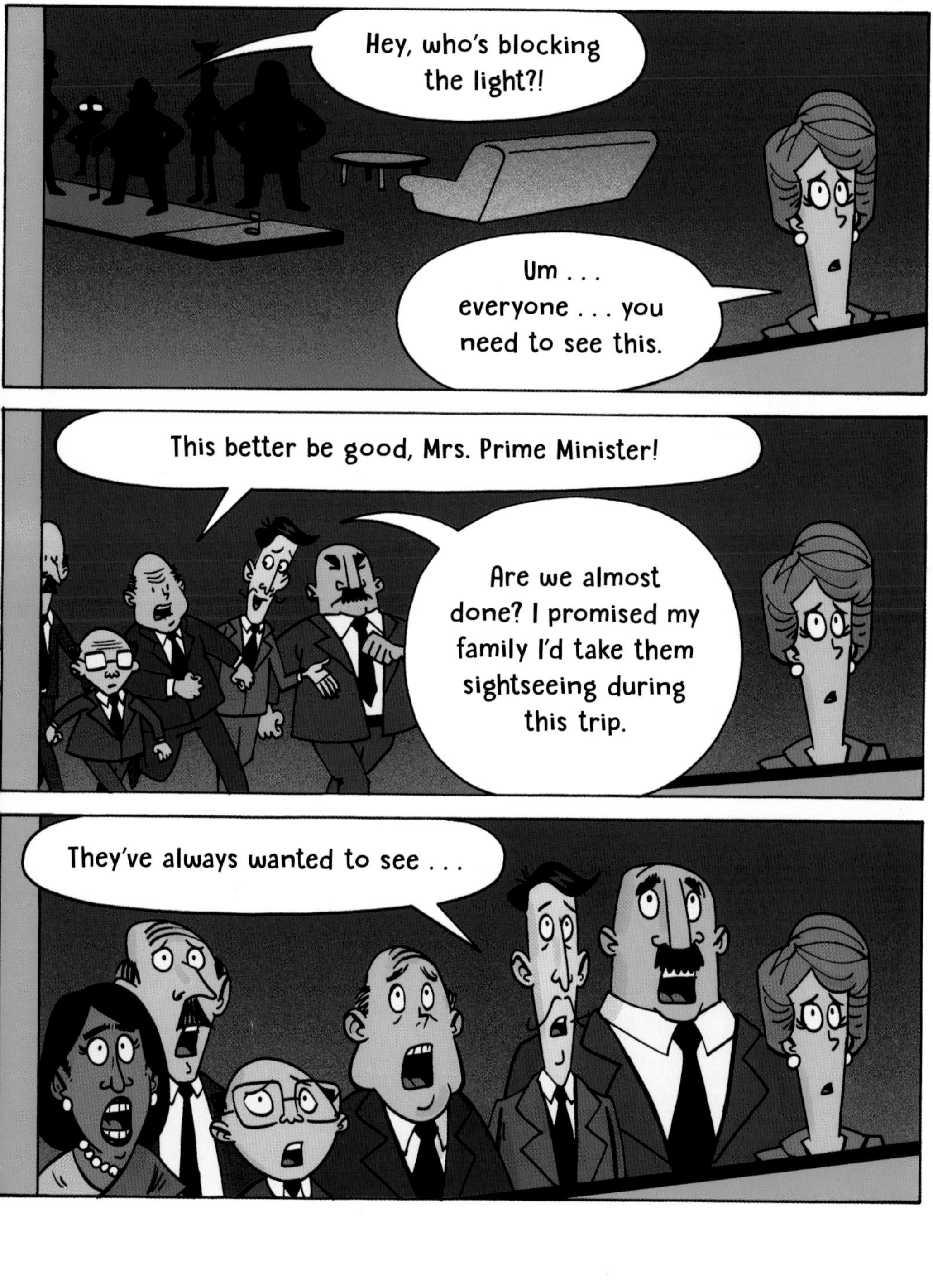
Hey, who's blocking the light?!
Um . . . everyone . . . you need to see this.
This better be good, Mrs. Prime Minister!
Are we almost done? I promised my family I'd take them sightseeing during this trip.
They've always wanted to see . . .

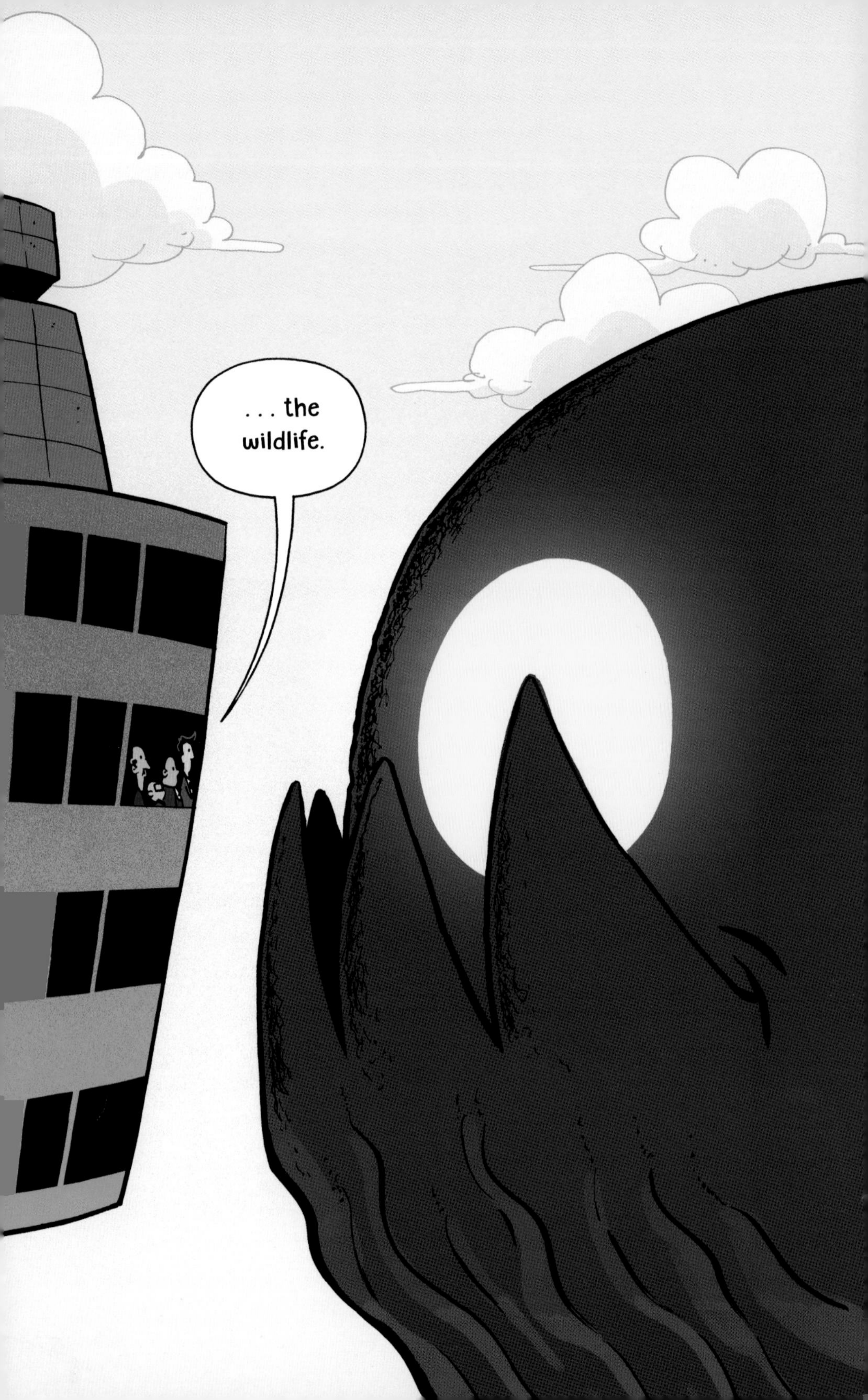
. . . the wildlife.

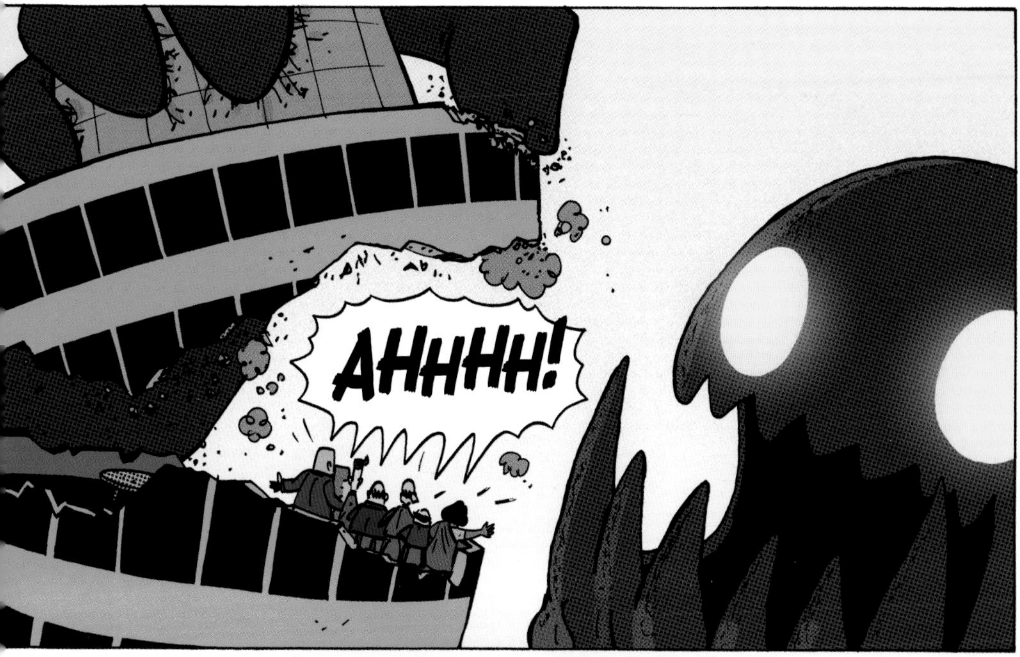
AHHHH!

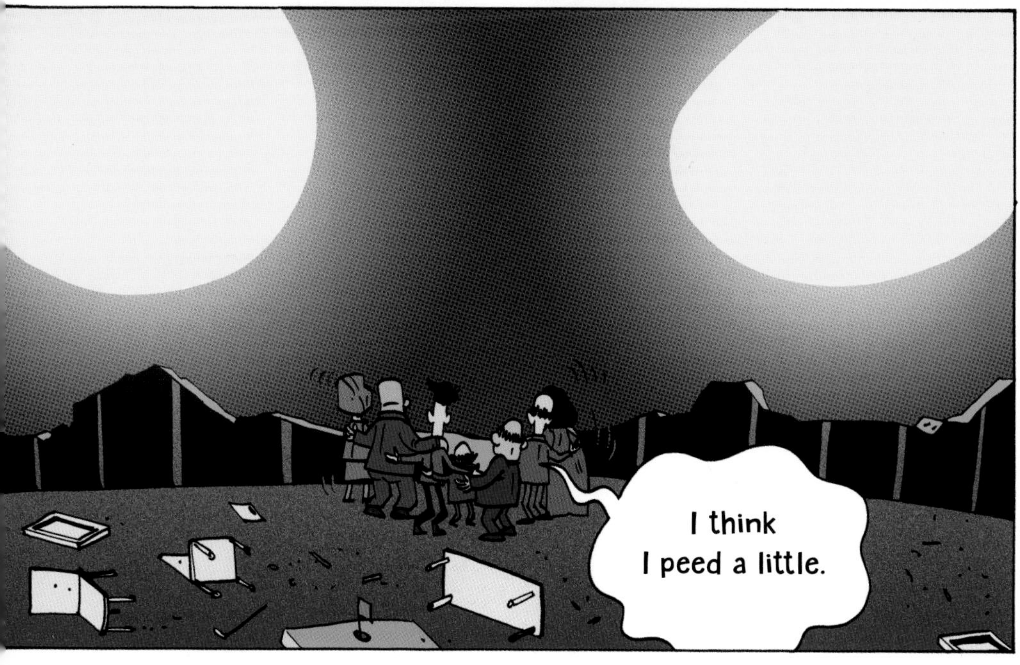
I think I peed a little.

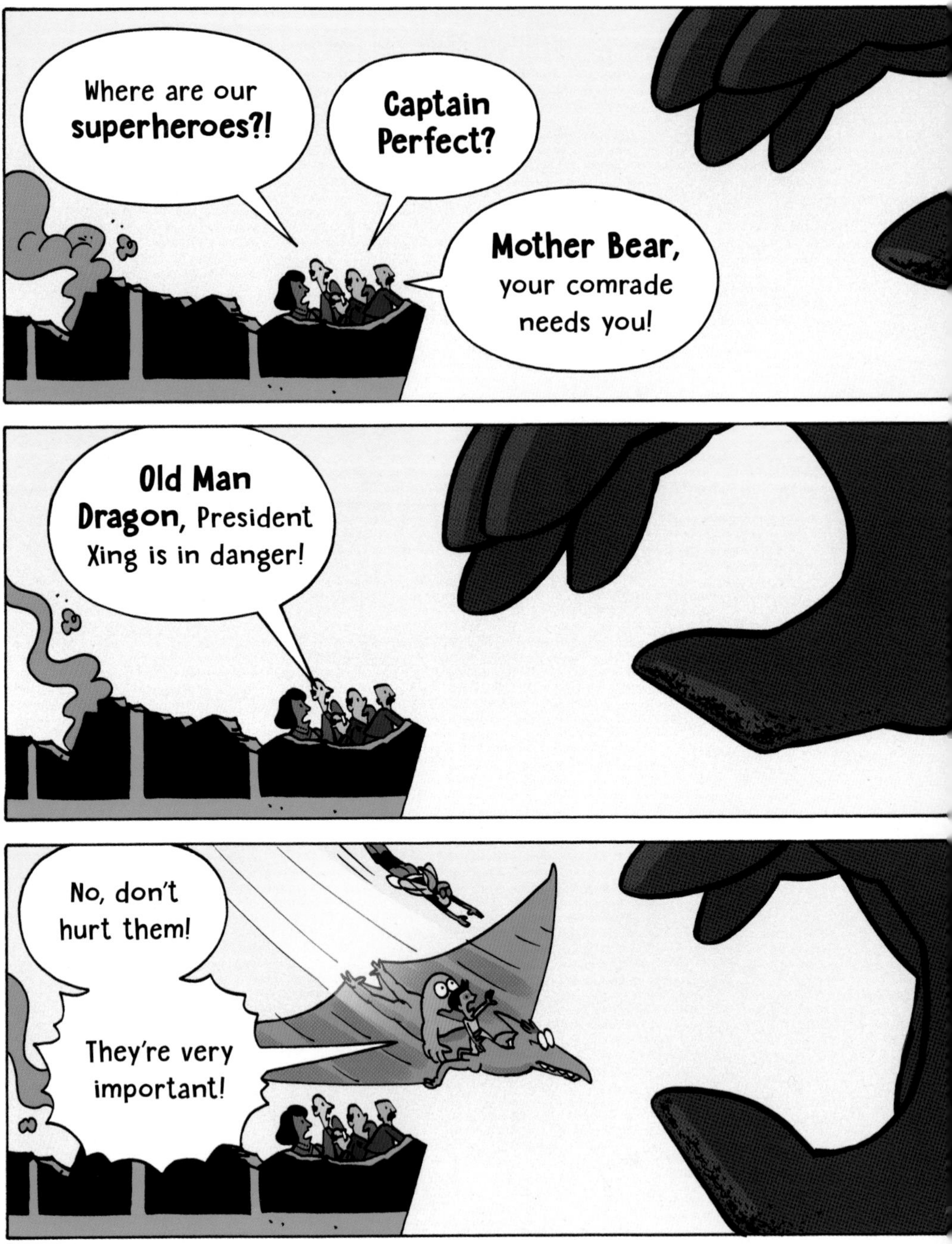
Where are our superheroes?!
Captain Perfect?
Mother Bear, your comrade needs you!
Old Man Dragon, President Xing is in danger!
No, don't hurt them!
They're very important!

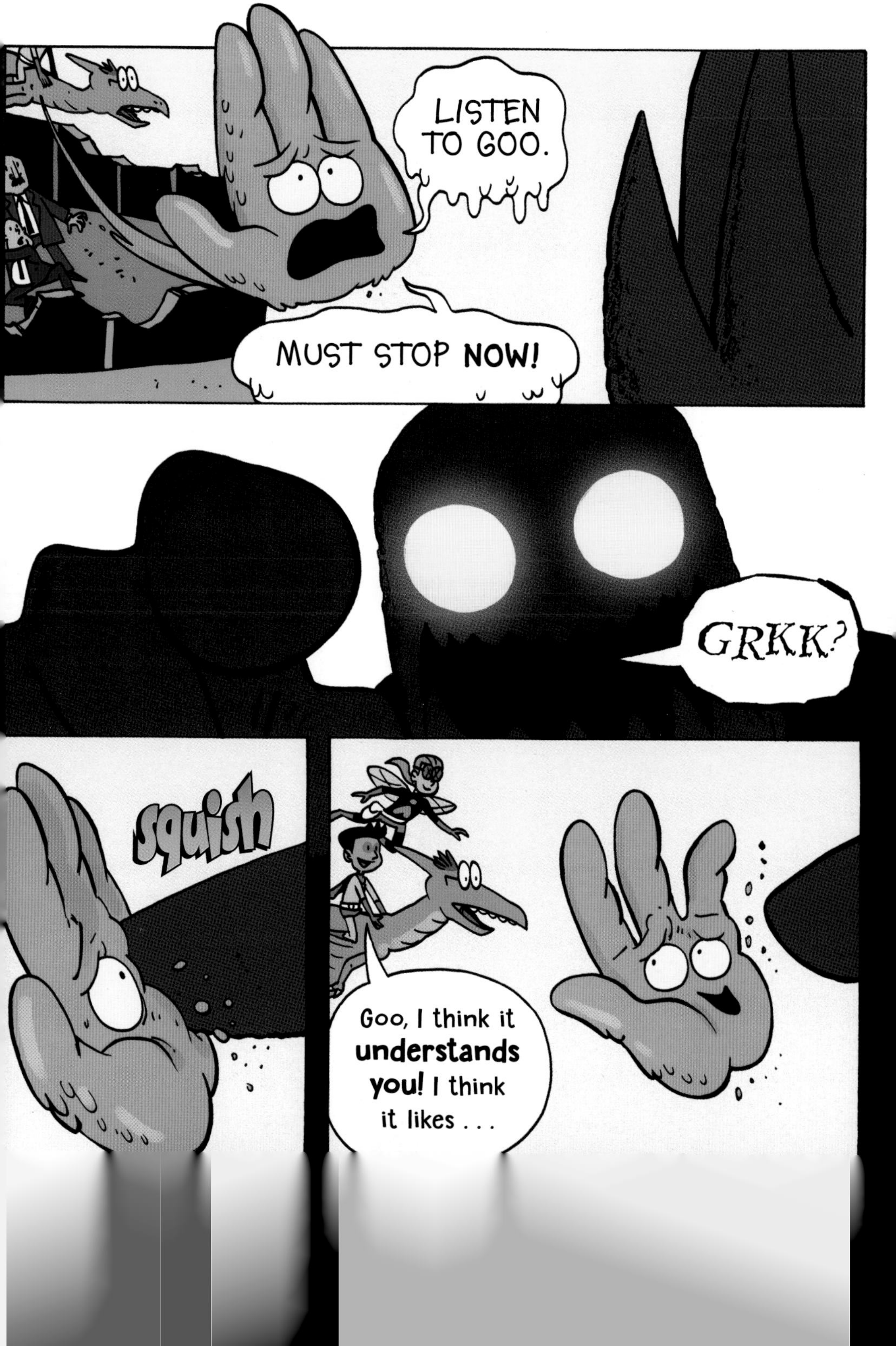
LISTEN TO GOO.
MUST STOP NOW!
GRKK?
squish
Goo, I think it understands you! I think it likes . . .

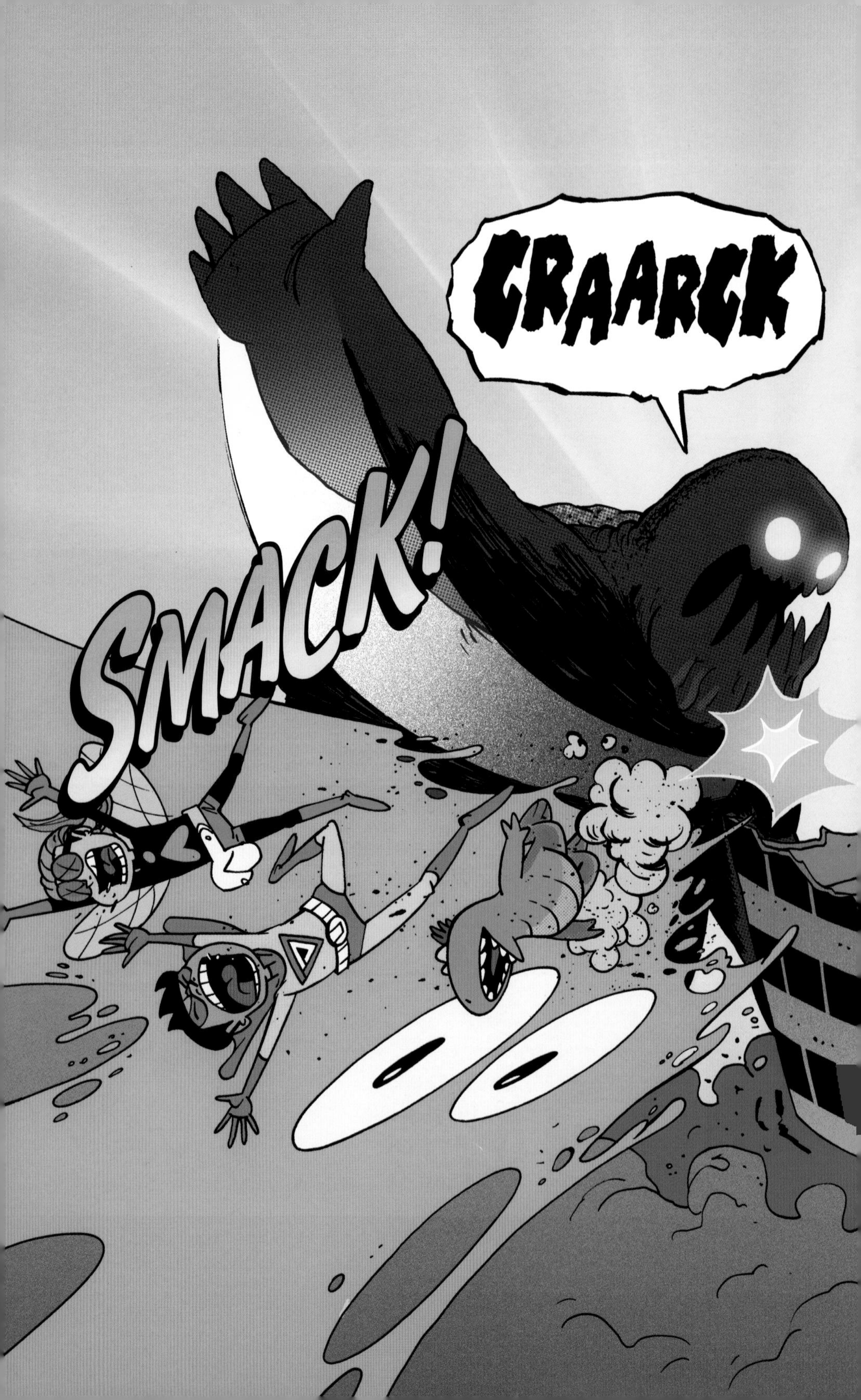
CRAARCK
SMACK!

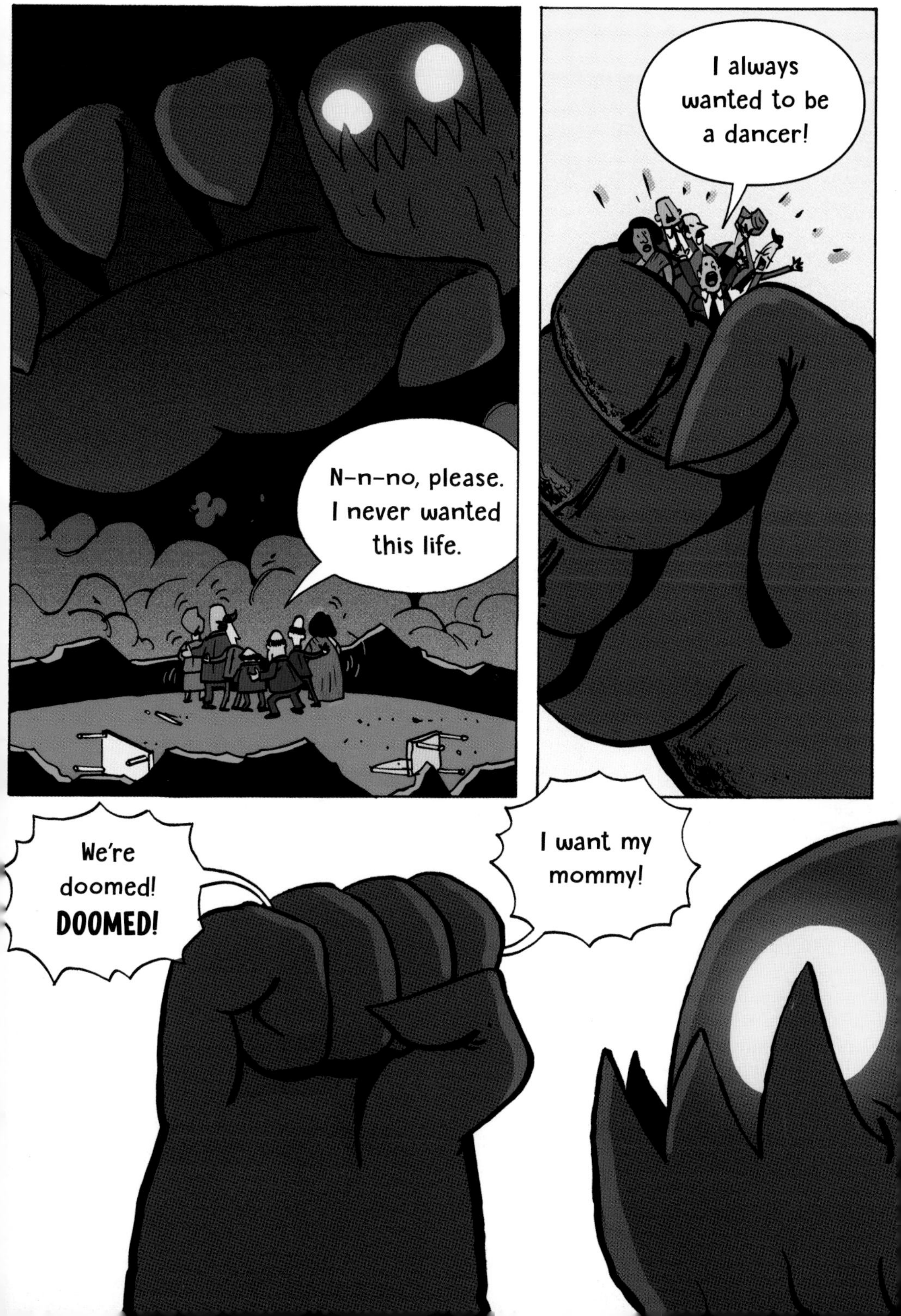
N-n-no, please. I never wanted this life.
I always wanted to be a dancer!
We're doomed! **DOOMED!**
I want my mommy!

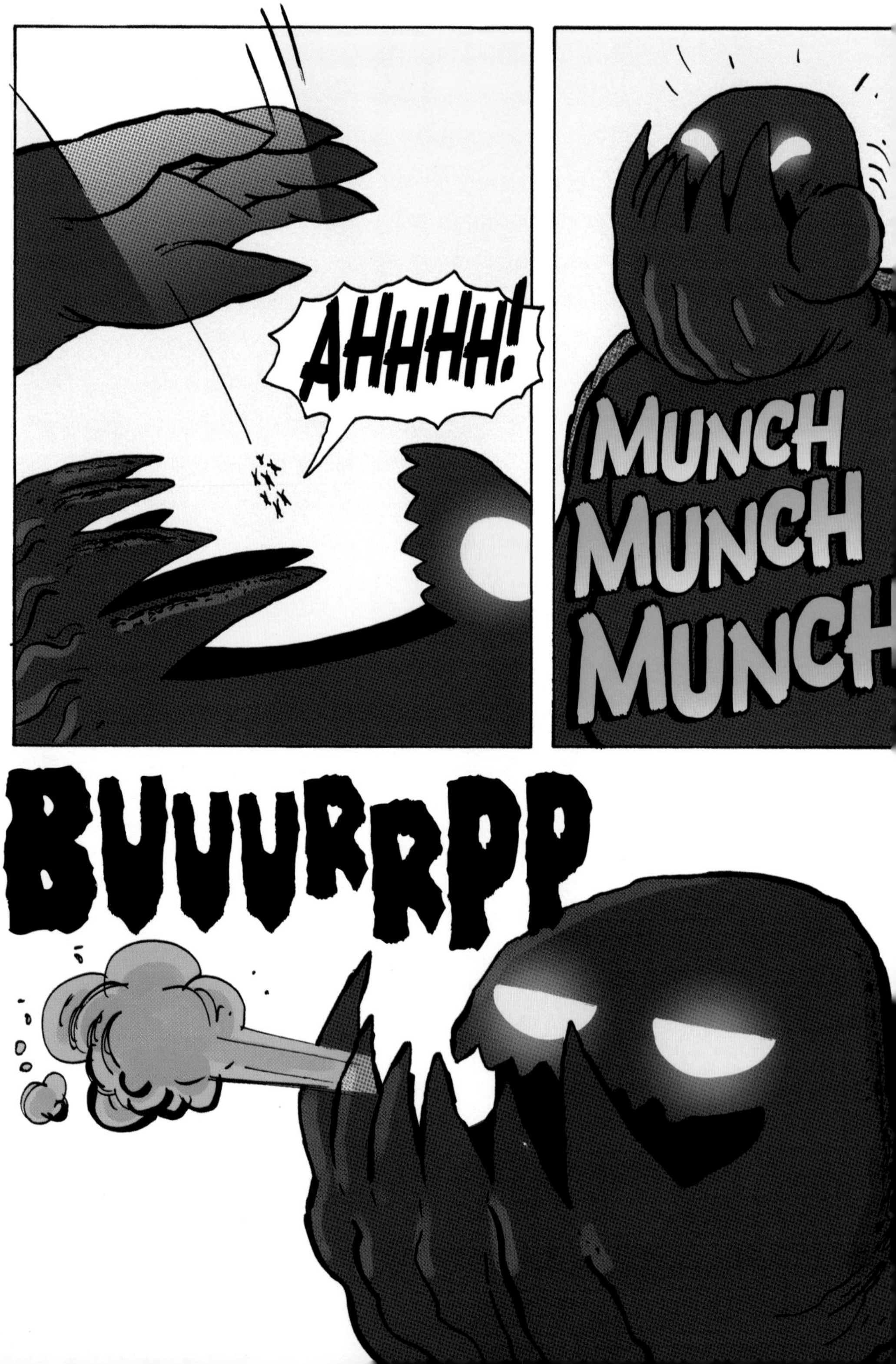
AHHHH!
MUNCH
MUNCH
MUNCH
BUUURRPP

Chapter

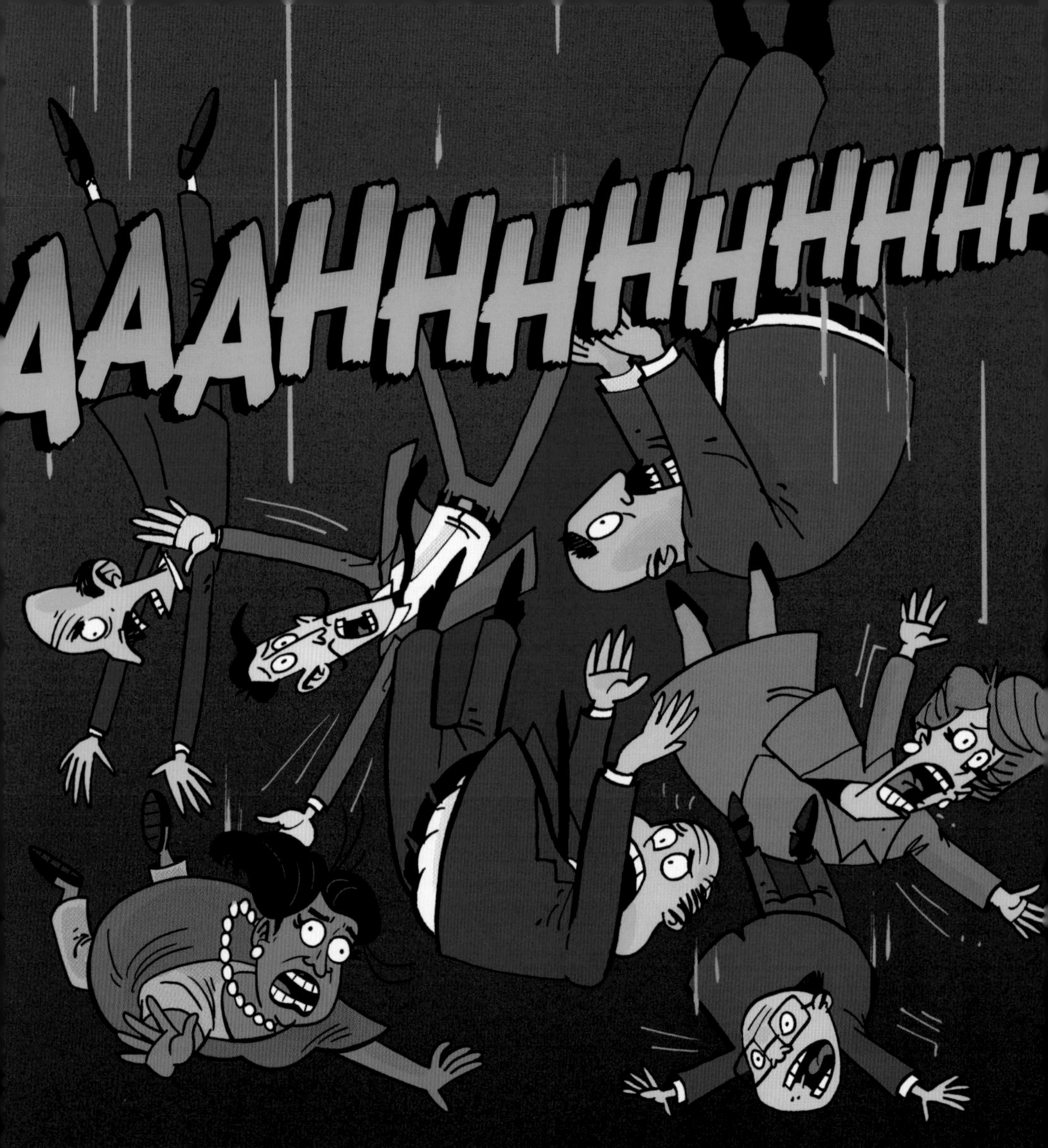
AAAHHHHHHHHHH

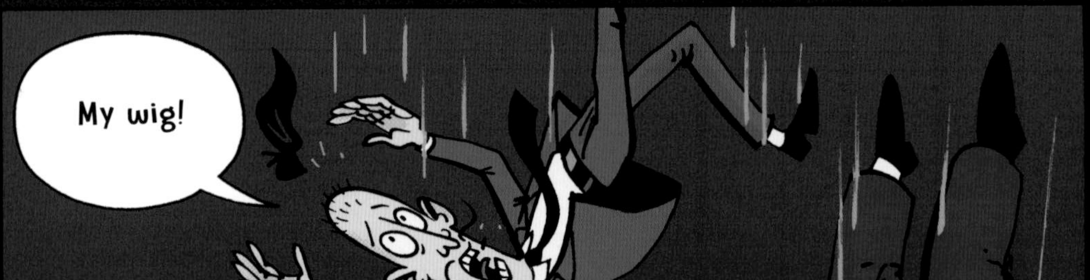
My wig!

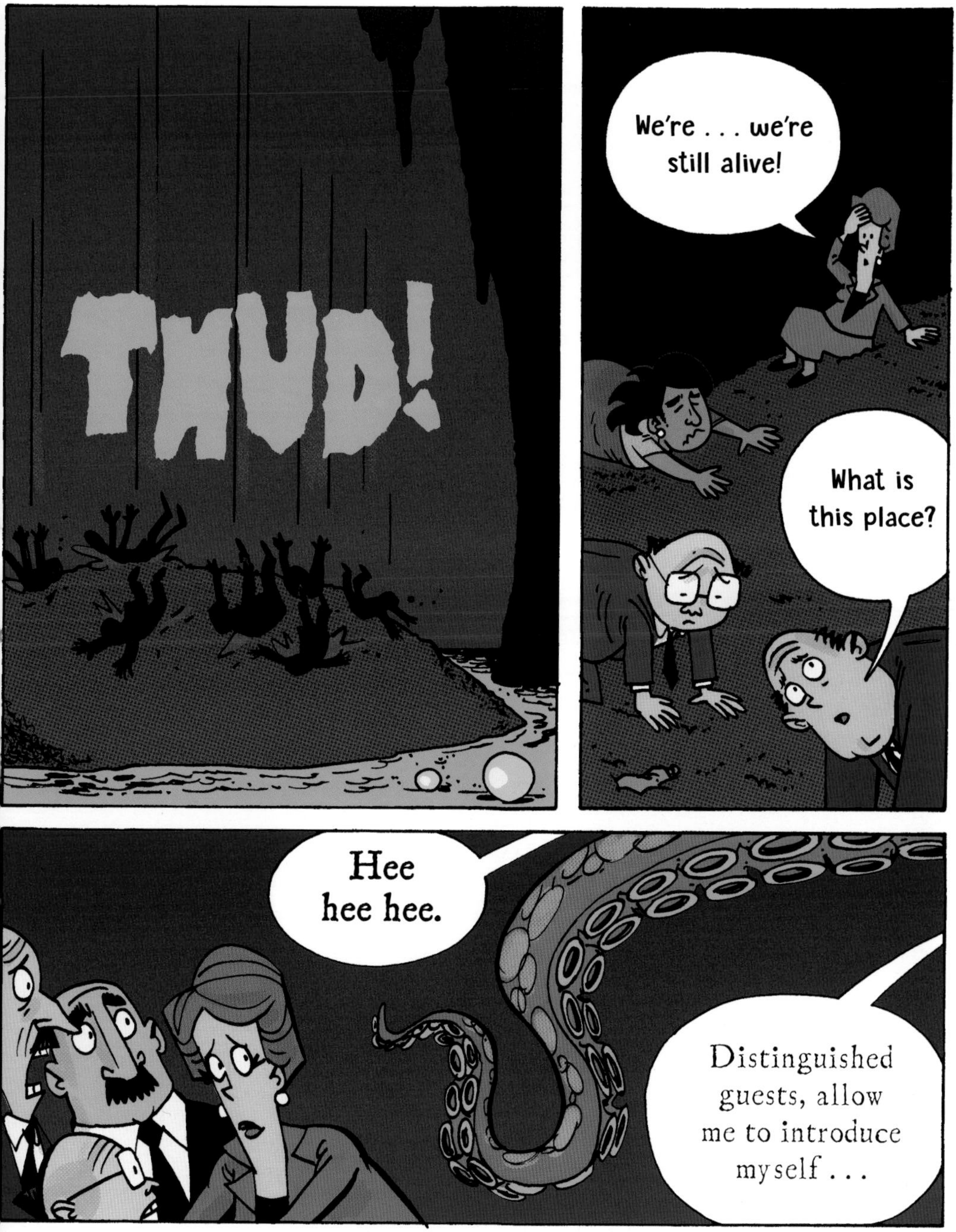
THUD!
We're . . . we're still alive!
What is this place?
Hee hee hee.
Distinguished guests, allow me to introduce myself . . .

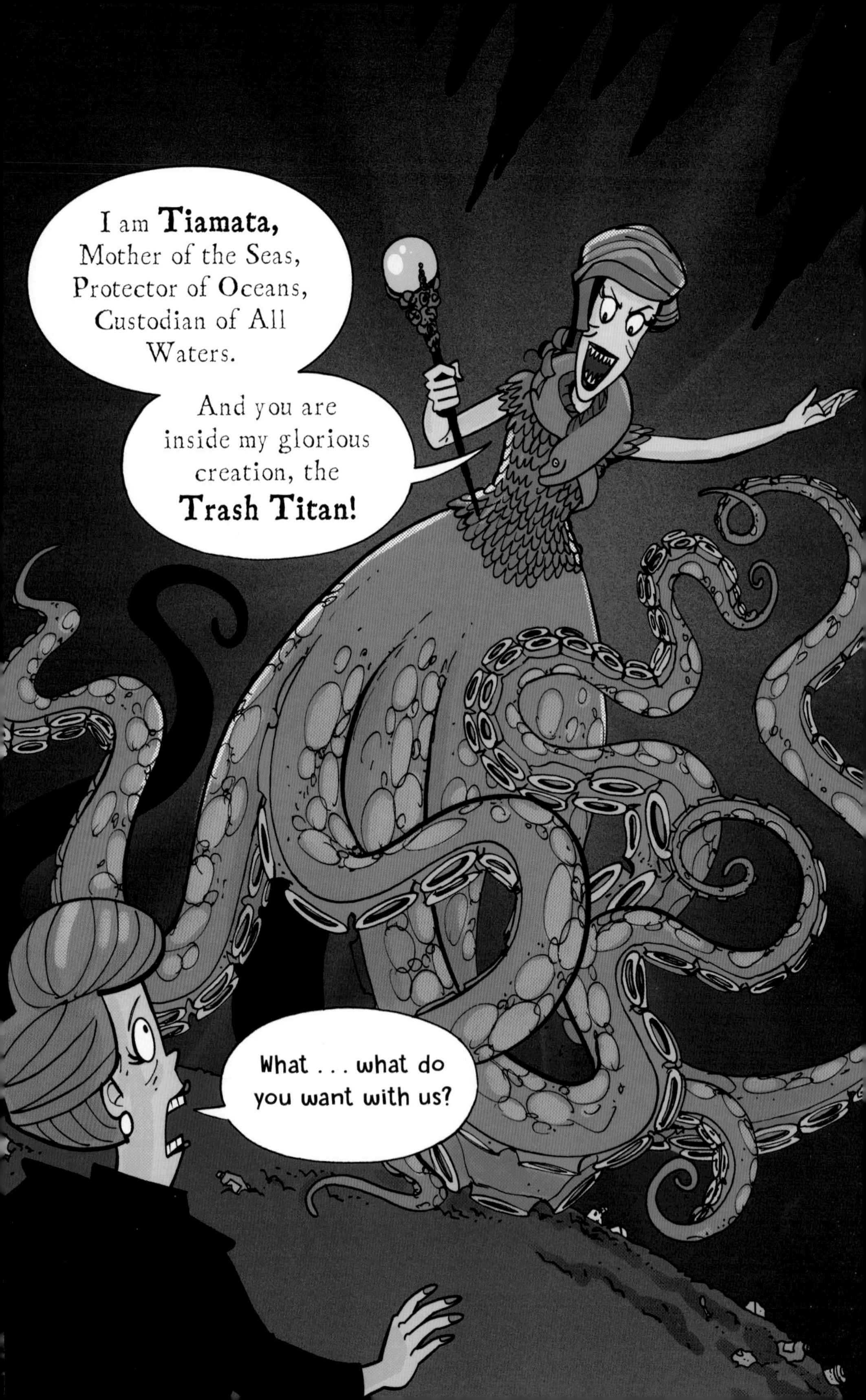
I am **Tiamata,** Mother of the Seas, Protector of Oceans, Custodian of All Waters.
And you are inside my glorious creation, the **Trash Titan!**
What . . . what do you want with us?

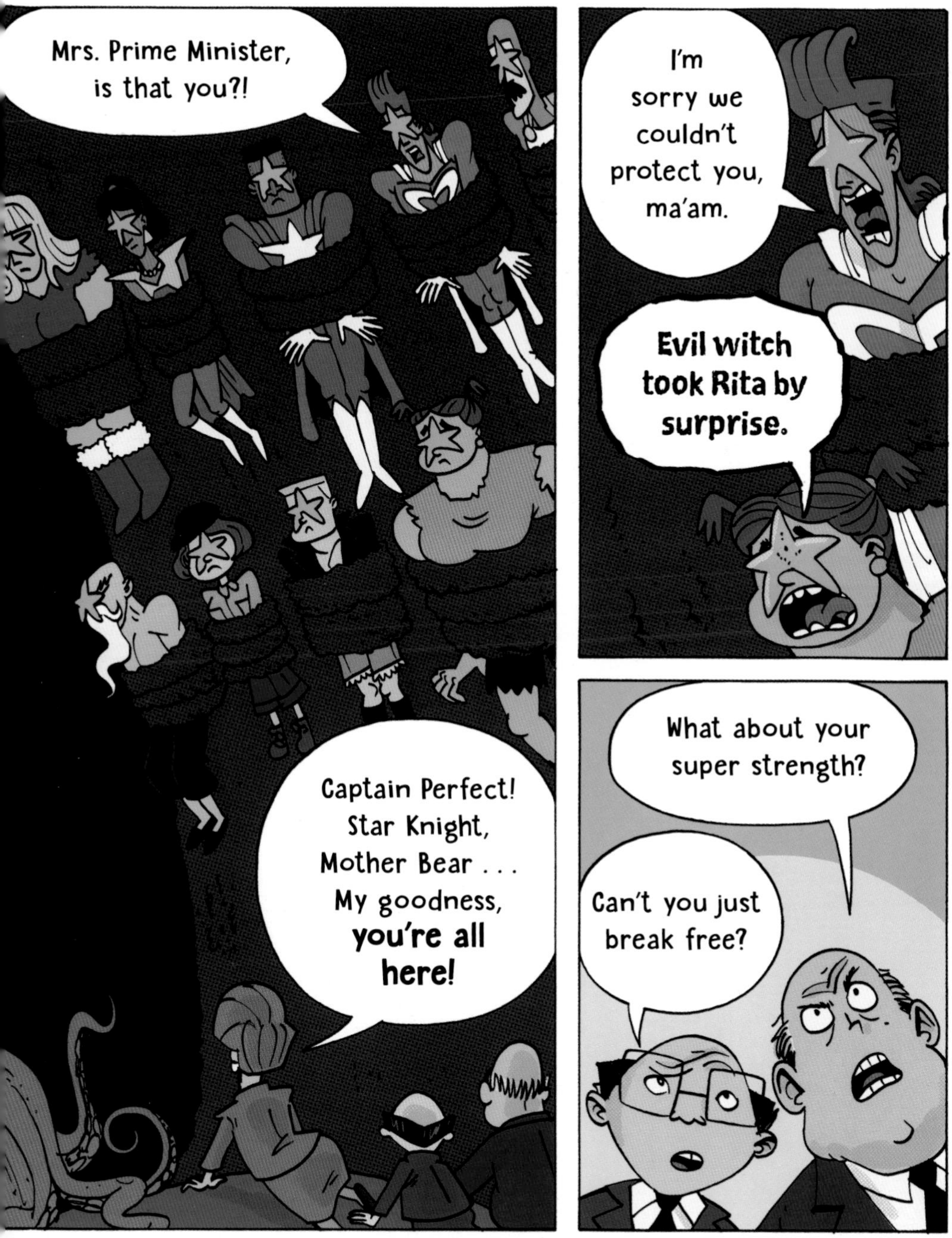
Mrs. Prime Minister, is that you?!
Captain Perfect! Star Knight, Mother Bear . . . My goodness, **you're all here!**
I'm sorry we couldn't protect you, ma'am.
Evil witch took Rita by surprise.
What about your super strength?
Can't you just break free?

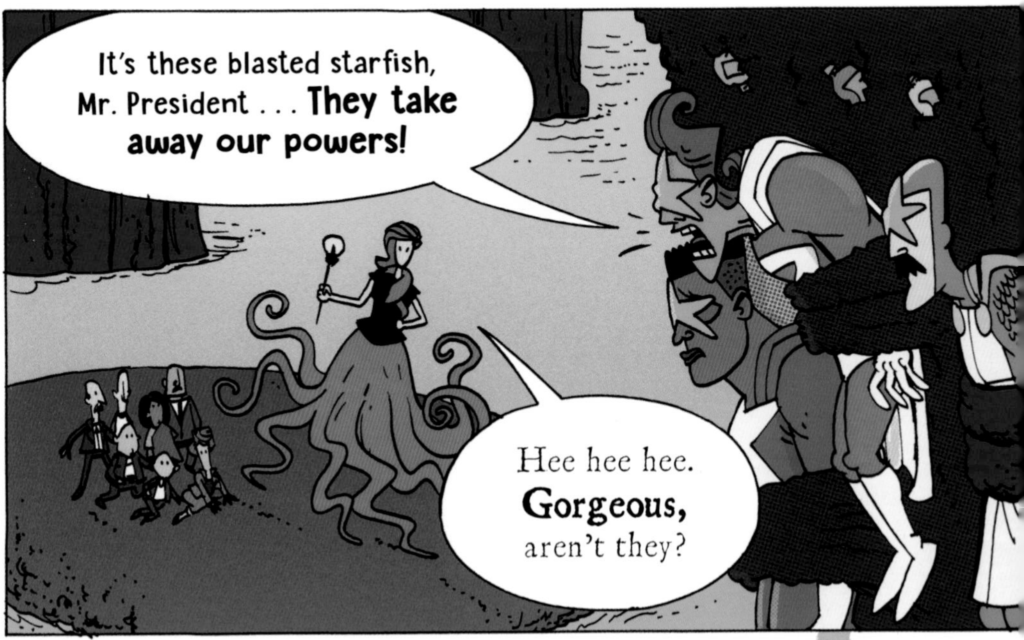
It's these blasted starfish, Mr. President . . . They take away our powers!
Hee hee hee. Gorgeous, aren't they?

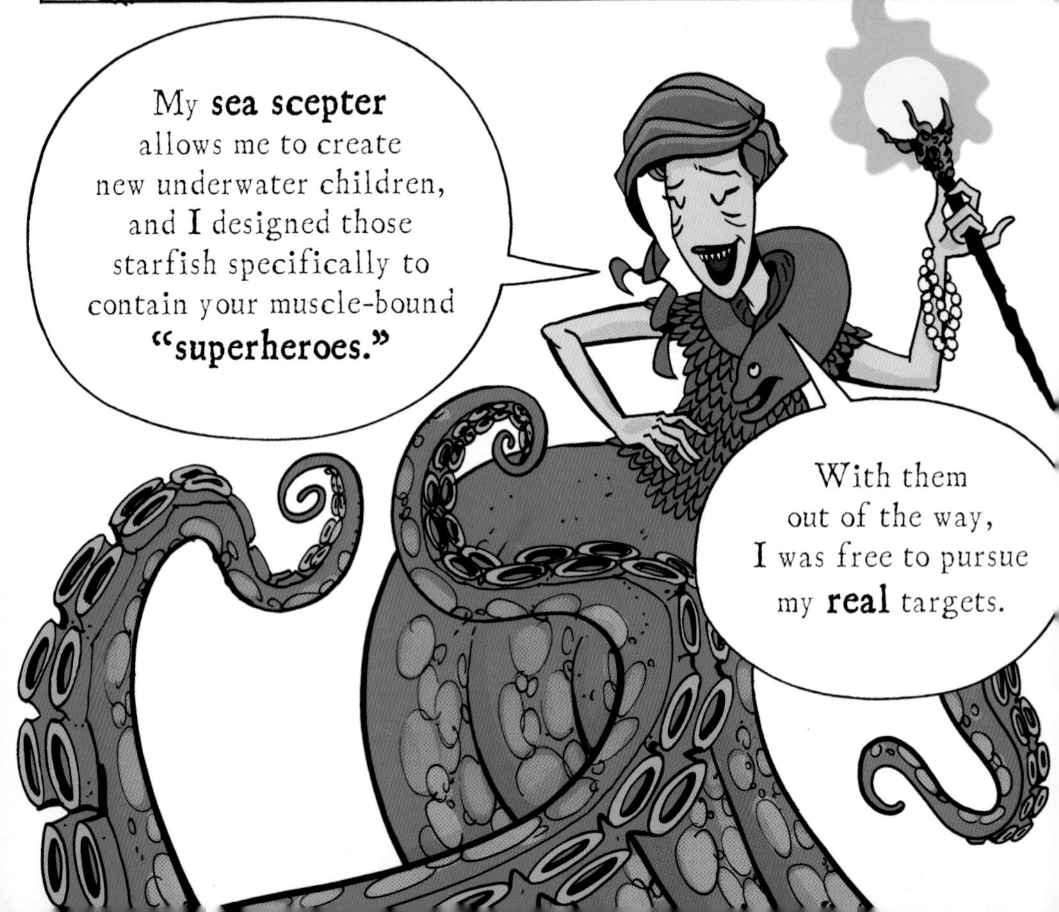
My sea scepter allows me to create new underwater children, and I designed those starfish specifically to contain your muscle-bound "superheroes."
With them out of the way, I was free to pursue my real targets.

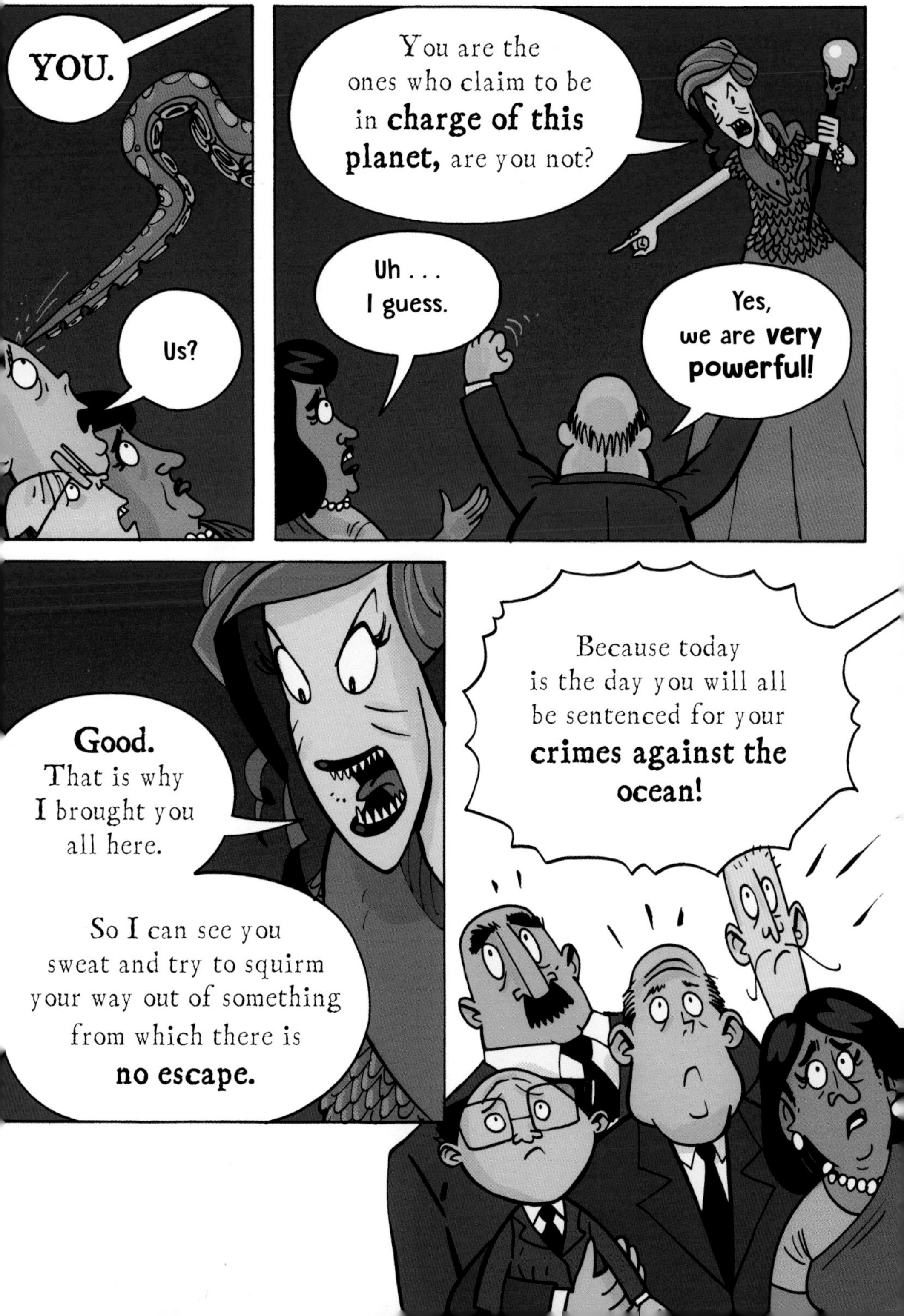
YOU.
Us?
You are the ones who claim to be in charge of this planet, are you not?
Uh . . . I guess.
Yes, we are very powerful!
Good. That is why I brought you all here.
So I can see you sweat and try to squirm your way out of something from which there is no escape.
Because today is the day you will all be sentenced for your crimes against the ocean!

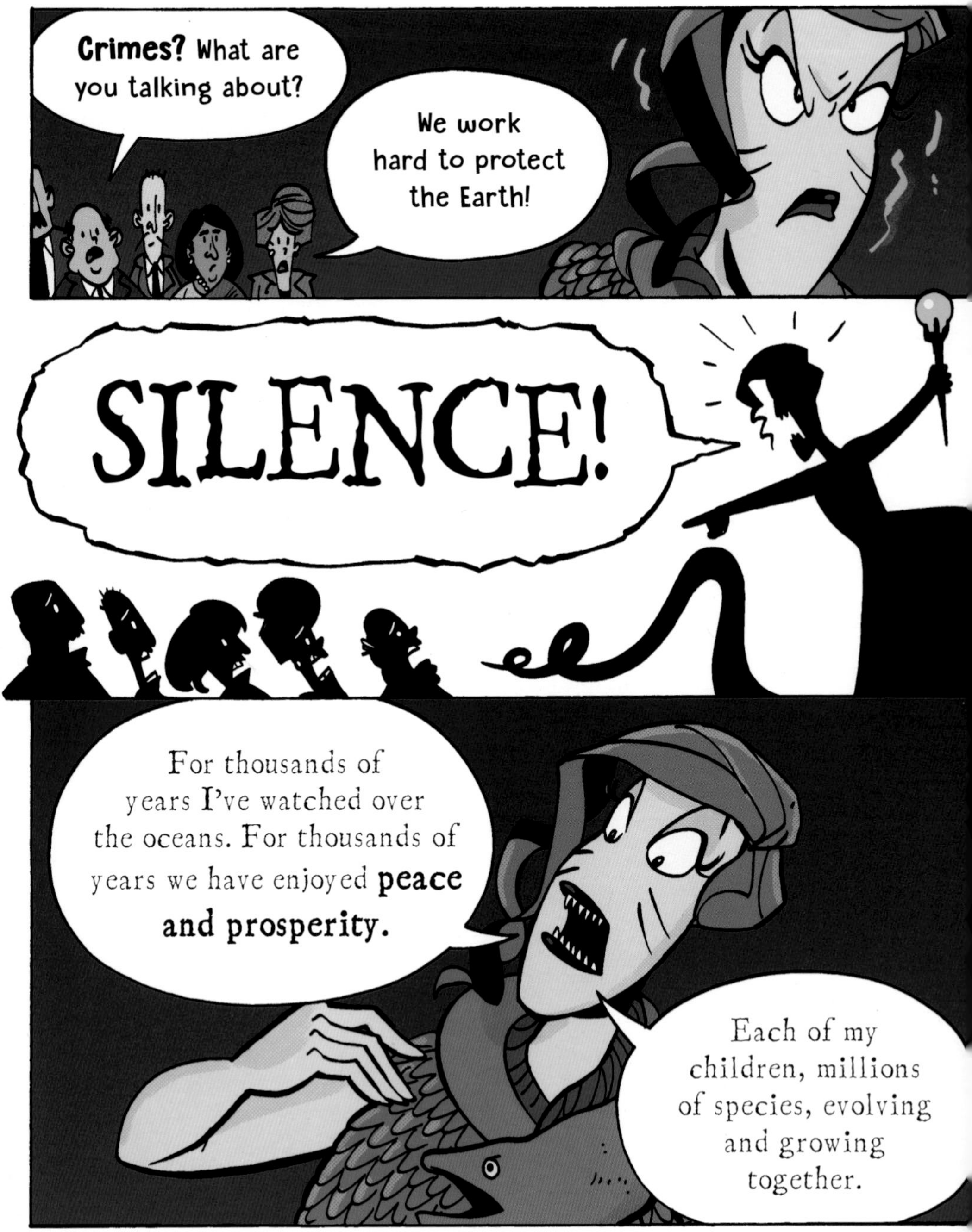
Crimes? What are you talking about?
We work hard to protect the Earth!
SILENCE!
For thousands of years I've watched over the oceans. For thousands of years we have enjoyed **peace and prosperity.**
Each of my children, millions of species, evolving and growing together.

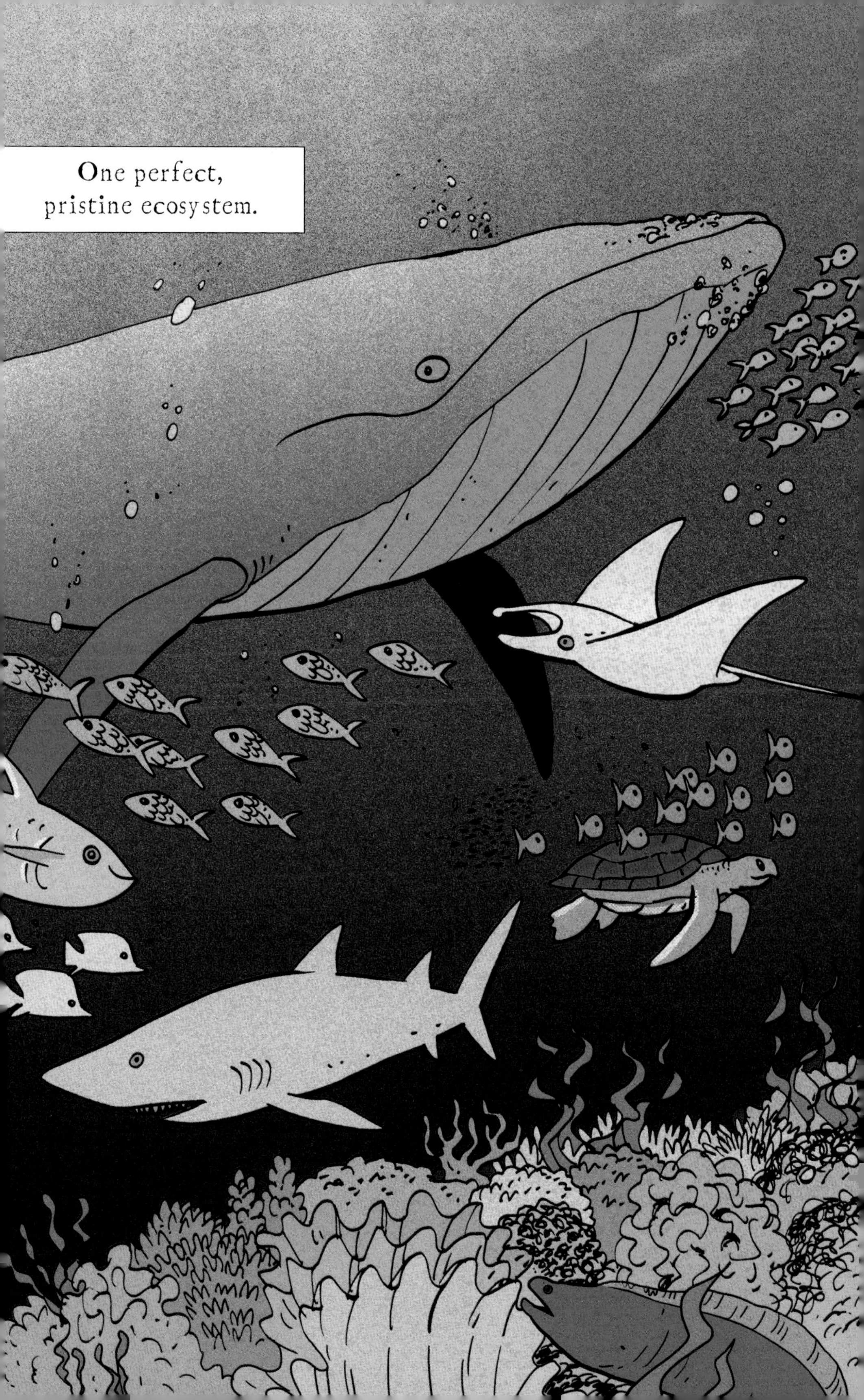
One perfect,
pristine ecosystem.

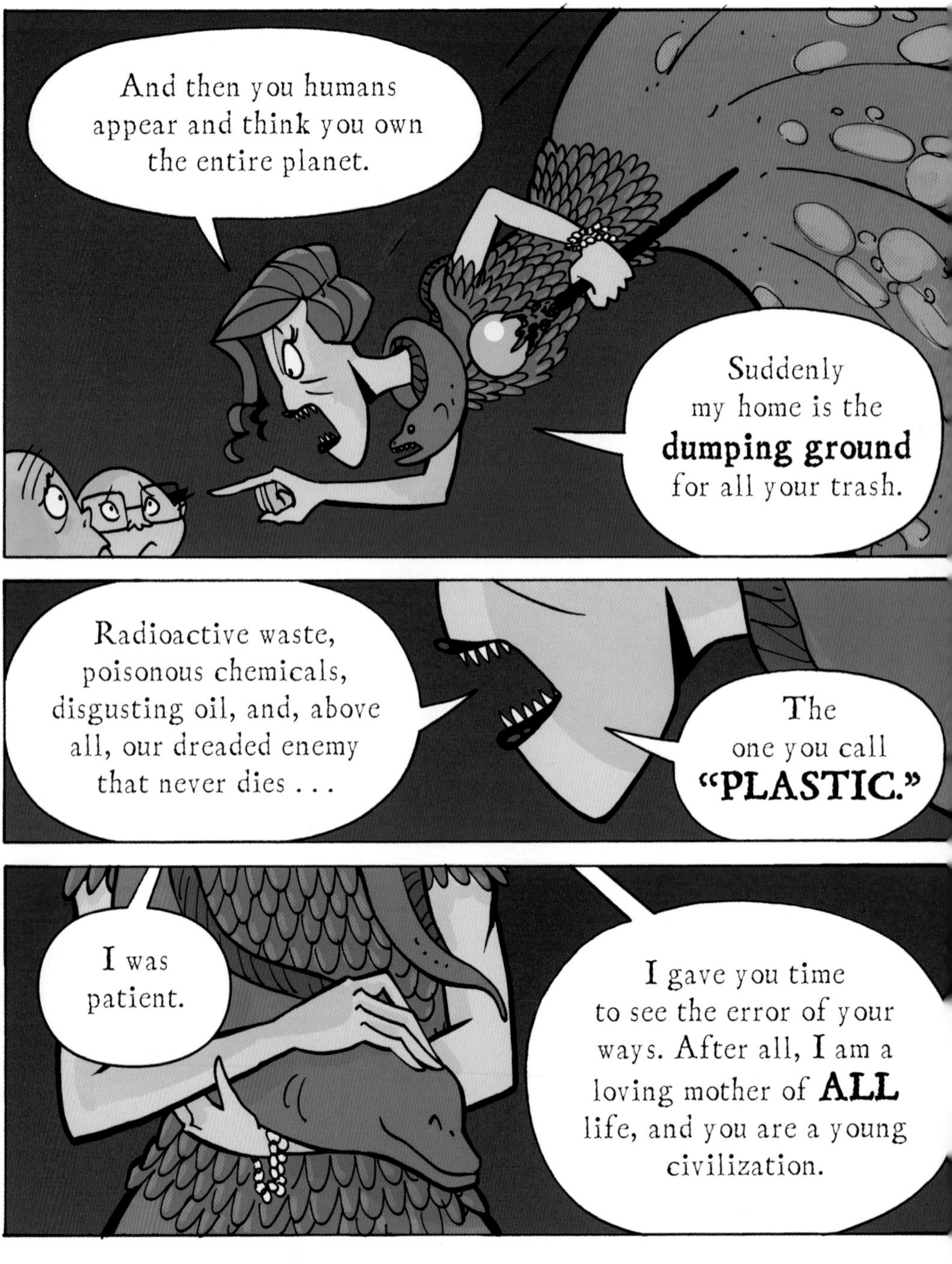

And then you humans appear and think you own the entire planet.
Suddenly my home is the **dumping ground** for all your trash.
Radioactive waste, poisonous chemicals, disgusting oil, and, above all, our dreaded enemy that never dies . . .
The one you call **"PLASTIC."**
I was patient.
I gave you time to see the error of your ways. After all, I am a loving mother of **ALL** life, and you are a young civilization.

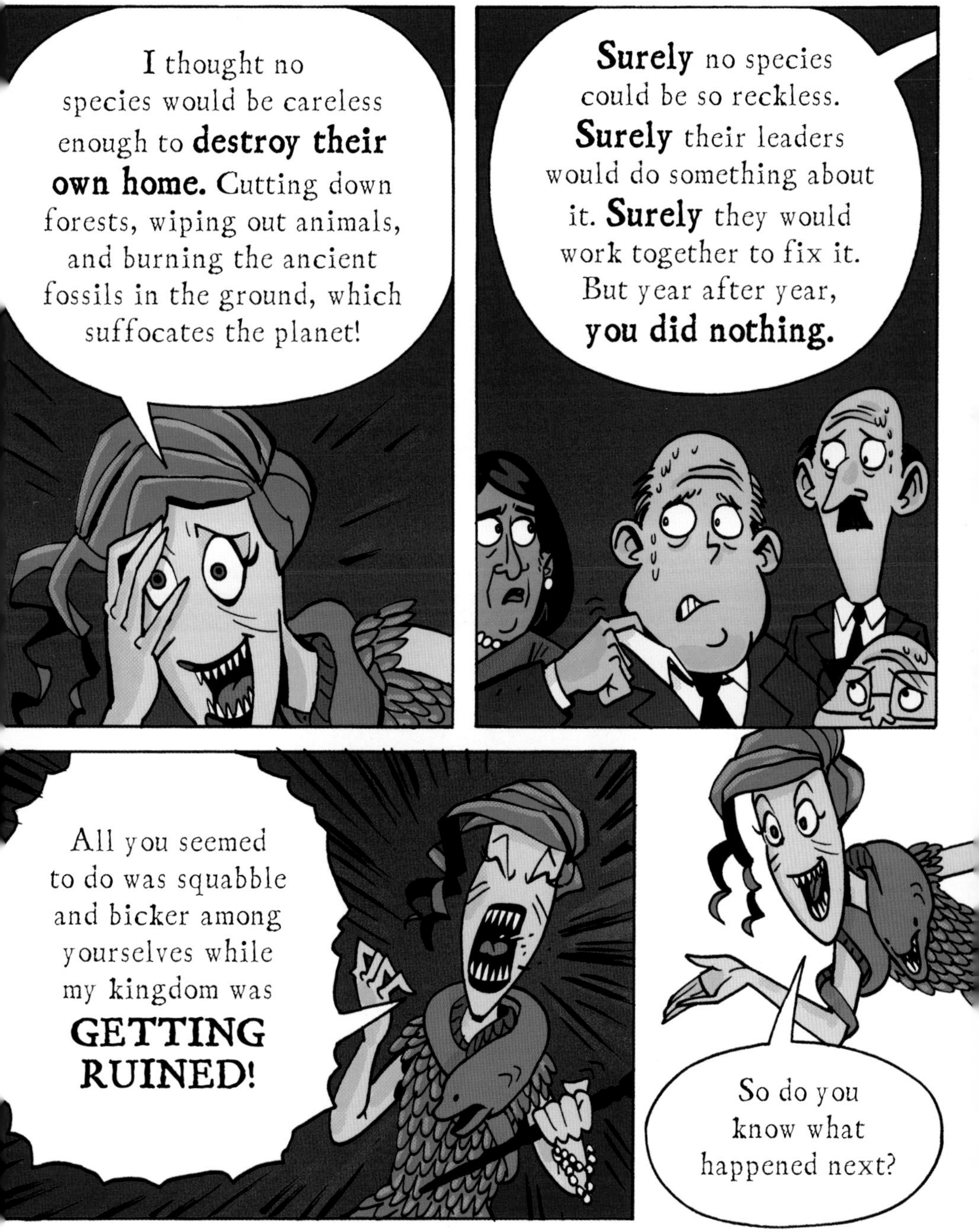
I thought no species would be careless enough to **destroy their own home.** Cutting down forests, wiping out animals, and burning the ancient fossils in the ground, which suffocates the planet!
Surely no species could be so reckless. **Surely** their leaders would do something about it. **Surely** they would work together to fix it. But year after year, **you did nothing.**
All you seemed to do was squabble and bicker among yourselves while my kingdom was **GETTING RUINED!**
So do you know what happened next?

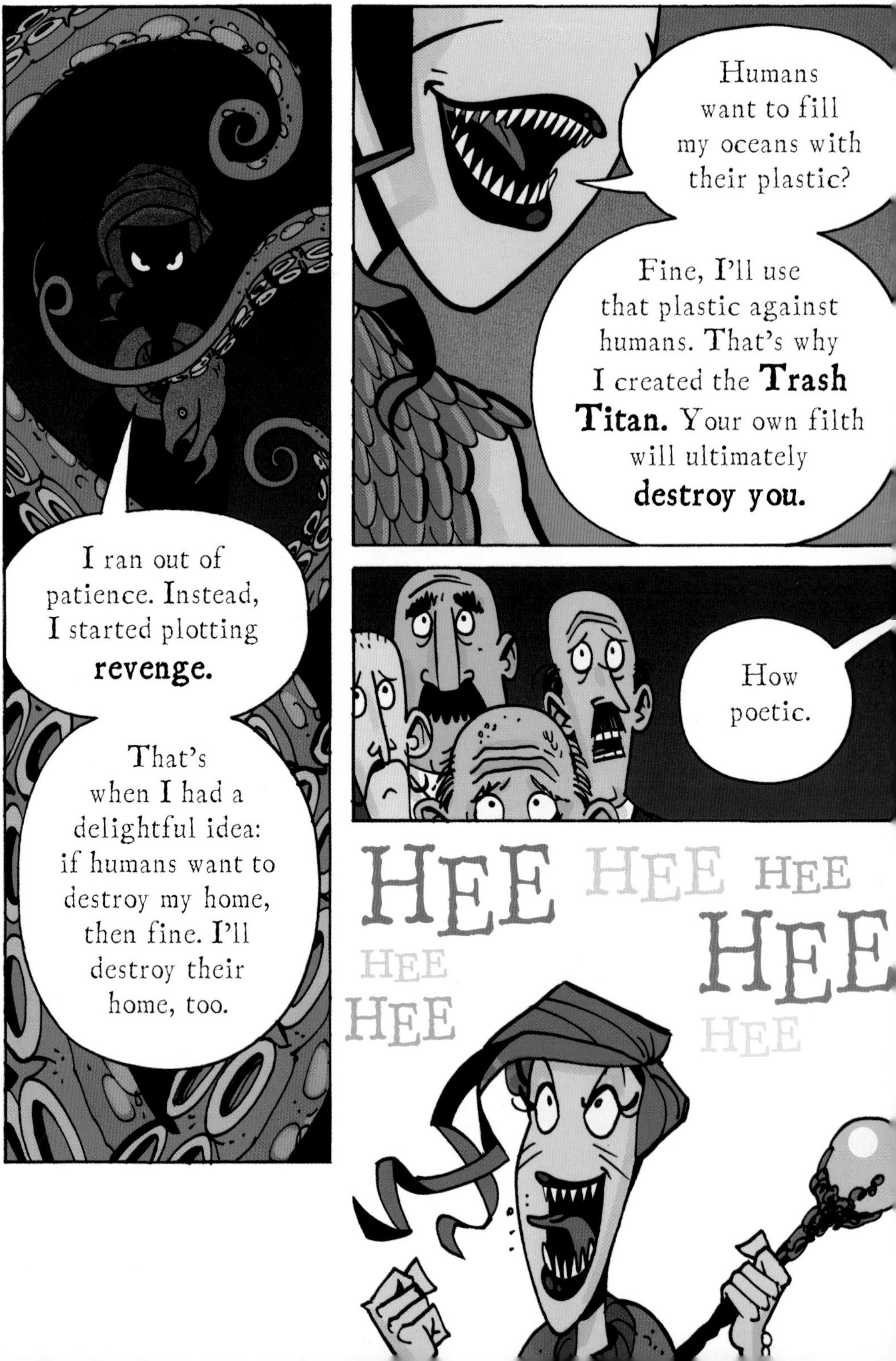
I ran out of patience. Instead, I started plotting **revenge.**
That's when I had a delightful idea: if humans want to destroy my home, then fine. I'll destroy their home, too.
Humans want to fill my oceans with their plastic?
Fine, I'll use that plastic against humans. That's why I created the **Trash Titan.** Your own filth will ultimately **destroy you.**
How poetic.
HEE HEE HEE HEE HEE HEE HEE

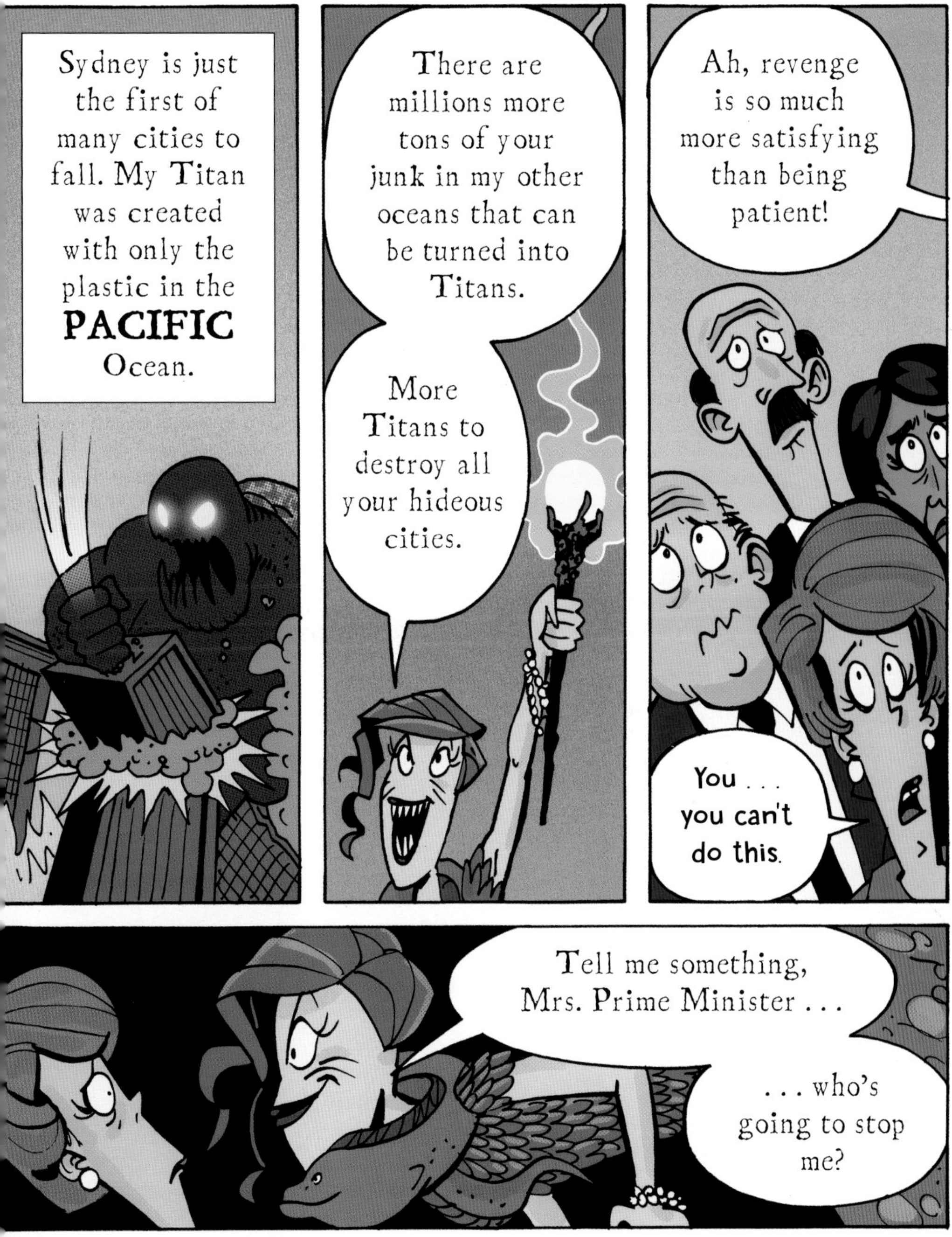
Sydney is just the first of many cities to fall. My Titan was created with only the plastic in the PACIFIC Ocean.
There are millions more tons of your junk in my other oceans that can be turned into Titans.
More Titans to destroy all your hideous cities.
Ah, revenge is so much more satisfying than being patient!
You . . . you can't do this.
Tell me something, Mrs. Prime Minister . . .
. . . who's going to stop me?

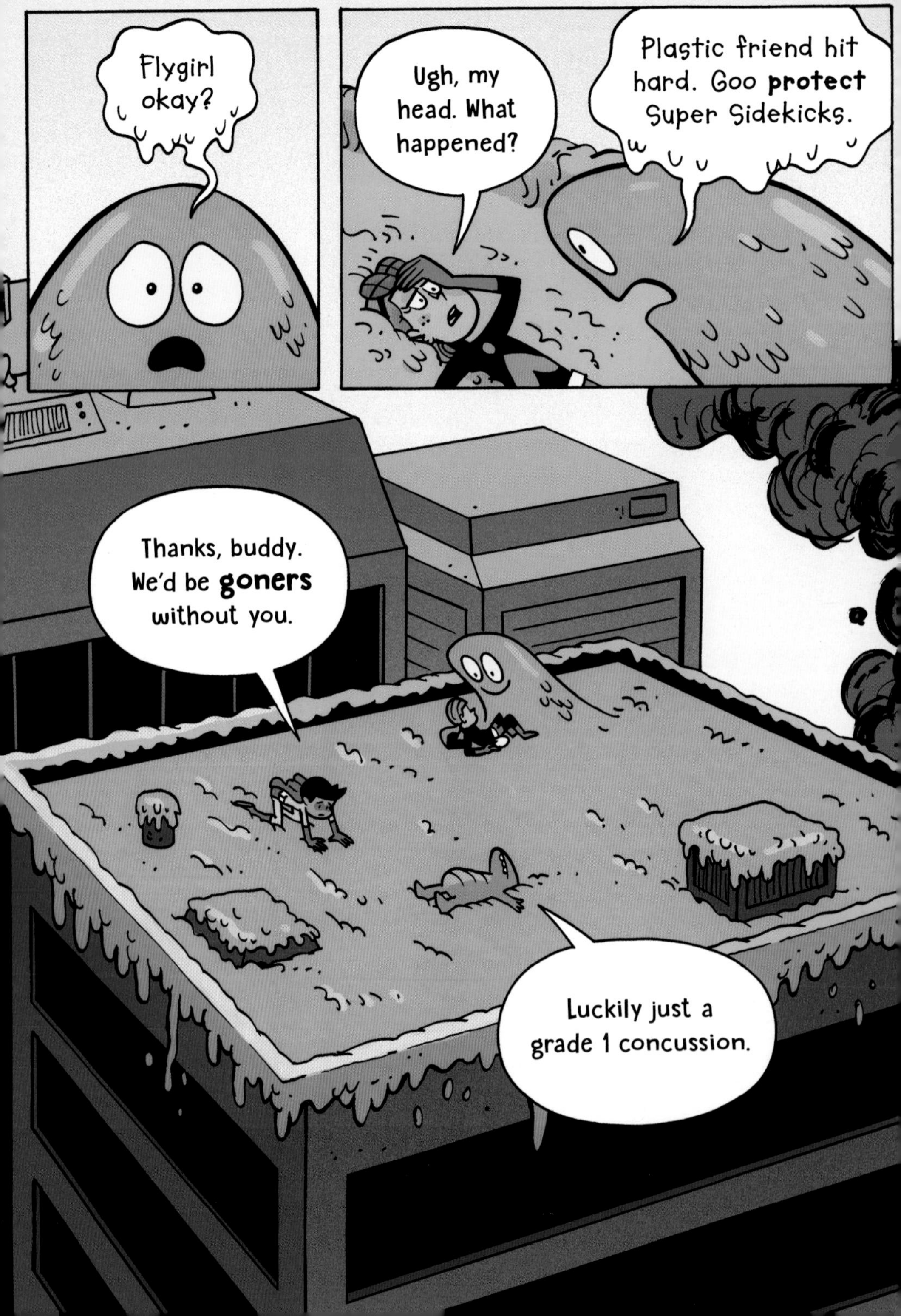
Flygirl okay?
Ugh, my head. What happened?
Plastic friend hit hard. Goo protect Super Sidekicks.
Thanks, buddy. We'd be goners without you.
Luckily just a grade 1 concussion.

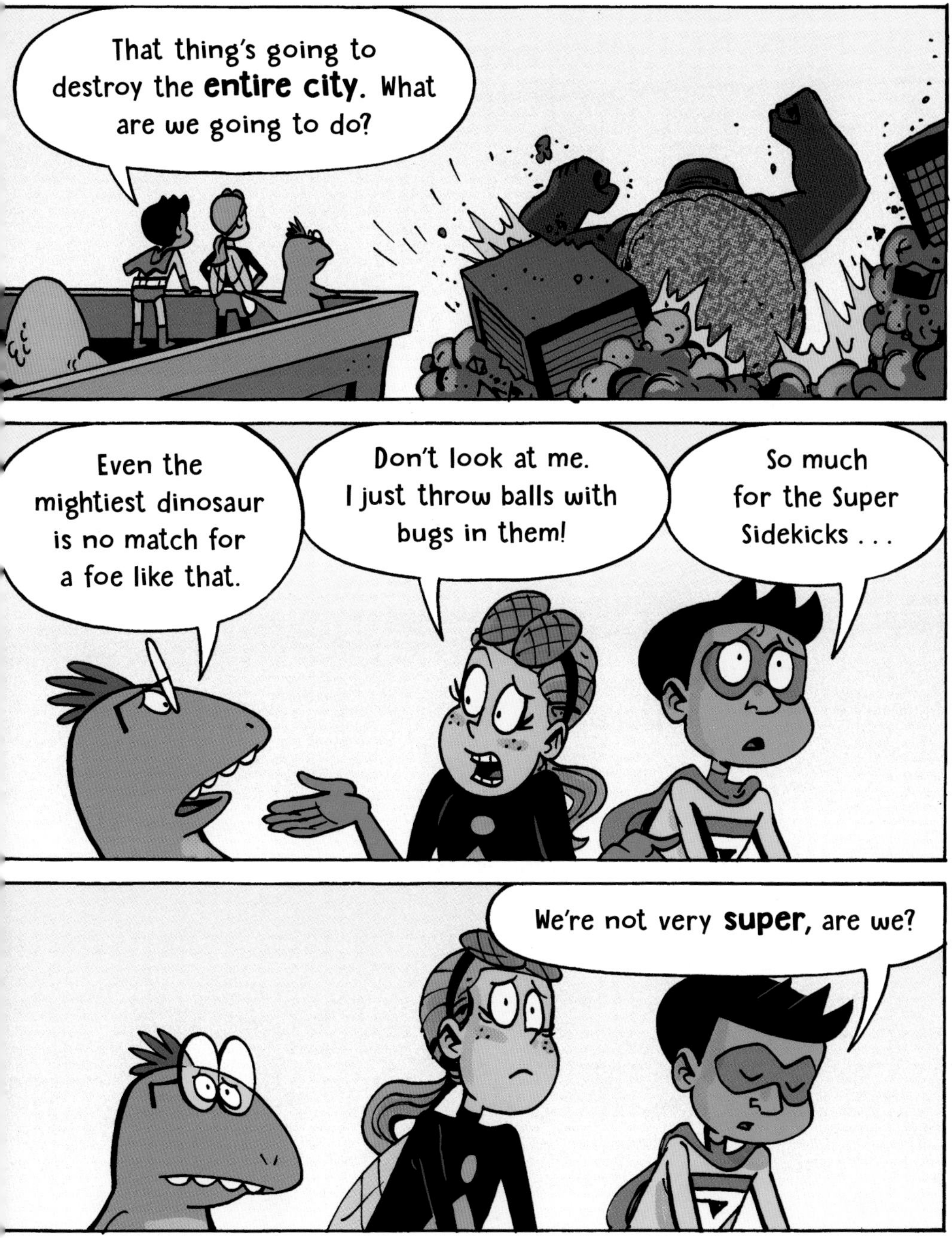
That thing's going to destroy the **entire city**. What are we going to do?
Even the mightiest dinosaur is no match for a foe like that.
Don't look at me. I just throw balls with bugs in them!
So much for the Super Sidekicks . . .
We're not very **super**, are we?

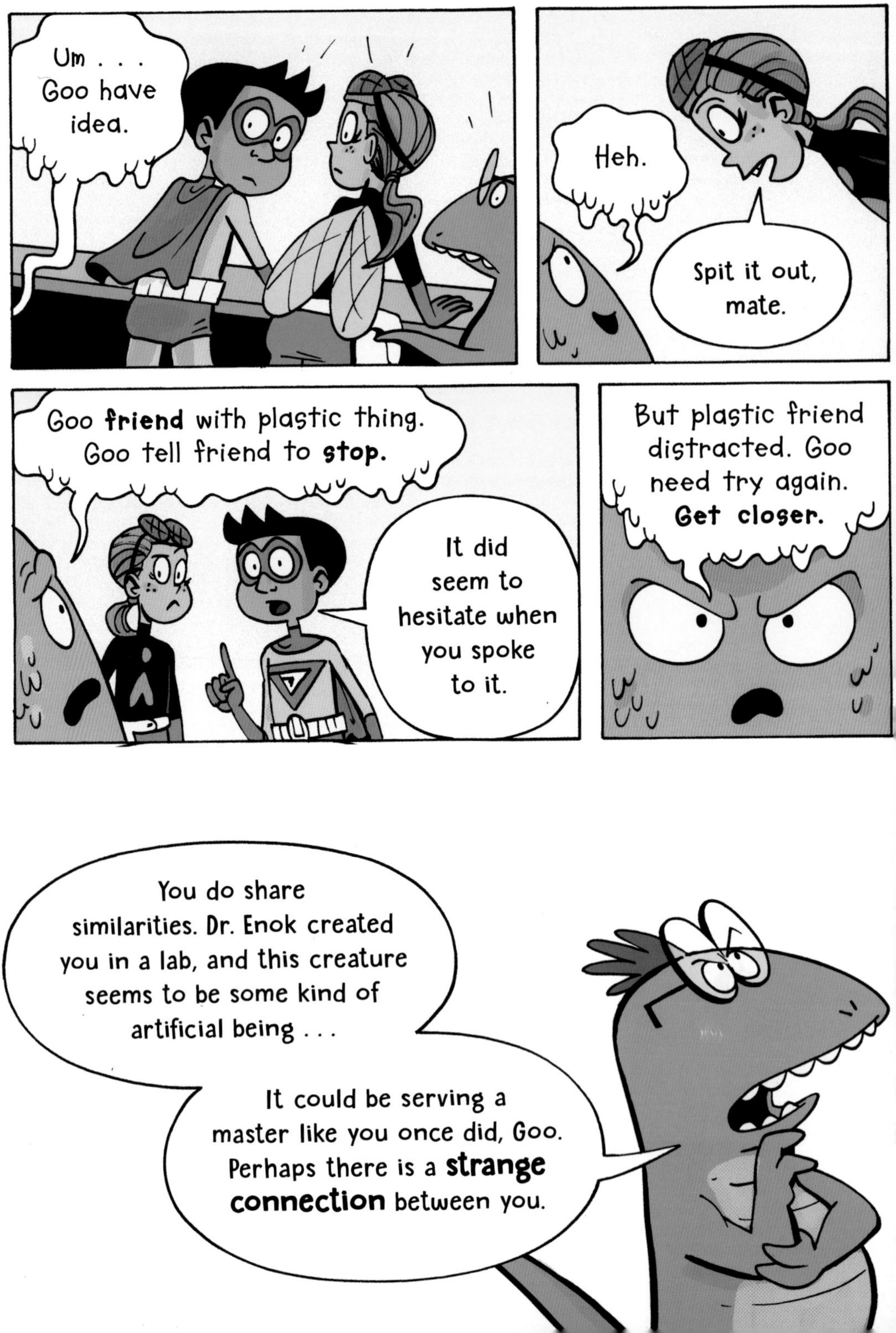

Um . . . Goo have idea.
Heh.
Spit it out, mate.
Goo **friend** with plastic thing. Goo tell friend to **stop.**
It did seem to hesitate when you spoke to it.
But plastic friend distracted. Goo need try again. **Get closer.**
You do share similarities. Dr. Enok created you in a lab, and this creature seems to be some kind of artificial being . . .
It could be serving a master like you once did, Goo. Perhaps there is a **strange connection** between you.

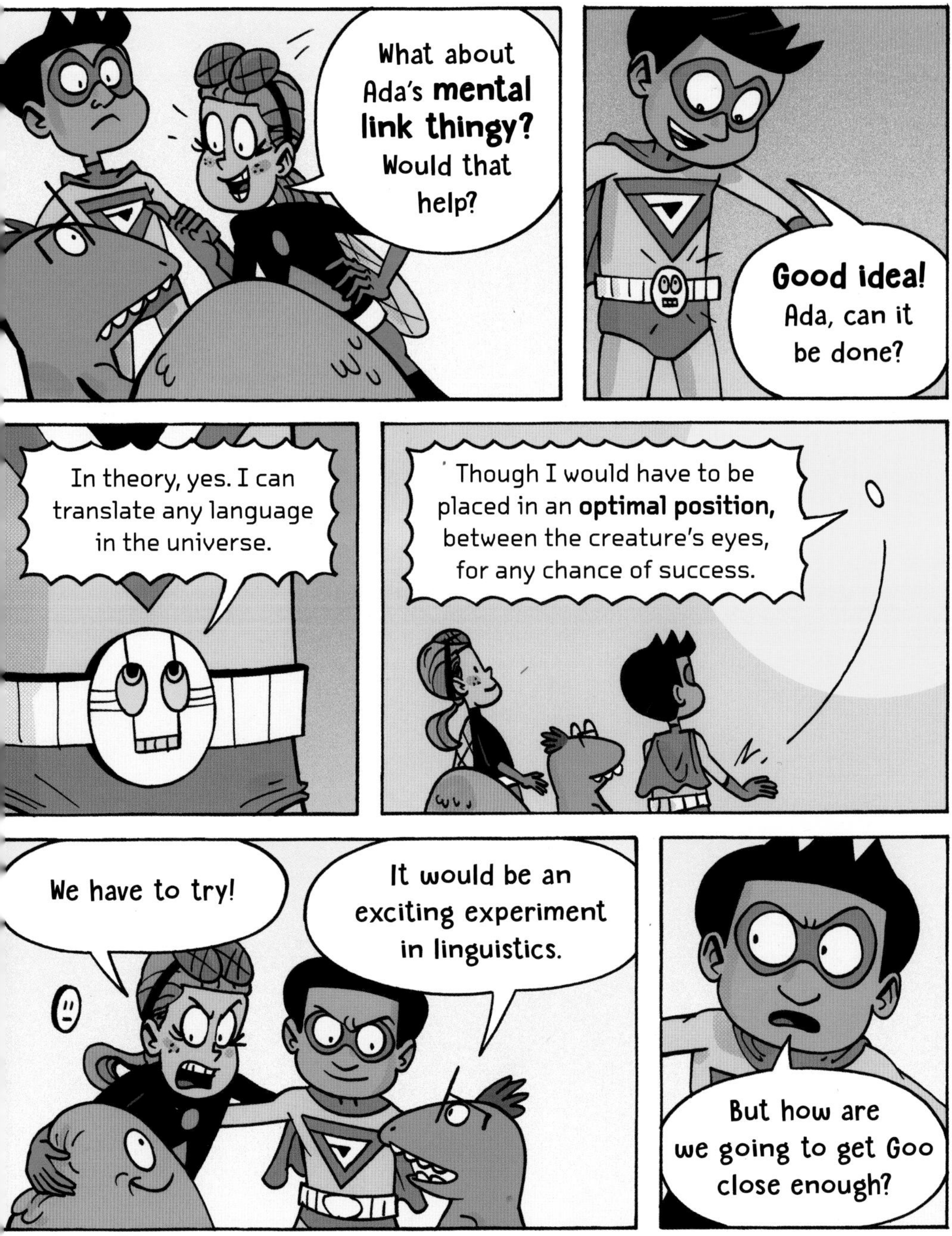
What about Ada's **mental link thingy?** Would that help?
Good idea! Ada, can it be done?
In theory, yes. I can translate any language in the universe.
Though I would have to be placed in an **optimal position,** between the creature's eyes, for any chance of success.
We have to try!
It would be an exciting experiment in linguistics.
But how are we going to get Goo close enough?

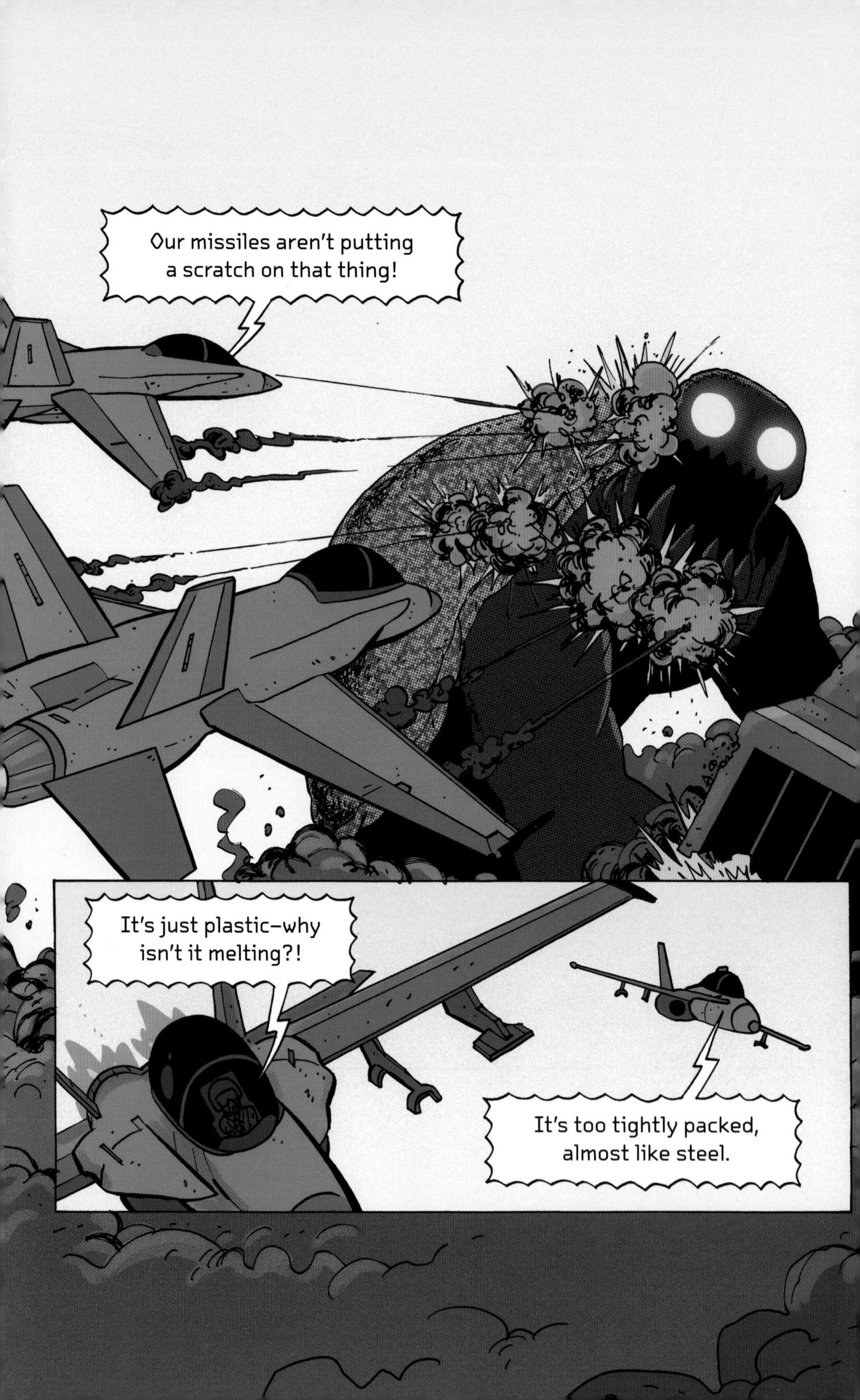
Our missiles aren't putting a scratch on that thing!
It's just plastic—why isn't it melting?!
It's too tightly packed, almost like steel.

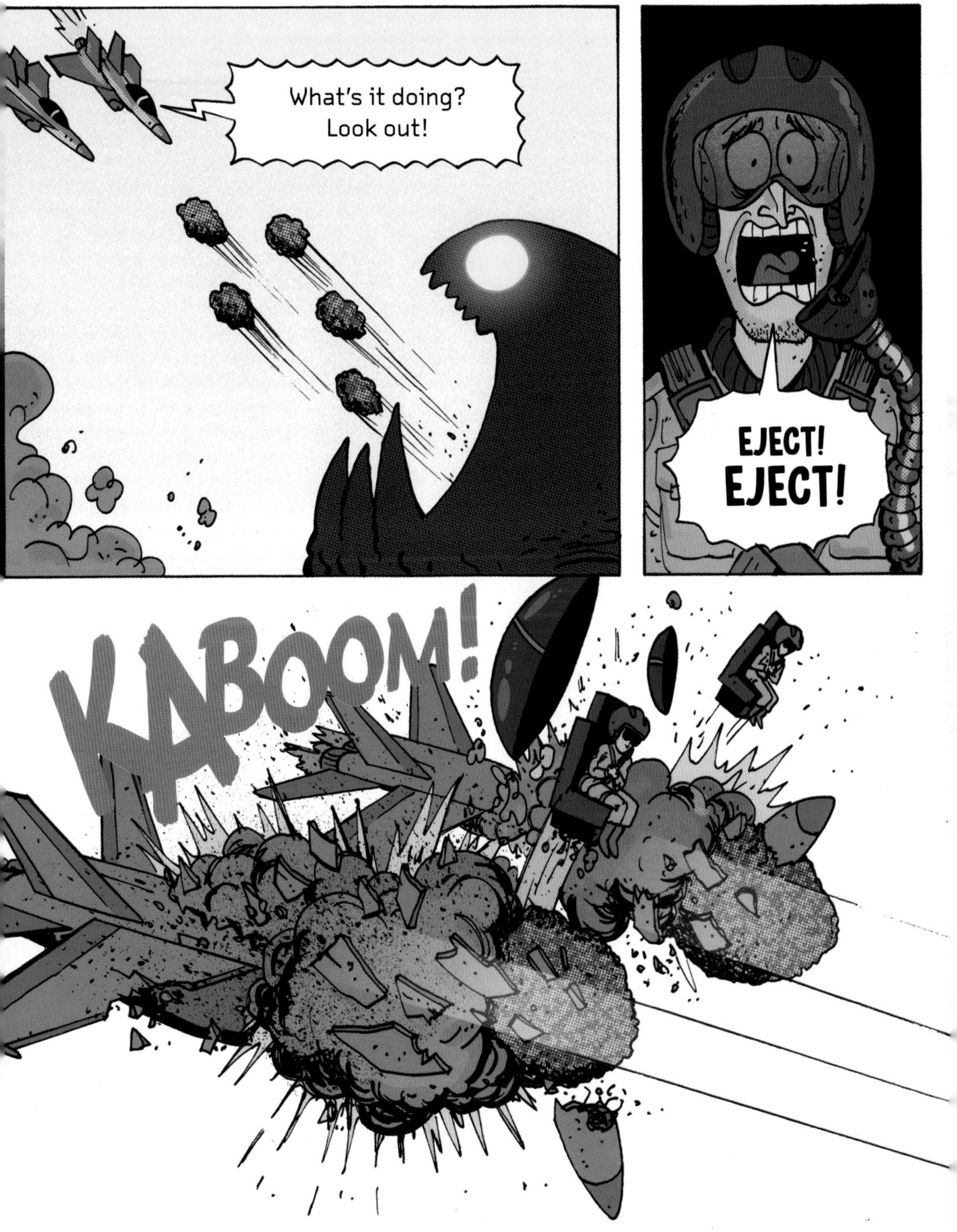
What's it doing? Look out!
EJECT! EJECT!
KABOOM!

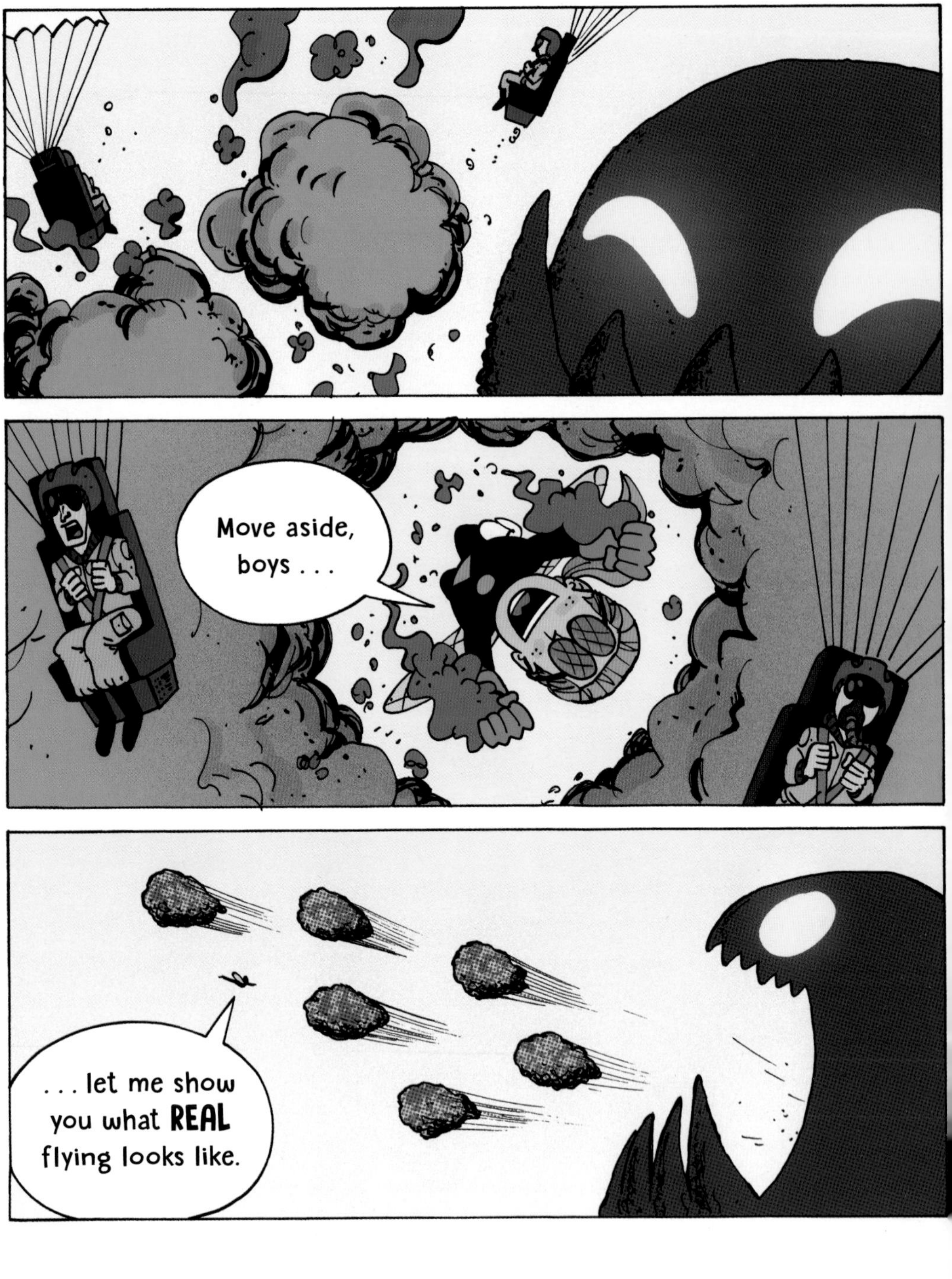
Move aside, boys . . .
. . . let me show you what **REAL** flying looks like.

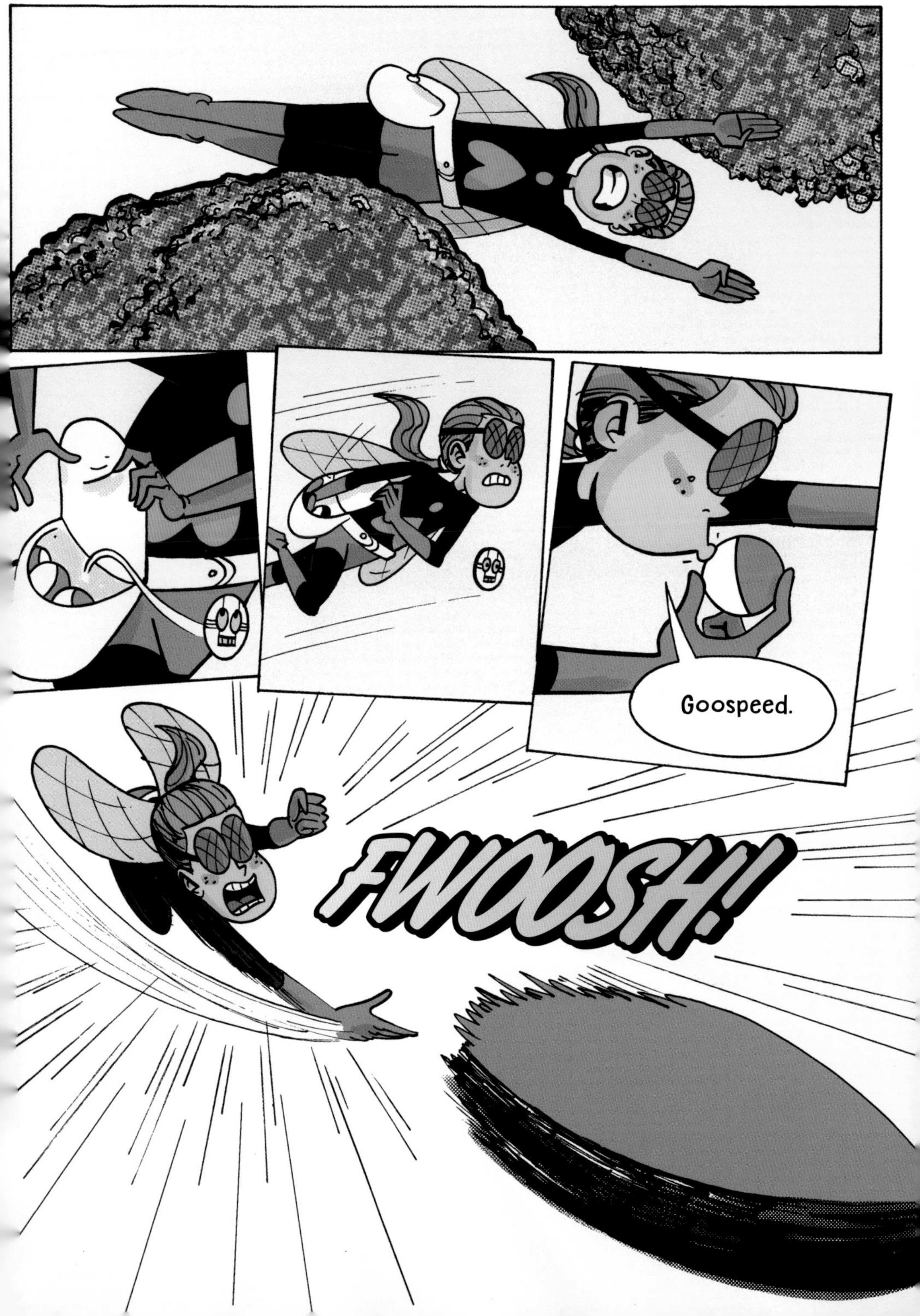
Goospeed.
FWOOSH!

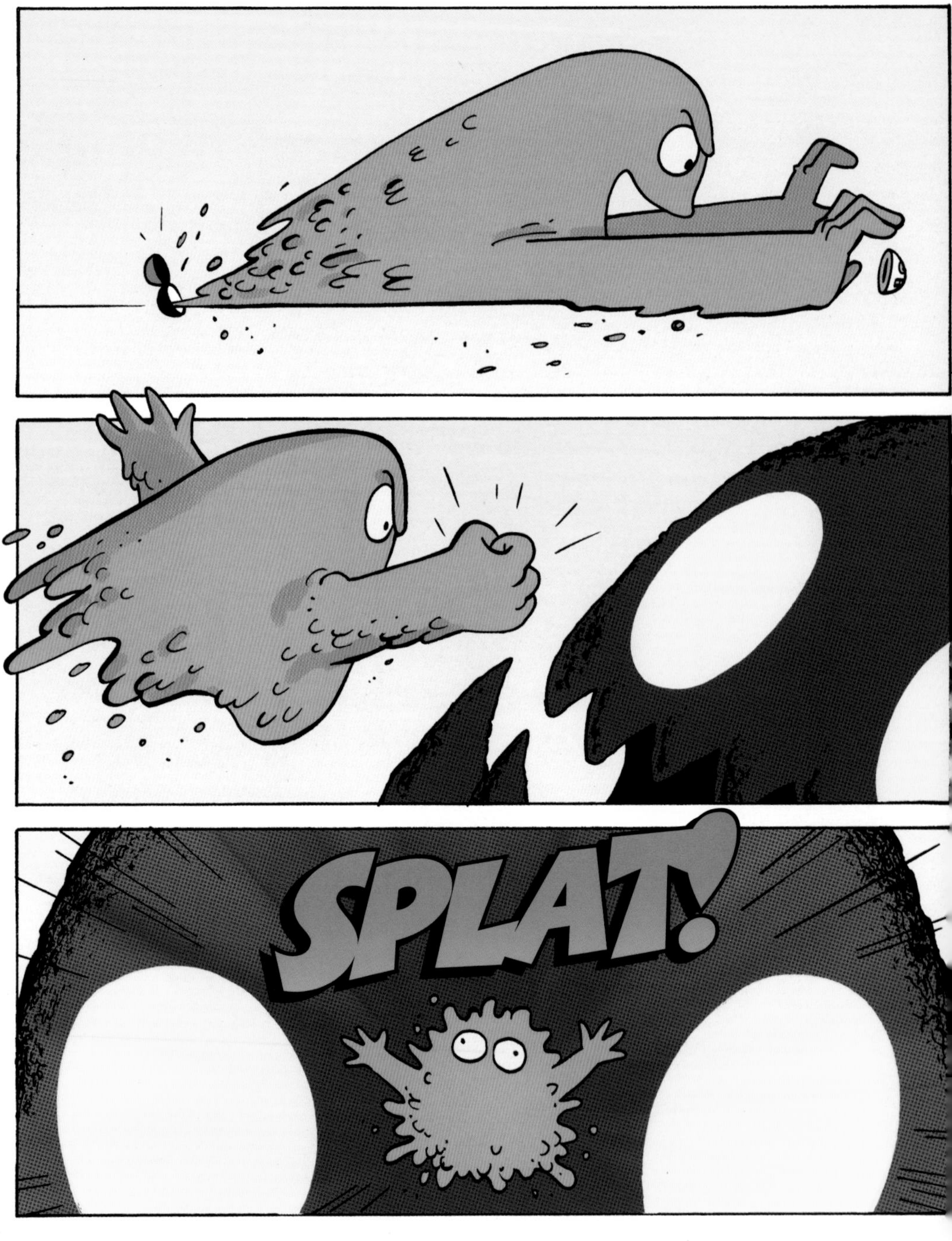
SPLAT!

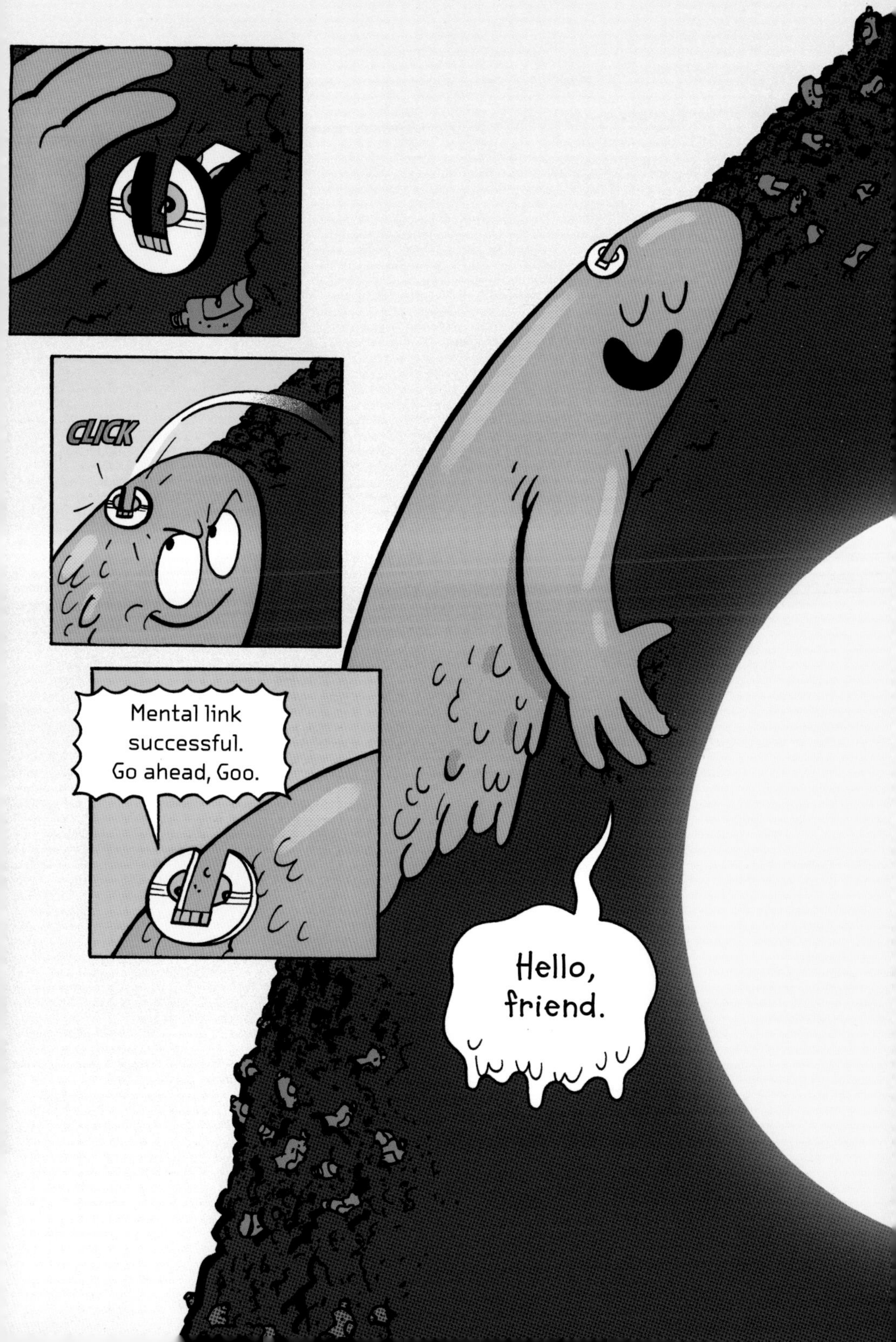
CLICK
Mental link successful. Go ahead, Goo.
Hello, friend.

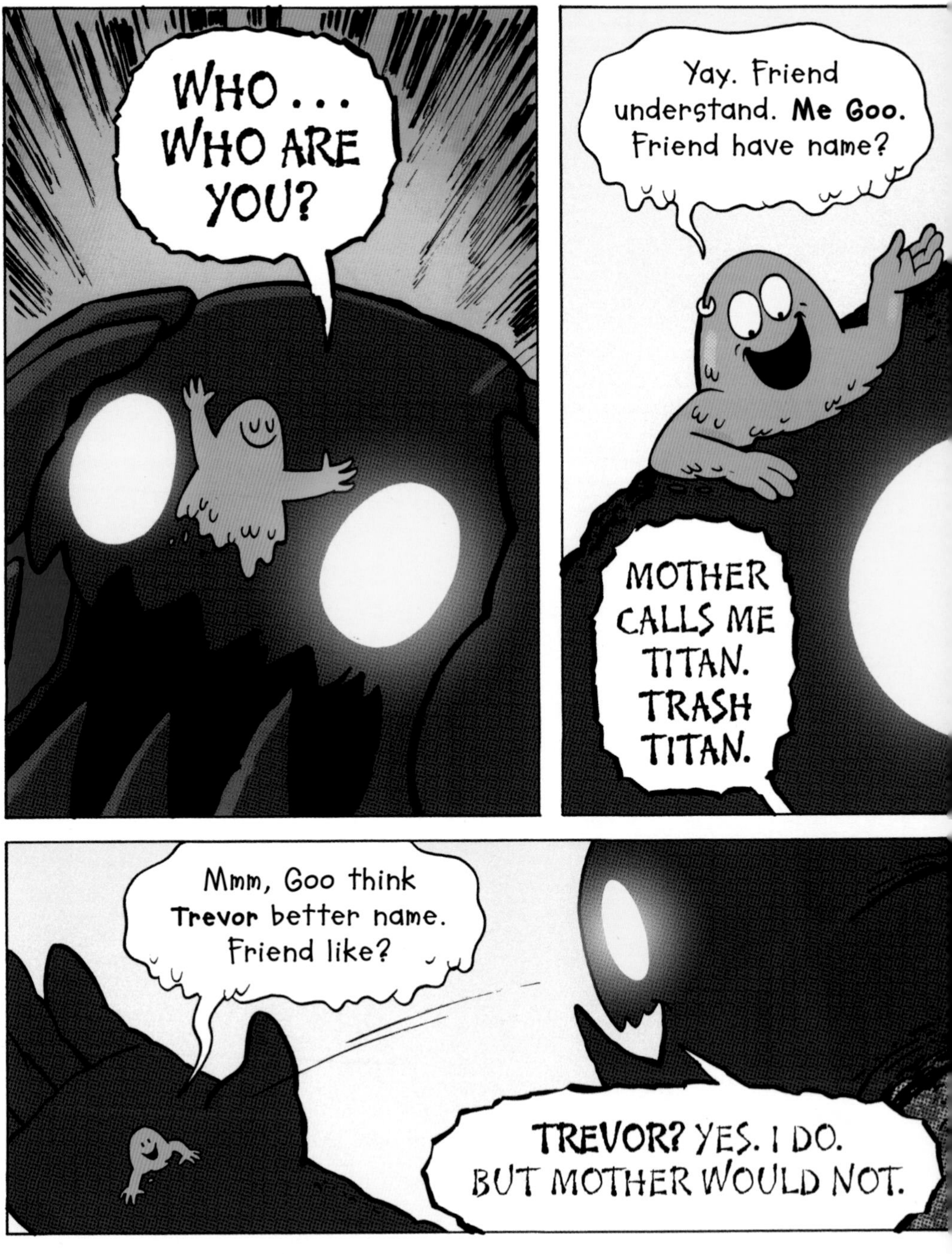
WHO . . .
WHO ARE
YOU?
Yay. Friend understand. **Me Goo.** Friend have name?
MOTHER CALLS ME TITAN. TRASH TITAN.
Mmm, Goo think **Trevor** better name. Friend like?
TREVOR? YES. I DO. BUT MOTHER WOULD NOT.

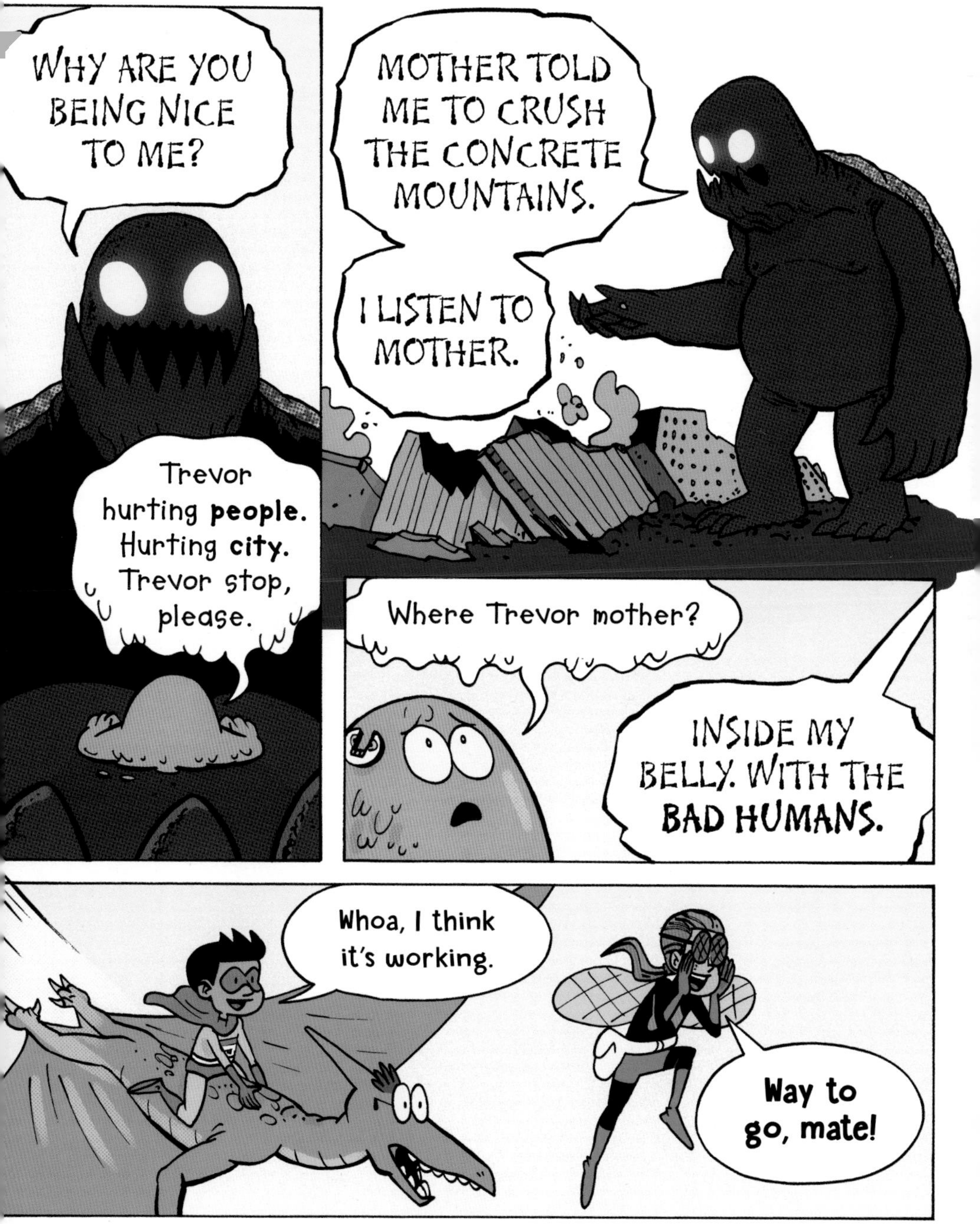
WHY ARE YOU BEING NICE TO ME?
MOTHER TOLD ME TO CRUSH THE CONCRETE MOUNTAINS.
I LISTEN TO MOTHER.
Trevor hurting **people.** Hurting **city.** Trevor stop, please.
Where Trevor mother?
INSIDE MY BELLY. WITH THE **BAD HUMANS.**
Whoa, I think it's working.
Way to go, mate!

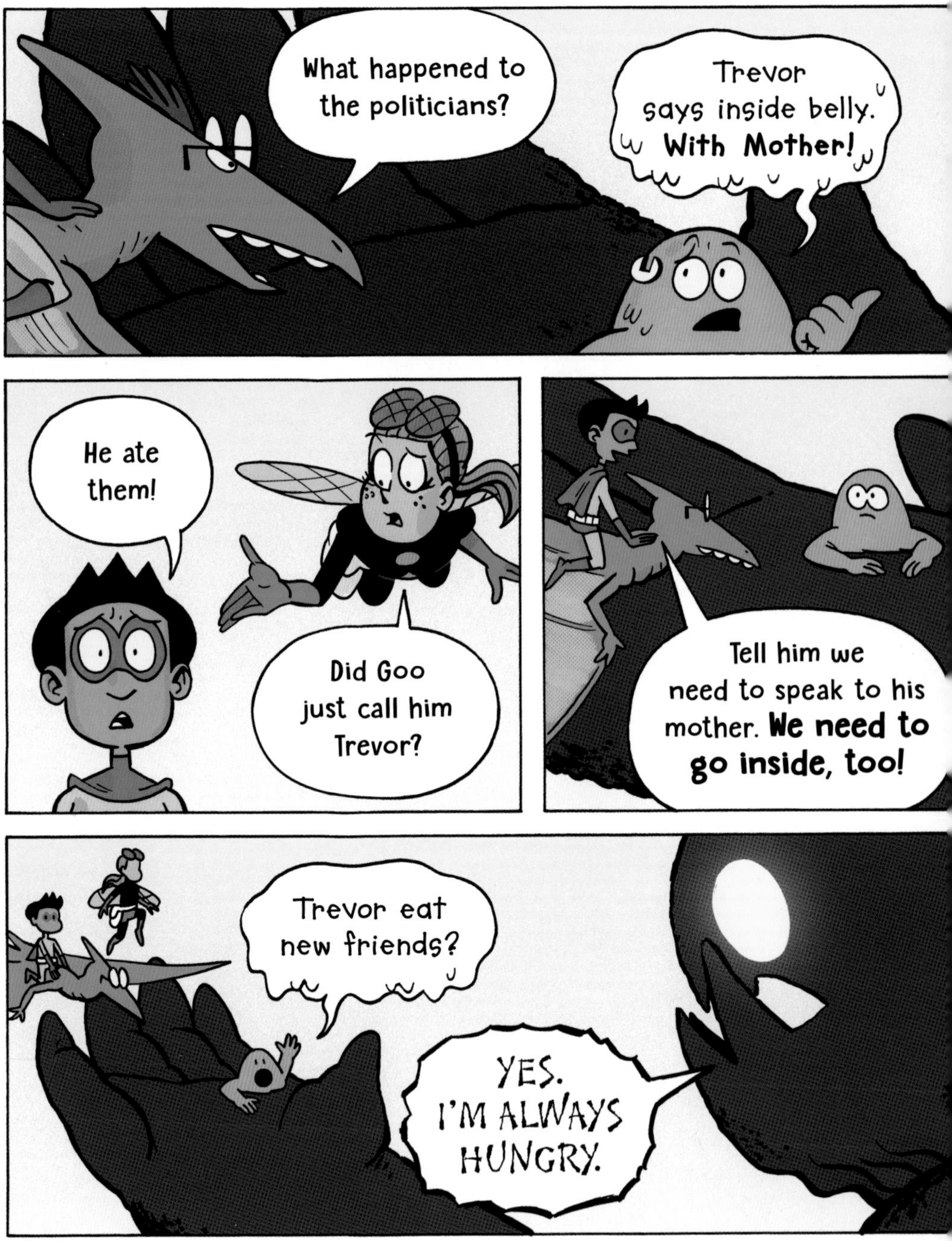
What happened to the politicians?
Trevor says inside belly. With Mother!
He ate them!
Did Goo just call him Trevor?
Tell him we need to speak to his mother. We need to go inside, too!
Trevor eat new friends?
YES. I'M ALWAYS HUNGRY.

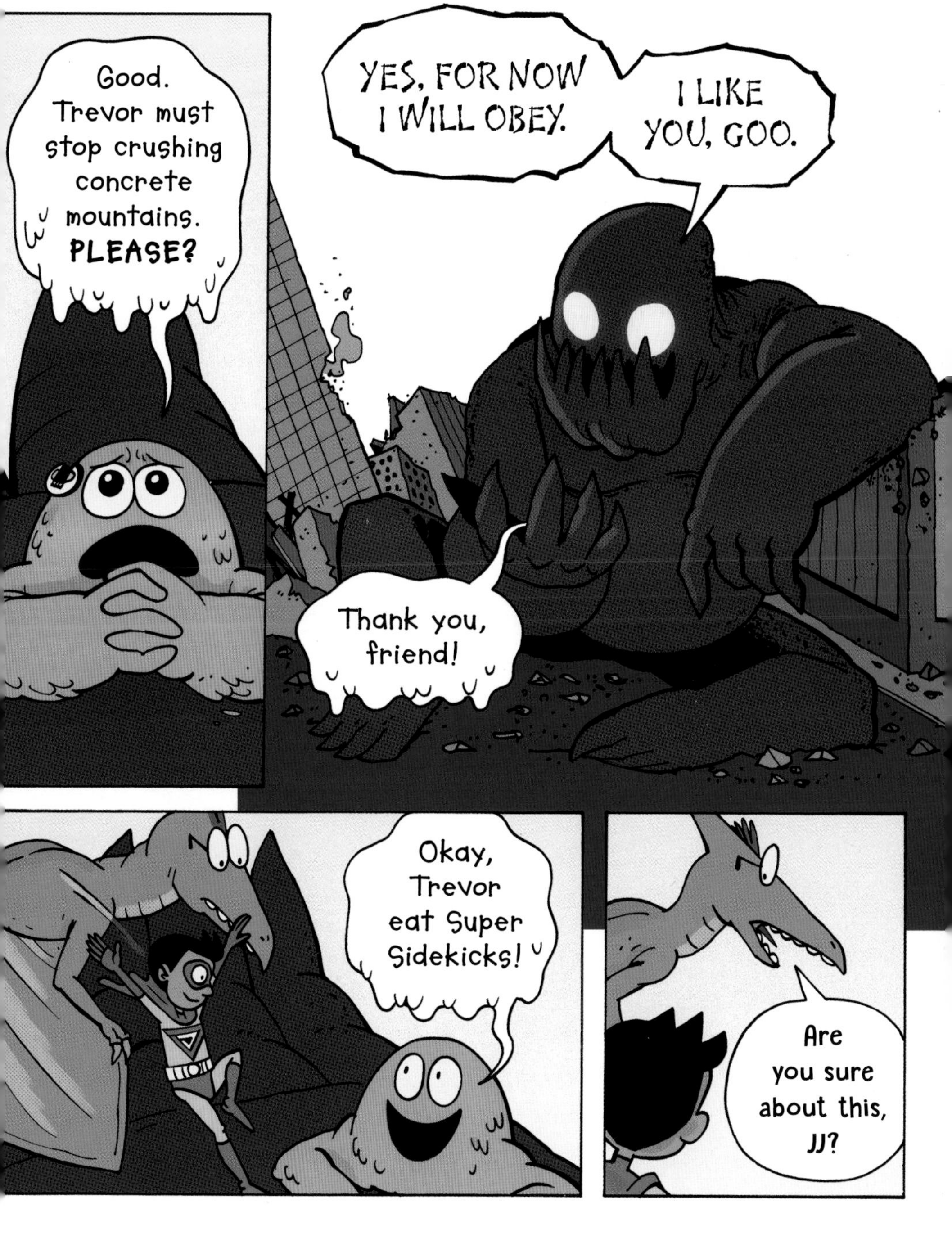
Good. Trevor must stop crushing concrete mountains. PLEASE?
YES, FOR NOW I WILL OBEY.
I LIKE YOU, GOO.
Thank you, friend!
Okay, Trevor eat Super Sidekicks!
Are you sure about this, JJ?

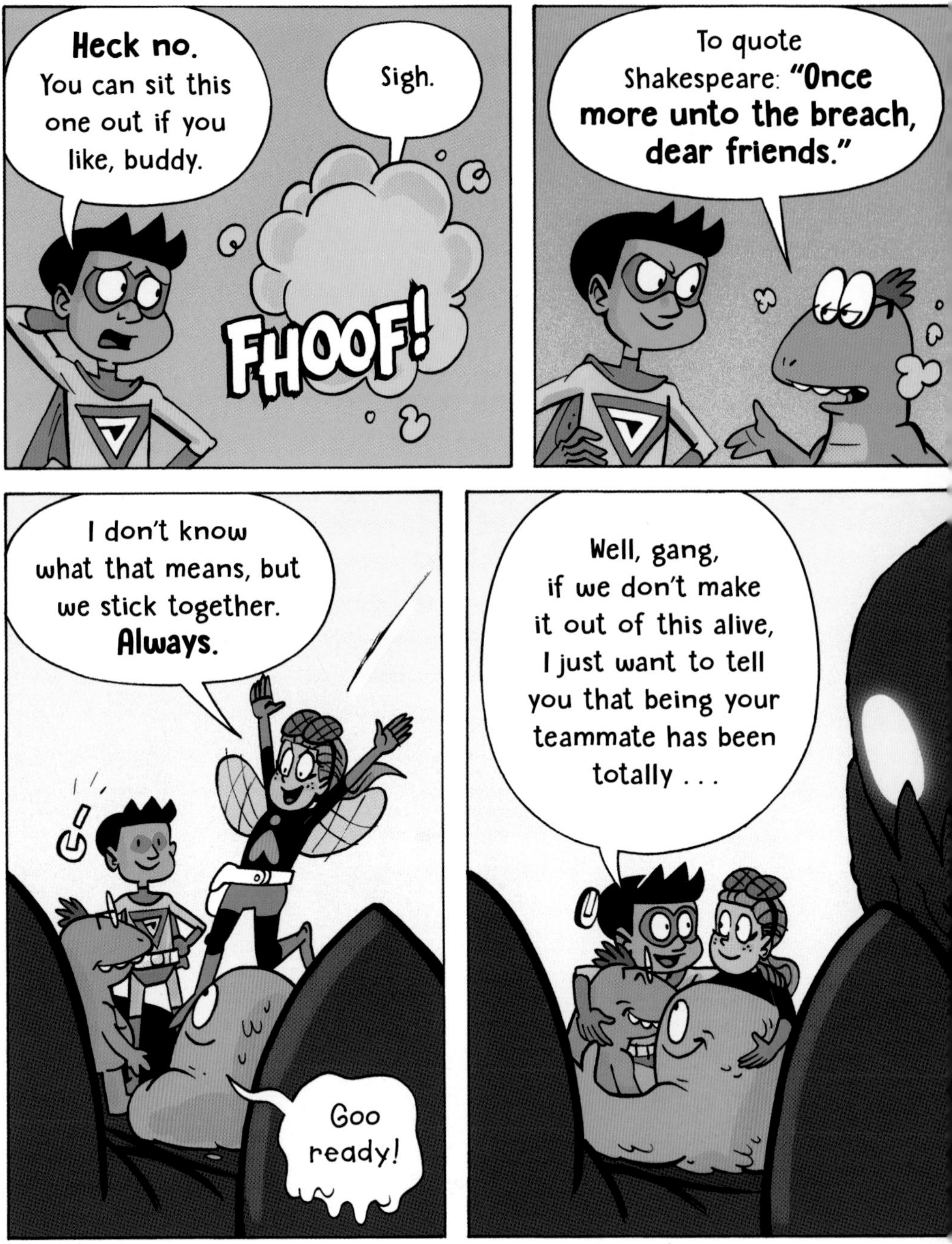

Heck no. You can sit this one out if you like, buddy.
Sigh.
FHOOF!
To quote Shakespeare: "Once more unto the breach, dear friends."
I don't know what that means, but we stick together. Always.
Goo ready!
Well, gang, if we don't make it out of this alive, I just want to tell you that being your teammate has been totally . . .

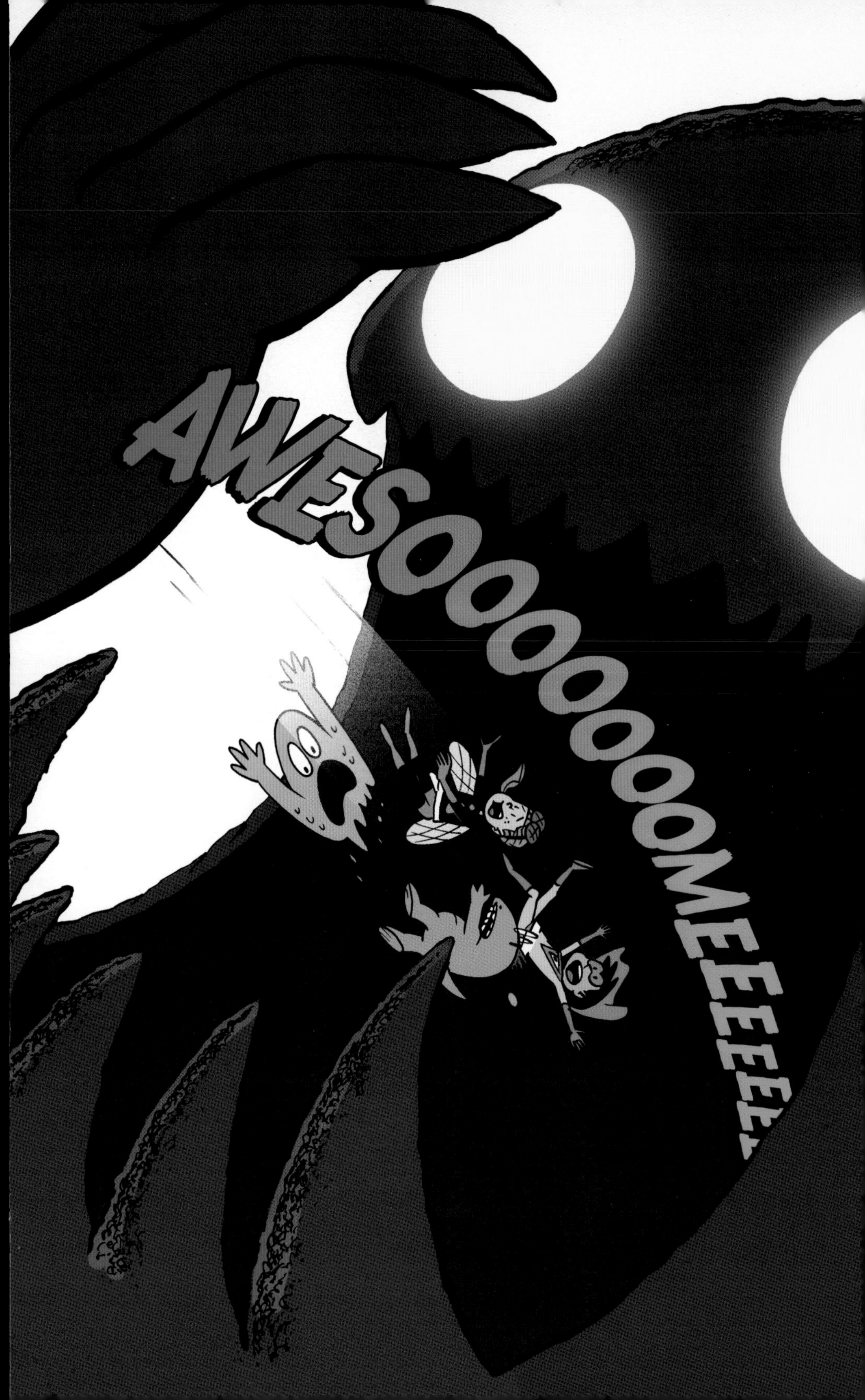
AWESOOOOOOOMEEEEEE

Chapter 5

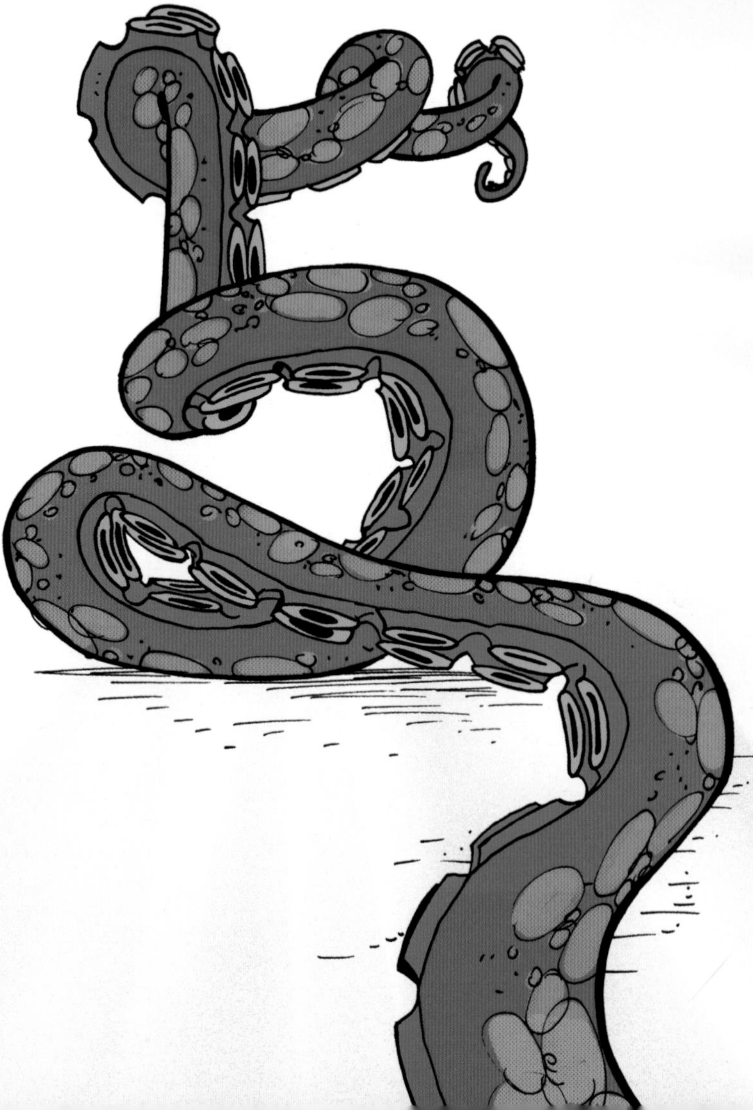

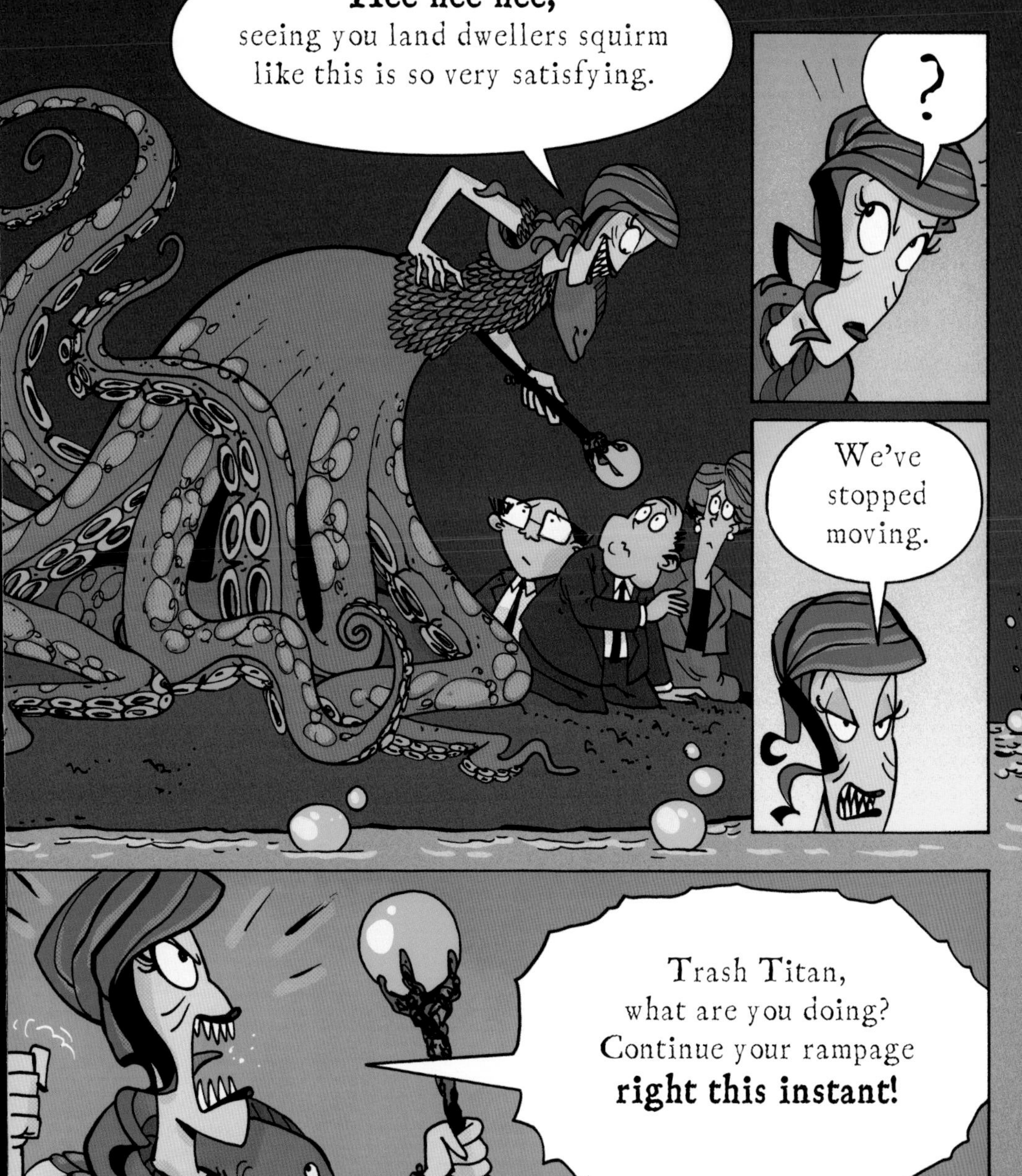
Hee hee hee, seeing you land dwellers squirm like this is so very satisfying.
?
We've stopped moving.
Trash Titan, what are you doing? Continue your rampage right this instant!

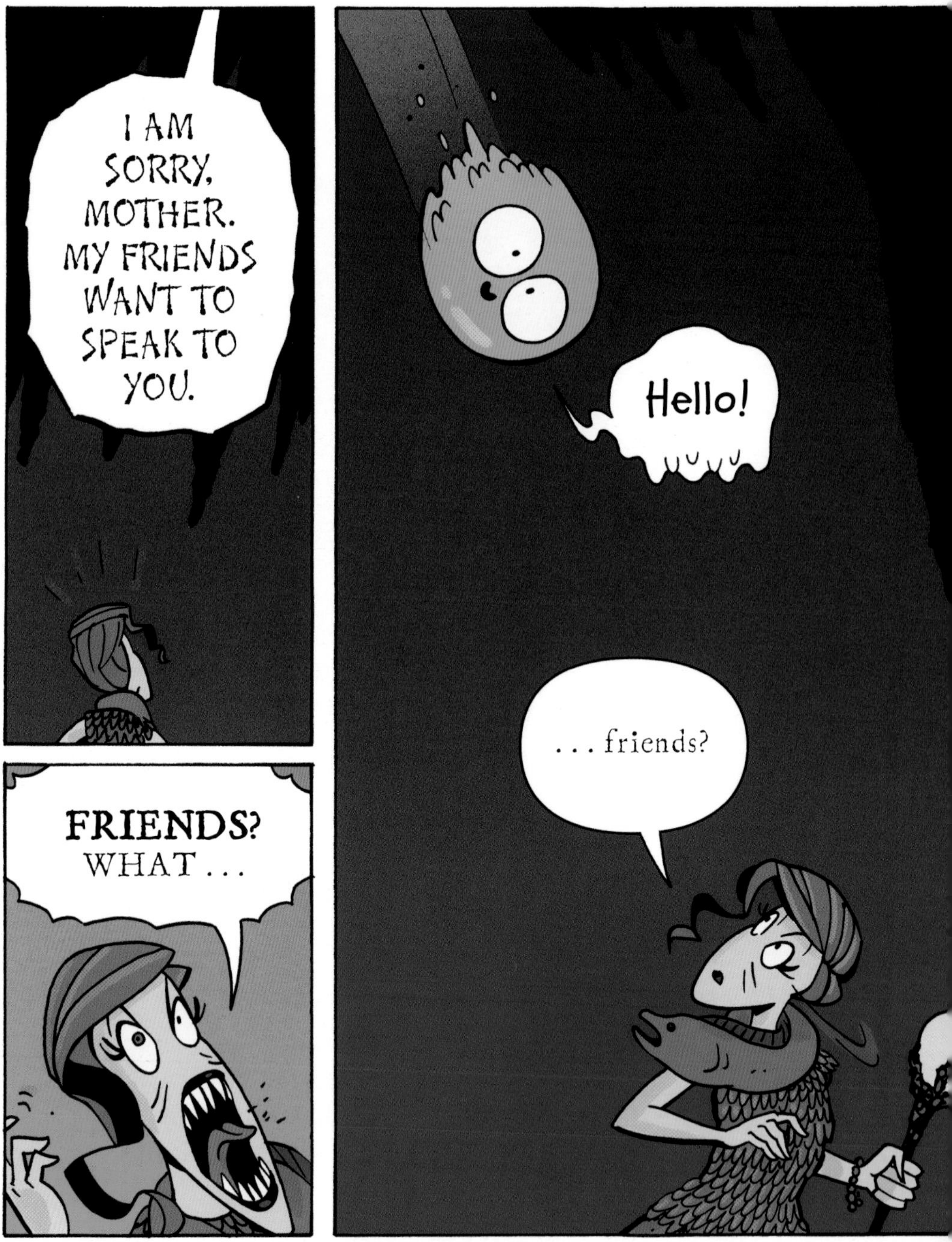
I AM SORRY, MOTHER. MY FRIENDS WANT TO SPEAK TO YOU.
FRIENDS? WHAT . . .
Hello!
. . . friends?

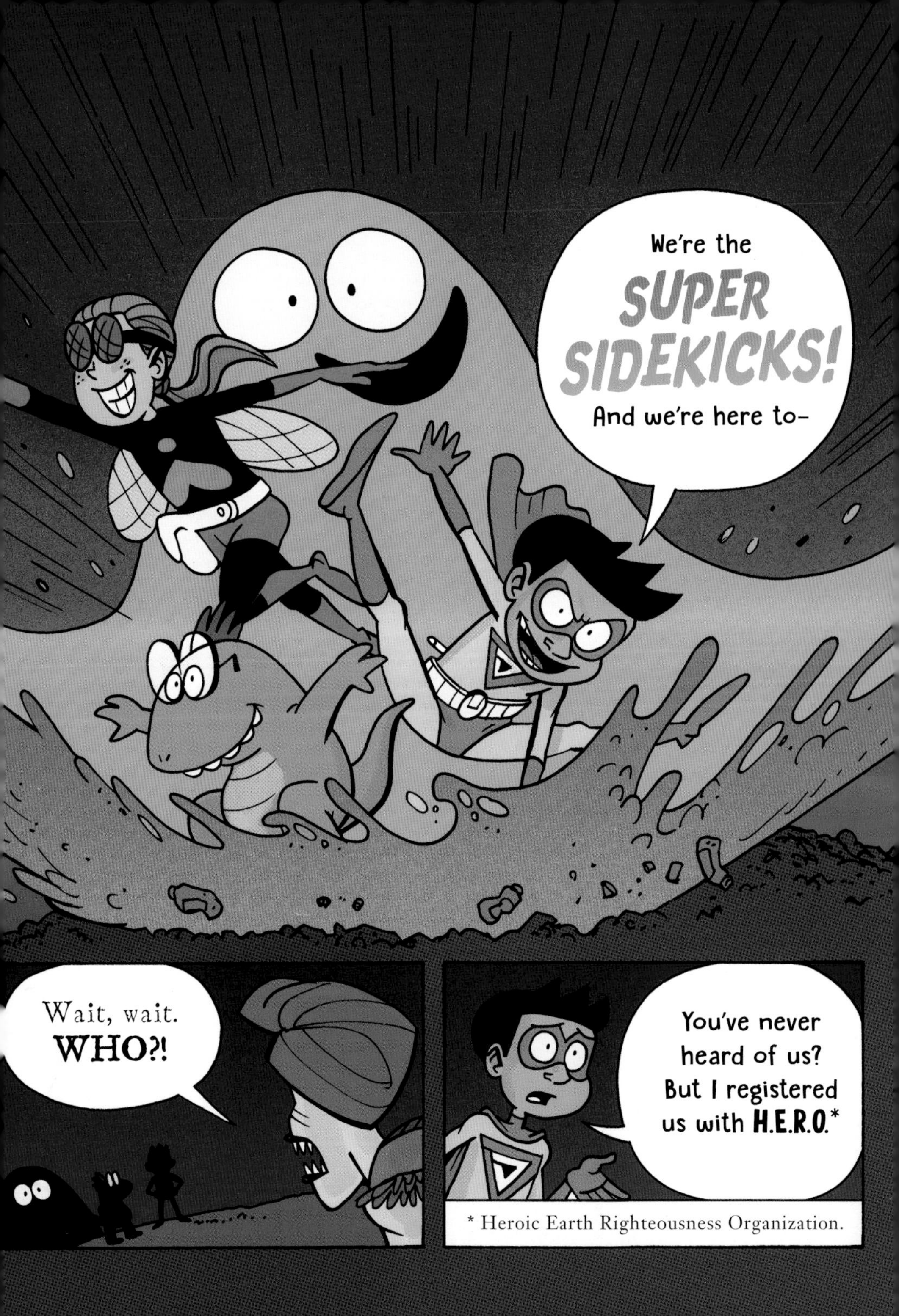
We're the SUPER SIDEKICKS! And we're here to–
Wait, wait. WHO?!
You've never heard of us? But I registered us with H.E.R.O.*
* Heroic Earth Righteousness Organization.

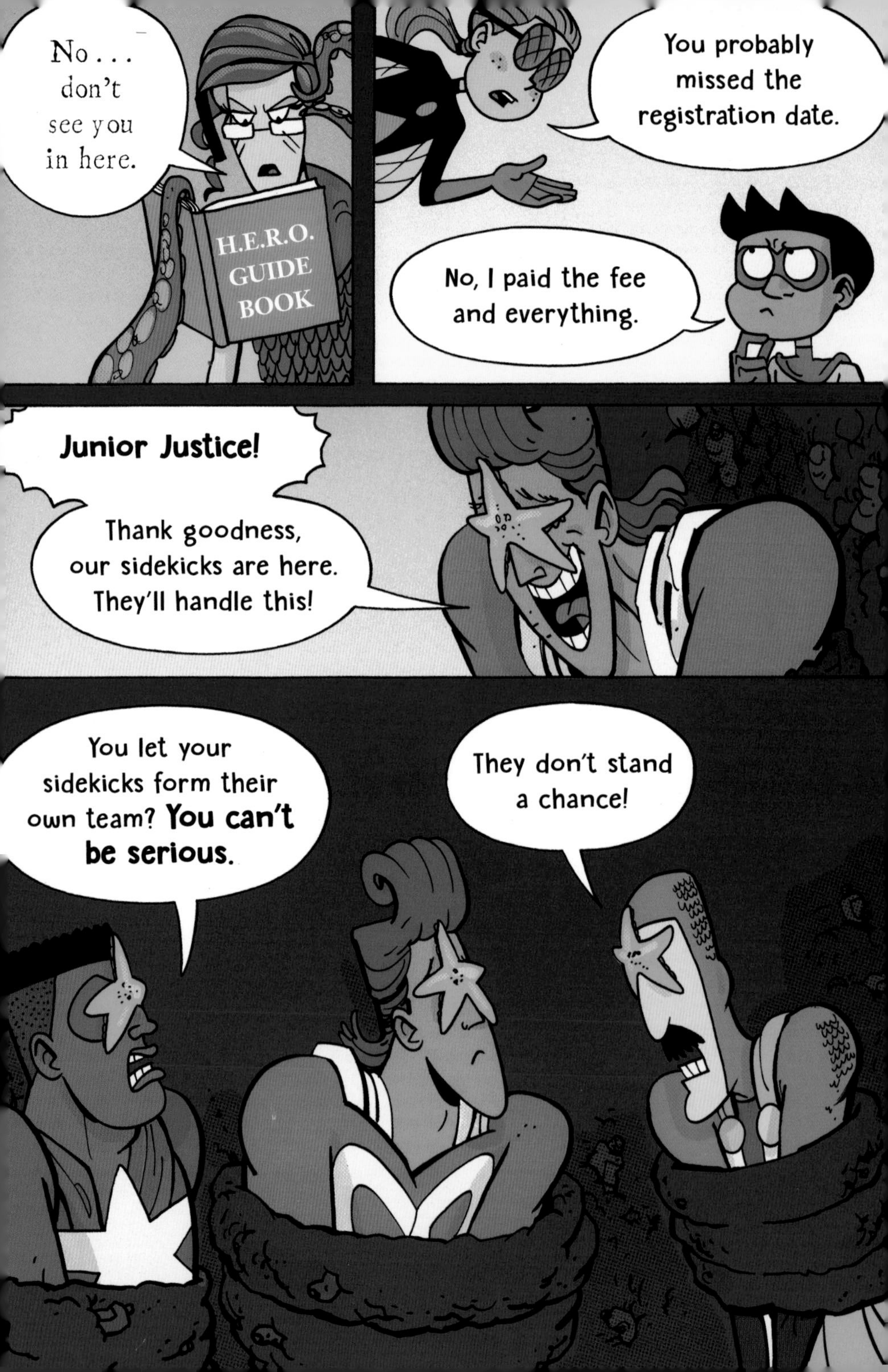
No . . . don't see you in here.
H.E.R.O. GUIDE BOOK
You probably missed the registration date.
No, I paid the fee and everything.
Junior Justice!
Thank goodness, our sidekicks are here. They'll handle this!
You let your sidekicks form their own team? **You can't be serious.**
They don't stand a chance!

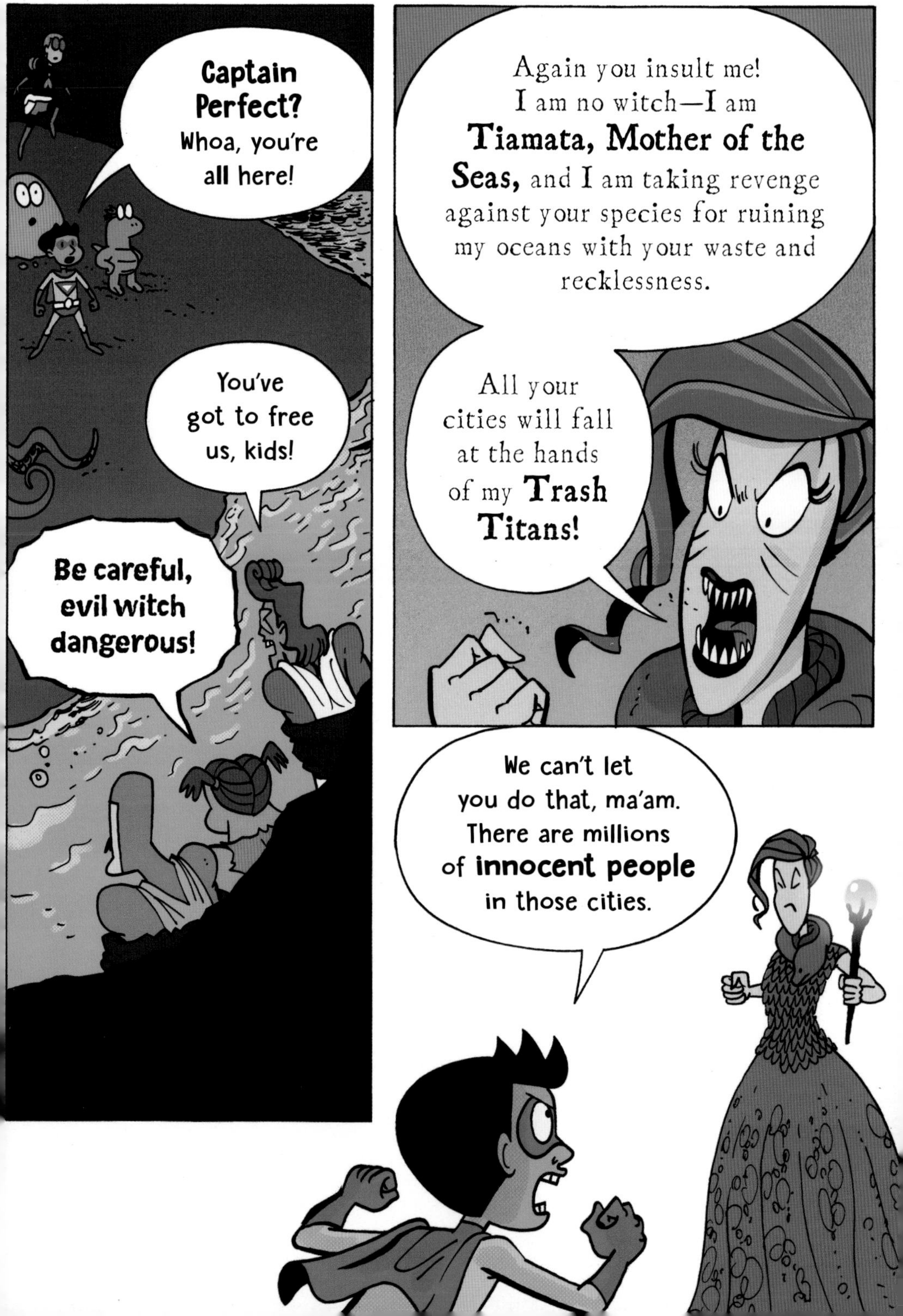
Captain Perfect? Whoa, you're all here!
You've got to free us, kids!
Be careful, evil witch dangerous!
Again you insult me! I am no witch—I am Tiamata, Mother of the Seas, and I am taking revenge against your species for ruining my oceans with your waste and recklessness.
All your cities will fall at the hands of my Trash Titans!
We can't let you do that, ma'am. There are millions of innocent people in those cities.

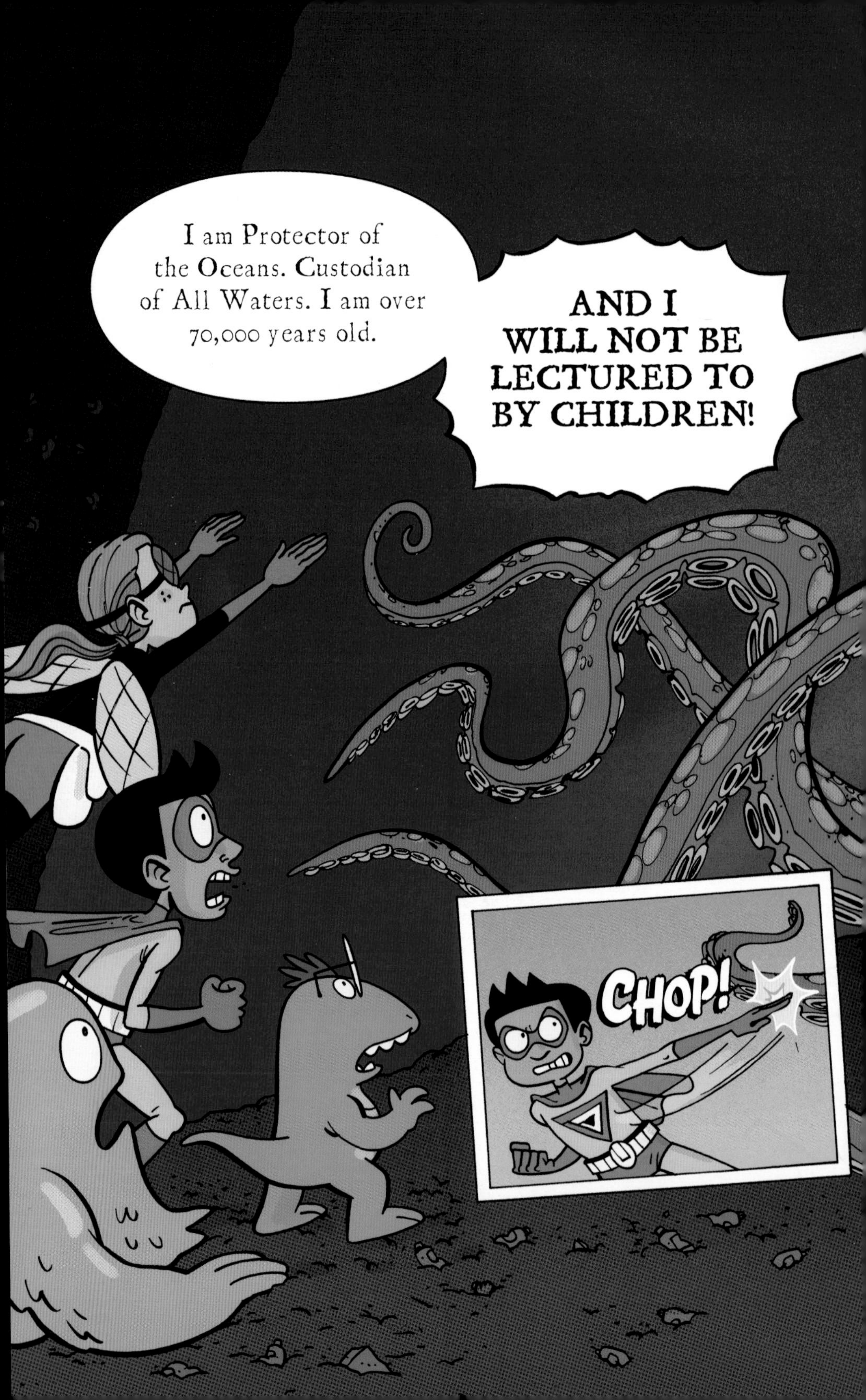
I am Protector of the Oceans. Custodian of All Waters. I am over 70,000 years old.
AND I WILL NOT BE LECTURED TO BY CHILDREN!
CHOP!

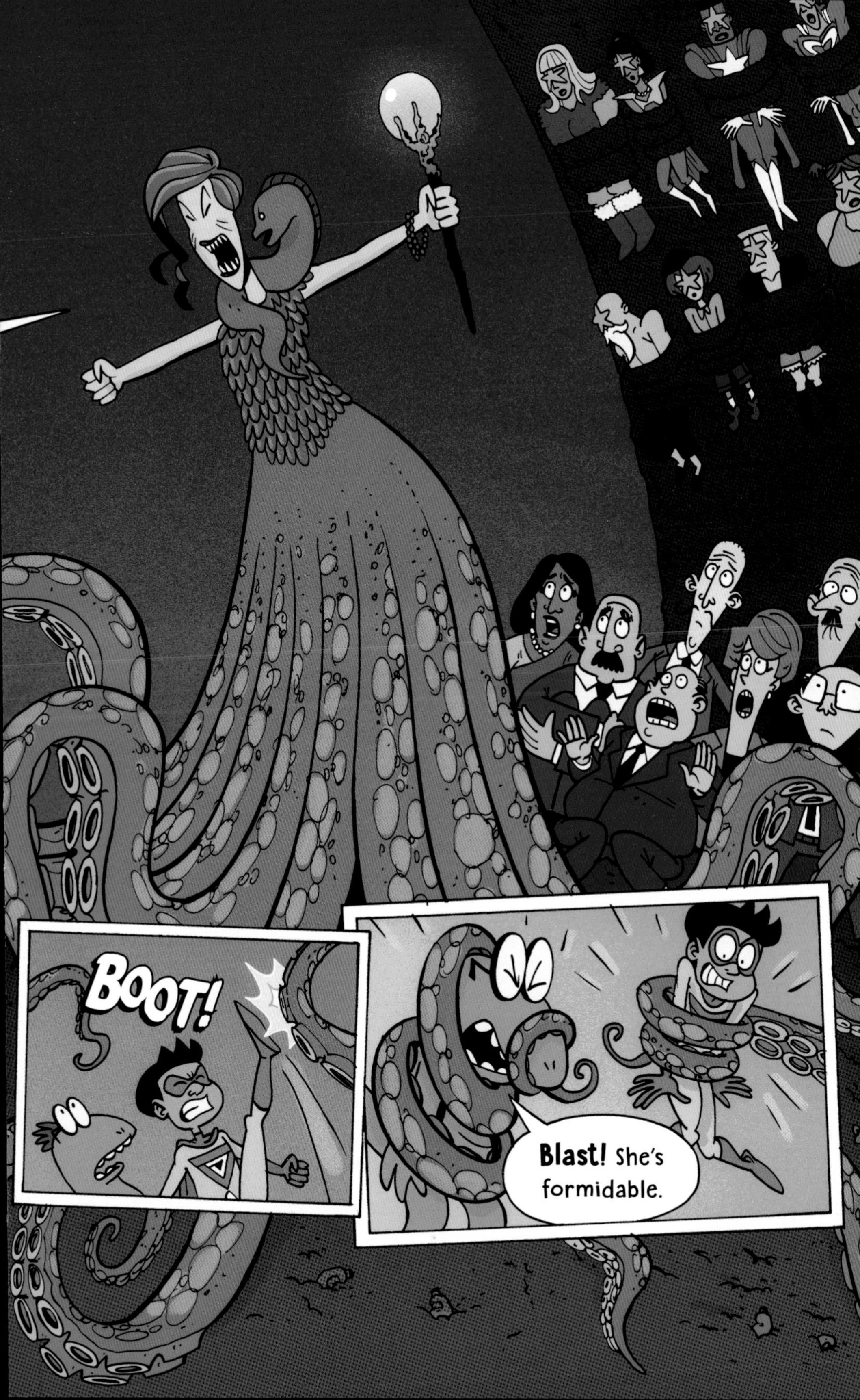
BOOT!
Blast! She's formidable.

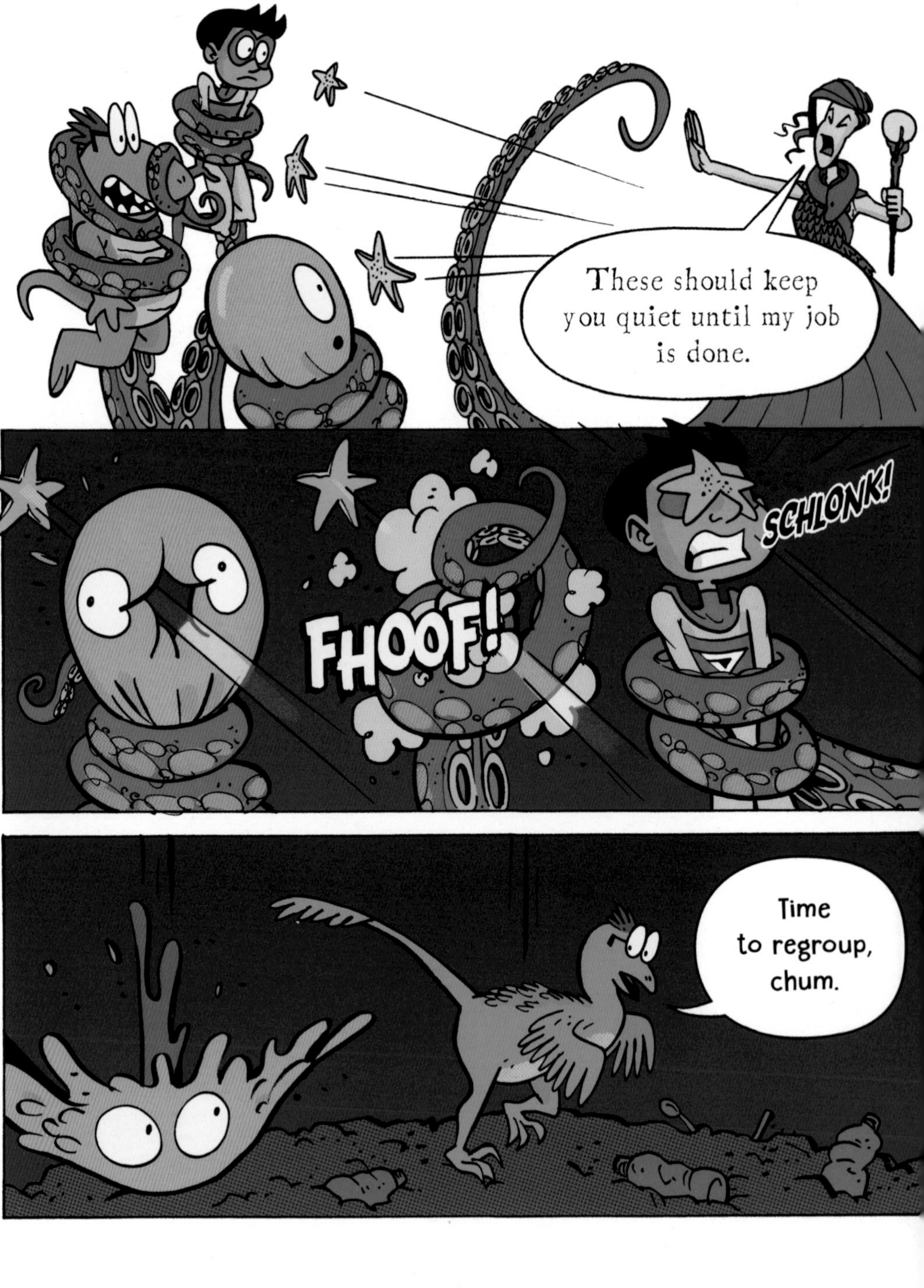
These should keep you quiet until my job is done.
FHOOF!
SCHLONK!
Time to regroup, chum.

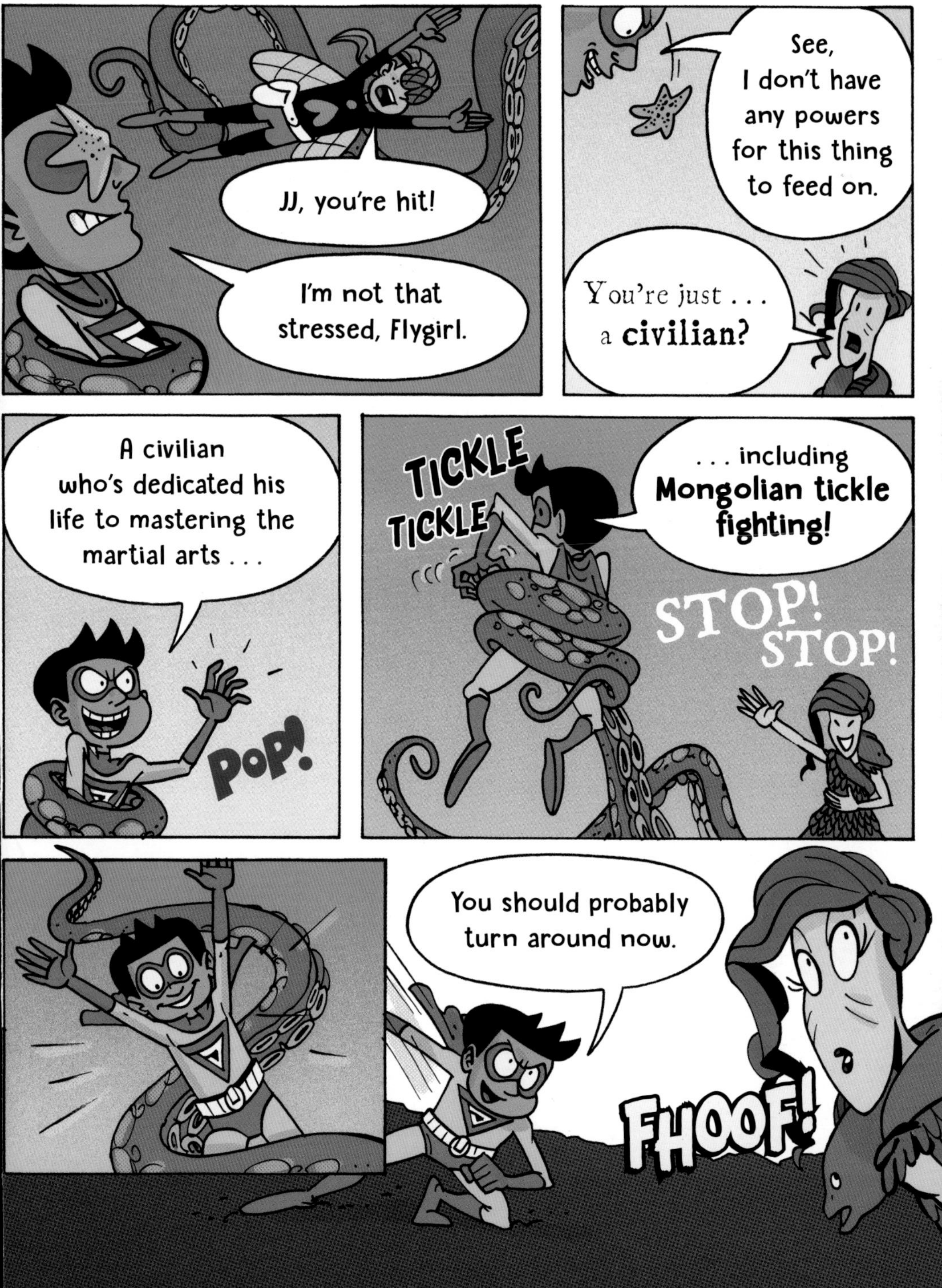
JJ, you're hit!
I'm not that stressed, Flygirl.
See, I don't have any powers for this thing to feed on.
You're just . . . a civilian?
A civilian who's dedicated his life to mastering the martial arts . . .
POP!
TICKLE
TICKLE
. . . including Mongolian tickle fighting!
STOP! STOP!
You should probably turn around now.
FHOOF!

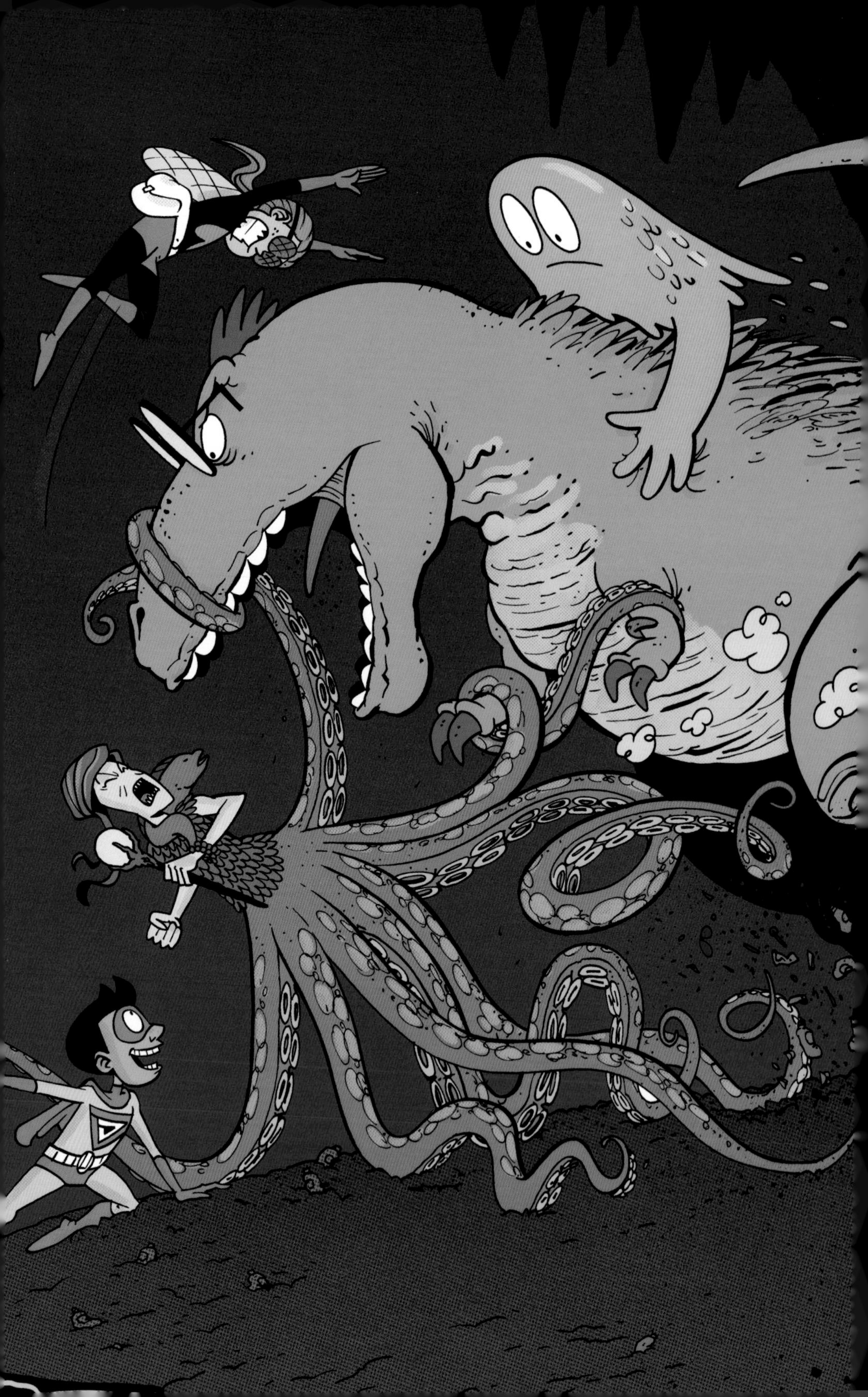

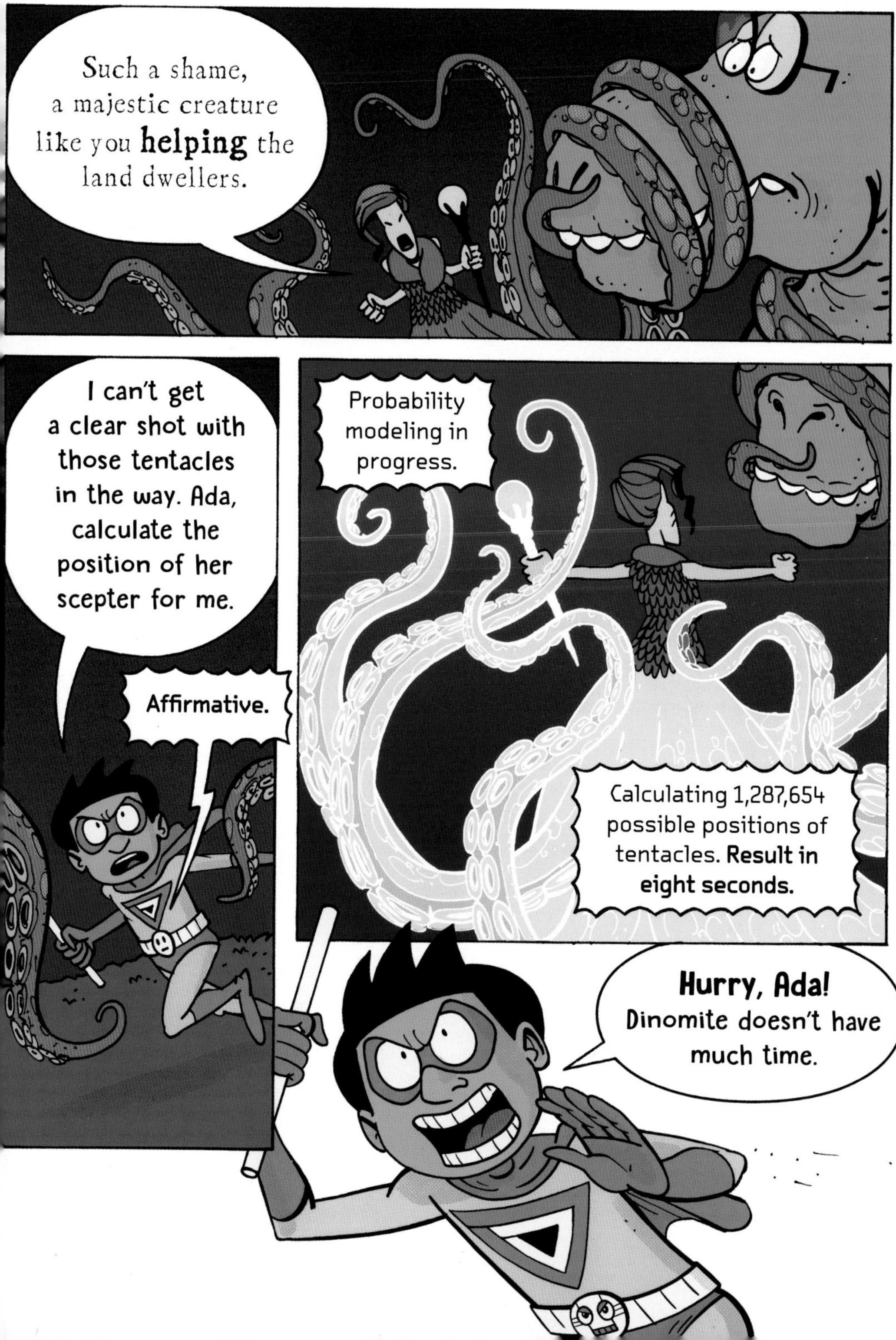
Such a shame, a majestic creature like you **helping** the land dwellers.
I can't get a clear shot with those tentacles in the way. Ada, calculate the position of her scepter for me.
Affirmative.
Probability modeling in progress.
Calculating 1,287,654 possible positions of tentacles. **Result in eight seconds.**
Hurry, Ada! Dinomite doesn't have much time.

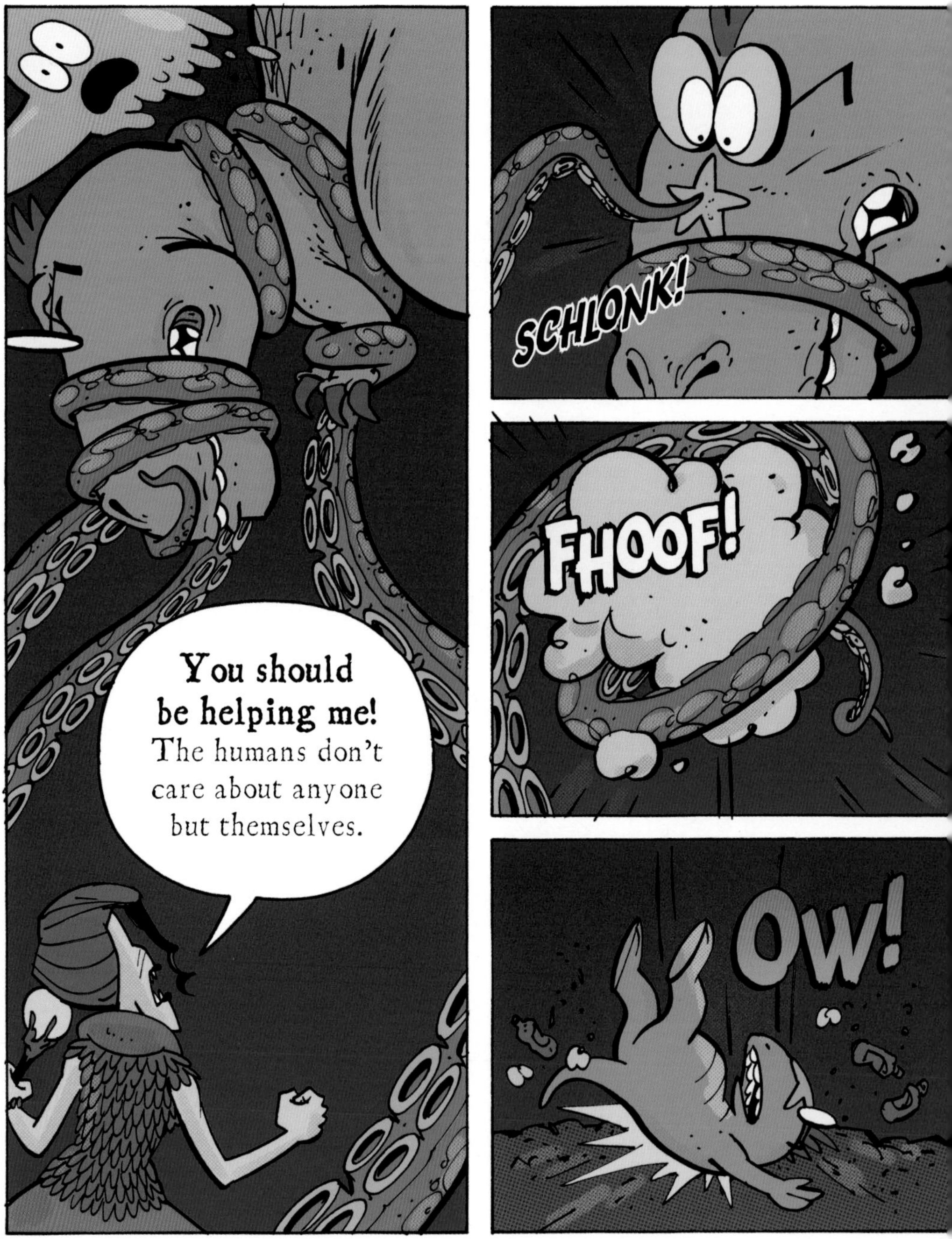
You should be helping me! The humans don't care about anyone but themselves.
SCHLONK!
FHOOF!
OW!

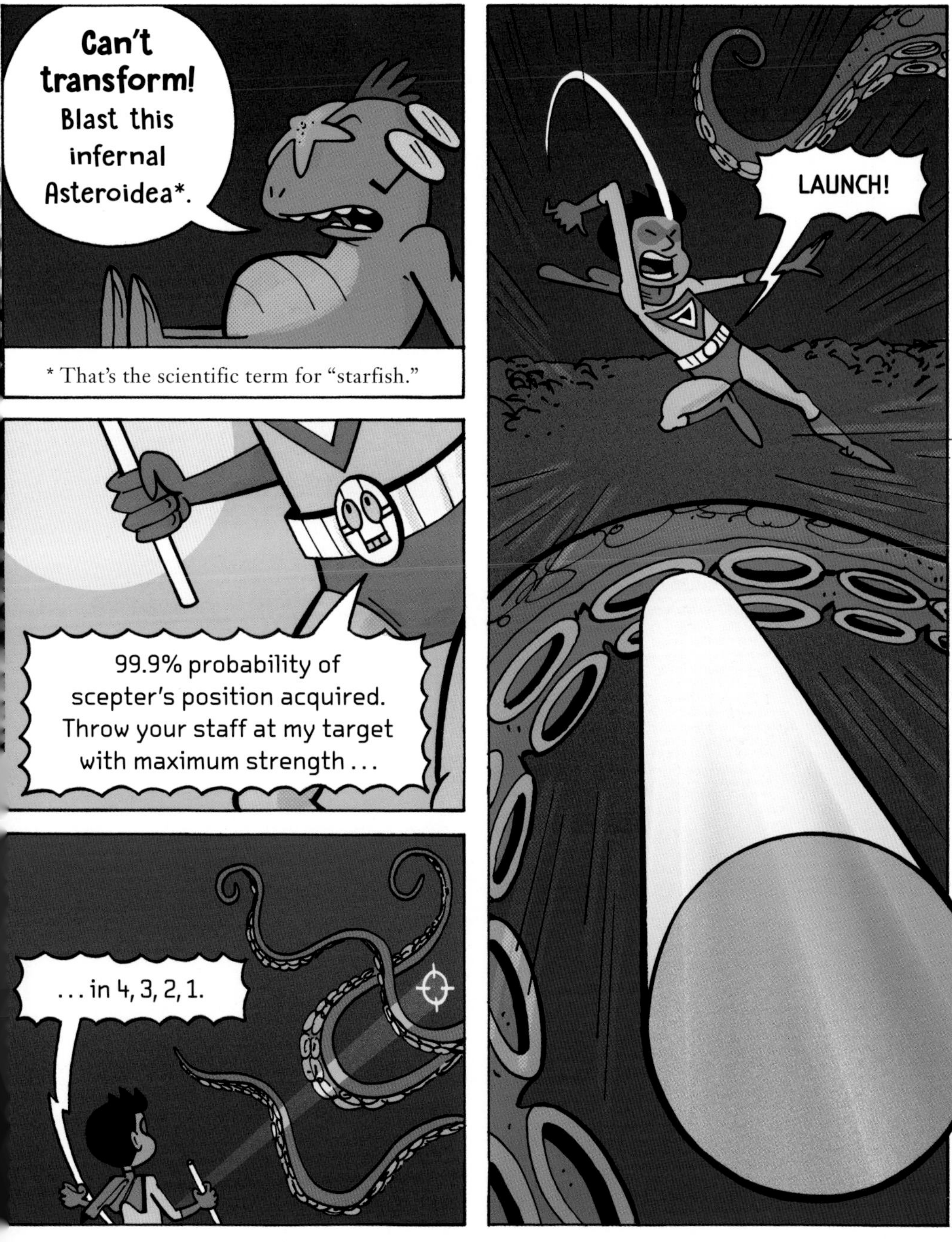
Can't transform! Blast this infernal Asteroidea*.
* That's the scientific term for "starfish."
99.9% probability of scepter's position acquired. Throw your staff at my target with maximum strength . . .
. . . in 4, 3, 2, 1.
LAUNCH!

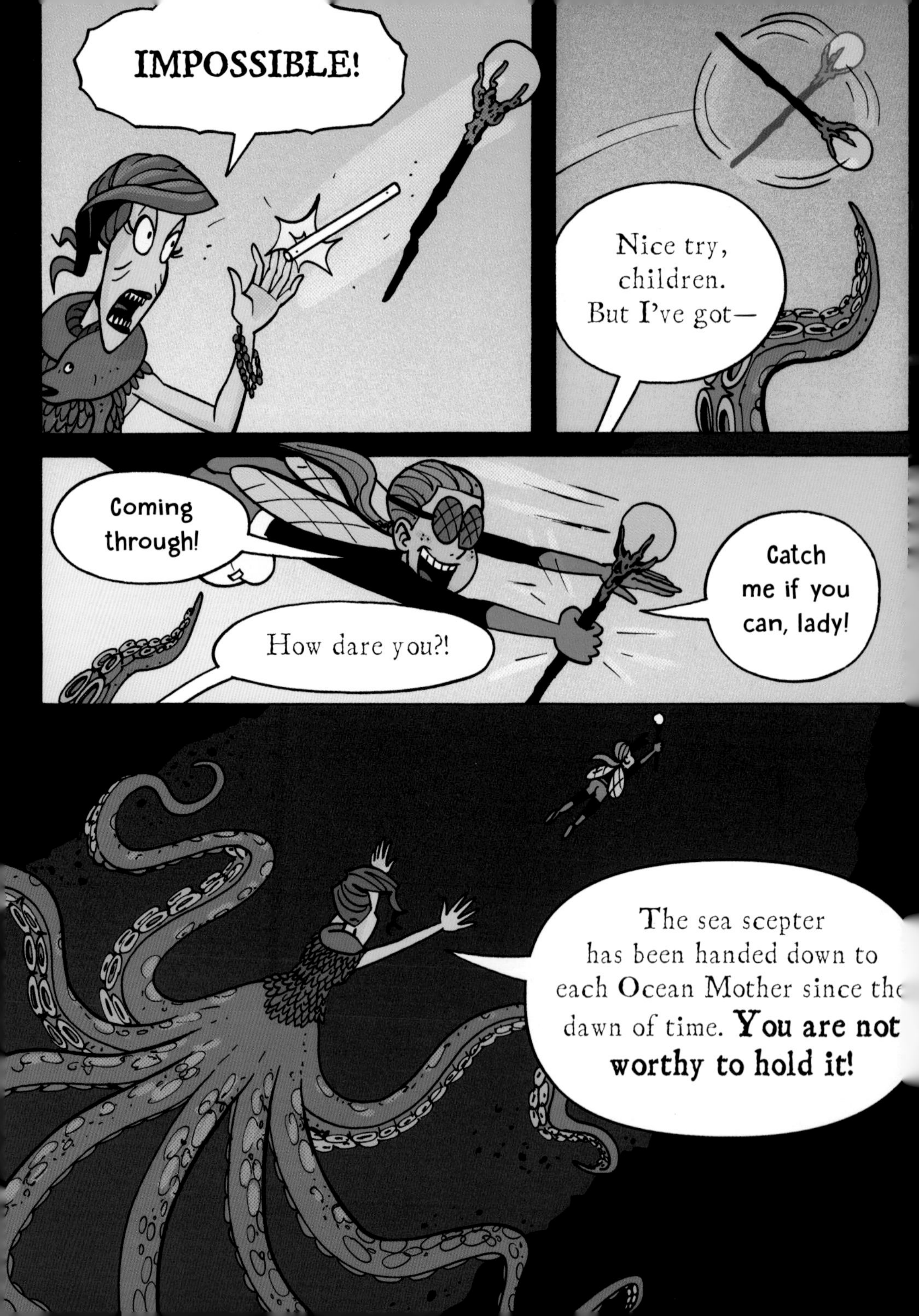
IMPOSSIBLE!
Nice try, children. But I've got—
Coming through!
Catch me if you can, lady!
How dare you?!
The sea scepter has been handed down to each Ocean Mother since the dawn of time. **You are not worthy to hold it!**

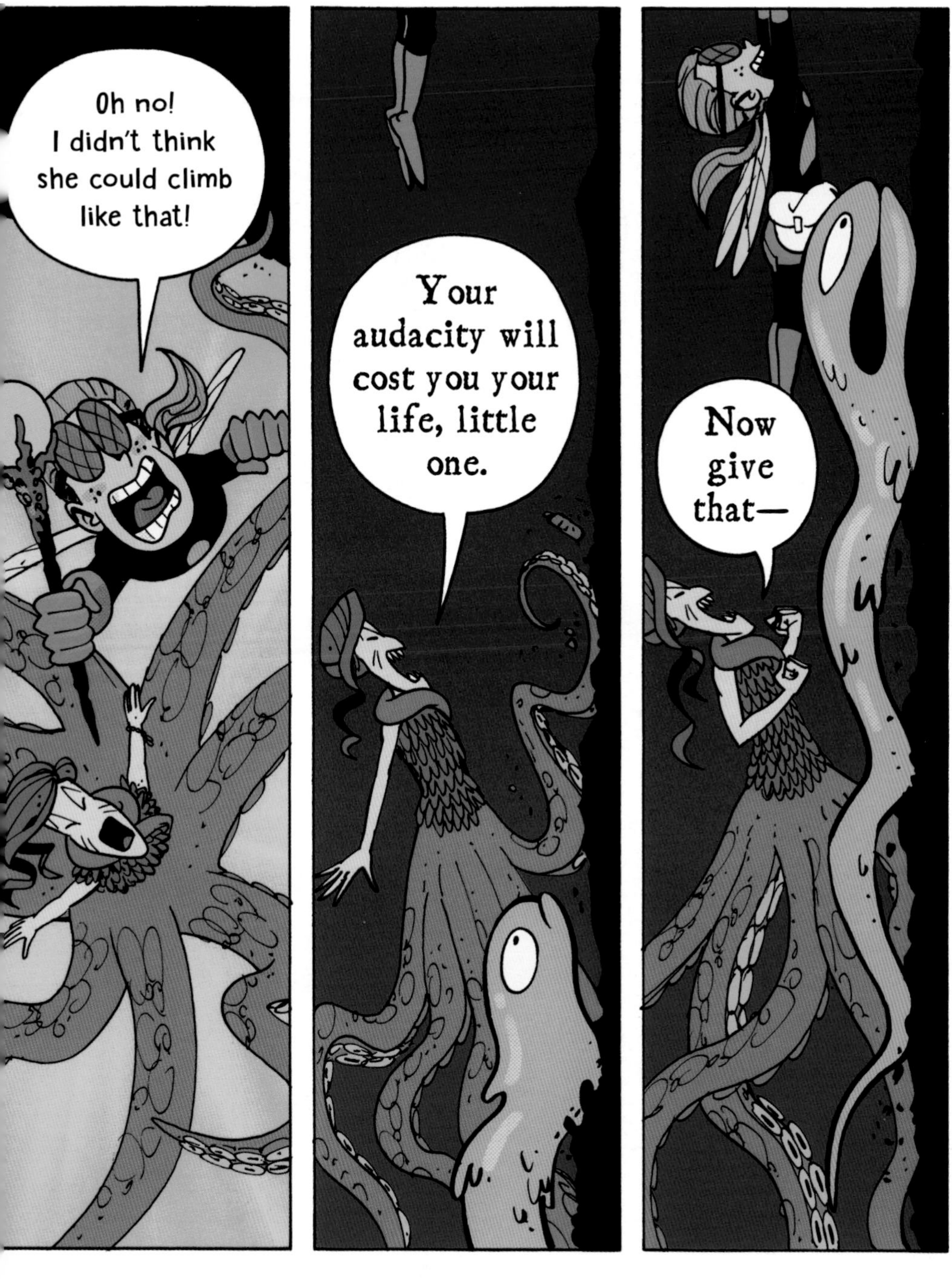
Oh no! I didn't think she could climb like that!
Your audacity will cost you your life, little one.
Now give that—

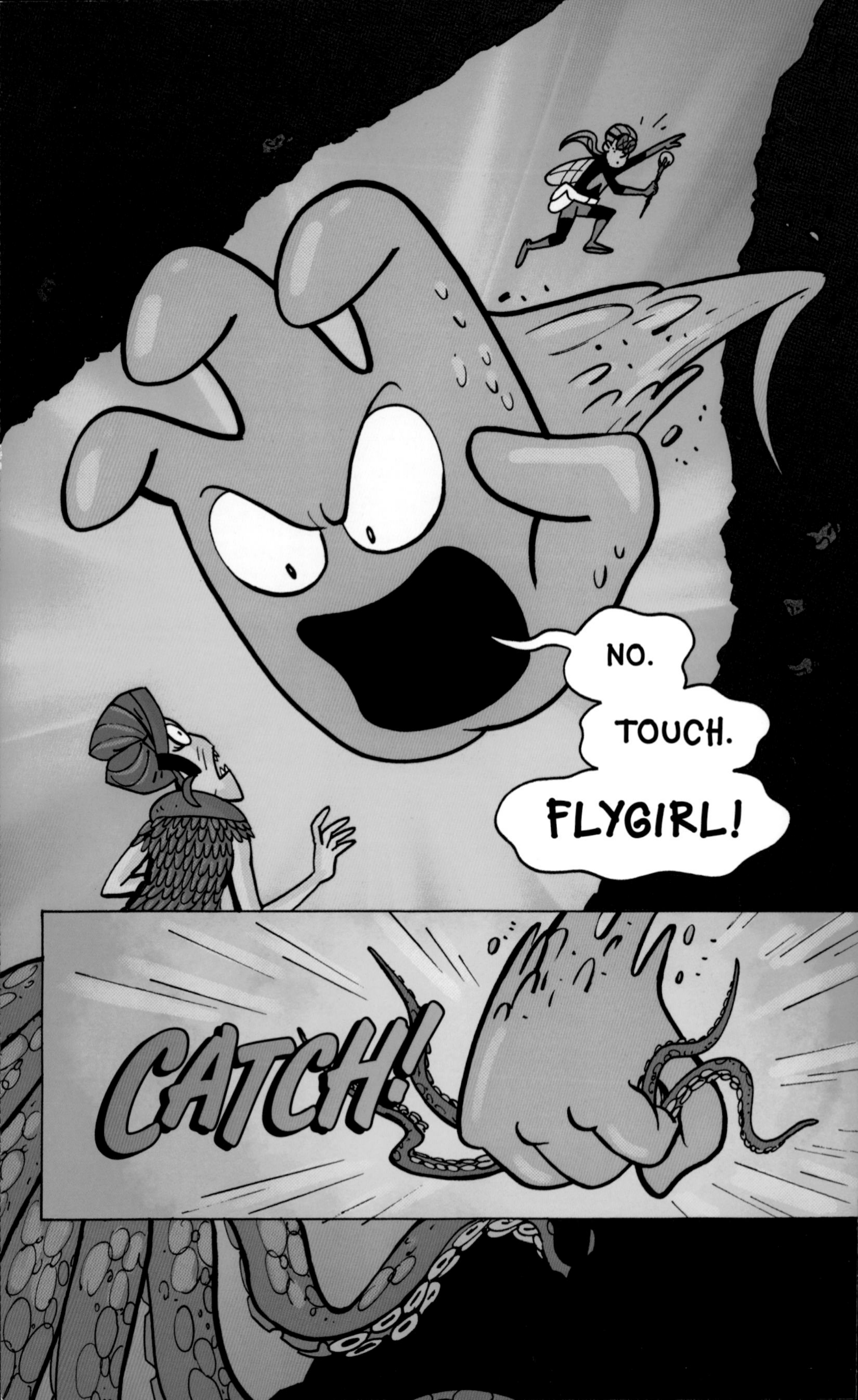
NO.
TOUCH.
FLYGIRL!
CATCH!

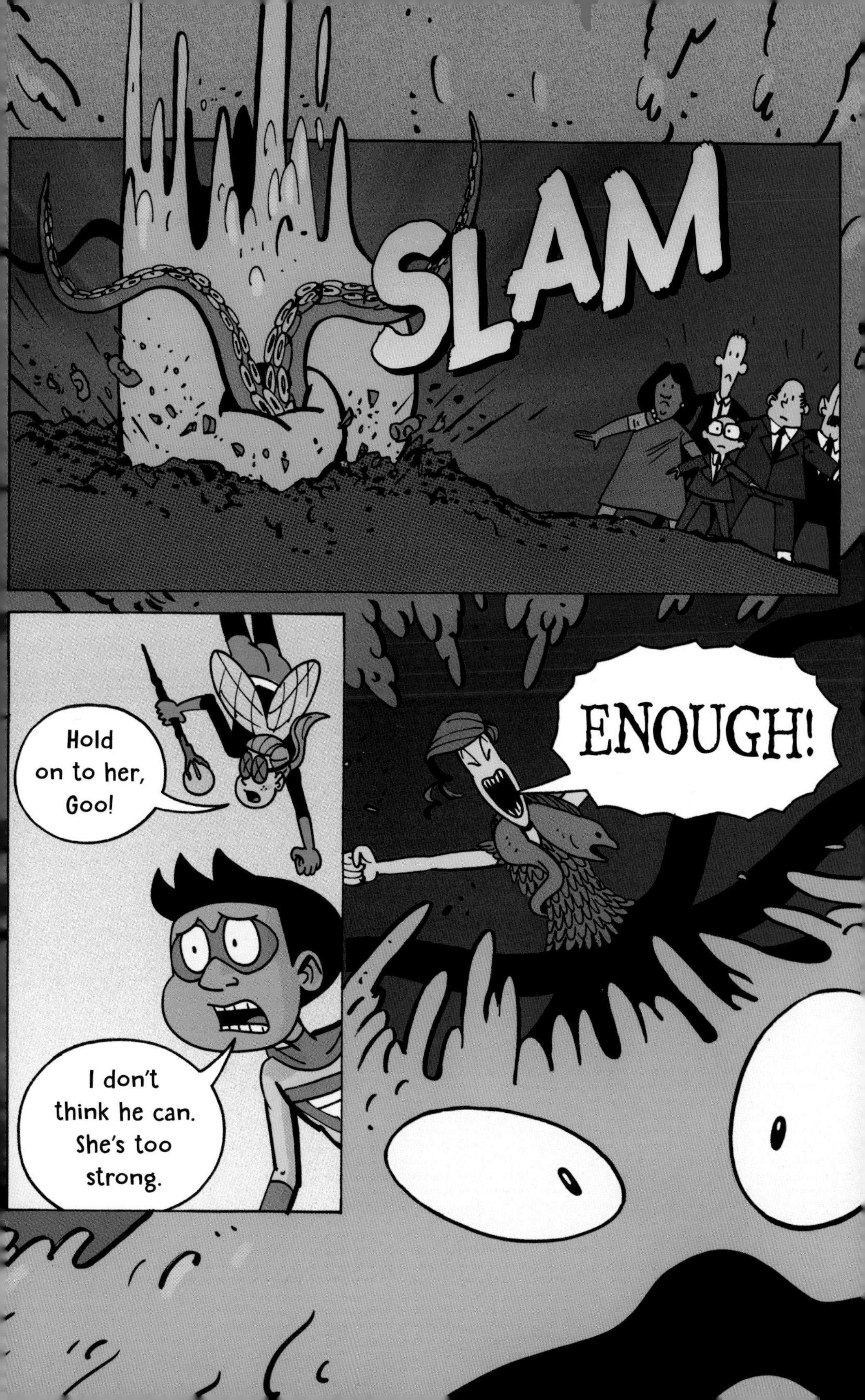
SLAM
Hold on to her, Goo!
I don't think he can. She's too strong.
ENOUGH!

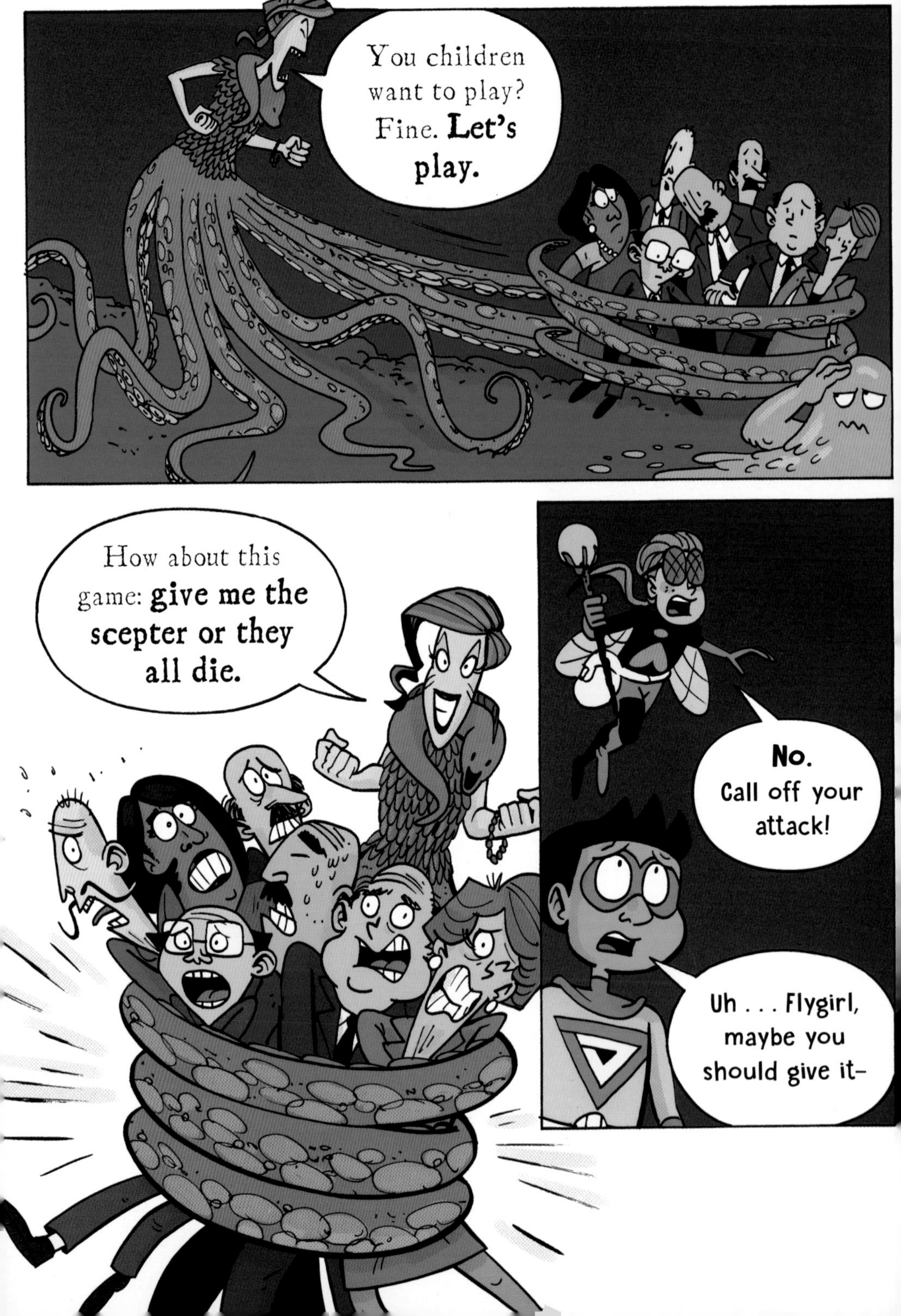
You children want to play? Fine. **Let's play.**
How about this game: **give me the scepter or they all die.**
No. Call off your attack!
Uh . . . Flygirl, maybe you should give it–

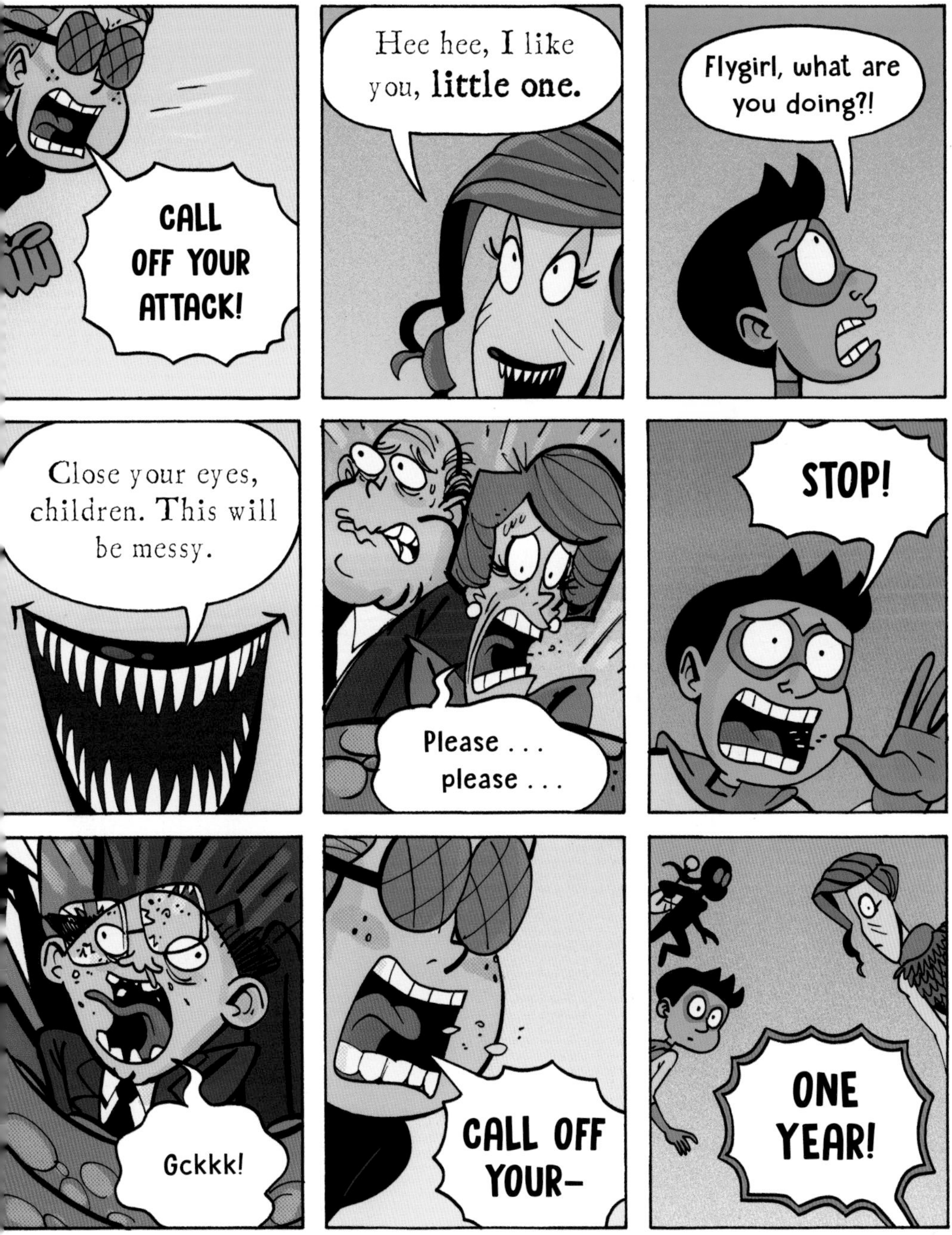
CALL OFF YOUR ATTACK!
Hee hee, I like you, little one.
Flygirl, what are you doing?!
Close your eyes, children. This will be messy.
Please . . . please . . .
STOP!
Gckkk!
CALL OFF YOUR–
ONE YEAR!

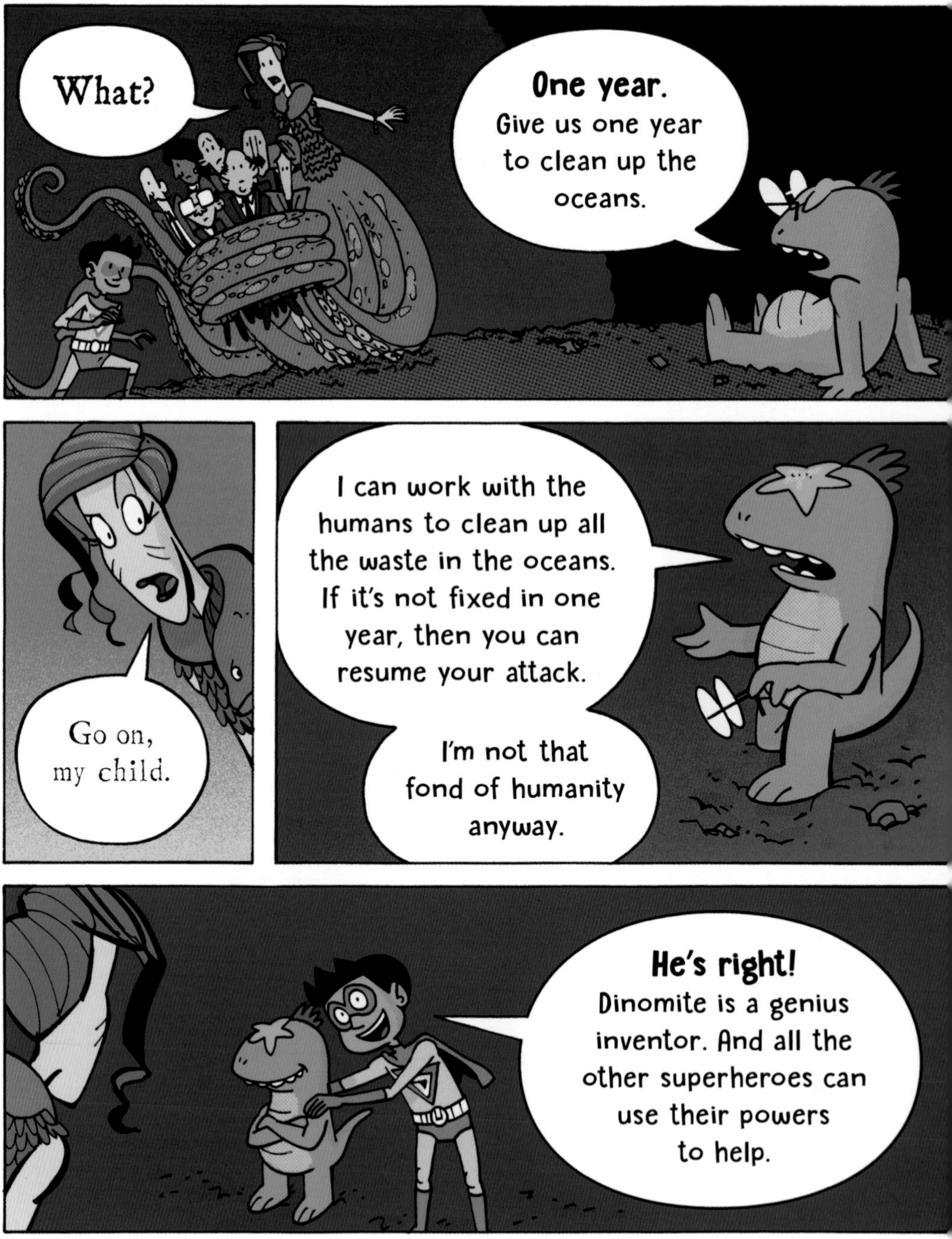
What?
One year. Give us one year to clean up the oceans.
Go on, my child.
I can work with the humans to clean up all the waste in the oceans. If it's not fixed in one year, then you can resume your attack.
I'm not that fond of humanity anyway.
He's right! Dinomite is a genius inventor. And all the other superheroes can use their powers to help.

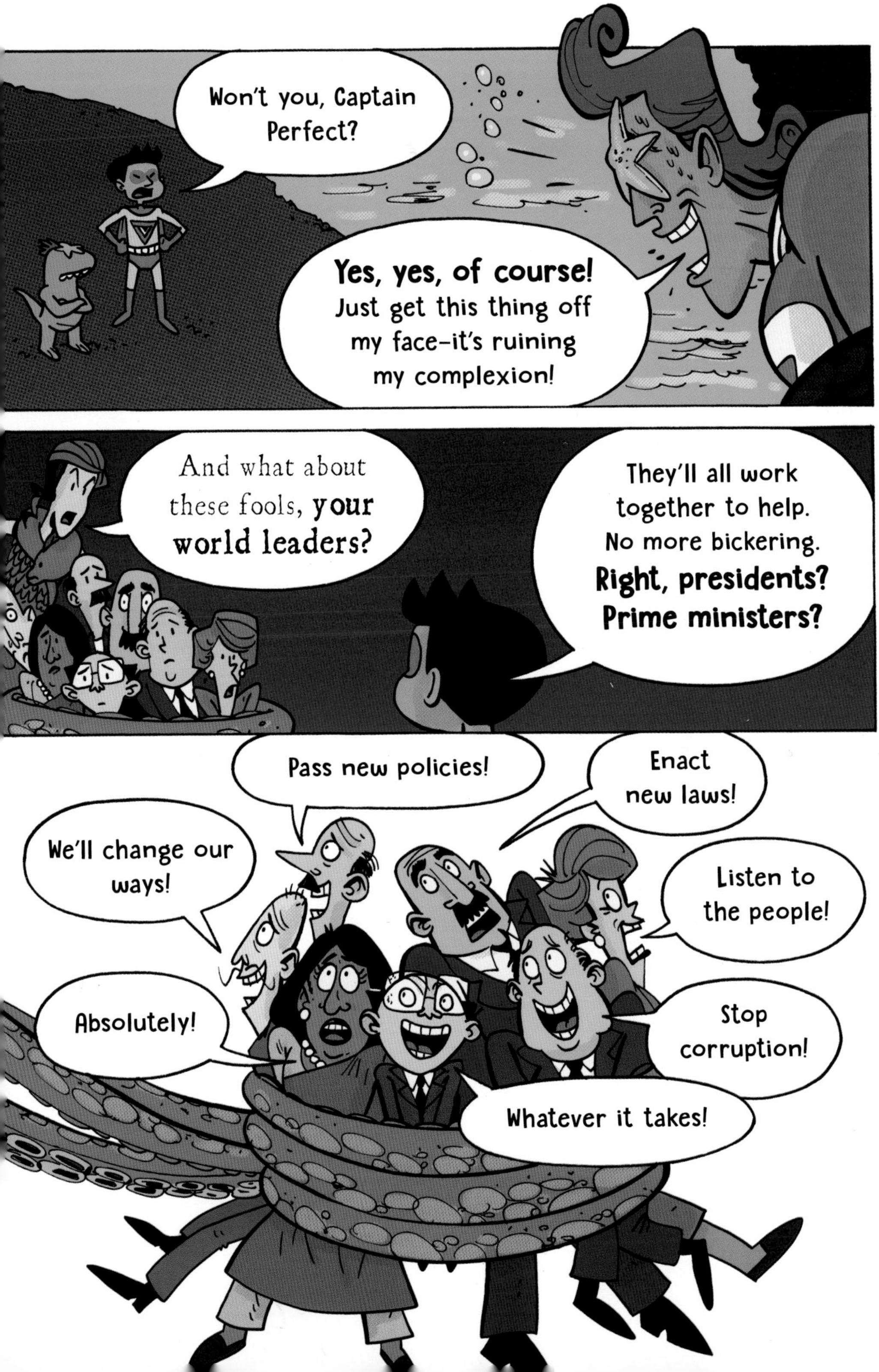
Won't you, Captain Perfect?
Yes, yes, of course! Just get this thing off my face–it's ruining my complexion!
And what about these fools, your world leaders?
They'll all work together to help. No more bickering. Right, presidents? Prime ministers?
Pass new policies!
Enact new laws!
We'll change our ways!
Listen to the people!
Absolutely!
Stop corruption!
Whatever it takes!

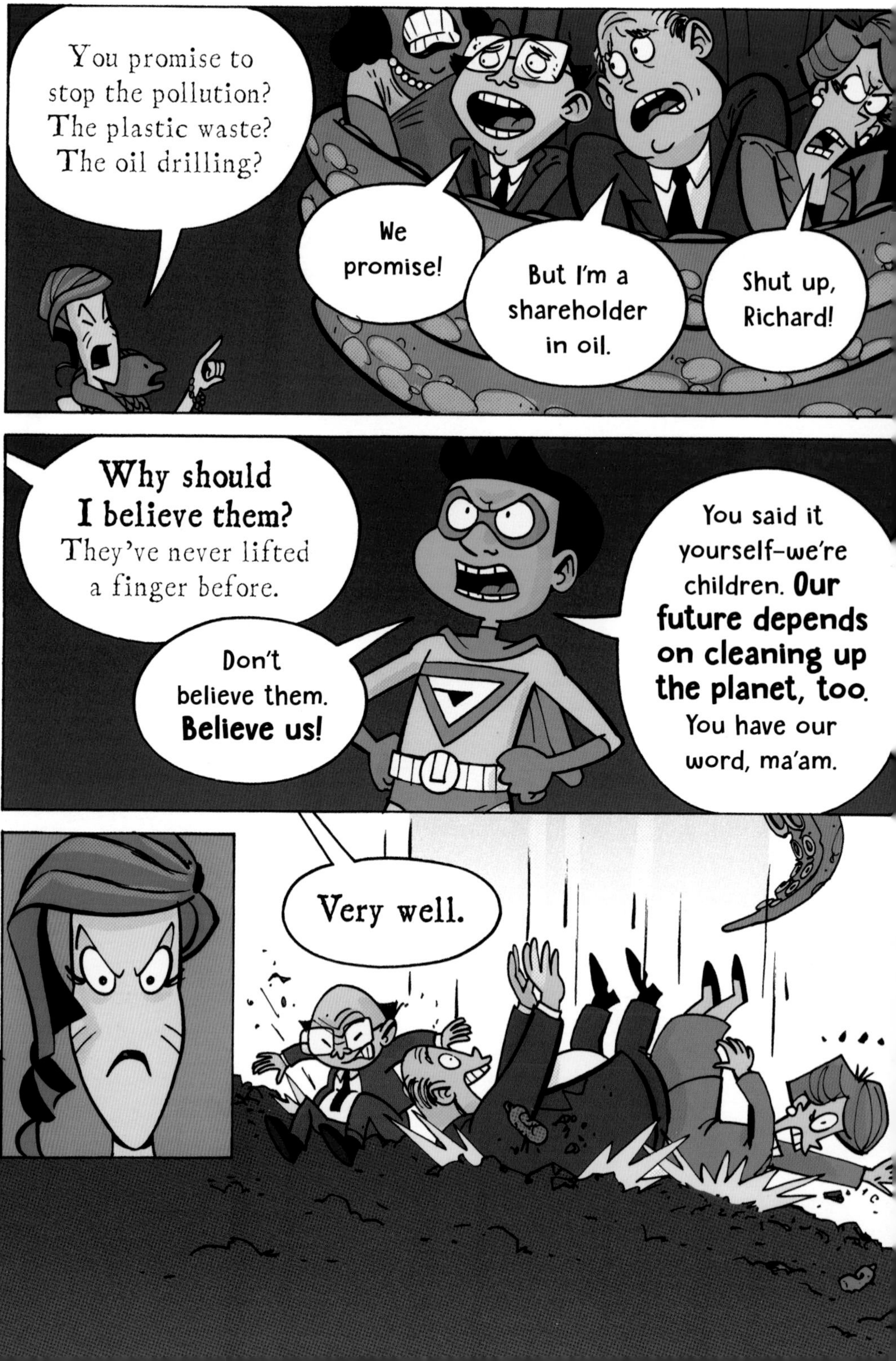
You promise to stop the pollution? The plastic waste? The oil drilling?
We promise!
But I'm a shareholder in oil.
Shut up, Richard!
Why should I believe them? They've never lifted a finger before.
Don't believe them. Believe us!
You said it yourself–we're children. Our future depends on cleaning up the planet, too. You have our word, ma'am.
Very well.

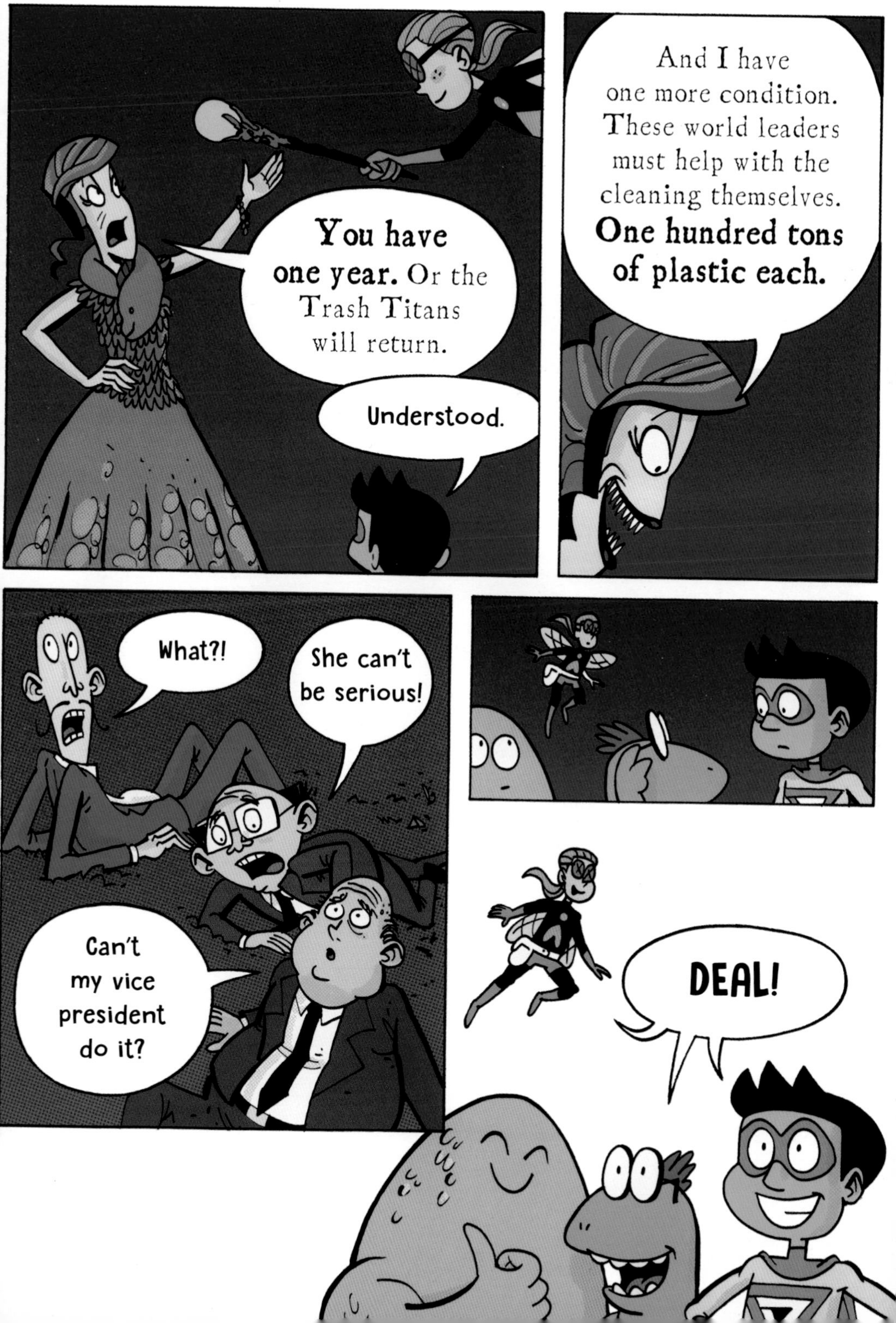
You have one year. Or the Trash Titans will return.
Understood.
And I have one more condition. These world leaders must help with the cleaning themselves. One hundred tons of plastic each.
What?!
She can't be serious!
Can't my vice president do it?
DEAL!

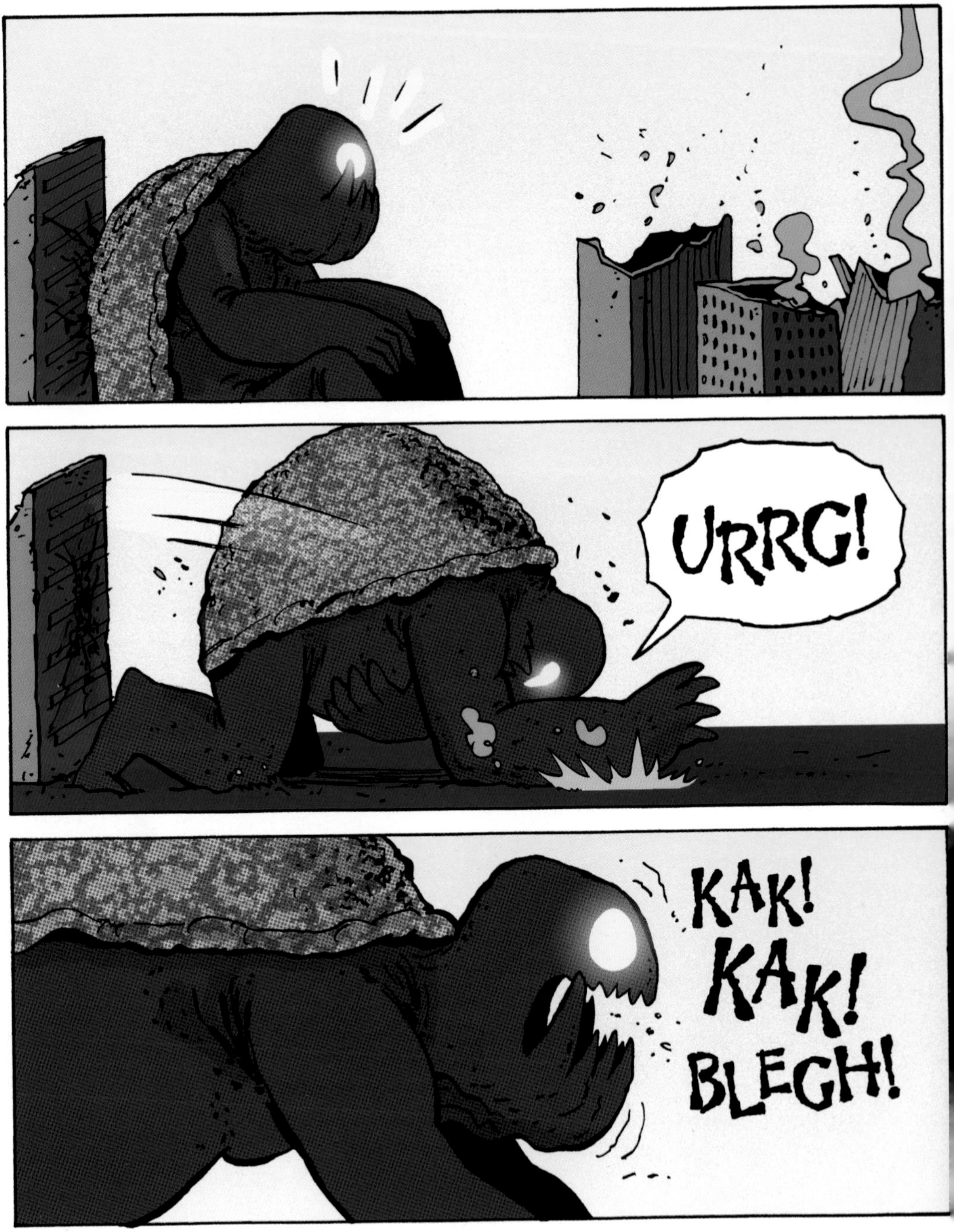
URRG!
KAK!
KAK!
BLEGH!

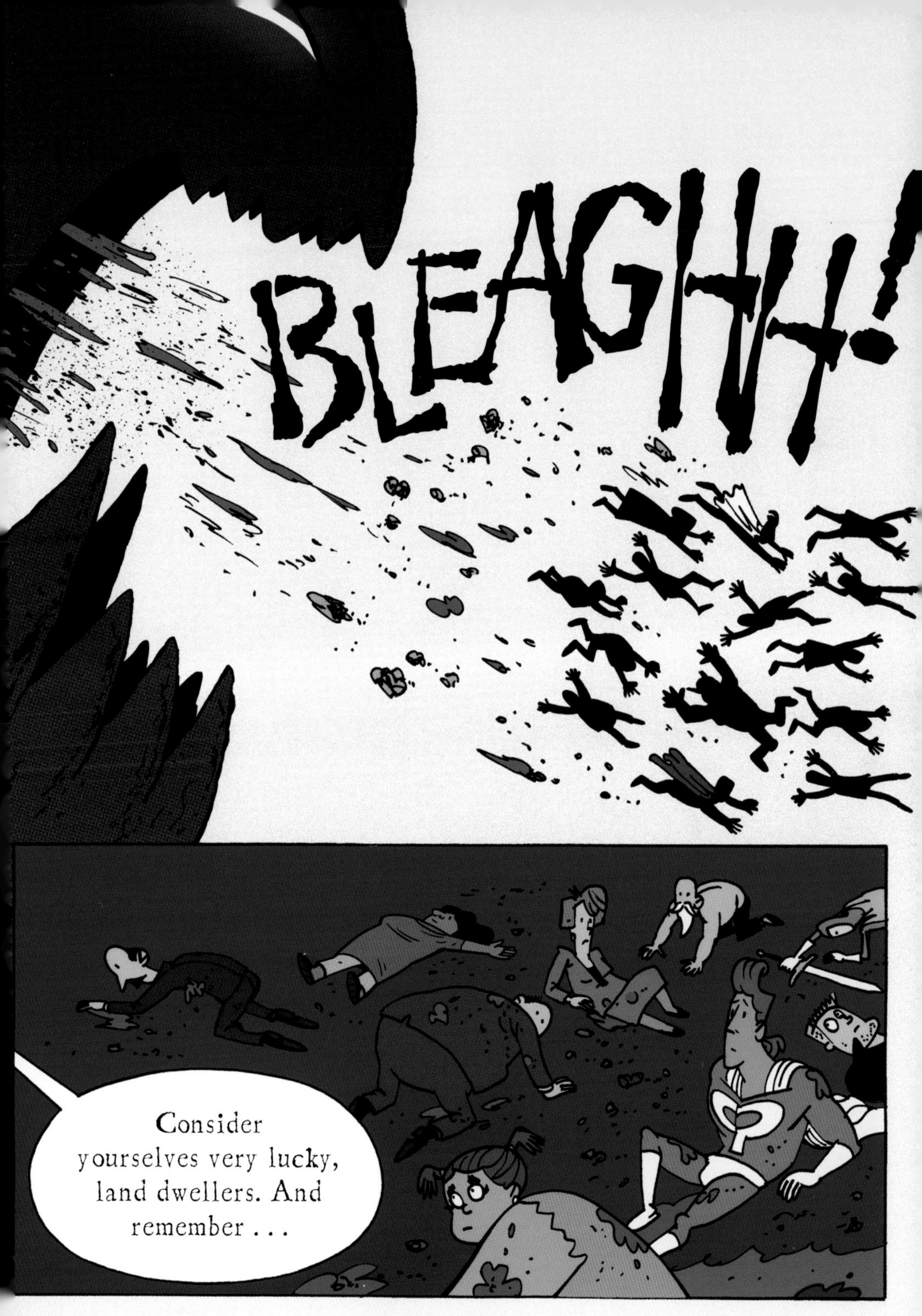
BLEAGHH!
Consider yourselves very lucky, land dwellers. And remember . . .

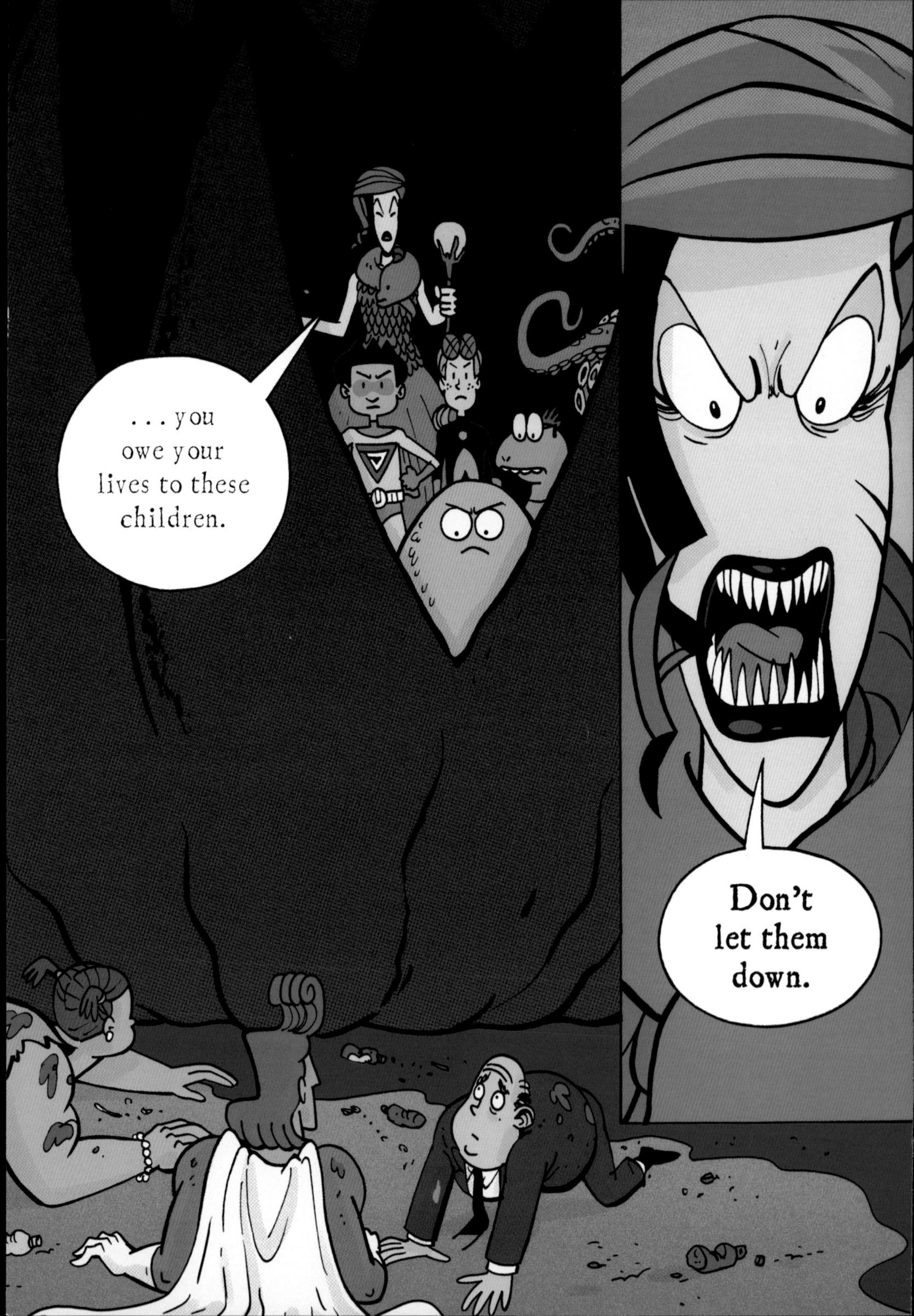
. . . you owe your lives to these children.
Don't let them down.

Chapter

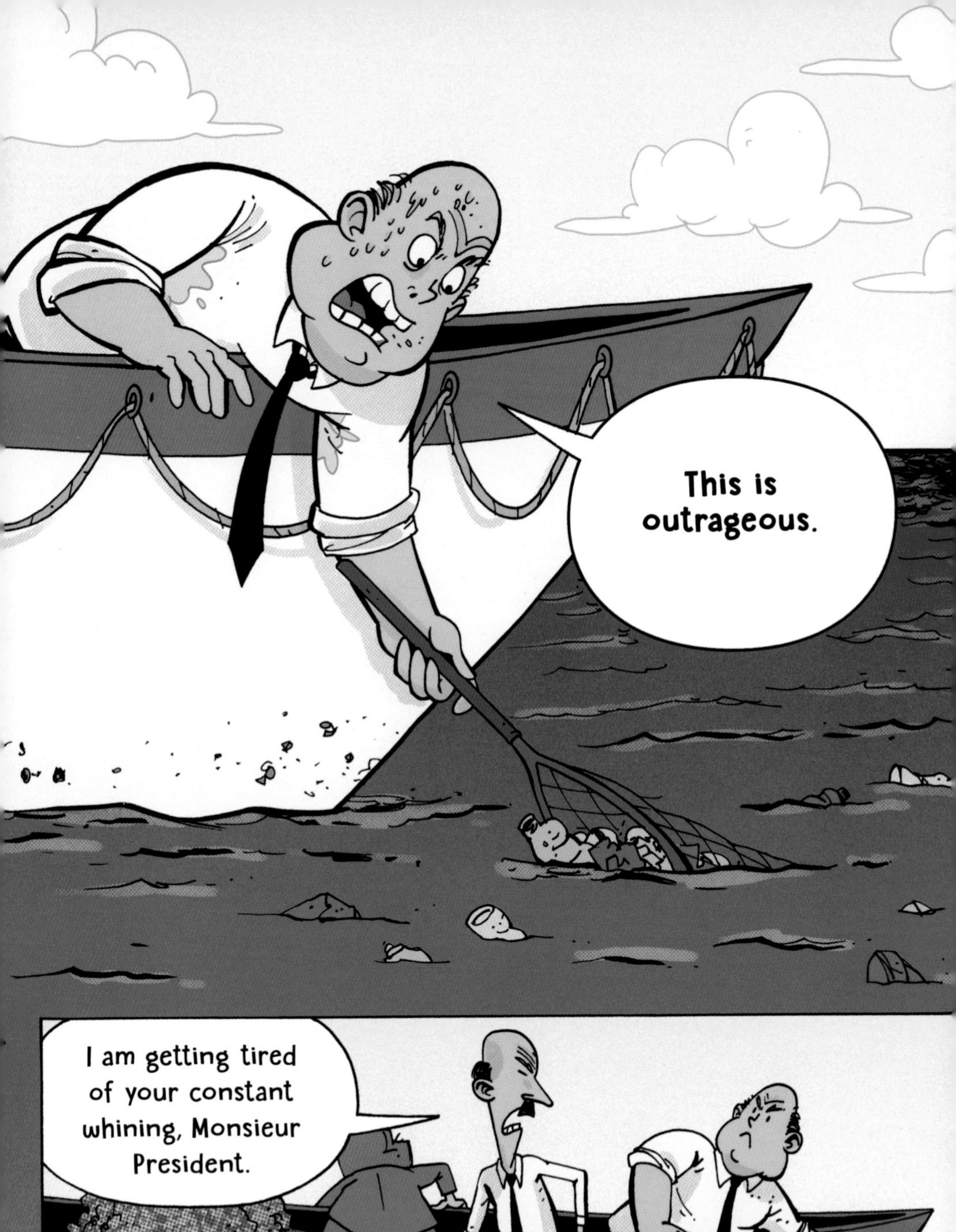
This is outrageous.
I am getting tired of your constant whining, Monsieur President.

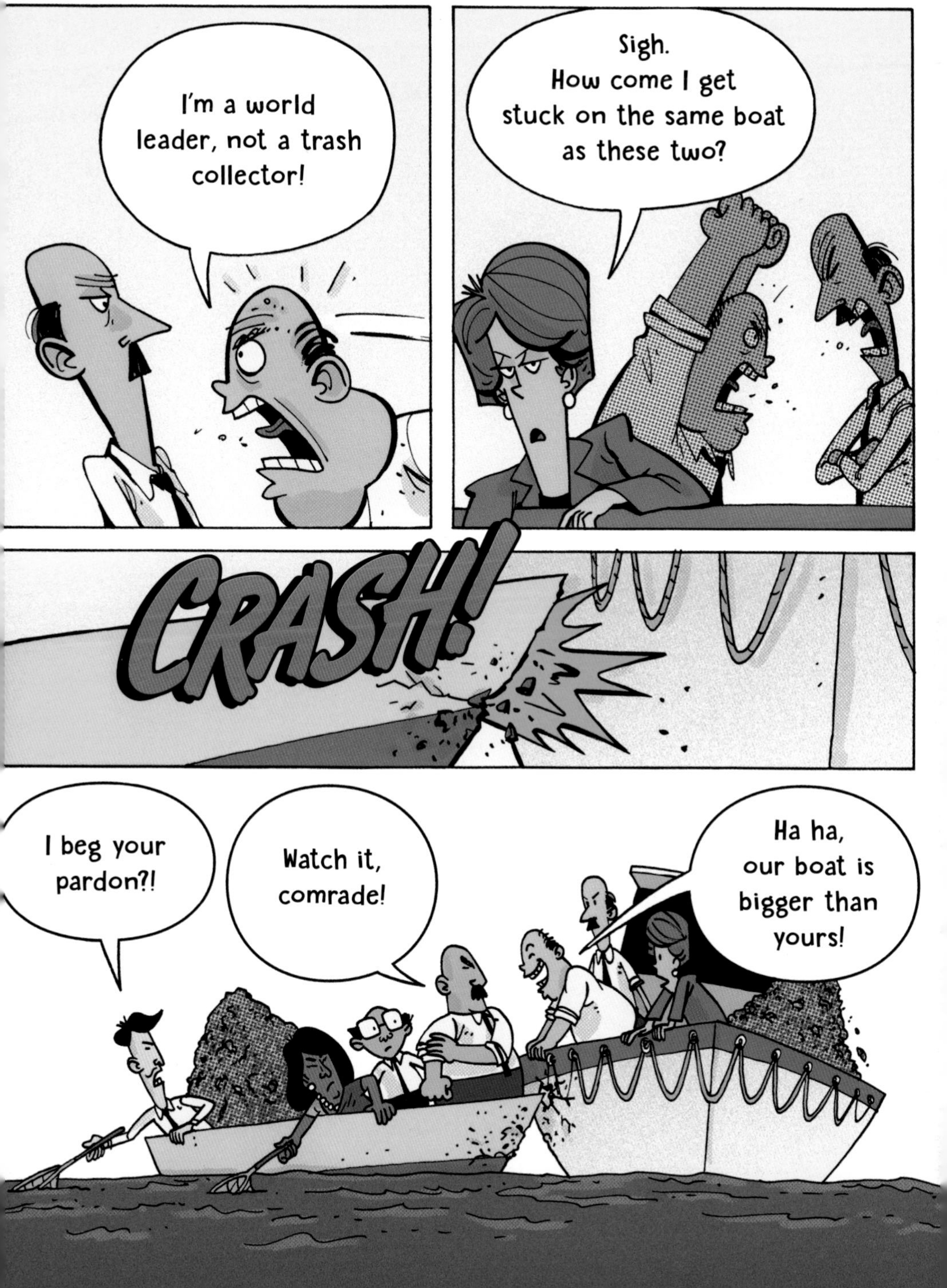
I'm a world leader, not a trash collector!
Sigh. How come I get stuck on the same boat as these two?
CRASH!
I beg your pardon?!
Watch it, comrade!
Ha ha, our boat is bigger than yours!

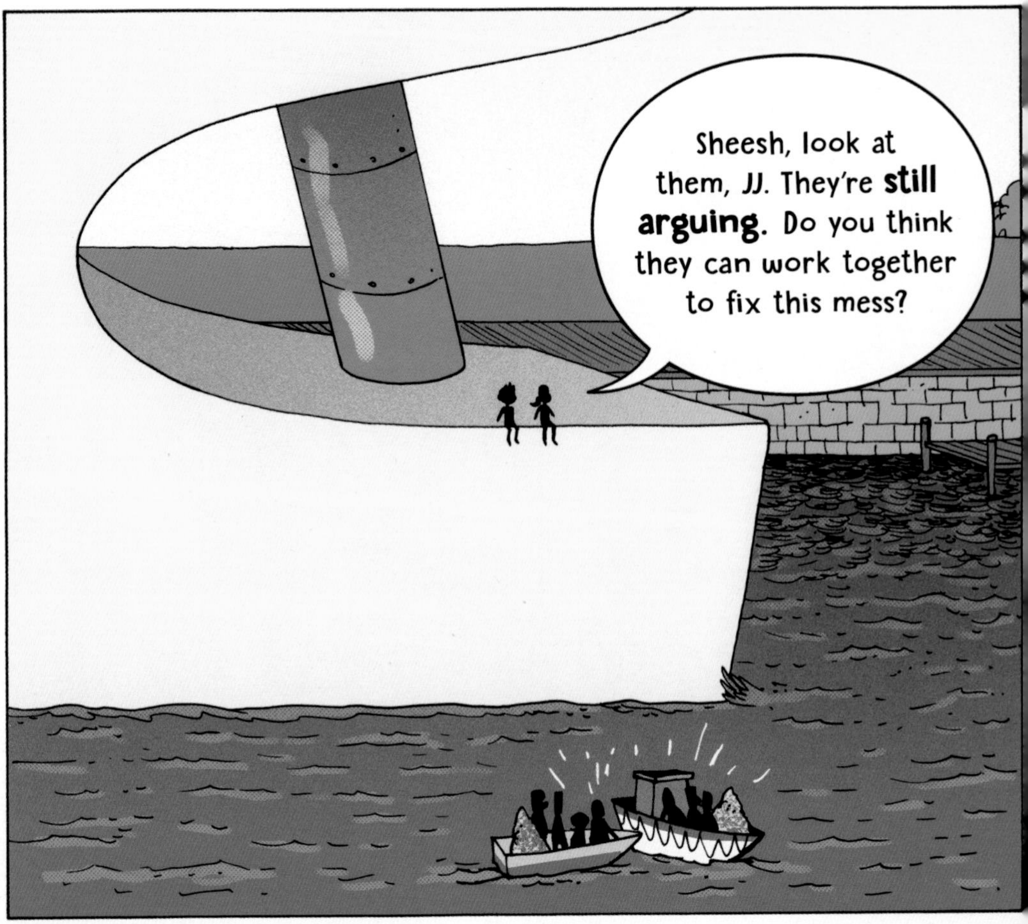
Sheesh, look at them, JJ. They're **still arguing.** Do you think they can work together to fix this mess?

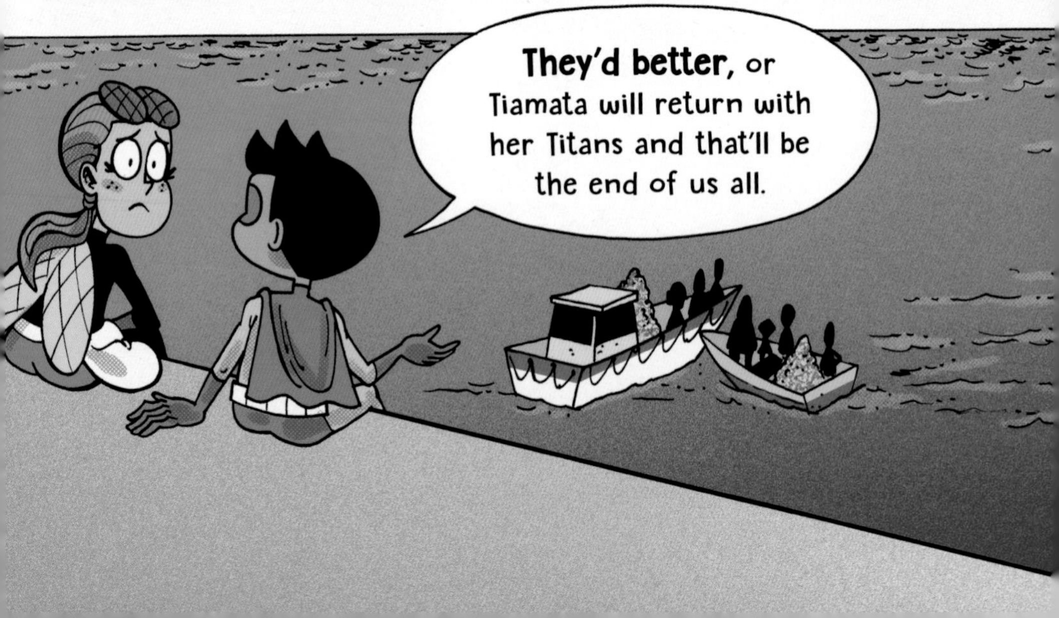
They'd better, or Tiamata will return with her Titans and that'll be the end of us all.

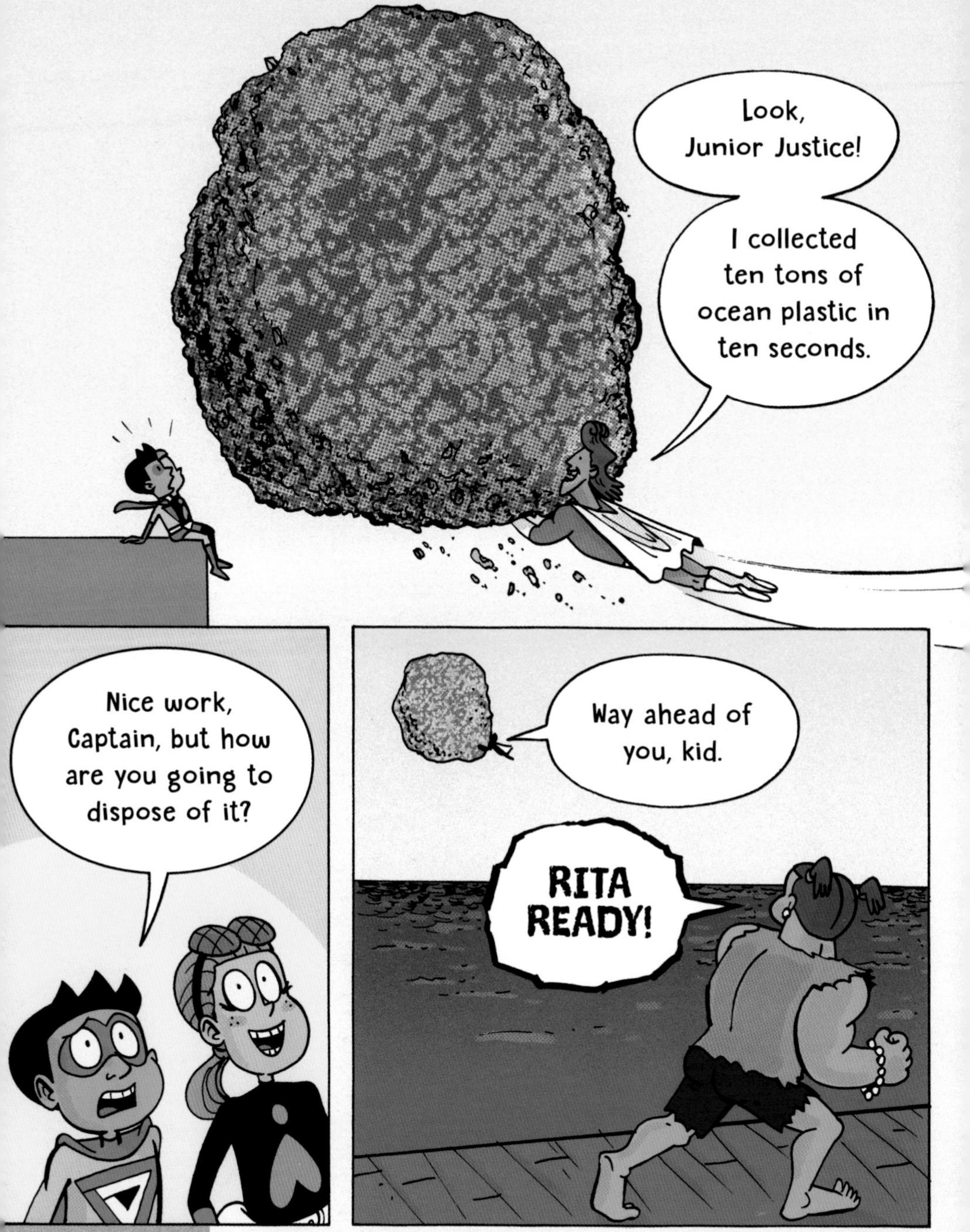
Look, Junior Justice!
I collected ten tons of ocean plastic in ten seconds.
Nice work, Captain, but how are you going to dispose of it?
Way ahead of you, kid.
RITA READY!

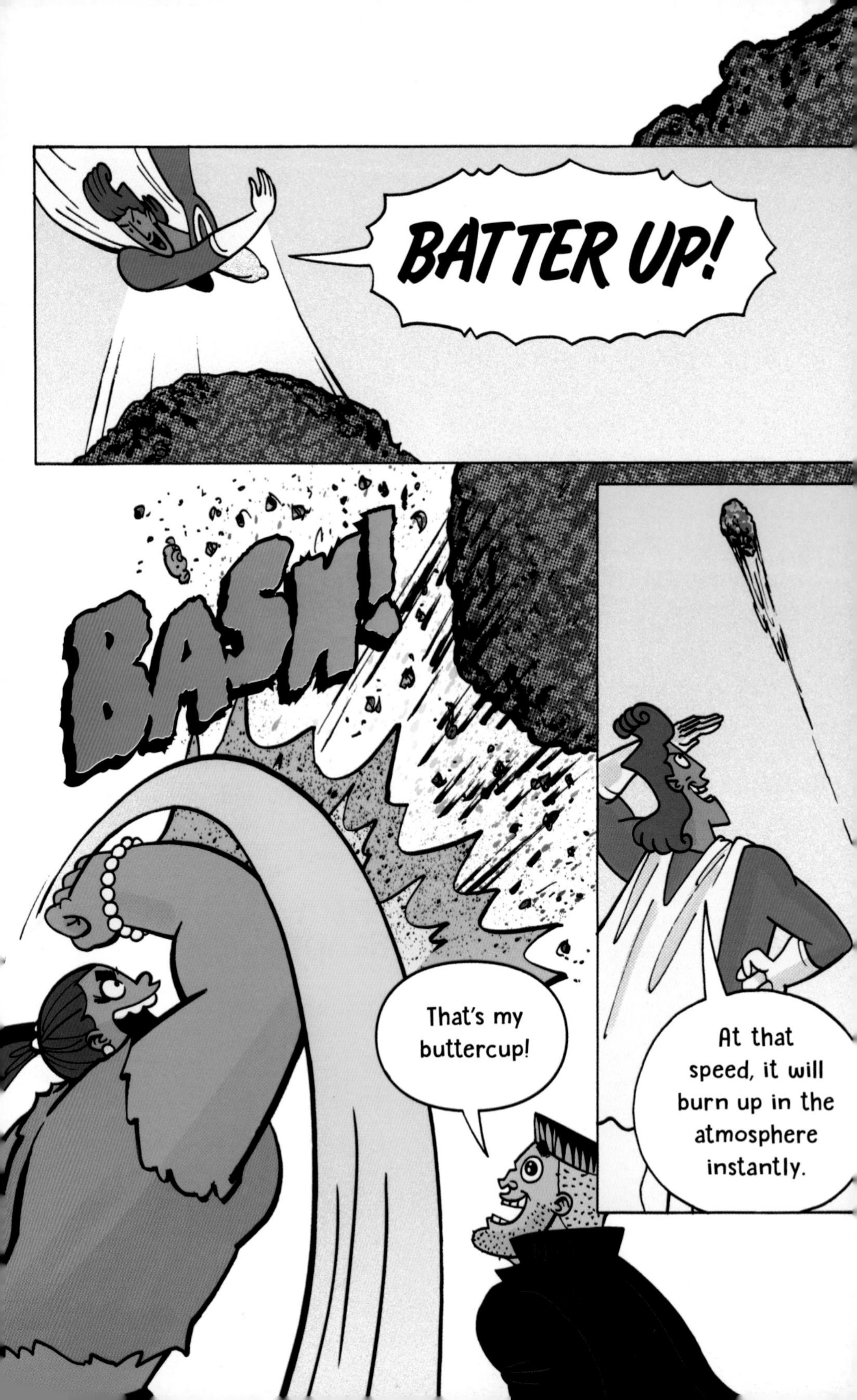
BATTER UP!
BASH!
That's my buttercup!
At that speed, it will burn up in the atmosphere instantly.

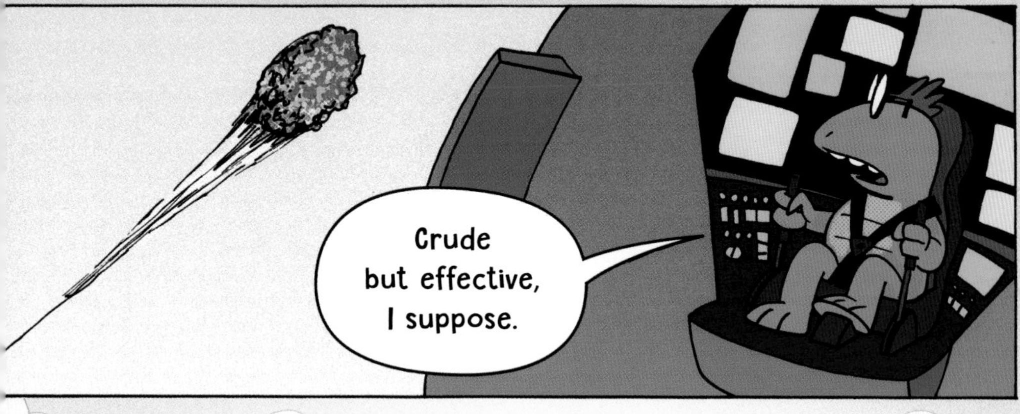
Crude but effective, I suppose.
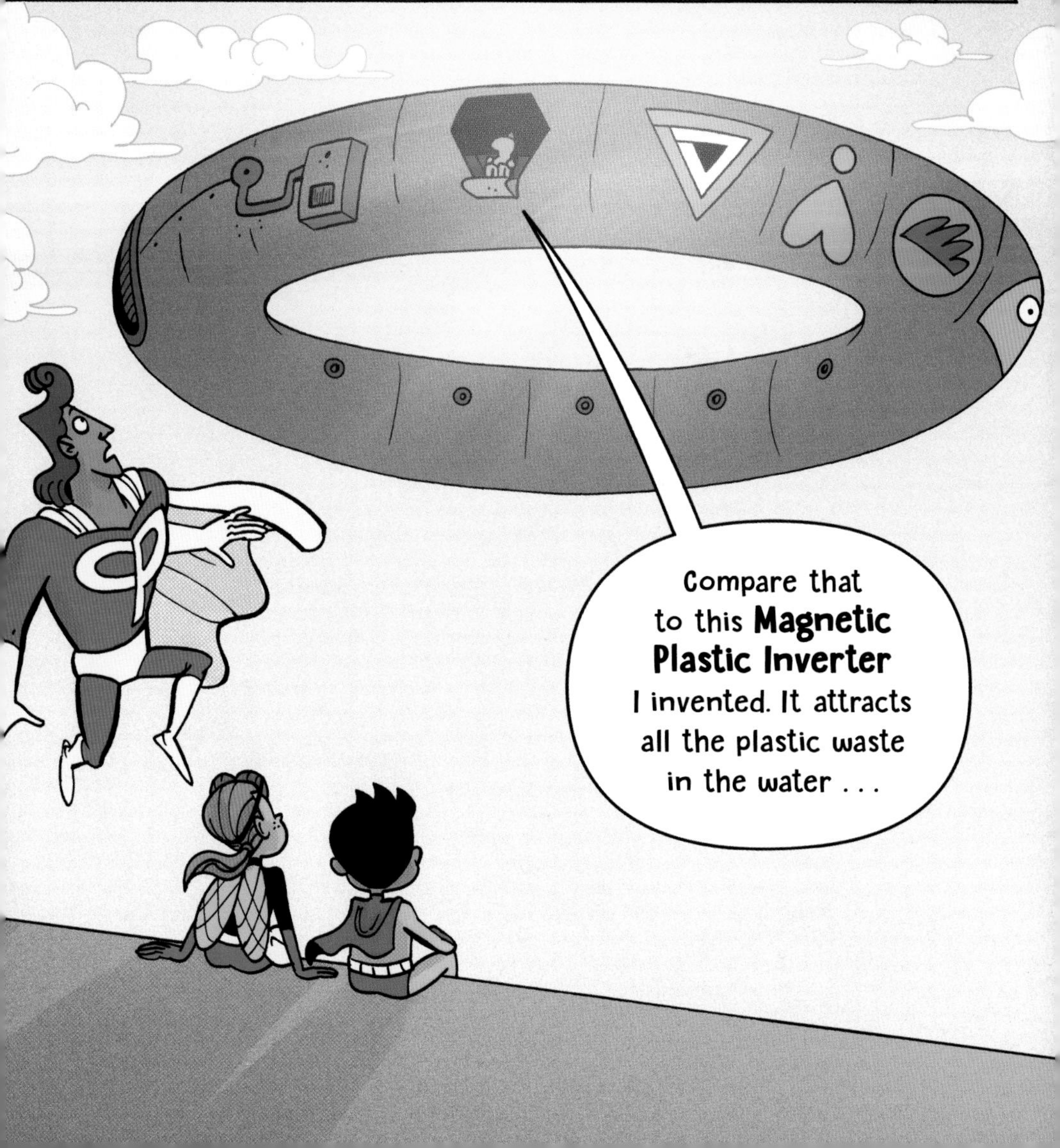
Compare that to this **Magnetic Plastic Inverter** I invented. It attracts all the plastic waste in the water . . .

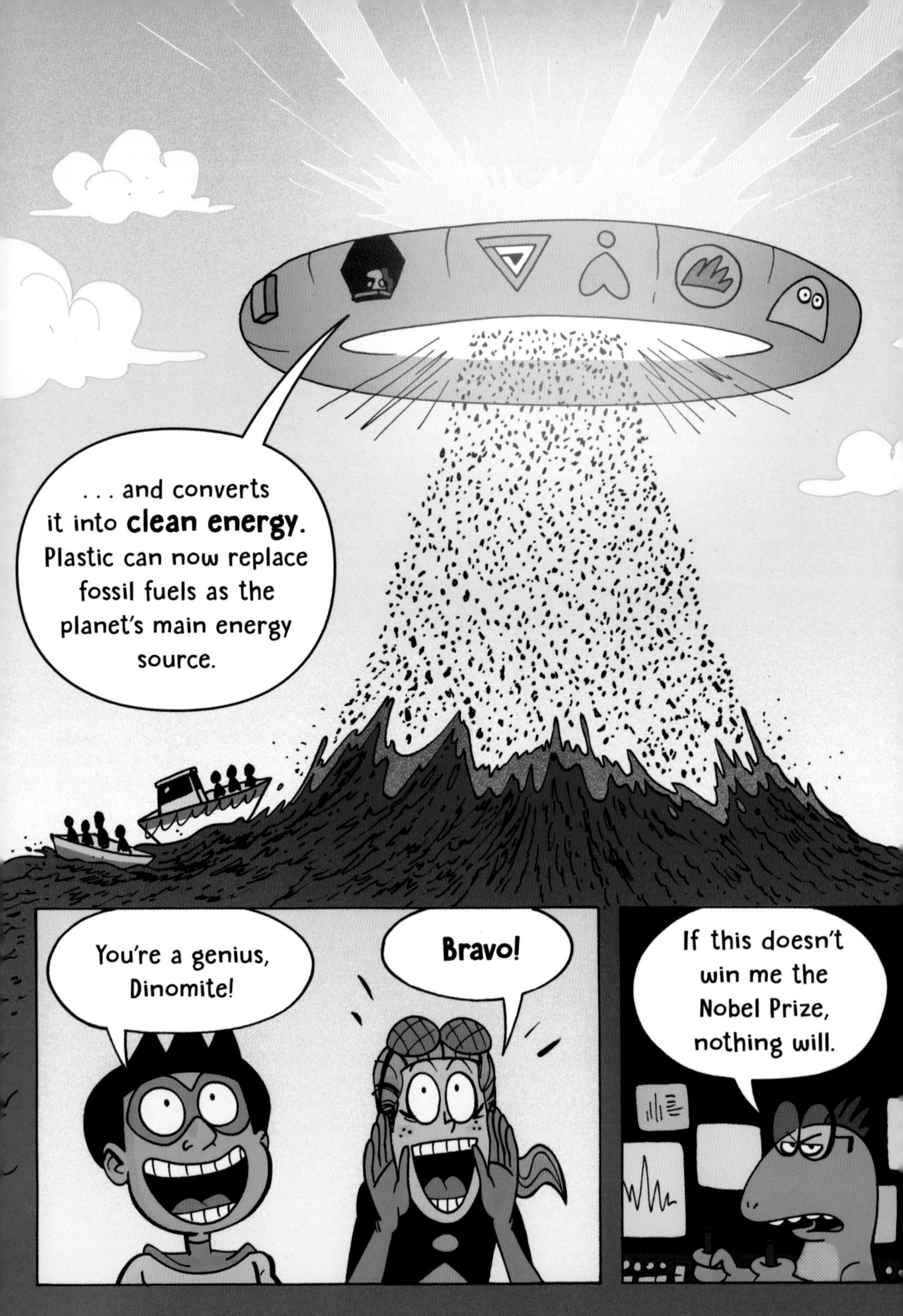
. . . and converts it into **clean energy.** Plastic can now replace fossil fuels as the planet's main energy source.
You're a genius, Dinomite!
Bravo!
If this doesn't win me the Nobel Prize, nothing will.

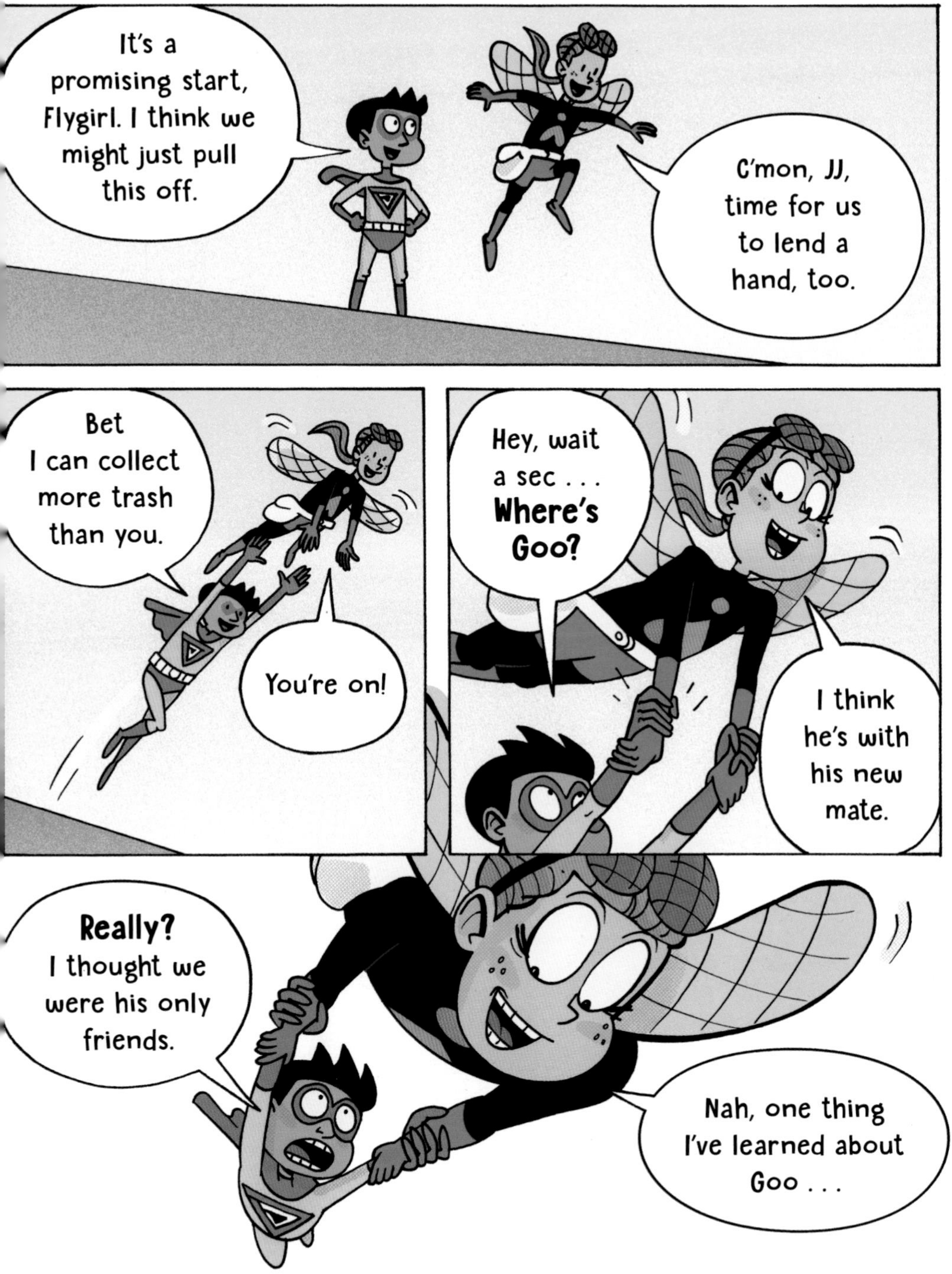
It's a promising start, Flygirl. I think we might just pull this off.
C'mon, JJ, time for us to lend a hand, too.
Bet I can collect more trash than you.
You're on!
Hey, wait a sec . . . **Where's Goo?**
I think he's with his new mate.
Really? I thought we were his only friends.
Nah, one thing I've learned about Goo . . .

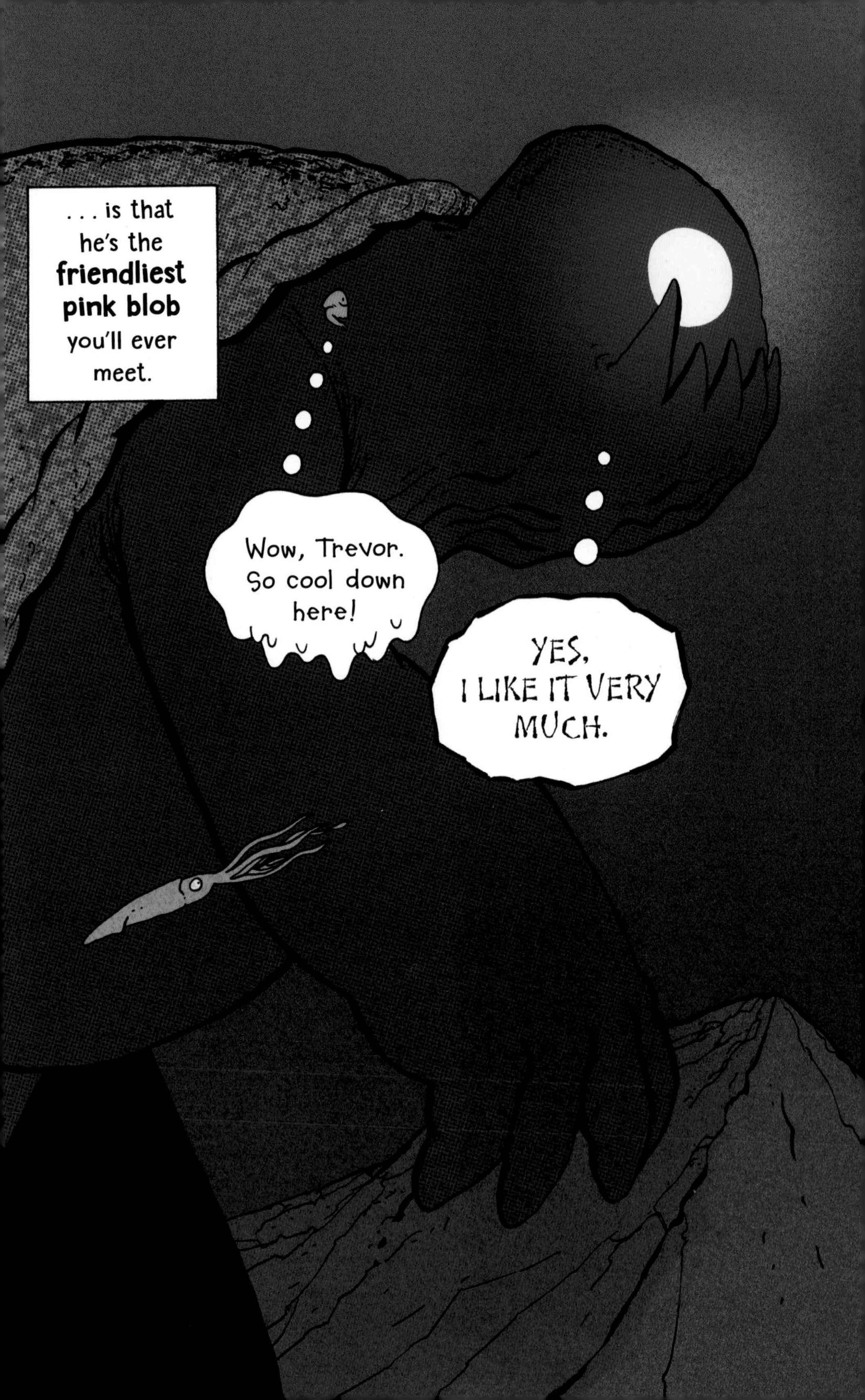
. . . is that he's the **friendliest pink blob** you'll ever meet.
Wow, Trevor. So cool down here!
YES, I LIKE IT VERY MUCH.

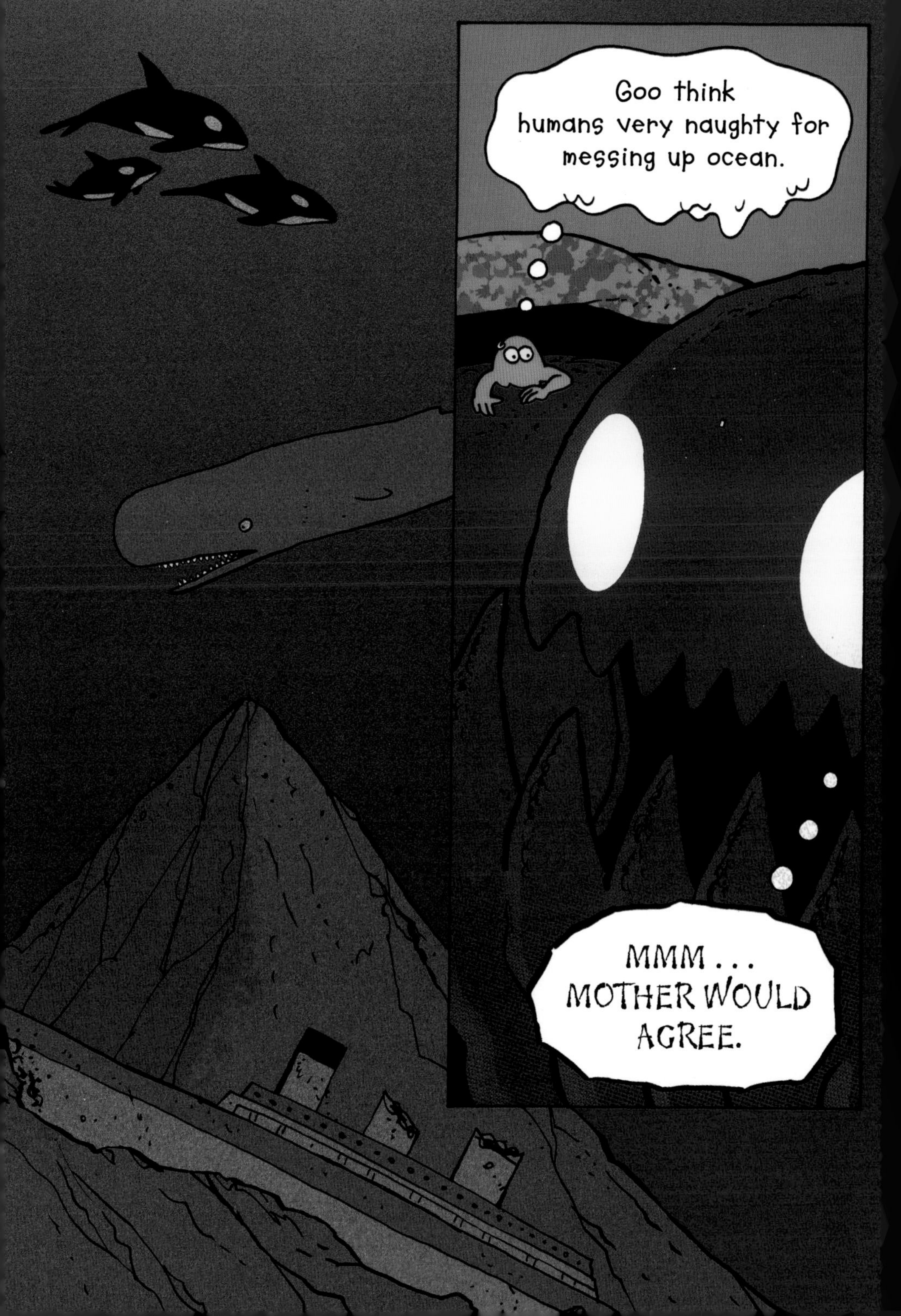
Goo think humans very naughty for messing up ocean.
MMM . . . MOTHER WOULD AGREE.

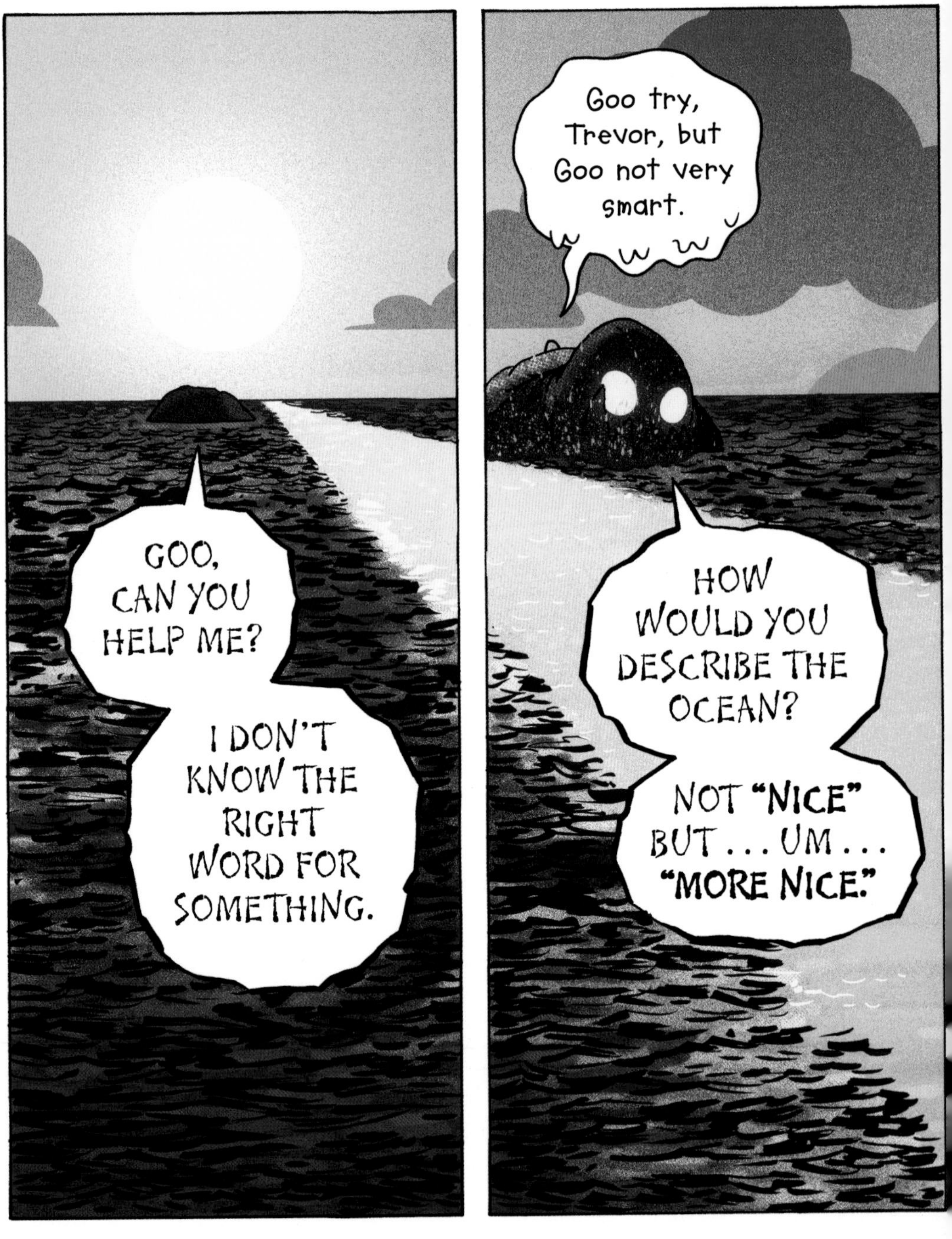
GOO, CAN YOU HELP ME?
I DON'T KNOW THE RIGHT WORD FOR SOMETHING.
Goo try, Trevor, but Goo not very smart.
HOW WOULD YOU DESCRIBE THE OCEAN?
NOT "NICE" BUT . . . UM . . . "MORE NICE."

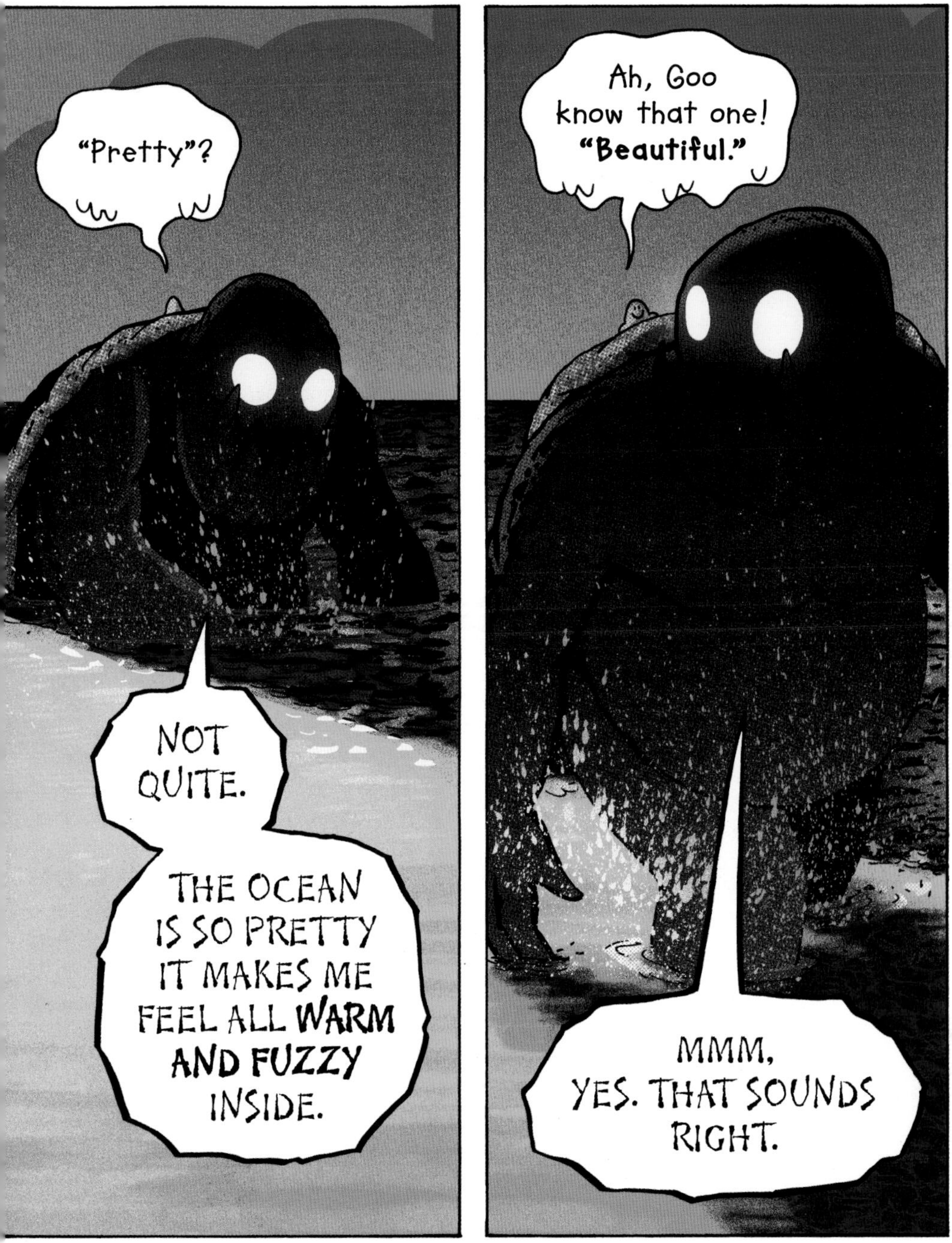
"Pretty"?
NOT QUITE.
THE OCEAN IS SO PRETTY IT MAKES ME FEEL ALL **WARM AND FUZZY** INSIDE.
Ah, Goo know that one! **"Beautiful."**
MMM, YES. THAT SOUNDS RIGHT.

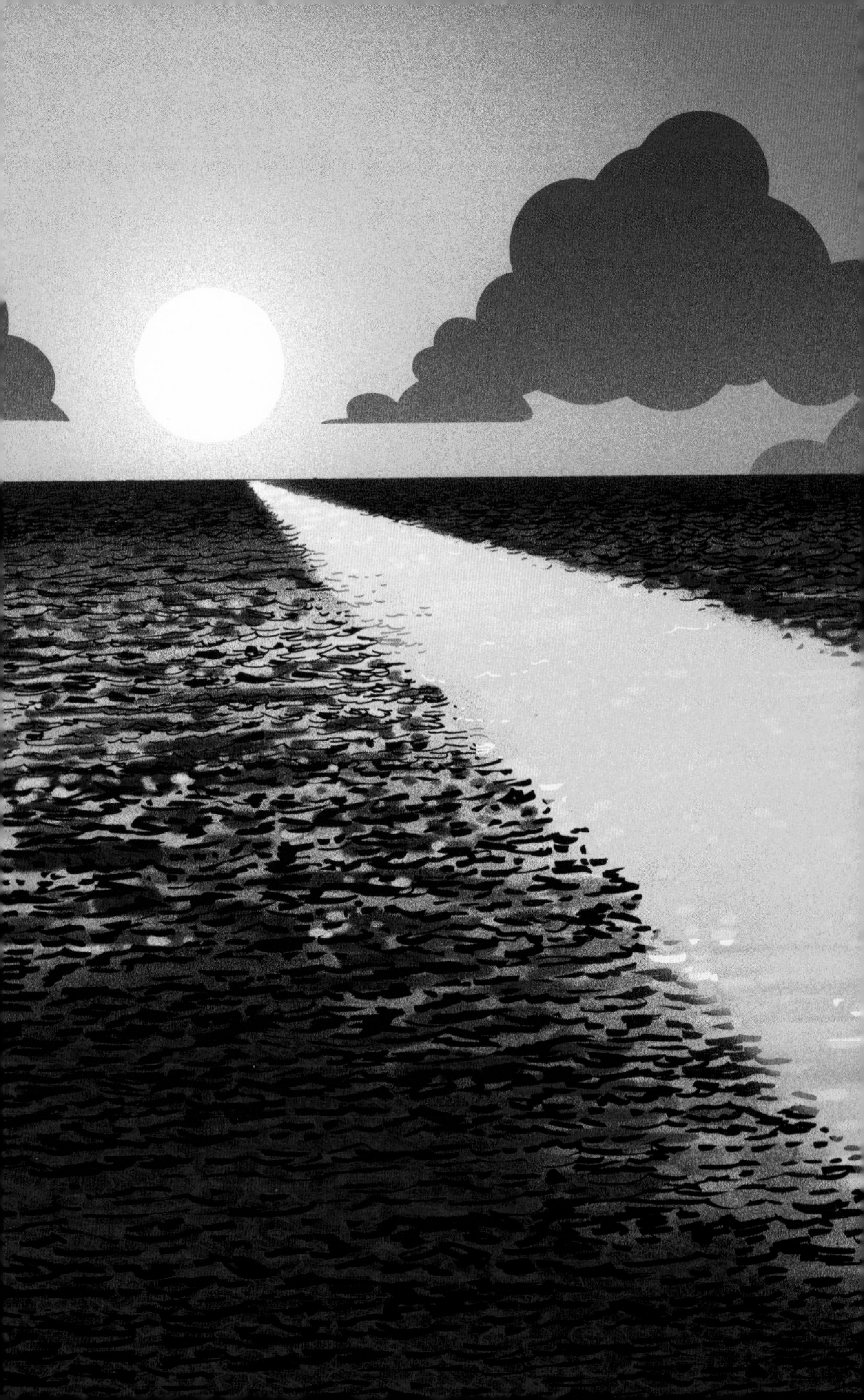

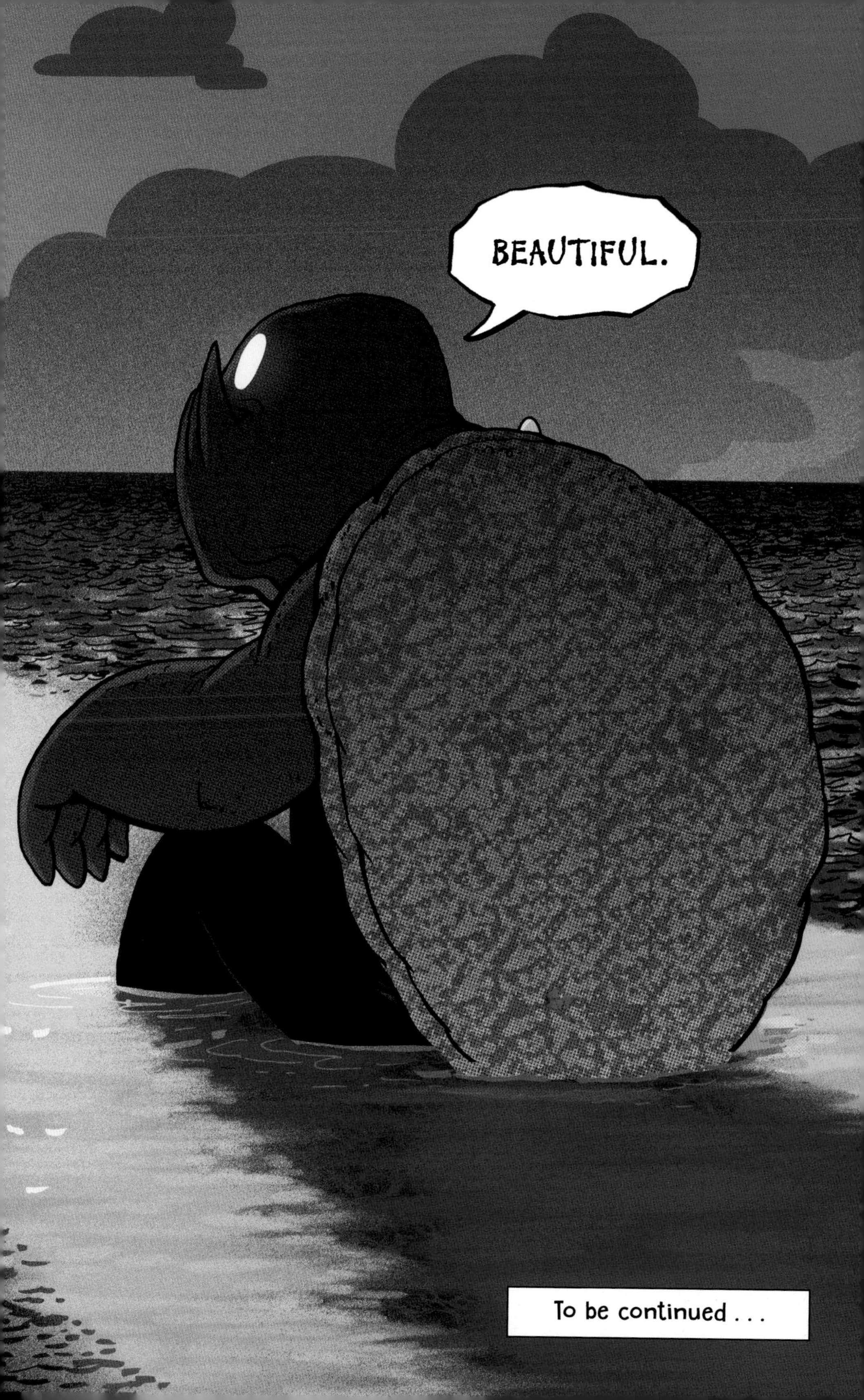
BEAUTIFUL.
To be continued . . .

Don't worry, the Super Sidekicks
will be back in

SUPER SIDE KICKS

BOOK THREE

TRIAL OF HEROES

The Super Sidekicks just saved the world and got invited to join H.E.R.O.—the Heroic Earth Righteousness Organization—an exclusive club for the planet's most famous superheroes. But before they can become members, the team must pass the hardest challenge in the universe, a test so scary and difficult only the truly heroic can survive.

COMING IN 2022!

Sounds like a must-read!

THE PLANET NEEDS YOU!

THREE GREAT WAYS YOU CAN ELIMINATE WASTE—AND BE A HERO.

Waste, and how we choose to handle it, affects our environment. It has to be carefully controlled so it doesn't harm Earth or our health. You can help the planet by learning and practicing the three Rs of waste management:

Reduce: Buy and use less! If all the other people on Earth used as much "stuff" as we do in the United States, there would need to be three to five times more space just to hold and sustain everybody. WOW!

Reuse: You can "reuse" materials in their original form instead of throwing them away. Plastic cups, plates, and utensils can be washed and used again.

Recycle: Don't just toss everything in the trash! Lots of things can be remade into either the same kind of object or new products. Things that you can recycle include aluminum cans, cardboard, electronic equipment, glass, magazines, metal, plastic bags, and plastic bottles.

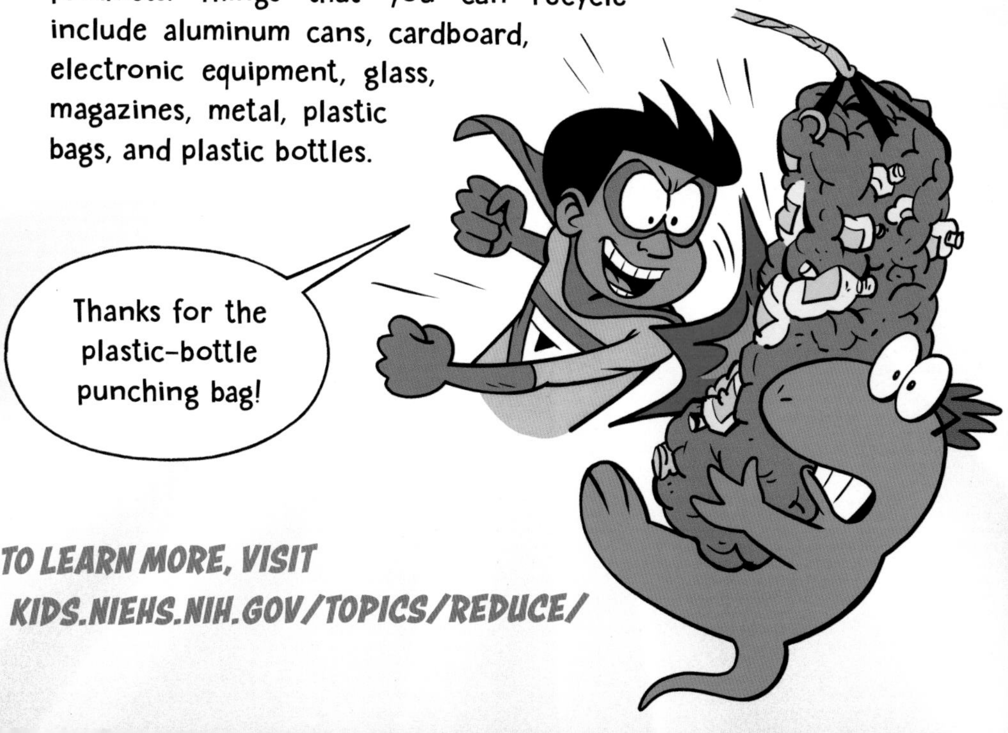
Thanks for the plastic-bottle punching bag!

TO LEARN MORE, VISIT KIDS.NIEHS.NIH.GOV/TOPICS/REDUCE/

THE FUTURE OF THE PLANET IS IN YOUR . . . LUNCH BOX?!

Did you know that a person creates an average of 4.5 pounds of trash per day? By reducing the number of items in your lunch that must be thrown out, you can:

→ **PREVENT POLLUTION**

→ **CONSERVE NATURAL RESOURCES**

→ **SAVE ENERGY**

→ **REDUCE THE NEED FOR DISPOSAL**

→ **BE AN ENVIRONMENTAL HERO AND MAKE A DIFFERENCE**

Practice the three Rs of waste management and work with your school administrators, teachers, and cafeteria staff to organize a Waste-Free Lunch Day. Encourage students to bring their lunch in reusable containers made of cloth, durable plastic, or glass. Work with the school cafeteria staff to plan a "waste-free lunch" for students who can't bring their own from home.

For a step-by-step guide on how to plan a Waste-Free Lunch Day, along with downloadable assets and other resources, visit epa.gov/students/pack-waste-free-lunch.

It's easy to reduce waste when you know Goo!

GAVIN'S DRAWING TIPS

START WITH SIMPLE SHAPES FIRST: For instance, Dinomite is mostly made of circles, rectangles, and triangles.

DON'T DRAW TOO DARK: Sketch lightly until you get the basic structure right.

ONE STEP AT A TIME: Once you have the structure done, it's time to draw all the cool details.

JUST HAVE FUN: Don't worry if you think you're not getting it right. Keep practicing—it takes time to get good!

DRAW DINOMITE

1.

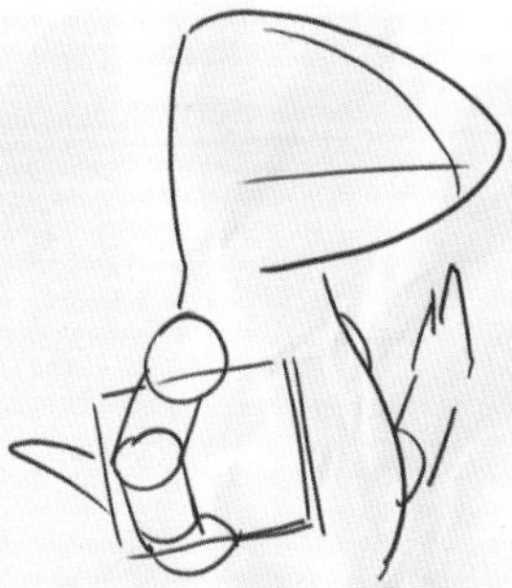

2.

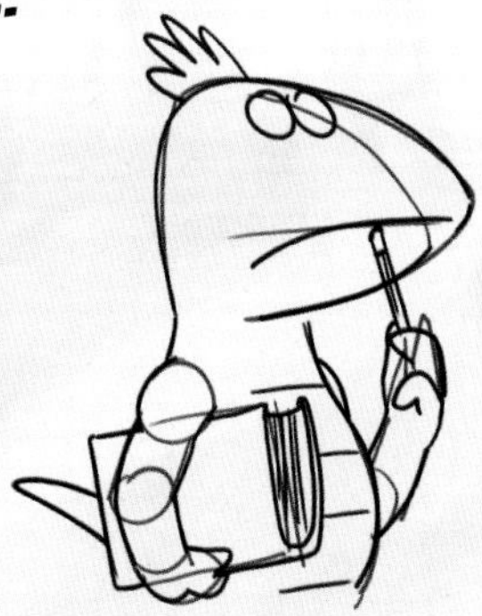

3.

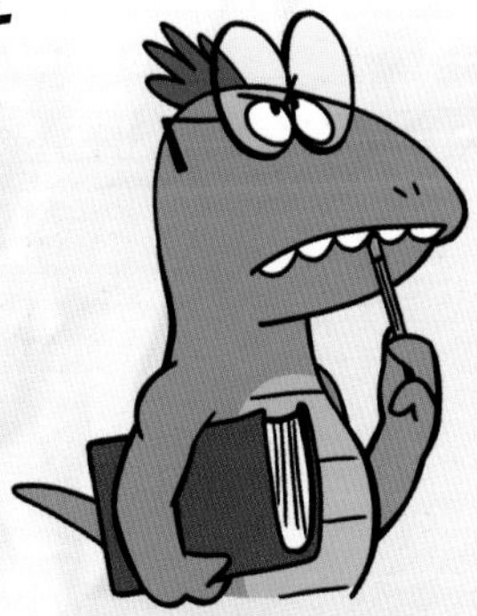

DRAW GOO

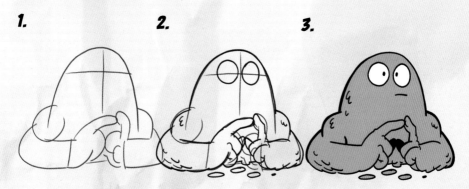

1.

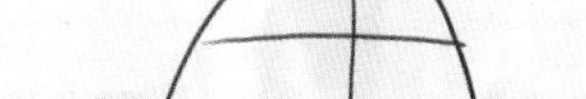

2.

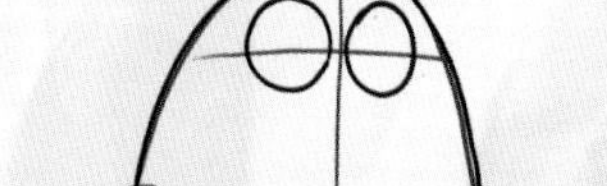

3.

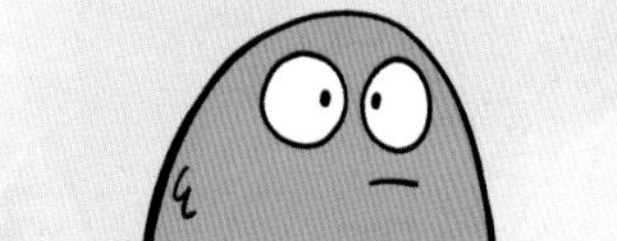

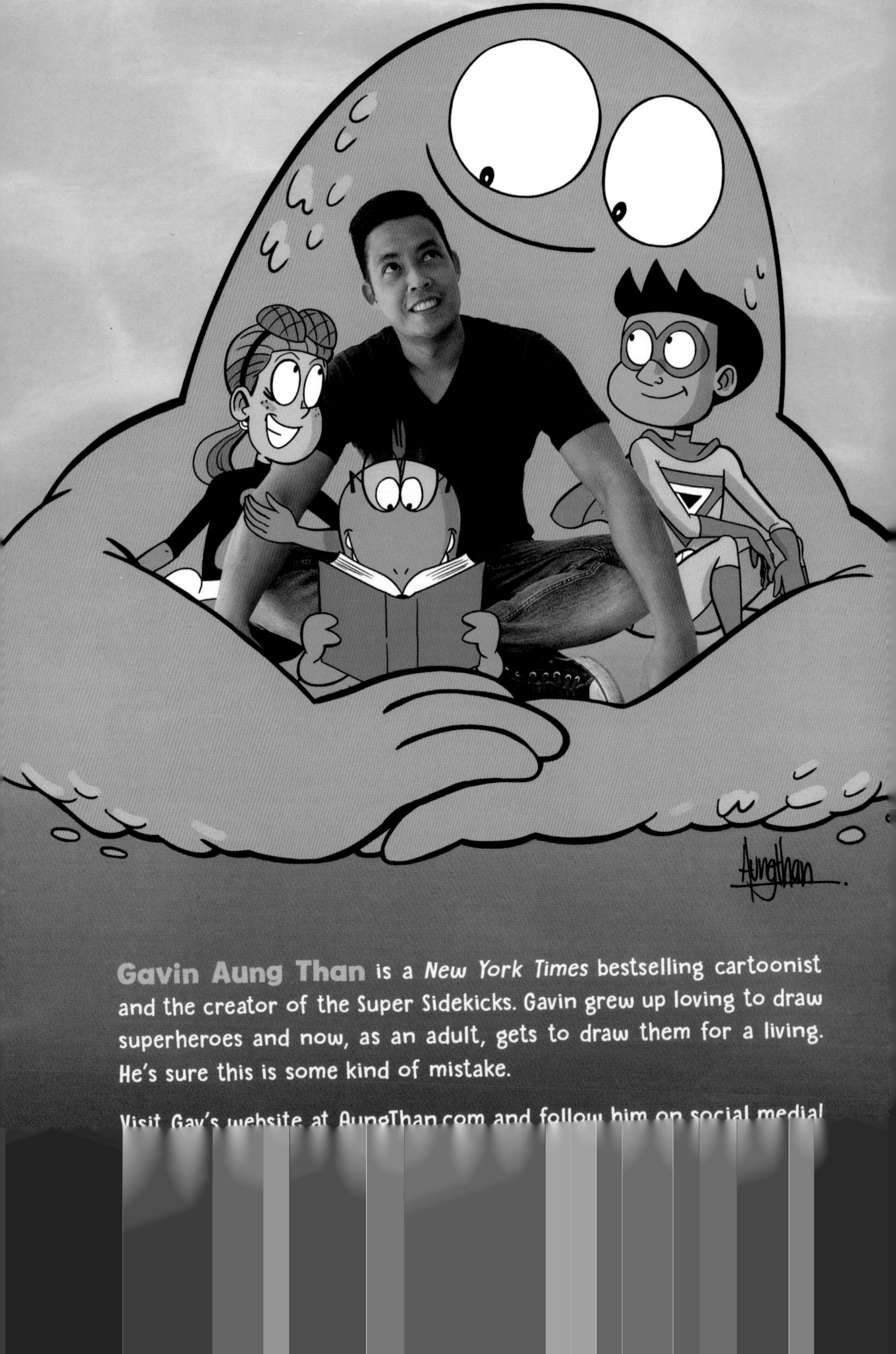

Gavin Aung Than is a *New York Times* bestselling cartoonist and the creator of the Super Sidekicks. Gavin grew up loving to draw superheroes and now, as an adult, gets to draw them for a living. He's sure this is some kind of mistake.

Visit Gav's website at AungThan.com and follow him on social media!